If Only

If Only

J. Anderson, B. Rowley, *and* J. Mulinaro

iUniverse, Inc.
Bloomington

If Only

iUniverse books may be ordered through booksellers or by contacting:

iUniverse
1663 Liberty Drive
Bloomington, IN 47403
www.iuniverse.com
1-800-Authors (1-800-288-4677)

ISBN: 978-1-4759-8061-5 (sc)
ISBN: 978-1-4759-8060-8 (hc)
ISBN: 978-1-4759-8059-2 (e)

Library of Congress Control Number: 2013904677

Printed in the United States of America

iUniverse rev. date: 04/05/2013

For the immense influences, guidance, wonderful people, and God's grace in our lives, the authors graciously and thankfully dedicate this book.

To The Redhead and to Emmitt Carney, Proverbs 27:17
-Bill

To my family, my mom, and dad, you guys are my best friends.
To Rowlo, thanks for taking me to Steak 'n Shake.
To all my boys, you guys are my brothers I never had.
Thanks for everything. I love you all.

-Joey

To Christ who provides the faith, memories, daily guidance, and the words for life
To Chuck and Ruth Mercer for helping to guide a young man in deep pain and providing great friendship
To Mrs. Phyllis Pearson, a fantastic teacher and counselor who took a lost young man under her wing and helped him to find himself again in a new school after his father's death
To Larry Midkiff, an amazing teacher who provided needed friendship, guidance, and fatherly advice
To all the Homecoming Queens who have blessed my life with their inner strength, intelligence, beauty, and grace
To Kathy Adams Vill and her parents, the best lifelong friends any person could ever have influencing and blessing their life
To Lita Foley Holler, a wonderful lifelong friend and homecoming queen who I miss dearly as the Lord called her home much too soon
To the wonderful Lindas who graced my life, My late sister; Linda Romine Bertram, a dear friend since high school who found a lost soul in a new school and made him feel as if she had known him

all his life; My wonderful wife who has blessed my life, is my best friend, and is the heart of my heart.

To Bob Bertram, A terrific high school friend and Linda's husband, thanks for the fun times and friendship

To Dave Girton, An amazing Christian brother, storyteller, singer, and friend; Beach Boys, cars, pizza, and great times

To Deb and Gene Coveney and Steve and Vivian Murrell for their counsel, friendship, and encouragement

To Rowlo for the great Friday lunches, discussions, and unlocking amazing memories in me

To all the beautiful friends who have touched my life in so many wonderful ways

To Herff Jones Inc. for a wonderful 35 year career and teaching me the beauty of heart-shaped stones

To Miss Mary Reed, a teacher who provided the drive and challenge to succeed in spite of comments by others to the contrary

And finally, to the Great Ormond Street Hospital for keeping the joys of childhood alive for many generations

-Jim

Contents

Present Day

Taking in all the attention to detail, Bill Denton studies the church's conference room while waiting. The ornate wood panels and soft lighting combine to create an air of old Europe. Tantalizing the senses, the aroma of the wood creates a magical atmosphere. It is a superb environment and setting for this day. Every facet of this room and the rest of the church demonstrate careful planning and design just as he lives his life. With everything and every possibility anticipated, as a quarterback would do, his attention to detail made him better than most others. Most people overlook these minutiae but he did not. Appreciating the artistry silently, he praises the carpenter who did the work. This is a room for important people and important decisions, not just a conference room.

Bill felt honored to be there especially because of the significance of why he was there. Many of his friends sit in the church and wait with anticipation. Soon, he will take his place beside his lifelong crush Sarah, his dream girl for nearly his entire life. He never married because she is the only woman with whom he had ever been truly in love, the only woman he wants most in his life. He amassed high school state football championships, a national championship in college, and four championships in professional football in his life. Those were great accomplishments but football is what he did not who he is. Simply, he has always been in love with only one woman. After high school, when he spoke about Sarah to people who did not know her, he just calls her "The Redhead." Not wanting the media or anyone else attempting to locate her, his description protects her privacy, wherever she goes.

Always strikingly handsome, he possesses leading-man looks, from his sandy beach-colored hair with dusky copper highlights to his deep brown eyes sparkling as the deep night. With his stature, he projects sheer confidence in his walk. Still possessing a strong, athletic physique, he is 6'6" and 245 pounds with a charismatic air of invincibility. Yet, as a person, he is caring and respectful, romantic and loving. Because of his fabulous looks, he could have almost any girl or woman. Many women dream of dating *the* quarterback. Being a famous quarterback, women want to be with him and guys want to be him. After all, Bill is a Professional Football Hall of Fame Quarterback and still has that "Rock Star" status.

Sarah Ormond is a drop-dead gorgeous red head with a petite swimsuit edition body. In Bill's mind, she is perfect in every way. Her personality is kind and generous with a caring and loving spirit. Possessing that "girl next door quality," a man could never want more in a girlfriend or wife than Sarah. Her skin glows like the soft light from a full moon while her eyes sparkle like fiery stars and her smile illuminates any room she enters. Like a fine wine, her red hair is a deep red that makes a man want to drink it in with a long second look. How could he even think about loving someone else? To Bill, there is no one else like her.

Sarah and Bill have been best friends forever, doing things, and having fun together constantly. Even after high school, they remain close. Sarah is his biggest fan. Other friends told him that on those rare occasions when the opposing team would hit him hard in a football game and he was slow to get up, her eyes would become teary. Wincing with his pain, she would close her eyes with fear that he might be hurt. However, Sarah never told him herself, not wanting him to worry she might be upset. It is Bill, the man, who is her best friend not the quarterback. During a conversation a few years earlier, the two of them joked about how their paths never crossed at the right time. Now their paths met at just the right moment, at the same place, and at the same time. Finally, after 45 years, he is taking his place beside her.

The door to the room opens and the priest, Father Doug Hunter, an old friend of Bill, told him, "Relax, Bill. You have a visitor."

It is the best man in his life. Other than Sarah and his "boys" he grew up with, it is his best friend since their first year of high school. Stone Scott enters the room and asks, "How ya doing buddy?"

"I'm scared to death. That's how I'm doing," he replies.

Amazed at his admission, Stony responds, "Nervous, *you*, Mr. Cool under pressure?"

"Yeah I'm nervous and a bit scared. I've never done this before," Bill continues, "I was always the guy that wanted to make the big play in the football game, lead the winning drive, and score the winning touchdown. I always wanted to take the last shot in basketball, to be *the guy*, but *this*. Man, I'm really nervous and scared and I just don't want to mess it up. I don't want to forget what I'm supposed to say. I don't want to mess up and embarrass Sarah."

Stony offers words of assurance, "You'll be fine." However, his words do not make Bill feel any less nervous. So, as he had done many times with his close friend when he senses this, Stony just starts talking to him, "When did this lifelong quest for Sarah even start? How did you two even meet? I mean you two were best friends from the first day of high school yet you went to different junior highs. I remember hanging out after games with you and the boys. You wouldn't even know what the final score was or how you had done. If someone asked how many touchdown passes you had, you'd say you didn't know and you really *didn't* know. You hardly ever wore your letter jacket because it just wasn't you. You didn't walk around and say look at me. You just liked hanging out and having a piece of pizza and a soft drink with everyone else. Sarah would be hanging with you if she didn't have a date. Really, I don't get it. You guys were best friends but had so many interesting times with each other."

Looking at him with a big smile on his face, Bill begins to unfold Sarah and his relationship to Stony.

1965

ill attends East Junior High while Sarah attends Central Junior High. Although the schools are only a couple of miles apart, they are worlds different. The Junior Highs consist of grades seven, eight, and nine. Both schools are rivals yet feed into South high school. Freshmen go to the junior highs while South High School is for sophomores, juniors, and seniors. Though Bill is still in the eighth grade, the high school football coach, Joe Mulinaro, comes to East looking for one person and the Principal calls that person to his office.

As Bill strolls toward the Principal's office, his thoughts race nervously, "What the heck did I do? Why is the Principal calling *me* to his office? Am I being punished for something?"

As he walks into the glass-walled office, he feels as if the whole world is watching him. Coach Mulinaro stretches his hand toward Bill and introduces himself, "Hello Bill. I'm Coach Mulinaro from South High School."

Shaking the coach's hand, he utters apprehensively, "Hello Coach."

As the coach begins talking, the next few moments become a blur to Bill. Coach explains, "I watched your performance in several games. In my opinion, you played very well. I believe that if you work very hard this summer you can improve your strength and agility greatly. I want you to dedicate yourself to hitting the weights daily. We can provide workout sheets for you to follow and open gym times. I would like to see you work on refining your throwing motion and range. I see great potential in you. I probably shouldn't say this but…" Then, after a brief pause, he said the only thing Bill caught in his foggy mind, "The coaching staff and I think you can be our starting QB in your freshman year."

The coach's words overwhelm Bill and send his thoughts racing and spinning. As he fumbles for the right words, those words escape his jumbled mind. While knowing he has strong skills but not to the point of arrogance, Bill carries a bit of a swagger onto the football field. After all, he is the quarterback and always believes his team will win any game on any day. It is his stage and the game is his show, the bigger the game, the bigger the stage. Just like a star performer, he loves a big stage. Off the field, he always strives to treat everyone with respect and never thinks he is better than anyone else is. Finally managing to collect his thoughts into coherent words, he utters, "Thanks coach. It's an honor to just be given a chance."

Interrupting the story for a moment, Stony adds, "Yeah that's how you are. Everyone knows you can do anything you want on the field. Off the field, you're just a regular person, no big head, and no arrogance. You're so humble and self-deprecating. I've spent years telling people that you're a great guy who will do anything for anybody. On the field, you *are* different. You'll stomp on 'em and rip their hearts out. Otherwise, you're just one of the guys."

"May I *continue*," Bill asks with mock frustration and a wry smile. That summer is like yesterday in his mind. The upper classmen are all over him, showing no mercy. Relentlessly, they continue forming his fierce metal in this crucible. As pre-season continues, he grows stronger daily. His air and swagger grow as he slowly takes control of every phase of the team's game. His passes come accurately and with speed on them. Their confidence in him keeps building and by the first game, he is their *guy*. The first game infects everyone else with butterflies of various forms while Bill dresses at his locker. The metal is refined and ready for public display. Team members come by his locker and tell him to fire up, thinking he is too mellow. The reality is, on the outside, he is Mr. Cool. On the inside, he is a trained assassin. Visualizing exactly what he is going to do and seeing the game progress in his mind, he is a freshman telling these upperclassmen to relax. In his mind, they are going to win and beat the number one ranked team in the state on the first Friday of the season. Not looking or acting like a freshman, he begins that soon-to-be-familiar walk from his locker. As he swaggers past the ivy-covered stadium walls, the dressing room fades from his mind. The fans begin to yell wildly as he moves through the gate, steeling his nerve. When he walks onto the playing field, a couple of opposing players look at him. Within his earshot, one of them says, "Is that him?" Looking at them with an icy glance, Bill does not say a word. Returning to his plan, he continues walking and then starts to warm up. Recalling that at every level he played 'til now, he always swaggered onto the field for warm ups, preferring the attention. After the games, he does anything he can to heap all the praise on his teammates. However, because of what he is, he has an obligation to do the non-game stuff too.

South has a freshman QB and Washington is loaded with seniors from last year's state championship team. South kicks off and Washington drives quickly down the field to score. Moving tentatively down the field, South appears to be playing afraid because of Washington's number one ranking. After scoring, Washington kicks off and South gets the ball on their 20. Five plays later, Bill takes charge and throws a 40-yard touchdown. The team looks at him with amazement yet they formed him together in their own crucible. His refinement process continues and he gives a fist pump while walking to his sideline. Everyone in the stands goes crazy yet Bill retains the same even keel he had before the game. Feeding off him emotionally, the team seems to calm down. It is a well-played ball game, tied at half 14-14, and Bill is 10 for 12 with two TD passes.

Sarah

At half time, all the fans are seething with excitement on the sidelines. As the team rambles to the locker room, Bill suddenly remembers the locker room is close to the concession stand and the crowd. The half-time throng ebbs and flows in the area like a giant amoeba. Jogging off the field and pumped to a high level of excitement, the team moves in an uneven line toward the locker room. At the end of the writhing line of players, Bill has his head down, wanting to get to the locker room without a bunch of commotion. Going through the gate by the concession stand, he continues to look down while moving forward. Suddenly, he bumps into a dream standing there and spills her soft drink all over her.

"Sarah," Stony asks visualizing the scene in his mind.

"Yeah, it was her," Bill continues.

Looking up yet still in a daze, his eyes fixate on her. Stunningly beautiful, he loses himself in her presence. She is more beautiful than any girl he has ever seen. As he gazes at her for what seems forever to him, he finally manages a feeble, "I'm sorry." Not really hearing his weak apology, she stares down at her feet, exasperated, dripping in soft drink. As she looks up, their eyes meet and he becomes lost in her eyes momentarily. Rising from the depth of her eyes, he begs,

"Please forgive me. I'm so sorry for spilling your soft drink on you. I have to get into the locker room but will you meet me by the concession stand after the game?"

Still frustrated, she answers, "Don't worry about it. I enjoy being soaked."

However, he insists and pleads with her, "*Please* meet me here right after the game with your mom and dad."

Yielding to his pleas, she commits, "Okay, I will if my mom and dad are willing to wait."

Relieved with her response, he exclaims excitedly, "That's *great*. I'll be here as soon as I change." Flying for the locker room quickly, he mulls over the encounter, "Wow, is she gorgeous. Shoot, I forgot to get her name." The whole incident takes only a few moments but seems like forever.

At the start of the second half, both teams score on their first possession. Trading possessions often, the teams march up and down the field until almost the fourth quarter. The crowd moves excitedly from standing on their feet to the edge of their seats. Finally, South breaks the scoring drought with a field goal at the end of the third quarter, up 24-21. The South defense digs in like Dragon's Teeth fortifications. Washington receives the ball in the fourth quarter slogging through nine minutes of torture to score. With the score now 28-24, much to their team's relief, and only 2:30 left to play, they think, "just dig in and we'll win." However, they did not consider the freshman QB opposing them to be an icy-veined assassin. On the ensuing kickoff, South receives the ball on its own 20.

As the offense hustles on the field, confusion and anxiety grip the huddle. Each player has an answer he needs to unleash on the rest as loud as possible. With the team stunned at what has just happened, Bill pushes into the huddle and says, "Ok, we have work to do and a short time to do it." While the others still go crazy in the huddle, the ice forms in his eyes and veins as he yells, "*Shut the heck up!*" Staring at him with disbelief on their faces, "Who does he think he is," courses through their minds. As the metal steels his physique, they receive an instantaneous answer to their thoughts. He glares at each of them, "Do your job the best you know how. Run your routes and block. Listen to me and we'll win." Due to speaking with an authority that belies his youth, a couple of his teammates roll their eyes at him. Grabbing their helmets, he yells, "*If you don't want to win this game, I'll get someone who can.*" Never has someone led them like this. He is calm, even icy, and that helps calm the others. In four plays, they march to the 50-yard line but stare at a 3rd down and eight. Coach sends in a draw play. Bill relays the play in the huddle but he tells the receivers to watch him. If he taps his helmet, they are to break down the sidelines. As South lines up, he reads the defensive set. Their corners' actions hint at a hard blitz coming. Bill reads their actions perfectly with the confidence of stellar persona performing at a concert. Tapping his helmet, he takes the snap and the receivers take off. He zips a fade to the right sideline for a 20-yard pass completion. With 45 seconds left, they reach the 30-yard line like an unstoppable juggernaut. Like a wizard weaving a spell, Bill takes the snap. He pump fakes to the right then throws to his left. As they reach the 10-yard line with 20 seconds left, the coach calls a timeout. Rallying his troops for the final assault, he calls the play. It's a sweep right but the team only gains 5 yards. The result forces them to use another timeout to preserve a chance to win.

With 8 seconds left on the clock and the ball on the 5-yard line, they must have a touchdown to win. Coach calls the same play again. Bill tells Steve Harris, the running back, "Make a good fake because you're not getting the ball." Coach has a tendency to sweep everyone to the right if South needs hard yardage. Knowing this, the Washington defense gambles to play the odds. Bill takes the snap, steps back, and fakes the hand off strongly. Steve locks his arms tightly as if he has the ball and rumbles ahead right. While the rest of the team drives hard to the right, Bill deftly hides the ball from Washington on his left leg. Running a naked bootleg to the left, he saunters untouched into the end zone as South wins 31-28. The entire stadium becomes frenetic as Bill jogs to the locker room, giving his fist pump on the way. The team is wildly ecstatic, as are the coaches.

Everyone presses around him lavishing praises, "Great game, Way to go." Finally, they exclaim to him, "You're *the man.*" It is an electric atmosphere. However, Bill thoughts are elsewhere, wanting to hang out with his friends and see the girl with the soft drink on her, of course. The game and the show are over.

While the lights begin to dim, it is time to be just Bill not the hero QB. Although he dresses quickly, he still has to answer a few questions from the media. With his thoughts near panic level, his mind races, "Let's get this over because I've got to go." Leaving the media room denizens speechless with his performance, he ponders fearfully, "*She left* because I took too long." While he runs toward their agreed meeting place, his mind sprints even faster that she *will not* be there. In the rushing distance, he spies her. "*She didn't leave after all,*" he considers with relief.

Sure enough, she is the same vision waiting with her parents that he bumped into earlier. Her dad and mom introduce themselves, "We're the Ormonds. Sarah asked us to wait with her because you wanted to talk to all of us."

"So *that's* her name," he muses. Looking amazed at her parents, he is thrilled they would wait with her to meet him and did not want to disappoint them. Then, gazing at her eyes, he says, "I'm so sorry I spilled the soft drink on you. It wasn't your fault at all. I wasn't paying attention as I made my way to the locker room. I wanted your parents to know that so you wouldn't get in any trouble. I'd be devastated if I caused that." His sensitivity and concern for her well-being touches her parents. Sarah's heart melts at this concern and her face glows with excitement.

Her smile turns Bill's night into day while her dad, recognizing Bill from the game, says, "Aren't you the quarterback?"

Somewhat embarrassed, Bill answers, "Yes sir. I am. I'm Bill Denton." Her dad replays the game highlights at length verbally with Bill thanking him graciously about twenty times.

Seeing the glow begin to leave Sarah's face, her dad thinks better of continuing his play by play. He probes intently, "You don't talk about yourself much do you, Bill?"

Revealing his character a bit, Bill replies, "No sir, football is what I do not who I am. God blessed me with great skills and I try to use them to the best of my ability every day."

Bill's candor for someone so young takes him back a bit but her mom comments, "My goodness, you're not like most teenagers."

Not certain of her meaning, Bill quickly replies, "Thank you Ma'am." During their conversation, the stadium lights dim to the point where ghostly shadows sit on the seats and benches. While everyone says goodbye to each other, Bill inquires of Sarah eagerly, "Are you coming to the game next week?"

Her look to her parents pleads for approval. To her relief, her mom says, "Yes, she'll be here." The friendship grows from an ember to an excited spark in one evening.

The Note

Bill hustles to school Monday morning and straight to his counselor's office. The office is a warm and familiar place to him. With mahogany wainscoting around the room, the environment always puts him at ease. The overstuffed chairs embrace guests with open arms. His counselor, Doug Tibbs, is his surrogate father, mentor, and friend.

Filled with excitement, Bill says to him, "Mr. Tibbs, you'll never guess what happened to me. Friday night at halftime, I wasn't paying attention and I bumped into the most amazing girl I've ever seen, spilling a soft drink all over her. Her name is Sarah Ormond and I even met her parents."

Of course, Doug Tibbs wants to know all about the game. "Bill, what about the game," Mr. Tibbs probes, "That was an awesome touchdown pass in the first half. That long gainer near the end of the game was truly inspirational. Did you come up with that helmet tap yourself? Was that naked bootleg your idea?" He continues to speak about the game even though he saw it in person. After a few uh-huh's and a couple of yes sirs, Mr. Tibbs figures out he is not going to get a lot of talk from Bill about the game or his performance. He says, "You're still the same kid that came into my office as a seventh grader, still very humble, and fortunate to be blessed with the talent you have."

"It's not about me, Mr. Tibbs. It's about my teammates. All I do is take the snap and hand it off or throw it. The rest of the team does the hard work," Bill reiterates to him. A big smile grows on Mr. Tibbs face, as he knows *this* Bill. He just likes to hear him state it again. That statement from Bill lets Mr. Tibbs know he is still the same person and he wants to be just a regular kid in school. Being a very good student, with usually A's and a B or two on his report card, he is a bright young man who thinks differently than the other kids.

Deciding not to prolong the visit longer, Mr. Tibbs questions, "How can I help you today, Bill?"

With Sarah dancing playfully through his mind, Bill recounts the soft drink story to Mr. Tibbs again then adds, "This is very important to me. I want to send a note of apology to her at Central. I have to let her know how very sorry I am for spilling the soft drink on her."

Slightly confused with his intent, Mr. Tibbs inquires, "You apologized to her parents and her already last Friday, right? So, why do you want to send her another apology?"

Quickly conveying his thoughts, Bill clarifies, "There is no one else like her. I can't stop thinking about her. She's so different from other girls I know. I got the feeling when I apologized that she was accepting it from Bill and not the quarterback. I want to do something very surprising. I want her to know she touched me deeply in one brief encounter. She has to know that I've done more than just say I'm sorry. This note has to tell her the person that I am because she's as beautiful to me as a spring meadow."

"You don't like her much do you," Mr. Tibbs quizzes jokingly.

Somewhat disappointed at his joviality, Bill utters, "Yes, I do like her but I'm not the kind of guy she would go out with. Being a freshman, without daily transportation, and going to different schools are not the ideal situations for dating somebody. I'll be happy if we can just be friends."

Wanting to impart fatherly wisdom, Mr. Tibbs responds, "It sounds as if you have a wonderful new friendship already. You shouldn't be afraid to build on that."

Jumping quickly on Mr. Tibbs statement, Bill declares, "I think every person needs that *one* friend with whom they can talk to about anything. I'm sure she's not chasing a quarterback. She was willing to wait for me after the game to apologize to her and her parents. I'm hoping we can be strong enough friends that I can confide my deepest thoughts and feelings fully with her. She blew me away. Most people want to talk about me as the quarterback and to hang out with the quarterback. When people introduce me to others, they always say this is my friend Bill. He's the quarterback on the football team. It's never just this is my friend Bill. I believe in my heart she can be that extraordinary friend because we didn't grow up together. Would you please do this for me, Mr. Tibbs?"

Mr. Tibbs asks carefully, "Bill, how would you like me to convey this?"

Breathing a sigh of relief, Bill sets his plan in motion verbally, "What I'd really like to do is hand-write a note and have you give it to her. If that's not possible, would you mind calling the counselor at Central and asking him to tell her that I'm sorry for spilling the soft drink on her. That would be ok as well, I guess."

Sensing Bill's saddened tone as he described the alternative method, Mr. Tibbs says, "Go ahead and write your apology to Sarah. I'll take it over and give it to her personally with her counselor at Central."

"You'd do that for me," Bill exclaims, almost in disbelief.

"Yes, I would because you're a good kid. If that's what you want, that's what we'll do," Mr. Tibbs declares.

Mr. Tibbs gives him a sheet of paper imprinted with the school letterhead. It looks very official and very classy. In the solitude of his mind, he has written this note many times since Friday's game. Now Bill writes the note from his heart:

> *Sarah,*
>
> *I want to apologize one more time for spilling the soft drink on you. I appreciate you and your parents waiting after the game so I could let them know it wasn't your fault. They were so nice about it and I'm glad they weren't mad at you. I so look forward to seeing you after the game Friday at the same place as last week. I would like to see your parents too if they want to wait. Again, I'm so sorry for spilling the soft drink on you.*
>
> *Your friend, Bill*
>
> *P.S. If you get to the game early give me a shout during warm-ups, I'd like to see you before the game too.*

Reading the note, Doug Tibbs shakes his head and says, "Bill, I didn't know you to be such a romantic. The note is very adult and stylish of you. I'll take it over right now."

As Mr. Tibbs leaves his office, Bill says with a wry smile, "Get me her number if you can." With a broad smile, Mr. Tibbs chuckles to himself and continues walking.

A short time later, Doug Tibbs walks into the Guidance office at Central and to his counterpart, Bill Chapel. After Doug explains the purpose of his visit, Bill Chapel responds, "This kid is a freshman? He thinks more like a man. I've heard a lot about him. How would you describe him?"

Doug answers simply, "He's just a great kid. He's the person you want your daughter to bring home and say, 'He's the one.' He's the person after whom you want your son to model his life. Forget football, he's just a quality young man." Doug accompanies Bill Chapel to Sarah's class. While the class works on their assignment, the two men walk into the room. Mr. Chapel calls Sarah to the door and Mr. Tibbs hands her the note in a simple envelope. The envelope reads a simple, hand-printed "Sarah" on it. Opening the envelope quickly, she still has some anxiety. After all, two Guidance Counselors do not come into your class every day to hand you an envelope let alone not stating its purpose.

After reading it, she whispers to Mr. Tibbs softly, "Did he write this?"

Recalling his earlier discussion with a smile, Mr. Tibbs replies, "Yes he did and I agreed to deliver it for him."

Gazing with amazement at Mr. Tibbs, Sarah exclaims, "*Wow*, how nice is that? Thank you so much. Please tell Bill thank you too." Lifted by euphoria, Sarah floats back to her seat.

Of course, everyone wants to know why two counselors came with an envelope for her and what was in it. She had relayed last Friday's soft drink story previously to everyone and Bill's kind actions after the game. Now, receiving a hand-written note from him, the emotional electricity flows quietly for Sarah through the class.

A girl in the class whispers, "Can you believe it? Sarah is now the quarterback's girlfriend."

Calmly but quickly, Sarah responds, "I'm *not* the quarterback's girlfriend. I'm just Bill's friend. He's so much more than a quarterback. He's the warmest, most caring person I know. How many athletes do you know that would even apologize let alone hand-write a note? He's just an amazing guy."

A girlfriend of Sarah's yells from the back of the room, "Yeah and he's gorgeous too!" While Sarah's face turns scarlet, her heart leaps to think Bill cares enough for her to send a hand-written and personally delivered note. The Counselor visit story flashes at light-speed from person to person throughout the day at Central. All the girls at Central beg Sarah to let them to see the note.

Doug Tibbs returns to East and after lunch, he calls Bill to his office. He hands him a piece of paper with a phone number on it when Bill arrives. Looking at the paper, his eyes become as big as silver dollars, his heart jumps, and his mind races deliriously. Then, shifting his focus to Mr. Tibbs, he thanks him profusely. Mr. Tibbs commands, "You can't tell anyone where you got the number. The school administrators wouldn't be very happy and I'd catch some heat."

Puzzled by the statement, Bill inquires with concern, "Why did you get it for me then? I don't want you to get into any trouble doing me a favor."

Mr. Tibbs expression turns serious as he says, "You're a good kid and a leader. The other kids look up to you and you're a role model for your peers. You probably feel as if you're under a microscope constantly. The pressure has to be immense and I'm sure everyone wants to be your good friend. I want to be here for you even if you just want to talk. If you continue to do as well the next four years as you did the first game, newspapers and TV sportscasters will call the school and want to talk to you. I just felt like doing something for you because of the kind of person you are. You have to deal with so much."

As his spirit fills with immense gratitude, Bill responds, "Thanks so much Mr. Tibbs. Thanks so much."

With a smile returning to his face, Mr. Tibbs chuckles, "OK, when are you going to call her?"

Thinking for a moment, Bill says, "I plan to call Sarah Wednesday evening. It's the middle of the week, a few days after the note, and a few days before the Friday's game. It'll give us a chance to talk and begin to build our friendship. Do you think she liked getting the note?"

Mr. Tibbs smile becomes very wide as he relates, "Yes, I'm certain she did. The look on her face told me the note impressed her very much. She whispered to me asking if you wrote it by yourself. When I said you did, her face glowed with amazement and sheer joy. One of her friends said Sarah is the quarterback's girlfriend. Sarah replied immediately that she isn't the quarterback's girlfriend. She's your friend and spoke of how thoughtful, warm, and caring you were to write the note. No athlete she knew would even have apologized but that you are different. I swear I saw her heart melt when she spoke about you. She didn't care that you're the quarterback. What I think impressed her most was how much of a gentleman you were about the whole thing." Thanking him again, Bill leaves Mr. Tibbs' office filled excitedly with joy and anticipation. It is not like big stage or big game excitement, but warmth that permeates his entire being. This was only Monday and Wednesday night's call to Sarah seems light-years away. For him, the call cannot come fast enough.

The Phone Call

As Bill dials the last number, his heart races. Barely talking to girls at school, he has never called a girl on the phone before tonight. Though not shy at school, he always excuses himself and moves on when the conversation turns to football. He has a few female friends who have known him since elementary school. Knowing him as Bill Denton and not a quarterback, they see his great personality and a person whom everyone likes. Never talking about being a football star, himself, or his accomplishments in any manner, he loves what he does but avoids situations that call attention to that fact.

"Hello," the soft voice says at the other end of the line.

Ever the gentleman, he says, "May I speak with Sarah please?"

"Who's calling," her mom asks, not yet recognizing his voice?

"It's Bill Denton ma'am," he replies.

"Hold on and I'll get her," she responds with a smile he could hear through the phone.

Bursting with anticipation, he hears her mom say, "Sarah, there's a call for you."

As she comes to the phone, he hears Sarah ask, "Who is it?"

"It's Bill. He asked to speak with you," her mom replies watching emotion pour over Sarah like a wave immediately. Taking the phone quickly from her mom, she begins to speak but no words come out. Excitement and nerves race for control of them both simultaneously.

Regaining some emotional control, Bill's words pour out, "Hello Sarah. How are you? Did you have a good day at school?"

Smiling at the situation, Sarah responds, "Hello Bill. Thank you so much for the note. I was amazed that you sent it to me at school." Giggling at her thoughts, she explains, "It took me back to elementary school immediately, passing notes in class. Your words were so warm and touched my very soul. How did you get your counselor to do it?"

Teasingly, Bill replies, "There *are* advantages to being a good student and doing the right things." After speaking together for 30 minutes about friends, classes, and their days at school, Sarah mentions she has a bit of a challenge in algebra, one of Bill's best subjects. Offering to help her study and be her tutor, they set a joint study time for her house Saturday afternoon. With words beginning to wane, sheer joy replaces adrenaline and excitement. Bill apologizes, "My homework is calling me and I don't want to stop speaking with you but I have to do so. I really look forward to seeing you Friday night."

Adding excitement to the conversation, Sarah promises, "I'll be at the game early to see you and say hello." Not speaking about dating or going out, they are just two friends exchanging ideas. Their only sports discussion is that Sarah will be at the game early on Friday. Saying good night to each other, they both hang up their phones with elation in their hearts. The full conversation is a warm memory to their budding friendship.

As parents will do when a boy calls their 14-year-old daughter, her mom questions, "What did you talk about?"

Glowing from deep inside, Sarah answers, "Bill is coming over

Saturday to help me with Algebra." While their friendship grows rapidly, they both are very comfortable conversing with each other. As a small forest stream winds through the trees, words and thoughts flow easily between them. Their feelings about each other warm them both like a sunny spring day.

Friday Night

South High School feels very good about the upcoming game. The team had a good week of practice and increasingly, it is Bill's team. Emerging steadily as their leader, he has done the same thing at every level on which he ever played. Pre-game in the locker room is a repeat of last week. Team emotions flash like lightning with excitement at a fever pitch while Bill is the eye of the storm at his locker, calm and cool. It is soon time to leave the lair and unleash the fury. The team rushes out whooping and hollering. As usual, Bill is the last person out strolling with that walk and swagger. He is Merlin driving the whirlwind before him to greet the fans arriving early and packing the stands for warm-ups. As he swaggers out, the crowd reacts with a steady thundering to the magician's wand. They know he is *The Maestro* and he generates excitement just walking out. Giving the fans his fist pump, the crowd yells and pumps their fists in orchestrated response. Looking in the stands for Sarah, Bill doesn't see her. Though disappointed, the siren call of the magic draws him out to warm up.

As he stops to get some water, the soft lilt of Sarah's voice calling, "Bill, Bill," tugs at his heart. Turning quickly to the sound, he sees a dream standing at the railing next to the field. Bill moves quickly to speak with her as the *Wizard* hides, "Sarah! I'm thrilled to see you. I don't know about you but Friday could not come fast enough for me."

Sarah practically sings back to him, "I feel the same way. Friday seemed an eternity away."

The *Wizard* returns quickly and changes the subject, "How is Algebra going?"

Exasperated with her subject confusion, Sarah replies, "I'm just lost."

Giving her that wry, magical smile, he says, "We'll fix that tomorrow together."

Wanting to gain understanding, Sarah replies with some concern, "I sure hope so."

Gazing deeply into her eyes and touching her soul, he says, "You don't have to worry. You're in my care and you'll be just fine." With those words, Sarah begins to glow, her eyes sparkle, and her smile comes from deep in her heart. The *Wizard* says, "I have to go now but I'll see you after the game?"

Her words resonate back from within, "Oh yes. You definitely will."

As he walks away, her spirit calls to him. Turning back, he asks excitedly, "Sarah, where are you sitting? I'll look for you during the game." As she reveals her location in the stands to him, her heart bursts forth a delightful smile illuminating the night while Bill begins his warm up routine.

South wins the toss and decides to receive the ball first. Receiving the kick off from Columbus, South returns the ball to its 35-yard line. The offense storms the field like a squall line as the crowd roars its approval. Coach Mulinaro sends a draw play into the huddle and Bill tells his team, "Coach wants a draw but I'm sure they're blitzing on the first play. Receivers, watch for the helmet touch. Let's see what the 'D' has." The offense moves in its orchestrated dance to the line. *The Maestro* gazes over the defense as the corners creep up a little. He taps his helmet and conducts the opening strains of this symphony. The running back, Steve Harris, knows he has to hit the line hard in a great illusory effort. Bill takes the snap, the corners blitz, and the *Wizard* appears with smoke and fury. The receivers sprint down the sideline like fiery thoroughbreds. Standing defiantly in the pocket, the *Wizard* faces the approaching defensive onslaught. Suddenly, he unleashes the fury. The released lightning bolt of a ball flies down the left side as the blitzing cornerback hits him hard. The pass is complete and it's a 65-yard touchdown. As the pile of players extracts itself off him, Bill does not get up right away. Celebrating the touchdown in near frenzy, the crowd turns deathly silent when they see him still down on the turf. With the trainer starting to come out, Bill rises up slowly and begins walking off the playing field. The crowd roars in relief that Bill appears okay. *The Maestro* gives them his fist pump and then searches for Sarah. In all the frenetic excitement, their eyes and spirits connect. He points at her and gives her a fist pump. As his eyes shift back to the field, they catch the concerned look of Mr. Tibbs in the stands. Looking at him directly, he taps his helmet twice. Suddenly, Doug knows his favorite student is ok.

All Sarah's friends turn green with envy and amazement. She is enthusiastic but they notice a couple of tears on her cheeks. They ask her, "Sarah, are you okay? What's wrong?"

Revealing the depth of her friendship, she replies, "When Bill didn't get up immediately, I was afraid he was hurt."

A voice in the crowd interjects, "If he gets hurt, we're in big trouble because he's the best quarterback anywhere."

With fire in her eyes, Sarah retorts, "I don't care if *he's* the quarterback or not. He's my friend and I don't want him to get hurt."

Her friends relieve her concern teasingly, "He's ok, Sarah. He wasn't hurt. I'm sure he knows how much you care. Funny, we didn't. Oops!" Sarah hears but ignores them. Still worried, she notices the trainer and team doctor looking under his rib pads for signs of injury.

They continue while South kicks off and the defense swarms onto the field. Instead of the game, Sarah continues to pour over Bill's condition from the stands. Nothing misses the glaring light of her eyes. Continuing to choke back the tears softly, she stops as the doctor speaks to Bill and he nods his head affirmatively with a smile. After the doctor and the trainer re-strap his pads, he pulls down his jersey and puts on his helmet again. Bill looks at Sarah with a wry smile, points at her again, and gives her his fist pump. While he swaggers over next to the coach, the crowd exhales in collective relief.

The Dragon's Teeth defense holds for three plays. After Columbus punts, South takes over on their 20-yard line. The offense swarms onto the field while Bill receives the play from Coach Mulinaro. As he jogs out to the huddle, the crowd roars approval. Sarah allows herself the luxury of a deep breath and exhale, relaxing as much as she can. Calling the play as if nothing had happened, Bill sends the team in a sweep right yielding a 7-yard gain, 2nd and 3. South steamrolls down the field mixing running plays and passing plays. It's first down and goal on the Columbus 7-yard line. Coach calls an option right. Bill and the running backs are to run right with Bill tossing the ball to the runner who has the best path to the end zone. However, the *Wizard* has a bit of magic brewing for the cornerback that hit him hard on the first play. Bill tells the running backs, "Sorry guys, I have a plan and I'm keeping the ball. Tight end, just brush that 'tough guy' cornerback and let him through."

Several of the linemen interrupt, "That guy hammered you. You must have taken a harder hit than the medical team knew."

The *Wizard* responds with that wry smile, "I'm fine guys. Just do what I ask and watch the magic unfold." Opening the huddle's cauldron, the team sets its assignments. The spell begins to envelope the field as the center snaps the ball. The offensive line and then the backfield rumble right, led by the *Wizard*. Moving quickly under the spell, the Columbus cornerback feels its effect, seeing an easy prey again. Suddenly, Bill tucks the ball as Sarah sees the events unfold in slow motion expecting the worst. Just as the cornerback readies mentally to deliver devastation, the *Wizard* lowers his shoulder and powers the spell upward with the force of an enraged bull, hitting the cornerback square in the chest. The force of his spell drives the cornerback backward in the air towards the end zone. Continuing to run right over the cornerback, Bill saunters in for a South touchdown. This time the *cornerback* does not get up for a while. Being the humble person that he is, Bill simply hands the ball to the official. Jogging toward the sideline, he looks at the cornerback with his wry, magical smile exclaiming Bill just proved a point. Whipped again to frenzied levels, Bill gives the crowd a fist pump as he gets to the sideline. Taking his helmet off, he gets a drink of water and turns his head to look for Sarah. Making eye contact again, he points to her and smiles. Filling with relief, she knows he is ok now. Her friends go wild again because the quarterback pointed her out. Pointing back immediately, Sarah gets a big smile on her face, communicating her joy. Bill receives that joy from her, lighting his face in an ear-to-ear grin. Their friendship grows better by the minute although they have only known each other one week. There is a building connection between them. It is a special feeling they get only when they are together or see each other.

South wins 42-7 and Bill has a stellar game with 27-30 passing and 346 total yards. This type of performance is an infrequent event in high school yet he is only a freshman. While he dresses in the locker room after the game, the press assembly grows steadily waiting for Bill's appearance. The media begins to call him a phenom. Although only 14 years old, he walks into the media room calmly and politely answers every question while humbly praising his teammates. The press interviews other South players and receive similar responses from them, "Bill seldom speaks about himself or his talent. He comes to practice and games, does his job, and then just wants to be a regular guy. He *is* a great friend that all of us like as a person. He handles himself with unbelievable poise for a freshman. He's under tremendous pressure and expectations after only two games. He's our leader on and off the field and he'd do anything for any of us."

The post-game media session takes longer than last week. Filled with great concern that he missed Sarah and her parents, Bill rushes from the locker room. Following quickly where his mind has already flown, he begins looking for Sarah and her parents. Outside the locker room, he bumps into a waiting Mr. Tibbs and asks anxiously, "Have you seen Sarah tonight?"

Hoping to provide some assurance, Mr. Tibbs replies, "She was still waiting on you when I saw her a few minutes ago."

Relieved, Bill says quickly, "Thanks, Mr. Tibbs." The stadium lights continue to dim as he searches for her. Suddenly, amazed and ecstatic, he sees the Ormonds still waiting for him. Greeting Sarah's parents in his normal, courteous manner, he shows them great respect for being so patient with him. Then, his heart turns to Sarah. As he warmly utters, "Hello," she rushes at him unexpectedly with open arms. She wraps her arms tightly around him with a hug that begs, "Are you ok?" In her caress, she presses her cheek against his chest. Her warm, caring emotion surprises him and embraces his heart. Time slows to a crawl as he returns her affection.

Yet, it is only a moment as Sarah intones what her arms asked already, "Are you ok?"

He assures her, "I appreciate your concern so much, but really, I'm fine."

Then, her dad interrupts the moment saying, "Bill, you were on fire tonight. You seem more focused than last week if that's possible."

Clarifying with reservation, Bill responds, "After that first hit, I had to prove a point."

"What point did you need to prove," her dad probes eagerly.

Revealing his determination, Bill answers, "That they couldn't rattle me. No matter what Columbus did, South was going to win. I was going to do everything in my power to help us win."

"You sure did *that*," her dad exclaims!

Speaking from his heart, Bill replies, "Thanks, I appreciate your words very much. They mean a great deal to me."

Before he can say anything else, her mom states, "Sarah tells me you're coming over tomorrow to help her with her Algebra."

Nervously, he explains, "Yes ma'am. I *am* planning to do that. Is that ok with both of you?"

Her mom answers, "Yes, that's fine. I just want to know if you could come over about one o'clock and have lunch first. Besides, I won't have it any other way. You can help Sarah after that."

Turning to Sarah, Bill inquires eagerly, "If that's ok with you, I'm glad to do that. I don't want to take up your entire afternoon if you have other plans."

Filled with excitement, Sarah bubbles, "It is just fine with me. My plans are to spend time with you learning Algebra better."

Responding to her mom's request, he answers, "Mrs. Ormond, I'll definitely be there at one."

Not wanting her time with Bill to end, Sarah asks him boldly, "Do you have any plans tonight?"

Enthused by her request, Bill responds, "I'm just going to get some pizza and hang out with the guys." Suddenly picking up Sarah's intent, he asks her parents expectantly, "Would it be ok if Sarah ate pizza with us too? We won't be late at all when we finish."

Sensing their friendship, her dad offers, "How would it be if I drop both of you at the Pizza Inn? Sarah can call us when you're ready to come home." Realizing he had not asked her thoughts, her dad inquires, "Sarah, would you like to go?"

Hiding her excitement in her heart, Sarah says, "Yes, Dad, it sounds like great fun."

Pizza

Her parents drop them off at the Pizza Inn. It is a warm and noisy environment drawing students and families to meet often but especially on the weekends. The glass storefront allows everyone who is anyone to see and to be seen. With dark oak wall panels and the red cloth-covered tables creating a welcoming atmosphere, each table adds its own separate cheese and chili containers for patrons to satisfy their cravings. Surrounding the counter in a circus of activity, people order a variety of pizzas and receive soft drinks while the staff tosses pizza crust in the air. The colorfully lighted sign heralds the offerings and costs brightly. Presenting an operating theatre environment, the white block walls and stainless steel tables serve the remaining staff as they heap toppings on finished crusts. The stainless steel ovens complete the process quickly, producing a crispy cracker-thin pizza with a tangy sauce. While devouring the delicious faire, students engage in thought-provoking conversation about different people, sports, weekend haunts and excursions, fashion and the next big fad.

In the midst of this youthful din, Bill and Sarah walk in. With everyone yelling and screaming at him while stroking any ego, he says humbly, "Thank you. I appreciate it more than you know."

Running interference for Sarah, they juke their way through the crowd's repeated praise, "Nice game. Way to go." Navigating the corridor between the tables, Bill picks a spot at the back where his regular friends, Pete, Andy, D. J., and Jordon, are seated. As he introduces Sarah to them, his friends' thoughts sprint vigorously but silently to her beauty. While envious, they remain devoted to his friendship.

Drooling "Hi Sarah," simultaneously, they all laugh at their response. As the guys make room, the couple sits with Bill's friends. No one speaks about football, just stories of friendship and school. While speaking with Bill and his friends, Sarah learns two things about him immediately. He does not see himself as a football star and he is very humble. As she lays her head softly against his shoulder and sighs, her warm touch urges Bill to caress her gently in his strong arm.

Turning to his ear, she whispers, "Why don't you talk about the game or how you did?"

Bill's response is his usual, "Football is what I do, Sarah, not who I am."

A bit confused by his words, she replies, "I don't understand."

"I love playing football but as I told your dad, God blessed me with wonderful skills. He asks me to use those skills to honor Him. In practice and games, I try to use those skills to the best of my ability. When I'm not on the field, I just want to be myself. I'm really nothing special," he explains.

Impressed his explanation, Sarah treasures his words in her heart and responds, "This is the reason I like you so much. You play your heart out, give the credit to God and your teammates, and still, you want to hang out with me." She continues in a whisper, "You could be with anyone you want and listen to them tell you how great you are. However, I can see you don't want that. You have only known me a week and yet you're willing to help me study Algebra. You took the time to apologize to my parents and hand-write a note to me. You *are* very special to me and I'm blessed to have a friendship starting with you." Sarah's words reach deep into Bill's heart and he embraces her tenderly. With their embrace, they experience tangible evidence of that special connection they share. Seeing the pair growing a strong friendship, his friends jokingly protest the whispered secrets between Bill and Sarah. Continuing to enjoy the time hanging out and eating pizza with friends, the two decide finally to call her parents. Making their way back though the adoring public in the restaurant, they reach the exit to wait for her dad to arrive.

Not wanting to leave his new friend alone, Bill waits outside the Pizza Inn with her. When her dad arrives, Sarah gives him another hug and walks toward her dad's car.

Suddenly, Bill says, "Wait a minute, Sarah."

Stopping at his request, she questions with a grin from her heart, "What are you up to?"

Walking to the car, he says, "A gentleman is supposed to open the door for a lady."

Another positive thought rushes through Sarah's mind, "Wow, I don't know anyone else who would be so concerned about my feelings."

As Bill closes the car's door, he intones, "I'll see you tomorrow."

Buoyed with anticipation, Sarah replies, "I'm looking forward to it."

During the ride home, Sarah and her dad have a wonderful conversation. However, the discussion is not about Bill being her boyfriend. As her dad listens with a father's love, Sarah's words are about Bill, the person. She explains, "Dad, he is a really nice guy and very humble, not arrogant or self-centered. Basically, he's a true gentleman. He's kind, caring, and willing to help me, a new friend, with Algebra." Thinking back to her friends' comments earlier in the week, she continues, "One more thing, dad, my friends are right.

He's a strikingly handsome ladies' man, every girls dream guy. I never gave any thought about him being a quarterback. Something about him when we're together makes me feel different than when I'm with anyone else."

At the same time inside the Pizza Inn, Bill rejoins his friends to talk further and have more fun together with them. Being frequent patrons, the owner knows them well and appreciates their business. He has no problem with them sitting and talking at length. After all, they are a fun group to be around and have around. Never causing any trouble, they are always respectful of other people. Additionally, they help keep the other kids under control too and never let anything get out of hand. After talking a while, finally D.J. asks bravely, "Bill, is she your new girlfriend?"

Surprised by the question, Bill responds back, "No, she's just my new friend."

Astounded at Bill's extremely myopic vision of Sarah's feelings, D.J. retorts, "Are you crazy? She's awesome. She has a great mind, a great body, and is downright beautiful. She even rested her head on your shoulder. At least, you have to be working on her becoming your girlfriend."

"Imagine that, Bill Denton has a girlfriend," Andy says with a laugh.

"No, I don't. I have a new friend and that's it. I'm not the kind of guy she'd go out with. She's way out of my league," he explains strongly.

Bill's friends burst with laughter simultaneously as Pete says, "You really don't get it, do you? You have no idea who and what you are?"

Exasperated, Bill replies, "Yes I do. I play football and I'm Bill Denton."

"Are you an idiot," Jordon inquires sarcastically, "You're the star on the football team. You're the smartest guy in school. Every girl melts when you walk by because you look like a movie star. You're the guy every girl wants to go with. We just hang out with you to get your throwaways, not because we like you." Everybody roars with laughter again.

Frustrated with Jordon's assessment, Bill exclaims, "What's wrong with you guys? You're crazy. I'm not that way."

Wanting to clarify his statement, Jordon continues, "When you're on the football field you're not the guy you just described, you are *the guy*. You swagger. It's your way of handling yourself. Confidence just oozes from you."

Wanting to add credence to the persona they see in their friend, D.J. chimes in, "We have known you all our lives. We know you better than anyone knows you."

Acceding somewhat to their idea of his persona, Bill offers, "Well, I do like the stage and the attention. I like to make the big play but that's a game. It's not my life. My life *is* different. I just want to be a regular guy and hang out with my friends."

Recognizing the need for some wise words, Pete interjects analytically, "Look, you need to adjust that philosophy a little. Take a piece of your on-field confidence and add it to your personal life. You can still do what you do when you're hanging with us and do it with a different girl every week. We can hang out with *her* friends. C'mon man, throw us a bone once in a while. We *do* know you and we know how you handle yourself. If we had a dollar for every time our parents said to us, 'why can't you be more like him,' we all could retire at 16."

Pondering for a moment, Bill says, "Sorry about that but that's me. My on-field character is completely different from who I am."

Frustrated with his friend's relationship blindness, D. J. presses the issue and probes impatiently, "Ok, if Sarah is just a *friend*, where do you see this *friendship* going?"

Thinking briefly, Bill bares his deepest thoughts, "I really like her. I like her a lot. I feel different when I'm with her. I've never had this feeling around a girl. It's as if we've known each other our whole lives. She's that one person I feel I can speak with and tell her everything. I'd like it to be more but I don't see it happening."

Stunned with his words, D. J. jumps on that last statement, "It *can* happen but only if *you* want it too. I saw it in her face tonight. Girls don't lay their head on a guy's shoulder if they don't like him. I don't want to be pushy but when *are* you going to see her again?"

With excitement charging his voice, Bill replies, "Tomorrow. I'm going to tutor her in Algebra. She's having a rough time and I know I can help her through it. Her mom asked me to come for lunch before we study. Her parents really seem to like me, especially her mom."

As D. J.'s jaw drops, he retorts, "Are you nuts, man? Her mom asks you over for lunch. You ask Sarah if that's ok and she says its fine with her. Man, I'm telling you, you guys are falling hard for each other but it's up to *you*."

"That would be great but I'm sure you're wrong. It's not going to happen. Hey, anyway we need to head home," Bill replies still unsure of himself.

Imparting food for Bill's thought, D. J. utters the evening's last words, "As I just said, man, she wants *you* for *you* and the next move is up to *you*." Moving toward the exit, Bill ends the discussion quickly.

When Bill arrives home, he has trouble relaxing. His body is tired but his mind refuses to relax enough to sleep. His thoughts dance with visions of Sarah. Visualizing her after the game in his mind, he rushes toward her and remembers losing himself in those sparkling eyes. His memory embraces her warmth as she rested her head on his shoulder at the Pizza Inn touching deep in his heart. Suddenly, he thinks, "*I'm* going to Sarah's house tomorrow. She needs *me* to help her with Algebra. She has such an amazing personality, so warm and giving. Wow, I *really* like her. I want to be more than just friends but I'm afraid to lose her friendship. I'm not sure I'm the kind of guy she would go out with. My *friends* believe I am and say they see it in her eyes and actions. I guess I must be blind not to see what they see." Sensing her warmth ghosting against his shoulder, he searches for a replacement touch. His pillow is a poor substitute but he caresses it anyway. As his thoughts ease their dance with Sarah, he slowly drifts off to sleep and dreams about her.

Arriving at home, Sarah floats up to her room too excited about the evening to sleep. Her thoughts dance with visions of Bill, "I still see the relief on his face turning into a broad smile as he rushed toward *me*. I saw his heart as he gazed into my eyes. I felt warm and safe as he caressed me and I nuzzled his shoulder at the Pizza Inn. *He's* coming to *my* house tomorrow and he wants to help *me* with my Algebra. Wow, I *really* like him and would love to be his girl but I don't want to rush my new friend. Tomorrow can't come soon enough." Her pillow caresses her as she drifts off to sleep and dreams about him.

Algebra

Bill arrives at the Ormond's home shortly before 1PM. Sarah's house is a charming, one-story, sandstone, cream, and red brick ranch. The pink trim enriches the red bricks welcoming all who come near. However, the front lawn is an intimidating green ocean to him. The stately ash trees guard her house strategically like silent sentinels, scrutinizing any newcomer's approach. To those foolhardy enough to get near the door, the sentinels come to life to challenge entry and protect the princess. The two semi-circular steps to the porch are daunting peaks to prevent access to her door. While Bill's eyes saw a traditional house, his nerves told his mind otherwise. At exactly one o'clock, Bill reaches the summit and knocks on her door.

Excitement overcomes Sarah as she senses him just inches away from her. Barely hiding her joy, she opens the door. "Please come in," Sarah requests with elation. Bill had breached all the defenses and now surveys the castle around him. His mind clears the clouds from his eyes as the room comes into focus. "I didn't think you were going to come. It was almost one and I hadn't seen you yet," she says with concerned relief.

"One o'clock is one o'clock. I like to be on time not early or late,"

Bill responds jovially. His words cause Sarah to burst with laughter suddenly. "What's so funny," Bill questions.

"I have only known you for a week and I knew you wouldn't be early or late. After a game, you have obligations but here you're different from everyone else. You're you," Sarah jokes playfully! Bill thinks, "There's that 'different' thing again," and then he laughs too.

Walking into the room where Bill and Sarah are talking, her mom says simply, "Hi Bill."

He replies politely, "Hello ma'am." As her dad strolls into the room, Bill says with respect, "Sir."

Outlining the activities for the next half hour or so, her mom says, "Your timing is perfect for lunch. It's ready and the table is set. Let's go to the dining room." Following the Ormonds toward the dining room, Bill's senses drink in the rooms as they go. To his immediate left, the fireplace with knotty pine above light wood wainscoting in the room conjures thoughts of future times with her. Proceeding down the hallway, he notices the same color wainscoting in much of the house. He can see her mom's design touches throughout as he walks. There is a liberal use of pink highlights everywhere.

While sitting down to the afternoon lunch of grilled cheeseburgers, baked crinkle-cut fries, and soft drinks, her dad exhibits his pleasure with the meal that he prepared for them while her mom set the table. In his mind, he is an excellent grill chef. Of course, he grills only for his family on special occasions such as this. Her mom and dad have several getting acquainted questions for Bill and they continue discussing various topics during lunch. Although a bit uneasy in this setting, he replies politely to all their questions. However, her parent's words fall on four ears clouded by thoughts of each other. While Bill and Sarah hear them, they really did not listen to her mom and dad's words. They focus their thoughts and eyes on each other, communicating without the need for words.

As lunch concludes, her mom says, "You kids need to get started on the Algebra. I'll clean up the dishes from the table."

Countering with kindness, Bill offers, "We'll get to the Algebra, Mrs. Ormond, but we need to clean up the table and wash the dishes first." Amazed at his words, Sarah thinks, "Wow, what a guy."

Her mom says graciously, "That's not necessary, Bill. I'll wash them."

Bill insists and begins cleaning the table, "Since you and Mr. Ormond prepared everything, the least I can do is clean up for you." Acquiescing, her mom shakes her head with a smile while Sarah and Bill take the dishes to the kitchen. After washing and drying the dishes, they put them away together. All the while, they talk, exchange warm glances and blushing giggles, and laugh with each other. Between looking out the window to the patio and backyard, they sneak glimpses into each other's eyes and share each other's thoughts.

Finally, they start the Algebra review. Surprisingly, after only 30 minutes of Bill's help, Sarah has an epiphany, "Wow that's all there is to it?"

Pleased with his pupil's rapid progress, Bill responds, "Yep, that's it."

"Well, why doesn't the teacher explain it that way," she inquires rhetorically?

Answering her anyway, he says, "I wouldn't know but you should be fine now. However, if you need any more help, just let me know. I'll always be here for you." With the planned lunch and Algebra activities complete, Bill nerves overcome his heart and he says, "I think I should probably go now."

However, Sarah is *not* ready for their day together to end yet. Thinking quickly, she questions, "Since it didn't take long, do you mind staying a while longer? You don't have something else you need to do, do you?"

Her words reach into his heart calming his nerves. Relieved at her question, Bill answers, "I don't have anything to do and would love to stay."

Since it is a temperate Midwest fall afternoon, he suggests they go for a walk to observe at the fall colors. Smiling at his suggestion, Sarah says, "Yes, I would like that very much." She muses in her mind, "I can't believe it. This guy wants to go for a walk, admire nature, and enjoy some special moments with *me*." As they shuffle around the backyard and eventually through the neighborhood, it appears as if God hand-painted each of the leaves on the trees just for them. It is an incredible feast for the eyes of red, gold, and orange color variations. Time drifts slowly by as they continue ambling between sun and shadow, viewing the beauty of God's handiwork, and discussing many things. They both are happy to have someone to talk with about any topic. Suddenly, Sarah probes, "Bill, do you attend any church?"

Opening his character further, he replies, "Yes I do. I know God blesses me daily and wants me to be a role model to younger kids. I try to do things God would have me to do. I don't go to church because people expect me to go. I go to church because I want to go. I owe it to God for what he does for me."

Wanting to spend more time with him especially at church, Sarah asks boldly, "Okay, would you like to go our church with my family and me tomorrow?"

Thrilled with the prospect, Bill answers, "Yes, I'd like that very much."

Drifting back to her house slowly through the sea of leaves, Bill trembles as he stretches his hand timidly toward Sarah's hand. As their fingers touch gingerly, she presses her hand into his hand softly. Emotion and delight overcome them as they share the joy of the moment. When they reach her home, Sarah rushes in to her mom excitedly and questions, "Mom, can Bill come with us to church tomorrow?"

Surprised yet pleased with Sarah's request, her mom answers, "Yes, your dad and I are happy to have Bill come to church with us."

Smiling at her mom, Sarah says, "Thank you so much mom. It means a lot to me." Returning outside the house to Bill, Sarah says, "We'll pick you up at your house tomorrow morning at 9." While bidding each other adieu, Bill realizes the house is no longer the daunting fortress that met him earlier.

Church

O n Sunday morning, Sarah and her parents pull into Bill's driveway to pick him up for church. As he comes out of his house and gets into the car, Bill's total presence stuns Sarah. Normally, she finds him quite handsome, but today, his appearance leaves her breathless. Arrayed in a grey/silver tailored suit, black belt, black shoes, crisply pressed white shirt, and a black tie, Bill is resplendent with his athletic physique. Her mind flashes one thought, "Wow, he cleans up well. Other guys would show up in just a pair of slacks and pull over sweater but he's dressed like a movie star today. He looks every bit the part." Sarah's parents notice she is as impressed as are they.

Grateful for the opportunity to worship together with the Ormonds, Bill says, "Thanks for coming by to get me. I look forward to a morning of fellowship and God's word." His words break her stunned psyche and she realizes he understands the meaning of being a Christian.

Calling her friends the night before, she told them Bill was coming to church with her today. In response to her call, her girlfriends sit in their customary spots in anticipation. As they walk in, Sarah holds onto Bill's arm. She smiles at her friends and they walk to where her mom and dad are sitting. Taking their place beside them, he leans over and whispers into Sarah's ear, "Do you think I impressed your friends?" Sarah smiles, as her face grows red because he caught her smiling to her friends.

Bill smiles while Sarah whispers back, "They are *very* impressed." He carries his personal, leather-bound bible with him to the service. As the minister delivers his sermon, Bill turns to the referenced verses immediately. Silently through the message, his attentiveness and understanding continue to reveal more of his character and impress Sarah and her parents. They are certain they see a deeply devoted young man with a strong character. Meanwhile, her friends are each speechless and silently envious of her. In their minds and on their faces, they remark at his persona. As the service ends, Sarah and Bill walk by them and smile. The girls return full-face smiles for her. They all nearly swoon at how handsome he is in his suit. The girls fawn all over each other but it appears his heart belongs to Sarah. They look like the perfect couple, meant for each other from Eden's dawning.

Sensing that Sarah wants to spend more time with him, her parents ask, "Bill, are you able to go to lunch with us? We'll take you home afterwards."

Looking at Sarah expectantly for approval, Bill inquires hopefully, "Is that was ok with you?"

Filled with excitement, she replies quickly, "Yes, I'm very happy to have you go to lunch with us." With a huge smile, he agrees to go to lunch with Sarah and her family. Her parents take them to a local steak house.

As they enter the restaurant, the host greets them warmly and asks, "How many people are in your party? Would you like a booth or table?"

Sarah interjects quickly, "A booth please." Hoping for a booth, Bill smiles at her request, which means the two of them can sit next to each other. Knowing it is not polite as the guest to speak for the group, he is glad she spoke up.

Being congenial, her dad says, "Bill, please order whatever you want."

Wanting her gastronomic opinion first, Bill inquires of Sarah, "What do you plan to order?"

Knowing her palate desires immediately, she answers, "The 6 oz. sirloin, medium-well, a baked potato with butter only, a side of green beans, and a soft drink."

Agreeing with her selection, he replies, "That sounds good to me. I think I'll get that as well."

The waiter comes to take the orders and asks Sarah first, "What would you like?" Before she can answer, Bill utters, "Sarah will have the 6 oz. sirloin, medium-well, a baked potato with butter only, a side of green beans, and a cola to drink. I'll have the same thing."

Impressed that he ordered for her, Sarah says, "I'm capable of ordering for myself. You didn't have to order for me."

Sensing some frustration, Bill explains, "I know but a gentleman should place a ladies order. It shows he cares about what she wants." As her mom and dad place their orders, Bill shows off a bit by taking Sarah's napkin and snapping it in the air. It lands perfectly on Sarah's lap. Her mom just smiles and shakes her head at his performance and at how well he treats Sarah. Before the waiter serves lunch, Bill gives Sarah another hand-written note. As she opens the note and begins reading, the words surprise her. While continuing to read silently, her smile grows from deep in her heart.

> *Sarah,*
>
> ***Thank you so much for sharing this time with me today. The fellowship at your church and you sitting next to me now at lunch, these things make this a very special day for me.***
>
> ***Your friend, Bill***

After reading the note, Sarah feels her heart race. Directing her beautiful smile Bill's way, she says, "Thank you. It is a very special day for me too."

On the way home from the restaurant, Sarah probes with clear intent, "What are you doing the rest of the day?"

Thinking for a moment, Bill replies, "I have some homework and extra credit work to do. It will only take me a couple hours and then I'll be done for the day."

Wondering aloud, Sarah says, "Why are you doing extra credit work? Are you behind in something?"

Attempting to clarify his reasons, he explains feebly, "Actually, I'm ahead of the rest of the people in my classes. I do extra credit to keep busy."

Looking puzzled, Sarah asks, "If you're ahead, why do extra credit?"

Chuckling, he replies, "I like the challenge and want to keep sharp in my academics."

Sarah inquires jokingly, "How smart are you then?"

Exposing more of his character, he confides in her, "I have a little game in my classes. It's another stage on which to perform."

Probing further, she asks, "Do you get straight A's, then?"

Surprised with her question but pleased with his abilities, he answers, "No. I usually get 2 or 3 B's a year."

"*2 or 3 B's a year,*" Sarah exclaims, "That's unbelievable. You're that smart?"

Sensing the need to explain, he says, "I work hard but as I said, I have a little game when it comes to academics. You know I think you're pretty smart too. I could tell when you picked up the Algebra so quickly. I see that in you."

Startled by his words, Sarah remarks, "I get A's and B's but definitely more than 2 or 3 B's a year. Would you like to come over and study together? I have some Algebra and Chemistry to work on."

Without hesitation, Bill says, "Yes but I have to be home by 9 o'clock to go to bed."

Curious, Sarah inquires, "Why do you go to bed at 9 o'clock on nights before school?"

Providing her more of his character and work ethic, he explains, "I get up at 5 am, hurry to South High School, and get in my weight work and running."

"Let me get this straight. You work out before school starting at 5 am. You attend class all day and then go to practice. Finally, you go home and do your homework. That's amazing to me," Sarah exclaims to him.

"That's pretty much my day," Bill responds.

Astonished, Sarah reacts, "I don't know how you can do all that and not sleep all weekend."

Looking deeply into Sarah's eyes with a wry smile, he chuckles, "If I slept all weekend, I wouldn't be able to hang out with you. I consider that unforgivable on my part."

She smiles at his words with a smile from deep in her heart and thinks, "That is so awesome and he is spending that time with *me*." Recovering quickly, she quizzes eagerly, "So, are you coming over to study or staying home? I could really use the help in chemistry."

Not wanting to refuse a friend in need or one so beautiful, he says, "I'll change quickly and get my books." Once they arrive at Sarah's, schoolwork starts immediately but so does the laughing, whispers, and giggling. Delighting in each other's company, they study vigorously. However, time passes much too quickly. When they look at the clock, it is 8:30 PM. Bill apologizes, "I'm sorry but I have to go. I wish I didn't have to do so but 5 am comes early."

Pleased with the help Sarah received from her new friend, her mom says, "I'll run you home, Bill."

Wanting to extend the weekend a bit further, Sarah exclaims, *"Mom, I'm coming too."*

When they arrive at Bill's house, he asks her mom hopefully, "Can Sarah come in for a minute to see my house?"

Allowing Sarah to get better acquainted, her mom says to them, "Yes but don't take forever. You have to get some sleep too. Remember, I heard your schedule for school days before we left."

Mom and Dad

Sarah follows Bill into the house and walks upstairs with him where he has a three-room apartment with a full bath, sink, and stove. As they reach the top of the stairs and walk inside the apartment, Sarah comments, "This is amazing. I'd never believe that a high school student would have their own apartment. I think it's great that you have a place this nice for yourself. Do your mom and dad live downstairs?"

With the pain of loss returning in his heart, Bill answers with a twinge of sadness in his voice, "No, my grandparents live downstairs."

Puzzled and intrigued, Sarah inquires, "Where do your mom and dad live?"

Bill shuffles his feet and stares dejectedly at the floor. His smile disappears as he explains, "My parents died a few years ago in a car accident. My grandparents allow me to live here with them. They could not bear to send me to a foster home. It would have been doubly hard on them to lose me as well but it *is* difficult for me at times. Even after a number of years, it seems like yesterday that I lost mom and dad." His eyes swell with tears as he continues, "I have a large trust fund from the insurance companies that I can use for my needs as long as I stay in school." Opening his character to Sarah a bit more, he expounds, "This is why I have to do things better on the field and I strive to get the highest grades I can achieve. This is why I perform the extra credit work. I have to maintain this strict regimen of workouts, studies, and leadership. I can't afford to take a chance of losing the trust my parents created for me and I don't want to burden my grandparents. I have to get a full-ride scholarship to college. When I graduate from college, I can access the trust for any reason. However, it's not about the money though it does help me. The trust fund is really just a tool to pay for the camps I attend to grow as an athlete, lunch at school, and pizza with a great girl."

"Oh Bill, I'm so sorry. I didn't know about your parents or your life. I hope I didn't bring back any bad memories," Sarah responds and hugs him tightly with great caring.

As he returns her hug gently, he responds, "It's ok. You're fine. You couldn't have known. The memories are always with me to keep my parents fresh in my mind and heart. However, I don't want people to feel sorry for me. Hey, on a brighter note, I'll get my driver's license next year. I can get a car and have some dates if there's a girl I want to ask on a date."

"So you're raising yourself," Sarah inquires.

"Not at all, my grandparents are super people and they work hard teaching me great life lessons. They're the reason I keep it together and why I am the person I am right now. My grandfather developed and refined my strong work ethic and my attention to detail. He's a fantastic carpenter and he taught me 'never let good enough be good enough.' My grandmother taught me to cook and clean properly. They both instilled a strong faith in me. When I need to talk with someone about school or life too, I rely on Mr. Tibbs, my guidance counselor, for advice. He's like a father to me and keeps me on the right path," Bill explains and continues, "My dad was tall like me and played football in college until he hurt his knee. My mom was dfd0df

a swimmer and won two National Championships. She was on the Olympic Team and won a medal." Bill notices Sarah's eyes becoming a little teary. Hugging her gently in his arms, he kisses her on both cheeks and assures her, "Sarah, it's fine. Please don't to worry about it. I'm glad I'm able to share my world with you." Gazing into each other's eyes, Sarah knows Bill is ok with their discussion. He walks her back to her mom's car.

As he opens the door for her, she says excitedly, "Call me in 15 minutes. I'll be home by then."

"OK, please listen for your phone to ring," he replies as he begins a countdown of the minutes until he can call her.

Goodnight Dance

arah's phone rings exactly 15 minutes after they left Bill's house. "What's up," Bill asks?

Very nervous and afraid to say the wrong thing, Sarah inquires, "I just have a question for you if you don't mind. It's kind of personal."

Confident they can discuss anything, Bill declares, "It's no problem. Ask away. Our conversation at my house pretty well established the fact we can talk to each other about anything."

With her confidence rising at his words, she continues, "Earlier, you said when you get your license, you're going to get a car. Then, you could have a date if there is a girl you want to ask on a date at that time. Do you have a girlfriend now?"

Opening his heart and character a bit, Bill responds, "If I had a girlfriend, I couldn't spend time with you. That wouldn't be right. It wouldn't be fair to you or the other girl. So no, I don't have a girl friend."

Relieved and emboldened by his words, Sarah questions eagerly, "Is there someone at East you want to ask on a date with when you get your license." Sarah rolls her eyes and pleads to herself, "Please say no. Please say no."

"No, there isn't anyone," he replies.

"Do you *want* a girlfriend," Sarah asks excitedly.

With his mind racing, Bill did not really hear the excitement in her question. "Yes I do," he replies meaning Sarah but afraid to reveal that to her plainly. He explains further, "The problem is most of the girls want to go out with me because I'm the quarterback. I know that sounds arrogant but I can tell when I speak with them. It's the quarterback they like not just me. I want a girlfriend who likes me just for me, not because I'm the quarterback." Suddenly, Bill has an epiphany and continues, "Take you for instance, you never ask me anything about football. We talk about all kinds of different things. *You're* the kind of girl with whom I want to go out."

Filled with great anticipation, Sarah misses what Bill just said. Quizzing him from her thoughts, she says, "Did I hear you say that you found someone like that?"

With his mind second-guessing his heart, he replies, "Yes I have, but I doubt seriously that she will go with me on a date."

Sarah, still contemplating rather than listening, quizzes, "Who is she? Maybe I can put a bug in her ear?"

Amused with her offer, he chuckles, "No thanks. I really need to ask her myself. If only I could find the courage to ask her."

Attempting to dance with his thoughts, Sarah inquires, "What's she like?"

Nervously teasing, he relates to her, "She's beautiful, smart, funny, and doesn't really care that I play football."

Making a bold challenge, Sarah interrupts, "Then what's the problem with asking her for a date?"

Voicing concern, Bill answers, "If I ask her and she says no, it would put this 'thing' in the middle of our friendship. I don't want to risk that. However, there is plenty of time." Fighting his nerves and summoning the courage, he blurts, "Sarah, do you have a boyfriend?"

Excited with his question, Sarah responds quickly, "I don't. Still, I have my eye on a guy but I feel like you do. If I say something to him, he might think I'm too forward." Struggling with her thoughts, she continues, "Really, I don't want my friends to tell him. I want him to ask me because *he* wants to ask me. I don't want someone to coerce him into asking me for a date." They continue dancing briefly with their words while both their hearts ache to confirm the words they heard are about each other. However, neither is brave enough to act and open their heart to the other out of fear of rejection. Compromising with their hearts, they agree to continue their Wednesday night calls. Disheartened, they say good night, leaving their hearts to yearn and their minds to dream about each other.

Before School

5 AM comes early but Bill gets up and hurries to South High school. Entering through the boiler room just as the custodians do, he meets the two custodians on duty.

"Mornin' Bill. You know where the weight room is by now," one of them says jokingly. Then he continues, "Oh, it's open and the gym lights are on."

Shaking his head, he chuckles, "Thanks guys," and rushes to the locker room. Changing into workout clothes quickly, he jogs to the gym to warm up. The gym at South high seats 7,000 people with a wide pedestrian path, two large concession areas, and restrooms around the top of the stands. Bill runs 3 miles around the path or 24 laps in 21 minutes. Then, he jogs to the weight room and performs the rest of his daily routine, which takes an hour and a half. Preparing his body for the rigors of the upcoming season, he executes this workout Monday through Thursday religiously. On game days, he performs only a half workout to conserve strength for the game.

Throughout the workout, his mind is free to roam. Reflecting on the impressions of Sarah created over the weekend, he muses liberally, "Man what a weekend. Sarah's amazing. I can't believe she spent so much time with *me*. Let's see Friday was the game and Pizza

Inn. Her head nestled on my shoulder as she sighed. What a night! Then, there was Saturday and lunch with her parents. We studied Algebra and she walked the neighborhood with *me*. I still feel the touch of her hand and that touch in my heart. She asked me to go to church with her the next day and she actually held my arm as we walked in the church. Then, her parents asked me to lunch with them and afterwards we studied together again. Whoa! She even came to my house and I could just be myself with her all weekend. I wish my parents were still alive to meet her." Reality and sadness bring his mind back to the work at hand and the day ahead. The phone call they shared races in his thoughts, "Was I the guy Sarah was speaking about? I can't be the one she wants to ask her out. Still, she did hold my hand as we walked and we did so much together this weekend."

Bill is in tiptop condition and his body fat is only 5%. At 6'6" 245 pounds, the workouts continue to build a ripped, physical specimen. Showering quickly in the locker room, he dresses for the days classes. Rushing for the bus parking, he catches the bus for East Jr. High. Once on the bus, he plans, "This will be much easier when I get a car and it's a perfect reason too. I can drive to the workouts myself."

The gossip machine starts as soon as he arrives at East. Walking into the cafeteria, he orders two chocolate milks, a couple donuts, and pulls out his two hard-boiled eggs for protein. His guys want to know how the "tutoring" went and question, "Did you kiss her or hold her hand? Are you making any progress with her?"

Disturbed by the nature of the questions, Bill says to them, "Listen up. I'm only gonna go through this one time. We had lunch, studied Algebra, and took a walk. She gave me a hug and we talked. She asked me to church on Sunday and I went with her family. We went to a nice steak house for lunch after church. I showed her my apartment and she asked a couple questions. I told her about my parents and she started to cry. She apologized for asking me about them. I gave her a big hug and kissed her on both cheeks. I walked her to her mom and dad's car. She asked me to call her 15 minutes later. I called her and she wanted to know if I had a girlfriend. I told her no and asked if she had a boyfriend. She said no. I went to the high school this morning for my workout and came here. End of the conversation."

"Did you even try anything," Andy asks incredulously.

Upset with his inference, Bill retorts, "First of all, you know I wouldn't do that. Secondly, I have too much respect for her to put her in that position. I wouldn't make her feel obligated to do something she didn't want to do. There is no way I would show any disrespect for her. She's my friend and I hope she will be my best friend at some point." Regretting his remark, Andy apologizes, knowing that is not in Bill's character.

Curious about their discussion, D.J. asks, "What did you say when she asked if you had a girlfriend?"

Avoiding the full discussion content, Bill replies, "I told her no but there is one girl. I said the girl is very special but didn't tell her who she is. Oh by the way, I'm not telling you guys either. She's pretty, smart, and a super person but I don't think I'm the kind of guy with whom she would go out. That's what I told her and that's what I'm telling you guys."

"C'mon man. You expect us to believe the girl isn't Sarah. We saw her at the Pizza Inn. What did she say about a boyfriend," Pete inquires wanting to know more about Sarah.

Still being somewhat secretive, Bill explains further, "She said basically what I said. She didn't want to say who her special guy is. *However*, she's glad she has a friend in *me* with whom she can discuss anything including him and from whom she can get advice."

Sarah's Morning

Sarah's Monday didn't start at 5 AM as Bill's did. However, as she dresses for school, her mind replays the same events of the weekend as Bill's did, "It was a wonderful weekend. Bill is an amazing person. I can't believe he wanted to spend so much time with *me.* He was so caring Friday after the game and at the Pizza Inn. He caressed me while I nestled my head on his shoulder. His touch was so gentle it made me sigh with contentment. What a very special night! Then, there was Saturday and lunch with my parents. He shows such respect for my parents and me. We studied Algebra and he walked the neighborhood with *me.* I can still feel his timid touch against my hand. It was so sweet that I had to put my hand in his. I *had* to ask him to go to church with me the next day. I wanted to see more of his character. I wanted my friends to see I cared for him. It was *so* cool I just had to hold his arm as we walked in the church. Then, my parents asked him to lunch with us. How did they know I wanted to do that? Afterwards, I *had* to ask him to study with me. I *didn't* want him to leave. Whoa! I couldn't believe he asked me to see his apartment and I could just be myself with him. I hope I didn't hurt him asking about his parents. The sadness in his eyes and face hit me hard. Mom seemed to like him so much but even dad liked him too."

At breakfast with her mom, Sarah questions curiously, "Why do you shake your head and smile so much when Bill does something?"

Her mom responds, "He's the type of young man you don't meet that often. He's respectful, caring, and polite. He's just a special kind of person."

Amazed with her mom's words, she exclaims, "I've never heard you speak about anybody like that."

Revealing her thoughts of Bill, her mom explains, "Well Sarah, it's because I've seldom met anyone like him. I keep looking for a character flaw but I haven't seen one yet. Do you like him?"

Filled with excitement, Sarah responds, "Yes, yes I do even though we've only know each other for about ten days. He makes me feel special every time we're together. He treats me so nice and he's so caring. Yes I like him a lot."

Breaking the moment's joy, her mom inquires with interest, "Does he like *you*?"

Contemplating for a moment, Sarah answers with hesitation, "I think he does. I *hope* he does. We have so much fun together and when we look in each other's eyes, it's special. I don't think it's a high school crush kind of thing. It's different with him. I don't want to go out with him because he has good looks. That's important true. It's hard to explain. I want to know more of *him*, more of his *character*. I know he likes being with me, just to be with me. I know in my heart that he doesn't have a hidden agenda or motive. Do you know what I mean?"

"Yes I do," her mom answers with understanding.

Opening her heart a bit more, Sarah continues, "I trust him totally when we're together. I know he respects me and wouldn't do anything to show a lack of respect towards me. I like the character he has shown me so far. He knows I don't care that he's the quarterback and he knows I'm his friend not the quarterback's groupie. He told me he didn't have a girlfriend. He confided in me that most girls wanting to be with him just want to be with the quarterback. He confessed to me as we walked Saturday what it was like being the quarterback."

"It has to be a lot of pressure. Remember, we have seen him on Friday nights," her mom adds.

Concerned, Sarah explains further, "He has so much stuff to do. You heard his daily routine. I'm happy to spend *any* time with him. He gets requests at school from newspaper reporters and TV sports reporters. Grade school kids want his autograph and he feels great pressure to do the right thing and behave in the right way. While wanting to *be* that role model, he's still afraid he might fail. He doesn't want to burden his grandparents or reflect badly on them. He doesn't want anyone to believe he's arrogant or privileged just because he's the quarterback. He's heard parents telling their kids that they should be more like him. Dealing with all that now, he knows it's going to become more intense if he continues his football career. He's pondering all that now. I've heard the girls at school all saying they want to be with the quarterback. When he bumped into me and spilled that soft drink on me, I thought he was just another bigheaded football player. However, the way he looked at *me* was so special when he asked if I would wait after the game with you. I knew then that he was a different type of person. When he met us, I did allow myself to admit he's handsome. When he apologized, I forgot how good looking he was and realized what a great person he was. Oh my goodness, what time is it? I need to get to the bus stop."

The Day

T he inquisition his friends gave him in the morning was bad enough. However, he receives notice to come to the office conference room immediately. Apprehensive and confused, he arrives at the conference room. Waiting in the room are two reporters from Ft. Wayne, IN. South plays Luers High School in Ft. Wayne this week for its first road game this season. Surprised and somewhat frustrated at the academic interruption, Bill says, "Gentlemen, I was unaware of this scheduled meeting." The reporters show him a confirmation letter from the South High School Athletic Director. After reading the letter, he states again, "While I was unaware of this scheduled meeting, I'll be glad to speak with you." It really wasn't the truth. He doesn't understand why his playing football is such a big deal.

The reporters explain to him, "We'll interview you and write an article in the Fort Wayne paper. We'll send you a copy too."

Indifferent to the offer, Bill responds, "Don't worry about that. You don't have to send me a copy. I don't have a scrap book and I don't really like reading about myself."

They inform him, "We'll do an interview for the local TV station."

Concerned about missing class, he says, "That's fine. By the way, how long will this take I've got classes to attend?"

"Not long," one of the reporters says as they start asking questions.

"South was 2 and 8 last year. This year with you at quarterback, so far, you're 2 and 0. You beat the defending state champions the first week of the season. Do you think your presence has turned this team around," one of the interviewers probes keenly.

"No it's not all about me. All I do is take the snap, hand the ball off, or throw it to somebody. The line blocks and our defense *is* stellar. We are a team. It's not about any one of us," Bill reminds them.

"This is your first road game of the season and it's a 3 hour bus ride from the Southside of Indianapolis to Ft Wayne. That's a lot of time to think about a game. Do you think, being a freshman, you'll get nervous and feel extra pressure," the interviewers continue.

"No, not at all, I'm where God wants me to be," he says frankly.

"So you don't feel any extra pressure being a freshman and going three hours to play," the interviewers probe.

"Nope, none at all," he replies with great confidence. Relentlessly, the interviewers fire the questions at him for two hours but Bill is a smart kid and adept at their game. Attempting to goad him into doing what he never does, the reporters try to maneuver him into talking about himself and saying something negative about an opponent. Through the entire interview, Bill puts all the praise and effort on his teammates constantly. However, he verbalizes his concern over the time being spent, "Guys, I'm missing important classes with this interview. I need to maintain my GPA. How much longer is this going to last?"

Finally, Bill receives permission to go back to class. The reporters turn to Doug Tibbs, who sat in on the interview in case Bill needed any advice. They interviewers state, "The kid puts on a pretty good game face, saying he's not nervous or feeling any pressure."

Amused by their observation, Doug responds, "He *doesn't* feel any pressure and I can promise you he won't be nervous. He is a unique young man who handles himself with a lot of class. What you just saw is really who he is. Oh yes, one more thing, he is as good as everyone says he is." With that in mind, the reporters headed back to Ft Wayne.

What a day. Grilled by his friends and suffering reporters' questions for two hours, now Bill thinks the rest of the day should be just fine. As soon as he walks into his 3rd period class, the girls start giggling. Two of them have *saved* him a seat and both hand him notes that say essentially the same thing. "Bill, you're a great quarterback. I would love to go to a game with you. You don't need to go to Central to get a girlfriend. You have one right here." He reads the notes and thanks them politely as class time allows. After class, he provides the explanation that Sarah is his friend, attempting to convince himself and others she is not his girlfriend. This only serves to make his girlish suitors more ardent. If he doesn't have a girlfriend, then he is fair game.

Lunchtime can't come soon enough. Two guys, who Bill has never met, slither up next to him and start asking questions about Sarah. They begin to say disrespectful and mean things about her as their insinuations about her raise his ire. Determined to stay out of trouble, he stands to move to another table. As he leaves, one of them says loudly, "How good is she," and they weren't talking about Algebra. Bill stops in his tracks and wheels back to them. By now, everyone in the cafeteria has heard the stench from their mouths. The cafeteria's gaze focuses on Bill.

Suddenly, the *Wizard* appears to protect Sarah's reputation with fiery eyes that only his closest friends recognized. Stepping back toward them, he leans in and says in a whisper laced with fire only they can hear, "If you *ever* speak about her like *that* again, you *will* answer to me." Fortunately, for those two, Pete and D.J. rush over quickly and tell him it's not worth it. While he is angry because these *jerks* spoke ill of his friend, he is angrier with himself for showing his anger publicly.

Protecting Bill's reputation with their intervention, Pete and D.J. speak quickly with the two guys and say, "Seriously, you don't want any part of him. He'll break you guys in two." Viewing the seething *Wizard*, the two get the message and realize they crossed the line. The mob mentality in the cafeteria had hoped to see him pound those two into oblivion. However, the girls all melt to see such a hero arise. They yearn for someone in their lives to defend them, as Bill did for Sarah.

After lunch, the *Wizard* fades from view and Bill returns to his calm self, thinking the rest of the day has to be better. Unfortunately, his thinking did not translate to reality. A local newspaper reporter wants to do a feature article about him and his rise to varsity quarterback. Bill hates this kind of stuff when the article focuses strictly on him. However, he knows if he doesn't concede to these interviews, rumors will spread that he's uncooperative and self-absorbed. To make the day worse, the distractions cause him to miss four questions on a 100-question test in History. "That's only 96%," he says in disgust with himself.

Finally, the school day ends and practice begins. Loving this part of the day, Bill has two hours of show time for him. Mentally relaxing, he works on his skills and hangs with his teammates. With the day he experienced, his mind flashes suddenly to Sarah and her day. Did she have the same problems? Even though it's only Monday, his mind persuades him to call Sarah and explain what happened in the cafeteria. He wants her to get the information first hand not rumor.

"Hello. Is Sarah busy," Bill inquires hopefully.

"Is this Bill," her mom inquires recognizing his voice.

"Yes ma'am it is," he replies respectfully.

"Hold on and I'll get her," she replies.

Somewhat confused, Sarah comes to the phone and says, "Hi Bill. This is quite a surprise. What is the special occasion? Is anything wrong?"

Nervous about his next words, Bill answers, "With the day I had at school, I wanted you to hear about it from me, not through the grape vine."

Concerned by his tone, she probes intently, "Are you ok? You didn't get hurt did you?"

Hoping to allay her concern, Bill begins to explain, "In the cafeteria at lunch, two guys asked inappropriate questions about you and me. I told them I didn't appreciate their lack of respect for you. When I stood to change to another seat away from them, they said one more very wrong and disrespectful thing. I stopped, turned back to them, and warned them forcefully if they ever talked about you like that again, they would have to answer to me."

His statements in defense of her reputation impress Sarah. While listening, she thinks, "He protected me even when I wasn't there. How did I come to deserve such a wonderful friend?"

Pausing for a moment to review his next thoughts, he continues, "They started to get up and I put my tray down as they approached. D. J. and Pete saw the fire in my eyes and stepped in before the two guys started something they would regret. My friends have known me a long time. They told those two they'd better mind their own business or I would break them in half. First, I want to apologize to you for letting them get me angry. If they continued, I would be in trouble and they would have been hurt badly. I don't usually ever get mad but their words were so hurtful toward you. I just didn't like their total lack of respect toward you. Also, I didn't want any rumors about you flying through the school. So I put a stop to it."

Hesitating for a moment to review his statements mentally, Sarah speaks softly, "I don't know what to say to you for defending my honor except to thank you for standing up for me. It's very special, more special than you can imagine. I'm *proud* to have a friend who defends me as you did. Thank you so much. I received a call earlier from some friends at East. They related what took place. I'm happy you didn't get into any trouble. Thank the guys for me that they defended you." With her last sentence, Sarah's voice quivers a bit.

Catching the shudder in his ears, he questions, "Sarah, are you crying?"

With tears welling in her beautiful eyes, she replies, "Yes, I am because you touched my heart deeply." Focusing her ideas, she continues, "Uh, so how was the rest of your day? I heard two girls gave you notes to be your girlfriend, did you tell them *yes?*"

Puzzled by her words, Bill replies with a lilt in his voice, "You *know* I didn't tell them yes. You *know* there's only one girl I want to be with."

"*And who is she,*" Sarah asks coyly?

Laughing in his heart, he continues the teasing dance, "I'm not telling you…until you tell me who your special guy is." Without waiting for her answer, he jukes verbally as if avoiding a linebacker, "The first thing this morning I had to meet with two reporters from Ft Wayne and one guy from a local paper. You *know* how much I like that. Will you be at the game Friday in Ft Wayne?"

Still spinning from his quick subject changes, Sarah answers, "I'll be there with my mom and dad too."

"That's great," he exclaims. Realizing he has not yet spoken of her day, Bill inquires with concern, "How did your day go?"

Hearing his concern over her day, she answers excitedly, "It was great. Everyone wanted to hear about our weekend in every class and at lunch. Of course, they talked about you and me being boyfriend and girlfriend. I kept telling them we're just friends. They asked me if you're the special guy I talked about with whom I wanted to go on a date. Of course, I didn't tell them who he is. But, I'm *sure you* can figure him out." She could hear his smile through the phone.

Through his smile, Bill answers, "Well, I just wanted you to know and make sure you're ok." They soon say goodnight to each other.

After telling her parents about their phone conversation, her dad comments, "I really like Bill. Most guys wouldn't do what he just did. They would have tried to hide the confrontation. Others would have just gone along with it and then the rumors about you would have started."

Her mom shakes her head and says, "He's a unique person. You know we rarely hear you kids talk about football or sports in general. We're proud that you two are loyal, supportive, and encouraging friends."

Luers

As the week progresses, the preparation for 7th ranked Luers becomes more intense but the practices proceed really well. Continuing the hard work and preparation diligently, the team pleases Coach Mulinaro immensely with each team member feeling very good about themselves, the team, and the upcoming game. Coach Mulinaro knows the difference in this year's team versus last year's team is Bill Denton's talent, but mostly, his leadership and football knowledge. Reflecting on his talk with Bill as an eighth grader, he enjoys watching him grow as a person and as a player almost like his father. Meanwhile, Bill is slowly making Joey Sanders his favorite receiver. He is his "go to" guy on big plays. All week long, Bill has the receivers stay an extra hour to practice their patterns and to perfect their timing together.

Finally, Friday arrives for the fans, the parents, and the players. Although South is 2-0, defeating the number one ranked team in the process, they are not ranked in the top ten yet. Talk circulates among the players that the pollsters have cheated them by excluding them from the polls. However, Bill stops that destructive discussion quickly. The *Maestro* arises, gathers the team, and verbalizes his thoughts emphatically, "It doesn't matter what we think. *We* have no control over the newspaper rankings. *We* have to change pollsters' minds and hearts and to do that, *we* go out and *win* games. If we *win* games, we *gain* their respect. We *control* the things that *we* can control. We *concentrate* on each of *our* jobs not the polls. We do *our* best with what *God* gave us. *No* worries! *No* bull! *No* foolin'! End of conversation!" The team hears and understands the *Maestro* and never brings it up again. Bill returns to his usual, calm, confident self but he projects an aura of leadership and confidence around him. When he speaks to the team, it is the law. That is the way it is with no questions asked.

The team leaves school early Friday afternoon for the three-hour ride. Arriving at Luers around 5:30 pm, the team dresses and prepares for the coming battle. Finishing warm ups, they are ready for the challenge. South has what the newspapers call a "high powered offense," averaging over 30 points a game. Luers has a tough defense and allows only 9 points a game. They are big, fast, and strong on defense. At opposite ends of the same scale, one or both of the teams will not meet their normal performance tonight.

Luers wins the toss and defers to South to be on defense first. If they keep South from scoring on the first possession, it is a huge psychological advantage to their team. By deferring, they get the ball to start the second half. If Luers has the lead, it is another big advantage for them. Of course, that is a couple of ifs and a roll of the dice. This is a serious coaching chess match. During Luers kick off, the ball travels past the end zone and South gets the ball on its 20-yard line. The offense hustles onto the field with Bill receiving the play call from Coach Mulinaro and as usual, trailing the rest of the team. As he swaggers onto the field, the South fans erupt in a thunderous roar.

Sarah and her parents have seats right at 50-yard line about 15 rows up. These are perfect seats in Luers stadium. Even Doug Tibbs and his family journeyed to see the game. While a special night for

Bill, Sarah beams with pride in the stands. Her heart knows the stands roar loudly for *her* friend. Calling the first play, he and the offense break the huddle. By now, the receivers know if Bill taps his helmet, they are to break deep. As Bill steps to the line, Luers formation has five down linemen and four linebackers. Reading the defense, he knows they plan to blitz on the play. Bill taps his helmet and takes the snap. As he drops back and before he can get set, his blocking collapses. Two blitzing linebackers and a safety crush him. Going down hard, he does not get up. While lying on the ground, he holds his ribs and by all appearances, he is injured badly. The trainer and team doctor rush out as Bill continues to lie on the ground holding his side. Doug Tibbs leans to his family and voices his concern, "I have never seen Bill stay down like this. I'm worried for his health." With big tears streaming down her cheeks, Sarah cradles her head in her hands. As fear about the severity of his injuries grips her, she becomes very concerned for Bill's welfare.

Sitting in stunned silence, the South crowd has the same question collectively, "Are all the hopes and dreams for the season vanishing in front of us?" The medical staff keeps talking to Bill. After about 5 minutes, he rolls over and gets to his hands and knees but still doesn't get up. Finally, Bill rises to his feet and walks off slowly. When he doesn't give the crowd his trademark fist pump, they know he is hurt badly. Deep concern overcomes Sarah as she cries intensely while her mom consoles her with a loving arm. It is second down and 20 yards to a first down. South runs two more plays with backup quarterback Ted Nalley at the helm and then they punt.

Luers runs the ball back to their 35-yard line. Marching quickly down the field, they score to take the lead 7-0. South runs the kick off to their own 15-yard line. Amazingly, Bill leads the offense onto field as the crowd erupts with roaring approval. Running their sweep, South gains five yards. During the play, Bill receives a strong late hit in the back after he hands off and goes down again. As a result,

Luers receives a 15-yard penalty for roughing the quarterback. The penalty moves South's possession to its 35-yard line but Bill is slow getting up again. As the South fans shower the Luers team intensely with chorus of boos, the team doctor and trainer start onto the field. Seeing the flurry of activity on his account, Bill rises quickly and waves them back vigorously. He determines in his mind that will not come out no matter what. In the huddle, the *Wizard* reassures his teammates, "I'm fine. While they hit hard and dirty, we *won't* be fazed. Remember who *you* are and who *we* are. Concentrate on your job. Lock and load! Let's take it to 'em." They know he's hurting but his toughness inspires his teammates. South bores downfield in ten plays and scores on a conjured touchdown pass from Bill to Joey. The play is a magical textbook fade to the right corner with Joey levitating flat out to make the catch and tie the score at 7-7. Before South's defense moves onto the field, the *Maestro* huddles with them, "Put the hammer on 'em D. Take it to 'em hard and get us the ball back." They know Bill's hurt too but his leadership stokes their competitive fires also. South holds Luers to a "3 and out" and returns the Luers' punt to the South 40-yard line.

Bill and the offense hustle onto the field as Coach sends in a pass play. Taking the snap, Bill drops back and is hit hard again as he releases the ball. Hiding her eyes in her hands, Sarah can't bear to watch him take hits repeatedly. The pass is good for 20 yards to the Luers' 40-yard line. After the play, Bill rises slowly but gets up nonetheless. After Coach calls another pass play, Bill drops back but the *Wizard* appears, sensing a presence rushing from behind him. Great quarterbacks have this "sense." As the *Wizard* cloaks himself and scrambles to his right, Joey, recognizing the scramble, breaks off his pattern. Cutting back hard for the ball, he leaves his defender grasping at air. Seeing Joey open suddenly, Bill throws a 12-yard completion just as he collects another hit. South has a first down at Luers' 28-yard line. The next play sweeps left for a 5-yard gain to

Luers' 23-yard line. With South running another pass play, Luers has all receivers covered. Scrambling for the first down marker, the *Wizard* takes a hit after 4 yards but falls forward for a 6-yard gain to Luers' 17-yard line and a 1st down. Sweeping right again, South reaches Luers' 15-yard line. As Bill drops back for another pass, the linebackers blitz from the outside, leaving a huge hole in the middle of the defensive line. Conjuring his magic, the *Wizard* tucks the ball and rushes for the end zone. With a tackler bouncing off him at the 10-yard line, he rumbles forward and bowls over a safety at the 5-yard line then whirlwinds another safety near the goal line. While scoring, he is hit hard again at the goal line by a linebacker.

South leads 14-7 at the half but Bill has taken a beating. Being sacked and knocked down five times each, he gets hit hard every time he runs the ball. Luers' game plan is simple, get the quarterback! At half time, Coach Mulinaro and his staff decide to throw deep to spread the defense and get more one-on-one coverage. While icing Bill's aches, the doctor and trainer bandage his injuries. Coach Mulinaro questions intently, "Bill, are you able to go in the second half?"

With his determination set, Bill responds, "I'm fine coach. Coach, can I say something?"

Expecting an excellent analysis, Coach answers, "Sure go ahead."

Bill continues verbalizing his idea, "If we go deep, our line is going to have to hold their blocks longer. Luers is fast and rushes hard. I think we should use short passes over the middle because the linebackers blitz almost every play."

Thinking for a minute, finally Coach says , "Ok, that's a sound idea. Let's use that approach and see how it works."

Explaining his recommendation further, Bill says, "If we get the short game going, then we can bust 'em deep because the linebackers will have to hold their spots."

"Sounds good to me," Coach says. As he walks away from Bill, he thinks, "How smart is this kid? I've never had one like him before."

South kicks off and the Dragon's Teeth rise to hold Luers to another three and out. South's offense hustles onto the field again. Aching from the hits, the *Wizard* purposes to work his magic on this stage. South has the ball at their 30 yard line and they work from the "shotgun offense" throwing short passes. Methodically, the *Wizard* weaves his spell flowing pass after pass over the field in eight plays. South scores and leads 21-7 while the Dragon's Teeth make yardage difficult to gain for Luers. With Luers accepting a field goal thankfully, South's lead is now 21-10. The strategy continues to function well in the second half for South, mixing short and deep passes to keep the Luers' defense off balance. During the second half, Sarah keeps fighting the tears and whimpering. Knowing Bill is hurt already, she spies blood on his jersey. After a painful first half, South makes it look easy and wins 48-17. Bill has an almost perfect second half, 21 for 23 with 4 touchdown passes but it comes with a physical cost. For the game, Bill is sacked eight times and is knocked down seven times. At game's end, he still feels each one of those hits. However, the cost is worth the pain in his mind.

While he earns total respect from Luers and their fans, the team earns its respect from the local media. Coach takes him out of the game with 58 seconds left. As he leaves the game, he gives the fans his triumphant fist pump and receives a standing ovation from both groups of fans, Luers and South. The Luers players applaud him as he acknowledges their accolades respectfully. Feeling great pride with Bill's performance, Mr. Tibbs has great relief because he felt every hit that Bill received too. Sarah rejoices inside that he is out of the game but emotion overcomes her with tears. His teammates shower him with praise because of his performance despite the beating he took. As the press blitzes him with questions in the locker room, he responds to their inquisition with aplomb, cordiality, and politeness. Putting all the praise on his teammates, he speaks with total respect for Luers. Every player interviewed speaks about Bill's toughness and leadership. To a player, they praise him to the press, "He's the man!" Gingerly, Bill showers and dresses to minimize the pain.

Leaving the locker room, he finds Mr. Tibbs waiting on him. "Bill, I want to know the truth. I can see the damage they inflicted. Are you really ok," he inquires with deep fatherly concern. The pain and their privacy cause deep reflection by Bill.

Lowering his emotional guard, he replies, "It means so much to me for you to be here. I wish my parents were alive to see the game. This was as much for them as my teammates. I'm really hurting but I'll be ready for Friday's game, no matter what."

Conveying the love of a father, Mr. Tibbs says, "I'm so *proud* of you, Bill. You fought for and led your teammates by your example. The pain will be temporary but what you gained here tonight will remain with you and your teammates for the rest of your lives. Now, go find that pretty girl of yours."

Brushing a tear from his eye as he smiles, Bill says, "Thanks Mr. Tibbs." Bill's ribs are so sore he can hardly breathe. He has a cut under his left eye and his right elbow, has bruises on his arms, and someone stepped on his left hand causing it to swell from the bruising.

After a brief search, he finds Sarah and her parents. Bravely fighting her tears at his appearance, she hugs him carefully because she can see he is in pain. Her dad disappears for a moment but returns quickly and says, "You're riding home with us. I asked the coach and he agreed. The bus ride would be rough on you and take longer than a car."

Bill nods his head in understanding but replies, "Thank you so much for the offer but I need to be with my teammates."

As he finishes speaking, coach comes up and interjects, "Please take this as a father not a coach. You're riding home with the Ormonds and that's the end of the discussion." Coach Mulinaro gets on the bus and tells the team he sent Bill home in a car with his friend's parents.

"How bad is he hurt coach," someone asks with great concern.

Coach Mulinaro answers, "I will be truthful with you. We won a big victory tonight but it was costly. Bill received the worst beating I've seen a player get in 20 years of coaching. If he plays next Friday, I'll be very surprised." The events of the evening and Bill's injuries weigh on the minds of each team member during the bus trip home.

Sarah's parents have a big car for the trip. They are glad they have the room to provide Bill some comfort. Bill and Sarah sit together in the back seat. Seeing Bill's grimace in his rear view mirror, her dad, being a concerned father, says, "Your performance tonight was amazing and you showed great leadership. We're very proud of your play but, Bill, we're concerned for your health because of the hits you took. We can see your visible injuries but what about the ones we can't see. Are you *truly* ok?"

His words and concern touch Bill and he opens his feelings, "I'm really hurting right now. I fought hard to play beyond the pain. My teammates needed my help to focus on the game and not my injuries. Luers thought they had us in the first half but I had to prove a point to them. I had to prove we're a strong team."

Sarah sits quietly and listens to him as tears stream down both cheeks. Seeing her tears at Bill's pain, her dad chuckles, "Hmm, it seems I heard that after the Columbus game, too. Well, sit back and relax as much as you can. We'll take care of you on the way home."

Her dad leaves Sarah to tend to Bill's emotional welfare. The darkness in the car welcomes them into a new world of their own. Despite his physical pain, his heart melts at her tear-stained cheeks.

Leaning to her ear, he whispers, "Sarah, I enjoy playing football but it hurts sometimes. You're so caring. God must have given you a servant's heart. Let me dry the tears you've shed for me. I'm here for you but right now but I can't put my arm around you to comfort you because of the pain." Flooded with so many different emotions, Sarah begins to cry softly again. "Hey now, what's this? More tears for me to dry," he chuckles. Wiping her tears away gently, he says warmly, "I have a soft shoulder to comfort you and a warm hand to cradle your hand." Laying her hand gently in Bill's hand, he cradles her hand in his. Nestling her head on his shoulder, she sighs contentedly and they both begin to relax. Elated with the warmth of Sarah snuggling him, Bill thinks, "I can't believe I only had to get pounded into the ground to get next to this wonderful girl. Maybe I should tell her now who my special girl is. After all, I've never seen anyone with such concern for me." Buoyed with confidence, he looks at her angelic face resting on his shoulder only to find her asleep in his care. Not wanting to wake her or interrupt the incredible warmth he felt right now caring for her, he thinks, "Oh well, I'm sure there'll be another time. We talk with each other every Wednesday. I have plenty of time plus she feels so natural on my shoulder." Time moves very slowly in this new world as they share each other's comfort and rest peacefully in each other's touch. Bill finally drifts off in slumber with Sarah's touch lifting him above the pain.

When they arrive at Bill's house, the mothering instinct in her mom takes over. Listening with a mother's ears to the earlier conversation of Bill's injuries, she also caught a glimpse of Sarah's care of Bill and his concern for Sarah's emotional pain. Pleased with what she saw, she knew the burden his grandparents would bear in caring for Bill's injuries. Last weekend's discussion with Sarah about Bill revealed his special lifestyle due to the loss of his parents. Before he can leave the car, Mrs. Ormond offers, "Bill, why don't you come over tomorrow and stay at our house? We can have lunch together and we won't allow you to do any work. You need special care and rest. We'll start you feeling better ASAP." Sarah has a "please come over" look in her eyes aimed straight at Bill's heart. She devises in her heart and mind to take care of his most minute need.

Unable to say no to two determined women, he answers, "How can I refuse such a gracious offer of care. I hope that going for a walk isn't in my recovery regimen, at least not immediately. I think your couch has my name all over it for tomorrow." Smiling from deep in her heart, Sarah knows he will be in *her* care tomorrow. With sweet remembrance, the thoughts of sharing each other's care on the ride home flood their minds.

Care

It's Saturday and the team has a short meeting to discuss how to improve their game performance. Coach Mulinaro addresses the gathered team, "I am extremely proud of the way we played. We held our ground in the first half against a strong team. We kept them off balance in the second half and won a hard fought battle. We must remember and visualize this fact in our minds. This is only one battle. We need to heal our wounds, set our focus on the prize, but look forward only to the next obstacle, the next challenger. We need to reach deep into each of our souls and pull out our best every game. *Take this to the bank*. Our opponents will bring their best each week against us. We cannot *hide* our talents any longer. We must meet each opponent head on and drive each team off the field. We will study and correct our weaknesses until we have none. We will search for and study the weaknesses of our opponents and we will use them to our advantage. That's all I have to say. This is what I want you to dwell on this and every week. I want to see the results in practice every day. You are our present and our future. Go have a good weekend and come back Monday ready for battle." Amazed to see Bill at the meeting despite his injuries, the coach knows Bill leads by example. Knowing that

Bill will not become a distraction to his teammates, he senses his team will be a singular mind this week and their focus is the next game not Bill's recovery.

After the meeting, Joey drops him off at Sarah's and asks, "Hey Bill, do you want to hang out tonight?"

Still experiencing pain, Bill chuckles, "I'll see how I feel, but I'll probably stay at Sarah's to heal. I'm really very sore. I really think I should rest for Friday's game."

Comprehending the entire situation, Joey laughs and says, "Friday's game? *Sure!* With a beautiful nurse like Sarah to help me heal, I'd rather be with her than with me too." They both laugh at his statement. As Bill turns from the car toward her house, Sarah is already outside to provide care, embarrassed at the accolades.

Looking at Joey, she says, "Thanks for bringing him over but don't to expect him to go out tonight. I prescribe complete rest and *I'm* going to make sure he gets his rest." Then with a smile, she adds, "and any needed attention it takes to make him feel better."

Laughing at the situation, Bill says, "Hey Joey, I hear my 'doctor' calling me to rest. You know what they say, 'Always follow your doctor's orders.' I'll see you Monday at practice." Sarah helps Bill walk gingerly into the house where lunch is in preparation and takes him straight to the living room.

As he starts for the couch, she says with a giggle, "Stay there a minute."

With Sarah blocking the couch from his full view, he snickers, "What are you up to?"

Placing a sign on the couch quickly stating, "Reserved for Bill Denton," she says with a smile big enough for him to hear, "Ok, come on in. This is for you." Looking at the couch, they laugh at her sign. He sits down as she removes the sign with a giggle and begins her doctoring duties by bringing him a soda with ice. Sitting on the couch with him, she puts a pillow on her lap and says in a commanding, mock serious voice, "Being your doctor, I order you to lie down here and put your head on this pillow. Rest is my prescription and rest is what you're going to get, along with my tender, loving care." Continuing softly, she adds, *"If you need anything, just ask."* As she holds him gently, she alternates between light massage to the aching muscles and ice for the bruises.

They continue the warm conversation started by his *doctor* and after a time that to them is altogether too short, her mom calls, "Lunch is ready kids."

Rising from the couch to get lunch, Sarah sees him wince in pain. "Oh, he's really hurting," she thinks to herself. "Need some help, Bill," she inquires with concern.

Smiling at her, he says jokingly, "Oh… all I can get." Laughing at his statement, she stands beside him as he holds onto her for strength. What a picture they make. Bill, the tall, strong athlete, helped to his feet by Sarah, the determined yet petite, rock of caring energy. He doesn't want to fall and hurt himself or her while he stands up slowly. However, his sore ribs make physical support difficult and breathing without pain almost impossible. Nevertheless, they amble to the dining room with Sarah providing support and nurturing. Lunch is Bill's favorite, roast beef and Swiss with mayo on wheat bread.

Amazed in his heart at the meal set before him, he voices his appreciation to her mom, "Thank you so much for lunch. That's my favorite sandwich." Then, looking at Sarah with surprise, he questions with curious confusion, "How did you *know*?"

Smiling wryly with confidence in her communications network, Sarah says, "I have eyes everywhere including East."

Joking with her, he says, *"So* you have them watching me. The plot thickens." "This is great. She really does care," he thinks returning a magical, wry smile of his own.

"Yes, but it's not like a jealous girlfriend or anything. I want to surprise you once in a while," she clarifies.

"You're the best. You take such good care of me. I couldn't ask for more," he reveals and kisses her cheeks. At that moment, Bill winces as he pulls an envelope out of his back pocket. It is another note from his heart to her.

> *Sarah,*
>
> *Thanks for allowing me to spend this time with you. I feel better just being here with you. You're my best friend and more special to me than you can imagine. I really enjoy spending time with you. I feel different with you than I do with anyone else. I have no answers for my feelings. I just feel an emotional bond with you and I hope you feel the same.*
>
> *Your friend, Bill*

Reading the note, Sarah eyes become teary. When she finishes reading, she whispers lovingly in his ear, "Yes, I feel the same way when I'm with you." While finishing lunch, they share tender glances periodically.

As Bill rises to his feet slowly, her mom, *his consulting physician,* jests, "Ok fun times are over. It's time to rest those aches. Now, get back on that couch." Ambling back to the living room per her orders, he lies down on the couch.

Realizing he left no room for Sarah to sit first, he says to her, "I'm sorry Sarah. I can move so you can sit down."

Seizing the opportunity, Sarah says, "That won't be necessary." Putting the pillow under his head, she says, "Just lie still. The doctor will be back shortly."

His second sense flashes a thought to his conscious mind, "What *is* she up to?" Returning with a light blanket, Sarah covers him gently. "Are you comfortable now," she inquires softly.

"Yes I *am*. Thank you so much," Bill replies, sacked emotionally by her care.

Then, making a surprise move, she lifts the cover gently and lies down beside him on the couch.

Looking deep into her longing eyes, Bill probes, "Sarah, are you sure about this?"

Looking back as deeply, she answers, "Yes Bill, you need my care and I can provide no better nurturing than right here beside you." Her warmth touches Bill deeply and his heart pounds with nervous excitement but she is right, he does feel better.

However, his head fills with jumbled thoughts and he questions, "Are you sure your mom and dad are ok with this?"

She assuages his fears with her response, "Bill, they are very fond of you. They trust me in your care and they trust my judgment as their daughter. They have no problem because they know nothing will happen."

His jumbled thoughts clear with her words. "They're right. I would never do anything to destroy their trust in either of us," he responds, opening his heart. "I have never done this with any girl in my life. You're so soft in my arms and your touch is so warm next to me and I sound like a complete idiot," he whispers.

Revealing her emotions, Sarah responds in kind, "I've never done this with any guy. I just wanted to care for you in the best way that I can. I've never felt as safe as I do here with your arm around me. I just hope I'm not hurting your injuries further."

Reveling in the moment, Bill whispers quickly, "No way. Your warmth makes my aches tolerable." His heart screams for him to expose his feelings further but his mind just can't muster the courage to vocalize them. She feels so safe that her heart begs her to verbalize her deepest emotions. However, her mind will not release the words from their locked gates. Still worn from the game, Bill falls asleep with Sarah in his arm. Falling asleep holding Bill, Sarah listens to his heart and dreams his heart is hers.

Waking up later in the day, he feels better at finding her arms still around him. It wasn't a dream after all and her soft whisper breaks his momentary stupor, "*Hi*. Did you sleep ok in spite of your aches?" Looking caringly, she gazes deep into Bill's eyes.

"You know it's funny but holding you next to me, my pains disappeared," Bill whispers in response, seeing the glow on her face and twinkle in her eyes.

"Do you want to watch TV? We can both see it while we snuggle here," Sarah offers.

"As long as I can hold you, I'm yours to command," he responds.

"This is just where I want you. You know my name means 'Princess' and you're my subject. I command you to stay here with me and heal," she jokes.

"Your wish is my command, Princess," he whispers the retort in her ear. Holding each other as the TV comes on, the current channel displays the Notre Dame vs. USC game, raising his excitement. After all, Notre Dame *is* his favorite college team but he continues to hold her. Hiding his excitement with the game, Bill asks calmly, "Do you mind watching Notre Dame play?"

Sarah answers with a laugh, "Sure, that's ok as long as you don't try to tackle me here on the couch." Secretly, she thinks to herself, "Why did it have to be a football game? Couldn't I nurse him back to health watching a different program?" Snuggling next to each other, they continue watching Notre Dame win the game. Meanwhile, the sunset paints the landscape outside with shaded brushstrokes of rose, purple, yellow, and orange.

The Evening

As it grows darker outside, Bill says, "I enjoyed being with you so much today but I probably should go home. I still need to rest these injuries although the solitary care I receive at home can't compare to the care you provided. By the way, are you going to church tomorrow? I'd like to go with you if your parents don't mind me tagging along."

Thrilled with the idea of worshipping with her best friend again, Sarah replies quickly, "Yes we always do and you're always welcome to come with us." Rushing to find her mom to verify his request, she asks her excitedly, "Bill would like to go to church with us tomorrow. Is that ok?"

Pondering for a moment, her mom answers, "We're always happy to have him come with us. I have an idea. If Bill would like to do so, he can stay the night in our spare room. Besides, you need to make sure he allows those injuries to heal further. In case he needs something, your room is right across the hall. Then, he can shower here in the morning before church."

Returning from her discussion with her mom, Sarah offers, "Bill, mom has a great idea. You can stay here tonight and go to church with us tomorrow. In the meantime, I'll tend to your injuries and needs before bedtime and then tomorrow after church."

Contemplating that special care, Bill replies, "You and your family have taken such good care of me today. That sounds amazing to me but I need get some clothes at home." Sarah and her mom drive Bill to his house.

Excited at the prospect of him staying, Sarah informs her mom, "I'm going to help Bill get some clothes for tomorrow."

Shaking her head, her mom laughs, "Ok Sarah. We'll all go together."

Once in Bill's apartment, Sarah asks, "Where's the suit you wore last week? You looked great in that."

Pointing to a cedar-lined, wood closet, he replies with a smile, "It's in there."

Opening the door expecting to get the silver suit, she finds five more suits as well much to her surprise. Seeing a visual feast from which to choose, Sarah inquires intently, "Which suit do you want?"

Sensing her surprise, Bill answers, "Why don't you pick the one you like."

Sarah reviews them quickly and picks a darker gray suit with pin stripes. She selects a baby pink shirt with a grey tie, black shoes, and black belt. "He'll look great in this suit tomorrow," Sarah visualizes to herself. Bill obtains his travel kit, fresh underwear, and gray socks. After gathering his clothes and other items together, they amble down to the car. When they arrive at Sarah's house, she shows him "his" room with great delight.

As Bill and Sarah hang up his suit and shirt, he suggests, "Sarah, I would like to change clothes, if you don't mind?"

Shifting her weight onto one hip, she folds her arms across her stomach and continues to stand with him in his room. Growing a big smile on her face, she says teasingly, "Go *right* ahead." A timid smile crawls across Bill's reddening face.

Looking with embarrassment, he asks with mock pleading, "Just give me a couple minutes, please."

Sarah closes the door with a playful backward glance and her eyes twinkling on her way out. Putting on his sweatpants without his shirt and filled with excitement, he ambles hesitantly to the door. "If I open the door without speaking, Sarah could still be dressing. I wouldn't want to embarrass her. On the other hand, she was such a tease as she left. She just might be waiting to 'surprise' me," he thinks as other thoughts race to choices and consequences. Shyly, he speaks through the door, "I'm dressed Sarah. Are you decent?"

Seizing on the joy of the moment, Sarah teases back, "I'm dressed but I'm definitely not decent." As a relieved Bill opens the door, she steps quickly into the hallway dressed in her pajamas. Abruptly frozen in her steps, the sight of a shirtless Bill in front her leaves her breathless. Quickly, her heart breaks her steps free as she rushes into his surprised arms. Clinging to each other for a good while, he winces in pain mixed with elation. Finally, noticing his wincing, she relaxes her hug and lays her head on his chest. Filled with the euphoria, he kisses her on both cheeks. Overcome with the emotion of the moment, she whispers in his ear, "Mom and dad's room is at the other end of the house. We can snuggle together here, if you want to."

Looking at her with surprise and love in his heart, he replies, "Sarah, I can't do that."

Filled with excitement, she questions intently, "Why not? We snuggled together on the couch today."

Taking her hands gently, he looks deep into her longing eyes and answers, "Sarah, if something happened in here, I would not be able to face you or your parents. They trust us both or they would not have allowed me to stay here. I can't put you in a position where emotions might coerce you to do something you'd regret later. I care for you too much. Mostly, for the rest of your life, I wouldn't want you to think I stayed tonight just to get you in bed with me. Those feelings would last a lifetime. I don't want that for you. I wouldn't want your parents to lose trust in either of us. God would sear my conscience for the rest of my life if I did that."

Sarah cannot believe the love poured out in Bill's words and hugs him again. Unable to bring herself to break the bond of love she feels, she keeps her deepest thoughts of her heart hidden. Finally, she intones, "Thank you so much for being you. I care for you more right now than you'll ever know. That said, I really should go to my room now." Taking a couple of steps toward the door, she turns quickly and leaps into his surprised arms. Wrapping her legs around him, she kisses him warmly and deeply on the lips emotionally jamming his injury pain. Just as quickly, she disappears across the hall into her room with eyes sparkling, saying teasingly, *"Goodnight Bill,"* as she glances back with a smile and closes the door. Hopping in her bed, her mind dwells on Bill's words as well as the care and the love he showed for her. "How could any other person care that much about me, my emotional well-being, or my life now or for my lifetime," she ponders. Lying down, she experiences the fondest dreams of her life. Meanwhile, her actions leave Bill in stunned silence. Confused totally by Sarah's emotional expression, he wrestles with his mind at her beauty, her friendship, and more. He loses himself in the whirlwind that left the room and the one remaining in his mind.

A Different Sunday

Sunday morning comes quickly for them both. Bill rises early and dresses by the time everyone else wakes up. Smelling a different type of coffee, Sarah follows the aroma into the kitchen. Last night, Bill brought some freshly ground, Columbian coffee with him from his personal collection. The pleasant aroma puts a big smile on her face and draws her mom and dad to the kitchen too. Her mom comments, "Bill, that coffee smells so good."

"Thank you ma'am, please have some. I hope you didn't mind me fixing toast and coffee for everyone," he says. Basking in the glow of last night's conversation, Bill and Sarah share some quality time with her parents over breakfast while everyone stands in the kitchen.

Breaking the warm atmosphere, her mom says, "We don't want to be late for church. Sarah, it's time to get ready. Scoot, scoot." As the family hurries to get ready, Bill has another cup of coffee since he is dressed and ready to go.

As mom and dad vanish down their hallway, Sarah returns to Bill and puts her arms around his neck. While her sparking blue eyes bore deeply into his soul, she opens her heart, "Thanks again for yesterday. It was so special to me. I opened to my emotions and followed them without question. I had you here with me alone, which is the stuff of my dreams. I was suggestive and hoped you would follow my lead. You did but realized I was unfair to myself and to you. I let my emotions rule my body and my spirit. It was a formula for disaster. You're my best friend and I feel very safe with you. I always had faith you would never try anything forward with me or pressure me into being intimate like that. That's one of the reasons I treasure you so much. You justified my faith in you last night. I'm so sorry and ask your forgiveness. I put you in an uncomfortable position. It was a position that might have led to something we both would have regretted later." As tears form in her heart and well up in her eyes, she continues, "You said no out of total respect for me. You give me more respect than I could ever expect from anyone."

Drawing her close and cradling her head gently in his hand, he holds her tight and says softly, "Sarah, I said no, but not because you're the most beautiful girl I have ever seen. It's not because I didn't want to be with you. It's because that, right now in our lives, it isn't the right time. The respect I have for you is greater than I probably would have for any other girl. You're everything to me. I think that you may realize now how very special you are to me. I'll always put your best welfare first in our relationship and I'll always be here for you. I hope this makes some kind of sense to you." While smiling at him with loving eyes and a glow from her heart, he dries the tears running down her cheeks.

"I have a surprise for you," Bill says and continues, "You should go get ready for church because I called my boys. Today they'll be at church with us. I'll be the one smiling because you'll be the best-looking girl in the church and I'll be with you."

"You didn't," she retorts!

"Oh yes I did," Bill says smiling wryly. "It's going to be 'Show Time' when we walk in," he says with a bit of swagger in his tone.

A question pours forth verbally out of Sarah's thoughts, "Would you help me pick out a dress because I want just the *right* one?" Agreeing excitedly, they walk to her room and look for the perfect dress. "Ah, here it is. What do you think," she says as she pulls a black one out.

Responding to visions of how she will look in it, he exclaims, "*Wow, it's perfect!*" The dress has a round cut front top, not revealing but still cut low enough to look thoroughly tempting. It is a full-body style dress with short sleeves, tapering in at the waist with no belt and stopping mid-knee. The cut compliments her assets perfectly. Bill picks up a pair of high heel shoes with straps at the ankle and states, "I think these will work impeccably with that dress and you."

Blushing at his flattering words, Sarah teases, "Ok Calvin, I will just for you." With Sarah looking for a necklace, he notices she has only a couple of necklace choices.

As he hands her a gold pendant with a cross on it, he says, "Wear this one please. I think it will be perfect." His search results put an idea in his mind. Because of the deep emotional connection they shared in the last twenty-four hours, he plans to get her something very special.

Arriving at the church, time begs them to go inside and begin worship. However, Bill and Sarah have a plan to be "fashionable" and make their entrance. Her mom and dad went in and found seats already. "Wasting" just the right amount of time, the couple continues talking outside. Now, as the clock makes the curtain call, their seats beckon at just the right moment. Reaching the entrance, the ushers open the doors with a smile for them. With Sarah holding his arm, Bill brings a bit of his pre-game swagger with him today just for fun but painfully so. Catching his approach mentally, she develops the same mindset. Looking at their friends, the royal couple projects a regal aura of future possibilities to their "subjects" as they pass by. Everyone smiles back in approval and the couple appears destined for each other as if joined through many lifetimes since time began. At that moment, they are the fulfillment of everyone's hopes and desires for perfection. After sitting down, Bill notices Sarah wants to say something to him. He leans toward her as she whispers, "I think they were very impressed."

"Me too," Bill whispers back through a big smile.

While bursting with pride, Sarah knows his rib injuries made that little show tough for him. Her prognosis is the healing progresses nicely thanks to all the ice and massage she provided. Quite satisfied with her healing techniques, she continues to monitor his progress nonetheless throughout the service. While observing him, she notices the pain on his face when he moves in the pew or stands for the hymns. Planning his care mentally for the afternoon, she continues to check her best patient through the remaining service. As the service touches both their hearts, God speaks to their consciences about their relationship. Throughout the service, their glances to each other convey right actions in overcoming their emotions. The glow in their hearts and on their faces says they received the message.

Together they tarry a little after church to speak with their friends but finally her dad says, "Hey kids, it's time to go."

Looking at her dad, Bill takes her hand and says, "C'mon Sarah, your mom and dad are waiting on us." However, she doesn't want to leave just yet, still basking in the glow of this day with Bill, her friends, the message, and the warm sunlight. His look pleads with her to leave the joy for now, joining her parents and him. Breaking out of her euphoria, she says goodbye to everyone, and gets in the car.

In the car, Bill inquires expectantly, "Would you mind taking us to the mall? I need to get something quickly and I know right where I'm going. I promise we won't be long." This weekend has been very special to him, as her care has touched his heart. In his mind, he wants to give Sarah a visible token of his feelings toward her.

Her mom and dad respond, "We don't mind at all. We can pick you two of you up in a couple of hours."

At this point, Sarah, the doctor, voices her opinion, "No that's not ok. We need to go home. Bill needs to lie down and take it easy."

Desperately, Bill interjects, "Really Sarah, I'm fine and I'd like to go to the mall."

Glaring right in his eyes, Sarah says, "Bill Denton, you can fool some people with that 'aw shucks ma'am' manner but not me. I can see you're not ok. Just that little walk to our seats at church and getting up and down in the church pews made you wince. Dad, please take us home. We can go shopping another time. The best thing for you right now is more rest and ice."

Interjecting words of wisdom, her dad says, "Bill, I've seen this before. When Sarah sets her mind, you don't want to go to battle with her logic." Being a very calm and strong-willed person, she believes in her heart she has Bill's best interest in mind and she protects him now as he protected her.

Looking at him sternly, she probes emphatically, "Bill, do you want to play Friday?"

Lowering his head slowly, he answers sheepishly, "I'm planning on it."

Revealing her mindset in her look, Sarah continues firmly, "I can tell you this. You won't play Friday if you don't take care of those ribs. You need that rib support to throw. The team counts on you and so do I. You need to rest and recuperate those ribs to do that."

"But Sarah, there is something I want to get at the mall," he pleads with her.

Finishing her reasoning firmly, she orders, "No buts, you can get whatever it is some other time. Right now, you need rest, ice, and massage."

With those words, he crumples in his heart and capitulates, "Ok doc, you win."

"Fine! Dad, we're going home," she says firmly, knowing in her heart that she is right.

"Yes, Sarah. I mean doctor," her dad laughs. Secretly, Bill really likes the massage idea.

Sunday Afternoon

O n the way home while holding her hand, Bill ponders, "This is another reason to like Sarah. She may be strong-willed but she's gentle and loving too. She doesn't have a problem making a decision or expressing her feelings. Now I understand why she's tells me I don't have to do this or that for her, that she can do it herself. However, she does enjoy my loving, respectful, courteous treatment, and allowing me to treat her like a princess too. There *isn't* anyone like her. I want to ask her out so badly but I'm afraid. I can stand up to a beating on the field but Sarah scares me. I wish my parents were here to ask them about her. On the other hand, I just told her no when she wanted to snuggle. *What have I done?* She's my best friend. Would I want one of the guys to do for me what she's doing? Absolutely not! Sarah is doing all this for me, her best friend. Would she do this for just anyone? I don't think so but…No, she wouldn't! If I didn't play football, it would be ok with her. She knows it's what I do but she doesn't care. She supports *me*, incredible. She's doing everything to make sure her best friend is ready to play his best." They continue to enjoy each other's touch and stolen glances of emotion as her dad drives homeward.

Arriving at her house, Bill's body informs his heart that Sarah is right. The trip to church, his swaggering, and the church pews all put a strain on Bill's ribs and he can't get his jacket and shirt off by himself. The pain is immense as he attempts to remove his clothes in his room. "Sarah, can you come in here and help me," he pleads.

After changing into her jeans and a t-shirt, she saunters teasingly into his room inquiring, "Do you need me to help you change clothes?"

Looking at her with his wry smile, he teases, "You can help me take my clothes off anytime."

Returning his tease with gusto, she scares him a bit saying, "It's about time!...Hold your arms down and I'll try to get your jacket off without causing you pain." Sarah removes his jacket gently. "Now let me have that shirt," she says with a big grin as she reaches to unbutton it.

Red-faced, Bill apologizes, "Thanks Sarah but I think I should do this myself. You're having *way* too much fun with this."

"You bet I am," she retorts with a big grin. Unbuttoning his shirt, he loosens his belt to get the shirt un-tucked. With his arms down again, she removes his shirt gently off his shoulders and arms. Now comes the hard part, extricating him out of his t-shirt. She questions, "Will it be easier for you to bend over or sit while I peel your t-shirt over your head?"

"I'd better sit, if you don't mind," he answers. While sitting, he lifts his arms painfully over his head to accomplish the feat.

All the while, she promises, "I'll be as gentle as I can." Seeing the look on his face, Sarah asks hopefully, "Are you ready?"

Anticipating the pain, Bill replies, "Go." Peeling off the shirt as gently as she can, he puts his arms down as the pain hits and he exclaims, "Dang that hurts!" Wincing in pain, he holds his left side for a while.

Getting his shirt off hurt him and Sarah knows it. Sitting next to him on the bed with her arm around him, she holds him until the pain dissipates. The sight and touch of Bill's shirtless body leaves Sarah breathless again. Finding no words to utter, her mind races to recover from the sensation her arm delivers to it. "His body is rock solid and I'm holding him," races around her mind. Overcome by the sensation and her emotions, she whispers, "We can lie here, just the two of us. Anything you need, I'll get for you."

Looking in her eyes deeply with love in his heart and holding both her hands, he says, "Lying here with you would be the most amazing thing I can think of. However, it will put us in a spot I don't want to put you in. It's this simple. If you were another girl, I might give in and say ok, but I don't want to be like that with you. You're everything I could want in a girl. Another guy would probably call your bluff to see if you'd follow through on your signals but I won't. I respect you totally as a person, a friend, and a girl. I don't want to do anything that might disrespect, embarrass, or obligate you. I can't show any lack of respect for you. I know we would thoroughly enjoy whatever we did and I really want to do this. *But*, I'll apologize now rather than after the fact." His real thoughts race past his uttered words ringing in his mind, "She's so beautiful and her touch is amazing. I *would* do anything she wants. I just can't trust myself alone with her, as she wants. I don't want to hurt her. I'll have to satisfy myself with being on the couch together as we were yesterday."

Sighing as she helps Bill to the couch near the fireplace, she thinks, "Ok, if he's never going to try anything that he feels wouldn't be right, how can I hold him in my arms like that again?" Planning her next actions for about a minute, she gets a huge smile on her face. Then, she reconsiders her frustration in her mind, "I mean too much to him for him try anything that would ruin our friendship. *Well*, I'll have to see how this proceeds. I love him for that respect and concern. With any luck, 'Love' is a word he might use referring to me someday. He *is* here today. *Well*, a bird in the *hand... However,*

I *still* have the rest of today with him. Let's see what the day brings with my TLC doctoring."

Reaching the couch, she puts the pillow down and gets "their" blanket. She says, "Doctor Sarah prescribes that you lie down, ice the bruises, take two aspirin, and stay here until the morning, to paraphrase." Holding his arm, she helps him sit on the couch. His face shouts the pain level still coursing through his ribs. Slowly reclining on the couch, he tries to get as comfortable as possible. She gets the ice, a towel, the aspirin, and some water. While he swallows the aspirin with water, she places the ice on his left side, which bore the brunt of the hits from the defensive blitz. With her mom fixing dinner in the kitchen, Sarah gently massages his back and shoulders for a few minutes. When she finishes to a chorus of his sighs, she inquires with great interest, "Do you need anything else?"

Responding to her care and warm touch, he says, "Yes, there is. Would you mind coming closer, please?"

With excited, delightful visions dancing in her head, she thinks, "*Oh yeah,*" and says, "Sure, I'd like that."

As she moves within his reach, Bill pulls her closer, kisses her quickly, and says, "Thanks for all your care of me. Would you mind watching TV and snuggling with me on the couch?"

Thinking, "*It's about time. TLC works well,*" she says, "I'll turn on the TV and be right there." Surfing the channels until she finds the movie "Brigadoon," she does not ask if this is ok but comes right to the couch. Lifting the blanket, she nuzzles next to him as they both face the TV. He puts his arm around her and pulls her as close as the pain allows. While the pain makes him a bit nauseous, he is *not* about to disturb the emotional bliss they both experience. Relaxing in the shared warmth, they fit together like spoons in a drawer. While sharing the spell she hoped the movie would weave, his pain magically disappears in the delight of the moment.

As Bill snuggles Sarah on the couch, he thinks, "I'm lucky to have someone to 'doctor' me like she does. Her touch drives me crazy and I have to be careful not to hurt her. My grandparents certainly couldn't provide *her* kind of care. Her parents are amazing caring for me like a son. Even if my parents were still here, I wouldn't feel this kind of love from anyone. I really need her in my life and I wish they could have met her. I know there's plenty of time for us but right now, this is amazing. When I'm on the field, I have ultimate confidence in my ability. I take chances and make good decisions. I can read a defensive set like a physics book. I understand every nuance and sense the opponent's thoughts and actions. Off the field, I'm an extremely smart, regular guy but then there's Sarah. She's a whirlwind of emotion. She has me swirling between exhilaration and defense with what she says and how she says it. I know we're best friends and I want even more than that now. But, there's plenty of time for us to grow together. To do more than that now would be a huge mistake. I have school and football ahead of me and maybe, just maybe, something here with her. My life would be unbearable if I hadn't bumped into her."

Snuggling in Bill's arm, Sarah thinks, "I don't want this moment to end. I love snuggling with him and I don't care where it is. I want our relationship to grow faster and I can't believe we've only known each other such a short time. If he hadn't spilled the soft drink on me and been so humble about it, I'd be lost now. He's so caring and protective but I'm not sure he wants our relationship to grow as fast as I do. I want much more of our relationship now. I just hope my care shows him how much I want him in my life. I want to hear him say more about us. It's getting embarrassing to have mom and dad drive us around continually. I know he has older friends on the football team with cars and girlfriends to double date with us. All he needs to do is ask. I'll find a way to show him what he's missing. I'll give us some time right now but the future sure looks bright. Maybe, it *is* time to ask a couple of questions."

Racing thoughts spur confidence as she lifts up his hand and asks excitedly, "Is it ok if I turn over to look into his your eyes. They twinkle when we're close like this."

Her words pierce straight to his heart and he says, "I don't mind at all. I want *you* to be comfortable too. Your eyes are like stars when I look deeply in them. I lose myself in those eyes of yours." As Sarah turns over, Bill responds to her words, the movie, the care, and the last day's events. Caressing her face softly, he brushes her hair out of her eyes and kisses her gently but quickly.

Responding to his caressing, Sarah thinks, "Well, it's a nice start. That he gave me a kiss is amazing. We *could* be more than just friends."

Deciding with his kiss to start their verbal dance again, she queries eagerly, "Bill, *please* tell me about this girl you like but you think won't go out with you."

He answers, "I will but only if you tell me about your special guy." The game begins anew as Sarah agrees and Bill starts, "She's wonderful. She's beautiful, smart, and doesn't care about me being a football player. She's so easy to speak with and actually listens when I speak with her. She's a caring person and a great doctor."

Sensing a hole in his shield, she thinks, "Got him. Finally, he is going to come right out and say it."

Providing a clue, he throws a curve as he continues, "She was at the game Friday."

Doing a rapid replay of Friday in her mind and certain that she was the only girl he saw, she sets a trap and counters, "Did you speak with her?"

Recognizing the gambit, he does not give her a yes or a no answer but counters, "I was with you and your parents the entire time after the game. So, what about this guy of yours?"

Countering his question with one last question, Sarah probes hopefully, "Where does she go to school?"

Bill replies with a wry smile, "I gave enough clues. I'm not telling you anything else to narrow down who this girl is."

Enjoying the intrigue and certain she's the girl, she begins her descriptive ploy, "He's really gentle and respectful of everyone. He treats everyone like they are special too and has a super personality."

Bill interrupts jokingly, "He must be a real bow-wow."

"Bill," she exclaims and gives him a playful slap. Then she retorts, "He's the most handsome guy I've ever seen but he's down to earth and not arrogant. He appreciates everything anyone does for him and would do anything to help anybody. Oh, he plays football too." While they did not give exact details, they gave enough information for great speculation and logical conclusion but not enough to end the game.

Halting the fun and verbal chess, her mom calls, "Dinner is ready."

Concerned with his ability to move without pain, Sarah inquires with concern, "Bill, do you want me to bring your dinner to you on the couch?"

Wanting to eat with her family, he replies, "No, I'd rather sit at the table with you. Besides, it's a little tough to eat lying down."

Filled with compassion, Sarah offers, "I'll feed you if you don't want to get up."

Losing himself in her eyes again, he says, "You're the best. You take such good care of me but I can make it to the table." After ambling to the dining room together, she and Bill sit down at the table with her parents. Shortly, Sarah excuses herself for a few moments. While she's gone, Bill states quickly, "I should have asked this earlier and I apologize for not doing so before now. Are you ok with us lying on the couch together?"

With protective thoughts filling his mind, her dad replies firmly, "I'm ok with it to a point. I'm sure you understand my meaning."

"I do sir," Bill replies fully catching the implication of his words.

Responding in kind, her mom adds quickly, "If it was anyone else but you, it would not be ok but we trust you totally with Sarah. We can tell you have total respect for her. We know you wouldn't do anything of which we would not approve. To bring it to a fine point, if we *didn't* trust you, we *wouldn't* have allowed you to stay all night, especially in a room right across the hall from Sarah."

Returning to her seat across from Bill, Sarah questions curiously, "What did I *miss*?"

Smiling, her mom answers, "Nothing at all, dear. Bill thanked us for allowing him to come over, helping him recover, and for you taking such good care of him here."

During dinner, Bill and Sarah exchange stolen glances and giggles while playing footsie occasionally under the table. After dinner, Bill questions expectantly, "Sarah, would you like to go for a walk with me?"

Responding with indignation, she says firmly, "You mean would I like to pick you up as you stumble around? Absolutely *not*! You *sir* are going back to the couch!" Her look of loving care says her concern centers on his health right now and not her desires. With an alternative plan in motion, she thinks, "Besides, I can have him closer and all to myself on the couch anyway. We both win." He doesn't argue with his "doctor" as he respects her too much and her reasons for helping him. While he lies on the couch, Sarah helps her mom clean up dinner. Then, coming to Bill on the couch, she lies down face to face with him. Knowing how to get him better fast, she probes attentively, "Would you tell me about your close friends from the Pizza Inn?"

Puzzled by her question, he asks, "Why would you want to know about them?"

Showing her strong interest, Sarah explains, "They're your

friends, an important part of your life, and I want to get to know them. Your friends should be my friends too." Her response touches Bill deeply, as he feels she truly is his best friend. His heart whispers to him of her depth of caring.

The Dirty Boys

B ill begins with Andy Worley, his life-long friend. Detailing their close relationship, he explains, "Andy lives next door to me, always has my back, and knows why many people want to hang out with me. He's the guy they have to get through to hang out with me, not as a bully or in a threating way unless you mess with him. Although, he *has* kicked people's butts for saying things about me that aren't true, he can read people better than any person I know. He can discern quickly if they want to be my friend or the quarterback's groupie. If you didn't know him, you'd think he's a sarcastic jerk but after all, he is protective and my best childhood friend. He sees people trying to take advantage of me just for their popularity. That may sound arrogant of him but Andy does that to keep me on track and avoid needless distractions. He knows I have a good future ahead of me whether it's football or a career somewhere. He prevents anyone from messing that up for me. I tell him all the time to lighten up on people. While he promises to do so, he never does. He is a great bodyguard."

Curious about the lack of Andy's protective nature with her, Sarah queries with a curious tone, "Why didn't Andy say anything to me at the Pizza Inn about being with you?"

Bill chuckles, "Andy could see the look in our eyes immediately when we came in together. Our eyes said it all to him. You were perfect and he did not have to concern himself with your intentions. As I said, he can read people and believe me when I tell you this, he knows you're my best friend. So he has your back too."

Telling Sarah about D.J. Dylon and Pete Mallay, who are other childhood friends, Bill continues, "They're the good time guys and I'm fairly stiff compared to them when measured by their standard. They do their best to help me loosen up once in a while. D. J. can be gutsy and direct, even pressing, with his questions. He seeks answers to a person's intent when they suddenly appear and want to get close to me. Guess what, he really likes you. Pete is the analytical one who views people and events for their whole effect. He's a straight shooter and the thinker of the group."

Sarah interrupts jokingly, "I thought that was you."

Chuckling at her words, he continues, "Ok point taken. They always tell me they don't hang out with me because they like me. It's because they want me to have a date." "So do I," she thinks while he continues, "Then, they can hang out with my date's friends. They're funny like that. They always tell me I don't realize who and what I am. They say I can date anyone I want to date."

"What do *you* say to that," she probes hoping to hear some reassuring words about their relationship.

Revealing his true character, he replies, "I tell them I know who I am and I'm nothing special." With Sarah laughing at his words, he quizzes with confusion, "What's so *funny*?"

She emphasizes with conviction, "They're right. You *can* go out with anyone you want *including* me. All of my friends want to go out with you. I'm sure the girls at East want to go out with you. I'm positive many girls at the high school want to go out with you."

Looking at her with his wry smile, he misses her inviting words and an excellent opportunity while returning to their verbal chess match saying, "There's only one girl with whom I want to go out and I refer to her often with you."

Receiving his obtuse answer with much disappointment, she contemplates, "I heard this too *many* times. Just pour out the words your heart tells you and stop thinking so much." She yearns to hear him say the words, "You're the one." Instead, she must rely on Bill's earlier description of her for now. His chess match leaves her with mixed emotions and deep longing for his words to caress her ears.

Finally, Bill begins to tell her about Jordon Lewenski. Laughing at the thought of Jordon, he explains, "He's just a goof ball and always joking around with everybody. He's always telling me, you're not that good at football. If I don't get at least an A-, he tells me that I'm an idiot. Jordon's a Polish kid who looks like he's Filipino but both his parents are Polish. He says he has no idea why he looks like he does. However, it's a great package and every girl should want it. You know what's so strange. I find him to be very insightful in spite of his joking manner. He quite often sees all sides of me as a whole. I guess I don't do a good job of that. Maybe I'm too close to the problem."

"That's pretty much my boys. I have other friends but we're the Dirty Boys," he finishes.

Curious about the name, she asks, "What do you mean about you being the Dirty Boys?"

"Well that's the funny part. We all grew up together and did everything together. When we went home, we were always dirty from whatever we did that day. Our parents and grandparents would say, 'You boys are always dirty.' So, we adopted the name The Dirty Boys. It's a small but exclusive club. You can be our friend but you can't ever be a Dirty Boy because you didn't grow up with us and do stuff with us then. Yeah, we're the Dirty Boys," Bill chuckles.

Evening arrives much too quickly and the time for Bill to return to his house. Sarah helps him off the couch cautiously. After gathering his belongings and taking them to the car, she and her mom drive him home. While Bill hobbles upstairs, Sarah carries his belongs into his house. Helping him take off his shirt and shoes, she questions wryly with a tease in her voice, "Is there anything *more I* can take off for you?"

Red-faced again, he counters, "No thank you, maybe some other time. Now *please* step out and let me finish."

"Oh shucks," she retorts and then closes the door behind her while he puts on his sweats. Attempting to weave a lasting memory, he comes out of his room without his shirt.

As her heart melts at the sight of him shirtless again, Sarah thinks to herself, "*Any* girl anywhere would go out with him but he chooses to hang out with *me*. If *only* he would ask me out or tell *me* I'm the one."

Instead, after giving her a hug, he kisses her goodnight quickly and says, "Sarah, no one can take better care of me than you did this weekend. I'm better only because of your care and your parent's kindness toward me. Our time on the couch was more than amazing. Your touch is so gentle and warm." "So is your kiss," he thinks and continues his praise, "I'll always remember this weekend and snuggling on the couch with you. You should probably go before your mom starts to worry."

As her smile rises from deep in her heart, Sarah says with a sigh, "You're right. One last prescription, your doctor orders you to bed right now." Pulling back his covers, she helps him get into his bed. She doesn't want the weekend to end and tears crawl down her face.

Brushing the tears from her cheeks and caressing her face, he inquires softly, "Sarah, are you ok? What's wrong?"

Visualizing her weekend with him, Sarah responds, "I'm sorry you hurt so much this weekend but I don't want this weekend with you to stop. I may never have another weekend like this in my *life*."

Attempting to comfort her fears, he assures, "Sarah, I'm positive we'll have many more weekends together. We have plenty of time."

Adding a sharp note of reality, she counters quickly, "We may have more weekends together but not like *this* one."

Reacting to her rapier-like words, he reflects, "You know she may be right. I didn't consider that before. Wow, she really *does* like me a lot." As Sarah starts to leave, he takes her hand and says gently, "Sarah, come here a minute. I don't want this weekend to end with you just walking out." Drawing her close, he kisses her goodnight warmly then says with a chuckle, "Now please hurry out of here before we start snuggling each other again. Scoot!"

As Sarah walks out the door, she looks flirtingly over her shoulder and says, "*Goodnight Bill,*" melting his heart. Gliding out to the car on euphoric wings, she thinks joyously, "That's more like it but I still wish the weekend didn't have to end." Reaching home, she floats to her bedroom and visualizes the amazing weekend she spent with her best friend.

Hurting

At 5:00 AM Monday morning, Bill gets up for his normal routine. His body pain conveys to his mind quickly that he's not going anywhere. Resetting his alarm, he returns to meet Sarah in his dreams. When the alarm interrupts his dreams again for school, he calls Joey and asks expectantly, "Would you mind picking me up for school today? I didn't go to my normal workout today."

Joey doesn't ask why Bill didn't go workout. He knows why already and replies, "Sure, how soon will you be ready? It's going to take me about half an hour, ok?"

Bill answers jokingly, "That'll be fine. I think my body will be limbered enough by then to ride in the car."

After dropping Bill off at East, Joey drives toward the high school saying, "I'll see you at practice."

During a break, Bill hustles in to see Mr. Tibbs and says, "Mr. Tibbs, you're the closest person I have to a father and I need to speak with you."

Attempting to discern the nature of Bill's visit, Doug Tibbs ponders, "What is he up to? I'll bet he wants me to deliver another note to that cute redhead at Central."

Bill continues, "Sarah and I are very good friends because of the note you delivered. Unfortunately, I'm not sure I'm good enough for her."

Stunned by Bill's lack of confidence, Mr. Tibbs interrupts quickly, "Whoa son, you stop right there. We know each other quite well now. I know your character, personality, and moral compass. I'd better not hear you putting yourself down again around me. Bill, I have seen you both. You two are great kids. I can definitely see you together if you choose to pursue her friendship further."

Struck by his candid words, Bill responds, "Thank you Mr. Tibbs. I appreciate your counsel. I'm just afraid to go too fast. She and her parents took great care of my injuries last weekend. They're a wonderful family and we have such fun together. I miss *that* type of family love but my grandparents are wonderful people who love me too. I'm sure Sarah and I have plenty of time to be together but I have football and school ahead of me. What should I do?"

Laughing as he answers, Mr. Tibbs says, "Bill, you're as smart as anyone I know. You're a great quarterback and team leader but you need to bring some of that quarterback sense into your friendship with her. You need that confidence with her. Don't split your personality into on and off field Bills. Listen to her words intently. Observe her actions when she's with you and for goodness sake, watch her expressions. I know you've treated her very well. That's your upbringing. Remember, there *is* room for football, school, and Sarah. Don't shut her out."

Realizing the wisdom in Mr. Tibbs' words, Bill says, "Thanks Mr. Tibbs. I need to do that with Sarah. I can always count on you. I'd better get to class."

At practice later, Coach Mulinaro requests privately, "Bill, tell me truthfully, what is your pain level?"

Still feeling sharp blades of pain sticking him, Bill answers, "It's pretty intense right now, Coach."

Confirming his fears, Coach replies, "I thought as much after what I saw on Friday. I know you hate this but I'm keeping you out of practice until Thursday. I want you to see the trainer. I hope he can get your body recovered for Friday's game." Bill doesn't even touch a football until Thursday and that practice is shoulder pads and sweats only. Bill wears the red "don't touch me" jersey. By then, he is still in pain and only takes half the snaps as a team precaution. After practice, Coach Mulinaro says, "Bill, you and I will talk tomorrow about whether you healed enough to play or not."

Apprehensive, Bill says, "I understand, coach, but I assure you, I'm good to go."

Friday night's game is against Manual. They're an average team on their best day. Coach Mulinaro knows this and tells Bill, "I'm not going to risk you getting hurt more than you are already." Bill has not healed completely as his left side is still sore. With the team in mental disarray, South kicks off and Manual runs the kick off back for a touchdown on the first play. Making multiple mistakes, both mental and physical, South is behind 21-0 at half time. With the Dragon's Teeth defense looking like pulled teeth, they make Manual's team look like championship caliber. During halftime, the coaching staff isn't very happy as they point out the team's mistakes, softness, and tentative play. Identifying and emphasizing Manual's weaknesses, they encourage the team to reach deep inside and begin to fight back. As the team starts for the field from the currently unfriendly confines of the locker room, Coach says, "If you leave it all on the field, the game is ours. Now get out there and show them your grit and spirit."

South receives the second half kick-off. On their first offensive play of the half, they throw an interception. Exhorting the defense, Bill urges, "Okay guys it's gut check time. Suck it up, hold 'em, and we'll win this game." The team has total confidence in Bill's abilities and his leadership. Firing up the team with his words, the defense hardens like steel again as they hold Manual to a three and out. He sidles up to Coach Mulinaro and says, "Put me in, Coach. I'll be fine. The line will protect me. If I get hurt, I'll take myself out."

Not wanting to risk further injury, Coach Mulinaro answers firmly, "No. It's too risky for your long term health."

Looking the coach directly in his eyes, he says, "Coach, life *is* a risk. *Now* is the time for us to take the chance. I *need* to be in there. I *want* the ball. Let me do what I do." With total confidence in his ability to conjure a victory, the *Wizard* considers, "Mr. Tibbs and Pete are right. I need to bring some of this confidence off the field with me to Sarah."

Coach Mulinaro concedes, "Okay Bill, I can't argue with that logic. Get in there and bring us home a win." The crowd erupts in a thunderous, rolling roar.

Giving a fist pump to the crowd, Bill jogs to the huddle. While jogging out, he looks up to the stands for a glimpse of Sarah. She always sits in the same spot so Bill can find her easily. Finding her quickly, his heart leaps as he points to her and gives her a fist pump. Then, tapping his heart, he points at her again. Her heart melts at his gesture and drives her friends crazy. On this stage, she knows his heart is hers. Bill, the Quarterback, just told her that but she still has doubts about the off-field persona. From *that* Bill, she needs verbal reinforcement. Still, he touched her heart deeply during the past weekend too.

With the first play a sweep right, Bill hands the ball off and avoids being hit. The play gains 5 yards and the next, a sweep left, only gains three. Needing 2 yards for a first down, Coach Mulinaro calls a draw. By now, when Bill taps his helmet, every team knows the receivers break straight down the field. In the huddle, Bill informs the receivers, "Manual is coming hard on a blitz because they think I'm gun shy about getting hit. Coach wants the draw and we're going to show that. But, you guys streak anyway as if I tapped my helmet.

Line, do the best you can to hold off the blitz. I *don't* want to get hit."
Visualizing the next play, he thinks, "I'll probably get hit anyway. It's
going to hurt but let's get it on." As he takes the snap from center,
Manual charges forward. It's a corner blitz and their defensive line
rushes hard too. The *Maestro* drops back and stands in the pocket
after orchestrating the fake draw. Suddenly the *Wizard* appears and
spots Joey flying down the left sideline from where the corner came
on the blitz. He sets and unleashes the lightning as the defense hits
him on his left side.

With the hit, collectively, the South crowd utters,
"OOOHHHHH!" Watching Bill go down from the rush, Sarah
knows they hit his bruised side. Covering her face out of fear for the
result, she replays mentally all the hits he received just a week ago. In
the meantime, Joey is in the end zone handing the ball to the official.
It's something he's picked up watching Bill and how he plays with
such a respect for the game. The crowd shouts and cheers for Joey
but their attention shifts quickly to Bill still on his hands and knees.
Remaining on the ground a minute, he gathers his strength. As
Coach Mulinaro and the team trainer start on the field, Bill jumps
up and waves them back as he starts for the sideline. His teammates
marvel at his toughness as confidence runs rampant throughout the
South sideline. It is a mental certainty they are going to win the
game now. Still, they have to finish playing the game.

While jogging off, he takes his helmet off and points to Sarah.
Giving her a fist pump and a smile, she knows in her heart that he is
ok. He's sore but the pain is *not* as great as his anticipation of it. The
Maestro is in the house and the score is Manual 21 South 7 with eight
minutes left in the third quarter. On the ensuing kickoff, the South
kick-off team is ravenous and unyielding, causing a fumble. The
crowd roars its approval and the *Maestro* returns to his stage for an
encore. Coach Mulinaro calls his favorite play again, a draw, but Bill
checks off because of Manual's blitz. Taking the snap and dropping

back, he does not waste time for a fake hand off. The *Wizard* spies Joey on a slant route in and throws a bullet right on Joey's numbers at the 10-yard line. Breaking a tackle with gusto, Joey scores again. While Manual's defense knocks him down again, Bill jumps up immediately this time. Running to Joey, he gives him a pat on the back. With the South juggernaut on-track and closing in, Manual leads 21-14 with 5 minutes left in the third. Coach Mulinaro doesn't have a problem with Bill checking off and changing plays. Besides, it's hard to argue against his success when doing that. He's never had a kid play for him who understands football like Bill does. The 3rd quarter ends with Manual punting to South.

The South Dragon's Teeth have taken over the game and Manual can't move the ball. Coach Mulinaro asks, "Bill, what play do you want to run?"

Filled with motivation, Bill replies, "I want to go deep and get this game tied."

Coach says, "Okay, that's the call guys. Let's do it." South lines up without a huddle, unheard of at this time, five receivers wide and no running back. The *Wizard* takes the snap and in his spell, Joey and Phil get behind their defenders. He unleashes a bomb to Phil, one play, one touchdown and ties the game at 21. Sarah cringes every time the defense hits Bill. She knows he's hurting but performing at his normal game, which means he's probably ok. Manual punts again and South scores on a long drive to take a 28-21 lead. Scoring late in the 4th quarter again, South wins 35-21.

Everybody in the locker room and in the stands knows they won because of Bill Denton's leadership and play. The post-game interview process continues. While very happy for him, Sarah feels every hit he receives as if they are hitting her. Still, she is anxious to see him and confirm his health for herself. Hearing him with her heart, she knows he's in the locker room heaping praise on all his teammates to the reporters yet saying nothing about himself.

Fielding several interviewers' questions about Bill, Joey answers, "Bill attempts to get us as many points a game as we can get open for him. He brings the game to himself. After the game, he's a normal person, just a goofy kind of guy. He *is* humble, *really*. He's not cocky or overconfident like some guys are. In fact, he can use some of that on-field confidence off the field."

Pizza Time

Sarah and her parents meet Bill in their usual spot after the game. After sharing briefly about the week, his health, and the game, her parents suggest, "Sarah, why don't the two of you go to the Pizza Inn. The two of you had so much fun together last weekend."

Agreeing with her parents, they comment simultaneously, "That sounds like fun," then break into laughter. Walking into the Pizza Inn, Sarah holds Bill's arm. Everyone congratulates them like a rock star couple and pats him on his back. In spite of the groupie environment, he maintains his usual aplomb and cordiality. The Dirty Boys are in their usual location at the back. Sarah greets them all with a smile that says, "Yes, he's mine. *I'm* the doctor that brought him back to health. You can look but don't touch." With a sudden wry smile, she quizzes teasingly, "And how are the Dirty Boys tonight?"

Awed that she knows about the Dirty Boys, they consider, "Wow, he must really be head over heels for her or he would not confide in her like that. After all that bull about not being good enough for her, he sure appears different on this stage."

With another stunning thought, Sarah inquires, "Would you

like to meet some of my friends? I'm sure you would get along with them too."

D. J. answers while the others are still speechless, "Are they as sharp as you?"

Delivering a quick-witted response, Sarah jokes, "Like a razor."

Looking directly at Bill with a big smile, Jordon jokes, "See, we told you it would work."

Laughing, Sarah says, "Since Bill and I are friends, my friends are his friends too." Pushing two tables together, they enjoy each other the rest of the evening.

Calling her parents when it is time to go, Bill walks Sarah out to her mom's car in the parking lot. She asks with an expectant tone in her voice, "Will I see you tomorrow?"

Logic overrules his heart as he says, "After our last weekends, I'd really like that if that's ok but I have morning practice first." He hugs her and kisses her quickly.

With her face showing some frustration, Sarah says, "Of course it's alright. Why wouldn't it be? I thought you enjoyed our weekends together."

Extremely nervous, he replies timidly, "I thought that you might have plans with somebody. I didn't want to assume you're always available to be with me. You're so beautiful and you have so many friends at Central. I'm the new kid here. I didn't want to monopolize your friendships with them."

She says calmly, "*Ok*, I appreciate your respect of my other friends but I look forward to these special weekends with you. I feel differently with you than I feel with any other person. Besides, I like hanging out with you. Going to different schools, we don't get to spend time together during the week." Her heart urges her onward emotionally and she pauses for a moment.

She takes a deep breath while Bill inquires, "Sarah, are you ok? Did I do something wrong?"

Opening her heart, she enlightens, "When I'm with you I feel totally safe and protected. I trust you in every sense of the word. Last weekend proved that to me and I hope it did to you. I know you'll not to do anything to hurt me, physically, mentally, or emotionally. I've never seen such respect from any of my friends that you show to me. I know you'd never let anyone disrespect or hurt me. When we're together, I have a warmth wash over me from my heart that no one else creates in me. You're the most special person in my life."

Sarah's words stop Bill's thoughts and overcome him with trepidation. He recovers his faculties and contemplates, "I've been waiting to hear these words from her. She must have been waiting on the same words from me. Instead of those desired words, I teased her with games about my special girl. I'm afraid now that I waited too long to say her 'longed for' words." He urges his mind to bring out the right words and he chooses them carefully. "Sarah, I know exactly what you mean. I've never felt the way I feel when I'm with you. I don't feel this way with anyone. We're the perfect best friends. I care for you more than I care for any other person and I can't imagine being with any other girl. I don't want to be with any other girl. However, we have plenty of time for each other. I have school and football but I want to be with you too." His words cool the loving warmth she felt in her heart moments ago. Suddenly remembering Mr. Tibbs words to him, he tries to extricate his whole leg from his mouth. Her eyes and expression say she needs more than sharing him right now.

Wanting to hear more, her thoughts flame in her mind, "Didn't he just hear what I said? I poured out my *heart* to him. Where are the words he spoke the last few weekends with me? I know they're in his heart *screaming* to come out and I still care deeply for him. I'll *bring* out those words and emotions when he's with me that I see him deliver on the field. I'll try a different plan and I'll *not* lose him."

Her expression change scares and concerns him as he says, "Sarah, are you ok? Are we still on for tomorrow?"

As Sarah gets in the car, she replies quickly, "I don't know Bill. I have some things to think about," and closes the door. As her mother drives away, Sarah hides her tears from his view. Standing in stunned silence, Bill watches the car pull away and thinks, "*What have I done?*"

The Plan

Saturday morning arrives early after a night of little sleep for either of them. Sarah has learned to weave spells herself from the *Wizard*. Realizing someone needs to make the first move, she ponders, "Well, if I don't call him first, he won't ever call. I'm *sure* he believes he's no longer my friend. Maybe, I shouldn't have reacted so strongly to his fumbling for words. Why can't he just call and ask if I'm ok? Where is the quarterback when I need him?"

As sleep runs from him, Bill rises early with his thoughts racing, "My gut aches from last night but not from the game. I've never taken a hit like that on the field and it still hurts. I still can't get the picture out of my mind of Sarah's car driving away last night. My heart aches to hear her voice, even if it only on the phone. Still, I have to focus. I have practice today and a season to finish. The team counts on me to be there for them." Suddenly, the phone rings and his heart trembles as he answers, "Hello, this is Bill Denton."

The voice on the phone says softly, "Hello Bill."

"Sarah! Are you ok," his voice breaks and crackles with emotion and excitement. He prays in his mind silently, "Thank you God! It's really her and she called *me*. She still likes me."

"Yes, I'm ok but I missed you all night. My heart ached for you," she confides.

"Mine too," he interjects.

Softly and warmly, she continues, "Please come over today. I want to spend this weekend with you."

"I want to spend the weekend with you more than anything," Bill adds. Opening his heart to thoughts of them together, he remarks, "I'll be there with bells on after practice."

Amused with his cliché, Sarah replies with her own, "I'll be here waiting with baited breath." The weekend is as magical as their previous weekends together. Walking through the woods behind her house, they cradle each other's hands and open their hearts just a bit more to each other. As Bill leaves for home, he hugs and kisses her apologetically for the previous night's verbal faux pas.

Smiling from her heart, Sarah thinks, "The plan is underway. Step 1 complete. Time will tell if and when I need additional steps but this one went well."

School Year

With the remainder of the season progressing better than people expected, the team finishes with eight wins and two losses despite being led by a freshman quarterback. It is an excellent record considering the last year's record was two and eight before Bill Denton came. However, the two losses are tough for him to accept. As a freshman, Bill receives the All-State team honorable mention status. The third team quarterback is a junior and the second and first team quarterbacks are seniors. So, there are some politics to overcome. Everyone speaks of the pressure on a freshman quarterback who isn't in the same building as the rest of the team. Bill has heavy expectations on him for his sophomore year and the team will continue to improve as his high school career moves forward. As a freshman, he receives letters from college recruiters already asking him to attend their school to play football. At this point, the schools are all small, Division III in the NCAA structure. After reviewing the letters, he wants to be gracious in his response to them. Asking Sarah to help him, she agrees to track each recruitment letter with him and from whom he receives it. Together they create a gracious declination letter to send back to the schools he does not want to attend or visit. In fact, the letters provide an excellent reason to see Sarah and be with her. Laughing and joking about the letters at first, they truly enjoy each other's company as the process progresses. Unfortunately, the task will become a huge but pleasing undertaking by their senior year.

The Dirty Boys and Sarah's friends meet and find common traits they like in the other person. Planning something every weekend and during school breaks as a group, they meet at one person's house for pizza or all of them go to a movie together. Sometimes, they hang out with each other, talk, and enjoy each other's company. As on the field, Bill leads this group of friends but Sarah becomes co-leader with him, a regal couple. Anyone watching them foretells this to be a permanent friendship. Other relationships forming within the group have the potential of becoming stronger than just friends. Although trying to hide the fact, the individuals always pair up with the same person whenever the group meets together.

Sarah is always with Bill and continues convincing him through various means to listen to his heart emotionally for her. When opening his heart to share, his mind overrules suddenly as reason and logic force him to withdraw slightly from her emotionally. Wanting him to bring some "on-stage" persona with him in their relationship, Sarah desires him to take charge with the passion in his heart. Jordon, Andy, Pete, and D. J. always remain with the same girl from Sarah's group. Envious of the guys' group name, Sarah's friends adopt their own name, calling themselves "Five Girls South" or the F-G-S. There are five girls in their group, who will all attend South High School next fall. Still, no one has a driver's license yet and their parents take them everywhere while enjoying meeting the great friends with whom their children associate. During the year, Bill and Sarah's relationship remains a solid one as they share their lives and learn about each other. Still, desiring a stronger emotional bond, she weaves her friendship deeper daily with him. While they have trouble meeting at the same emotional level, both want more from each other. It is the speed of emotional growth where they differ. Their freshman school year ends with Bill having all A's and one A- on his report card. Sarah did very well too with Bill's pride showing in her accomplishments and his help in them. With the A-, Jordon shows no mercy on Bill, telling him he needs to get a tutor and go to summer school.

QB Camps

During the first month of summer break, Bill attends two quarterback camps. Spending last-minute time with Sarah before leaving, he will attend the University of Texas camp first. Her plan with Bill proceeds on pace with her mental timetable and success expectations level. Experiencing Bill opening his heart to her slowly, she does see hope in how far his heart is opening. Wearing their emotions on their sleeves, they talk about how much they miss each other already. Speaking frankly, they discuss how empty their lives will be without the other person while he is at camp. Her mom, dad, and Sarah take Bill to the airport and at the gate, he says, "I wish camp was finished already. I can't believe I'll be away from you for a week."

Sarah promises, "I'll be at the airport next Sunday when you get back with a *big* hug waiting for you." Sarah thinks, "Boy, wait 'til you get back. Do I have a surprise for you! I'll knock your *socks* off." The thought brings a huge smile to her face. Not waiting for the "end of camp" greeting, they quickly hug each other now. As he walks down the boarding ramp, he continues to take mental pictures of Sarah over his shoulder. Catching his glances, Sarah makes sure she wears her biggest smile and changes "super model" poses each time he looks back. Blitzing his psyche relentlessly, she wants him to *remember* the girl he left at home.

A few weeks earlier, Bill called his uncle, who is on the Houston police department, to say that he is flying to Texas to attend the UT Austin quarterback camp. Since his uncle does not get to see Bill often, he takes a vacation week to see him workout at the camp. Bill's parents named him after his uncle, who is officially his godfather, William Denton. They spend the evenings together at restaurants or in the motel talking.

One evening with him, Bill says, "It's great to have family to talk with. I miss mom, dad, and telling them about my life. I met a wonderful girl named Sarah, who is unbelievably beautiful. I bumped into her during halftime of a game, spilling a soft drink on her. I met her parents, who actually like me."

"And why wouldn't they, son," Uncle Bill interjects in a strong Texas twang.

Bill continues his story, "I spent the last year hanging out with her. She's so amazing and even cared for me at her parent's house for a whole weekend when I was injured in a game last season. We have so much fun together and I really like her but *I* have *school* and *football* ahead of me. There is plenty of time for us to be together."

His uncle stops the story quickly, "*Boy*, I cain't believe what I just heard you say. Were you listen'n to yourself just now? Ya tell me about this beautiful girl, who nursed ya back to health, and all y'all can say is '*but* I got *school* and *football* ahead of me.' I thought you were the brains in the family. Maybe, *that's* what's *wrong*. Yer thinkn' *too* much. *Boy*, ya *gotta* make a *decision*. Is there room in your life for Sarah or are ya gonna give 'er to some other dude? I know how ya are on and off the football field. Ya believe there isn't anything ya cain't do on a football field. It's a stage for y'all. Off the field, yer too dang laid back and conservative. Y'all need to bring some o' that passion off the field with ya and into *her* life. *Son*, y'all have to '*cowboy up*' and tell *her* what ya said to me about her, how y'all feel, or yer *gonna* lose her to someone. Ya know me and I'm tellin' ya straight."

With his discussion hitting its target, Bill nods, "You're right Uncle Bill. I understand your words and their meaning."

"Y'all say that but are *ya* gonna do somethin'? Just think about it. Ya know I'm right," his uncle retorts.

Mentally organizing his "priorities", Bill thinks, "I know I need to tell Sarah how I feel but I have to finish this camp with my head on straight and focused. Maybe I *can* bring the stage to her." However, he does not reveal his action plan to his uncle.

At the end of the week, all the quarterbacks get a personal evaluation with one of the assistant coaches, except Bill. The head coach calls him to his office for his personal evaluation where the entire camp staff waits for him. Stunned by the size of the group, he keeps his emotion hidden from the staff. The Texas coach gets right to the point, "I'm going to make this plain and simple. You're the best quarterback to go through this camp in 10 years. You outplayed, outthrew, and outsmarted 50 other guys. You're a sure Division I prospect and right now as a freshman, I would put you in the top 25 players in the country. You'll be hearing from us and we're looking forward to you coming to camp next year."

Remaining in Houston on Friday and Saturday night, Bill stays at his uncle's home, needing family time desperately. Wanting to clear his head, he focuses his thoughts about Sarah, school, football, and his future. They discuss how much he misses his parents and how he wishes he could talk with them about Sarah. His uncle explains his great pride in Bill's camp performance, which he describes in detail. Flying home on Sunday afternoon, Bill thinks of Sarah, her beauty, and missing her immensely. At the airport arrival gate, Sarah waits expectantly until Bill is safely away from other passengers. Then, rushing him like a blitzing cornerback, she jumps in his arms and plants a huge warm kiss on his lips with all the passion she can muster. The other passengers begin cheering and clapping as Bill's face turns scarlet. "Do you think I missed you," Sarah quizzes teasingly and thinks to herself, "Got him!"

Still in emotional overload, Bill jokes, "No, not much."

After lightly slapping him on the shoulder, Sarah exclaims, "Bill!" Walking from the airport gate, she and her parents retrieve his luggage and offer to take him to dinner. Sarah inquires with love in her heart, "Did camp go well for you?"

"I have something I'd like you to read," Bill says with a wry smile. Handing her his camp evaluation form, she begins to read it intently.

As her smile grows to amazement, her dad asks with curiosity, "Sarah, you seem surprised by the contents. What does it say?"

Sarah replies, "His total score is 95% and the written comment at the bottom reads, 'You're the best we've seen in 10 years. Look forward to you returning next year.'"

Her mom inquires curiously, "Bill, were you the best player there?"

Uncharacteristically, Bill answers simply, "Yes ma'am, I was."

Amazed by his comment because he never talks about himself, Sarah says with surprise, "I've never heard you say how good you thought you were."

He responds seriously, "Really Sarah, I'm not bragging because it's written in the evaluation. I answered your mom's question politely." That wry smile he gets when he's proven a point grows on his face.

Loving the appearance of this side of him, she enjoys him acknowledging that he is very good and thinks, "I hope he brings some of that confidence and presence into our relationship." The rest of dinner contains desserts of stolen glances and shared smiles with each other.

Two weeks later, Bill attends the Notre Dame Quarterback camp where his performance at Texas and his reputation precede him. Sarah's parents offer to drive Bill to the camp, which he graciously accepts. The head coach, George Alan, and his staff welcome Bill personally. The camp's staff greets the remaining campers while the head coach reviews his notes for the week. As Bill unpacks his things in his dorm room, a few other guys at camp come by to ask, "Are you the QB kid from Indianapolis?"

Bill answers simply, "Yes, I am."

"Ok, we just wanted to know some of our competition. Thanks," they say and move to other dorm rooms.

Bill's special sense tells him he is the target and he considers, "These guys want to prove they're each better than me. Good luck if they think for one minute that I'm going to get overconfident and give those guys any edge. I'm not going to let *that* happen."

Several others come by and say, "Hey, we're going out on the town for a while. You want to come with us?"

"Thanks very much. I appreciate the offer but I plan to stay here," Bill declines.

"We know about a party off campus. We're going to go and want you to come with us too. You might meet some college girls and have some fun," they offer. Thinking about Sarah's beauty with his heart, he declines again. The group quizzes somewhat sarcastically, "Why not. Don't you want to have some fun?"

Determined to maintain focus, he explains, "Guys, I'm here for one reason and one reason only. I want to become a better football player plus I have a very special girl back home." Their jaws drop, looking at him as if he's a few sandwiches short of a picnic.

The devil in them rises, pleading, "Come on, man. It's a week without parents and we're planning to take advantage of that and you should too."

Bill, in his own polite way, responds, "Guys, I appreciate the offer but that's not my style. My parents are dead and I've come to camp for the camp, not for the parties. I need to get my rest for camp tomorrow." Shaking their heads, they apologize and walk away red-faced. After the group leaves, Bill lays on his bed thinking how much he misses Sarah. Reminded about his parents by their comments, Bill falls asleep praying about his camp performance in the coming week and asking the Lord to let his parents watch him this week.

The week begins and so does the camp. The first day of camp centers on conditioning, agilities, and overall body strength. As usual, Bill works extremely hard and is the top performer. Wowing the coaching staff, the other campers are envious of his physical abilities. With envy and jealousy flowing strong among the attendees, the target on Bill's back grows larger. Tuesday is accuracy and footwork. With each player allowed 20 throws, Bill throws last in view of his outstanding performance on the previous day. The other camper's scores range from 7 to 12 out of 20 and Bill is ready for his turn mentally and physically. After his 20 throws, he leaves the other campers shaking their heads as he scores 17 out of 20. Wednesday is timing drills like those Bill practices with his receivers at South. Making every throw perfect, he delivers on time and on target exactly to the camp receivers who are from the Notre Dame Football team. Bill amazes everyone that he is this good and yet only going to be a high school sophomore. The end of the third camp day has everyone wondering who will be second because of Bill's performance the first three days. Thursday is finesse day with long throws, fades, and putting the ball right where it is supposed to be on a 50-yard pass. Again, Bill astounds everyone including coaches, campers and the Notre Dame receivers. Friday morning is just for fun. The rules allow each attendee five throws and the person who can throw the ball the farthest wins. When Bill's turn arrives, the longest throw in the air is 65 yards. Bill uses his first four throws to warm up and they are in the 65-yard range already. Bill decides to stun the crowd one more time. The *Wizard* makes his appearance and uncorks a magical throw for number five. In the air, the ball flies from the goal line to the other 22-yard line, 78 yards in the air. Everyone gives him high fives and pats his back. As he meets the first guys he met when unpacking for camp, they shake his hand and confess, "You're as good as everyone says, congratulations."

The usual coach and player meetings take place the rest of the morning. Again, Bill meets with the head coach and the entire camp staff. Coach Alan shakes his hand and says, "Bill, we're extremely impressed with your performance this week. We hope your experience here at Notre Dame was an enjoyable one. We're very interested in keeping an eye on you for the next couple of years. Please send me your game schedule so we can watch you play." Coach Alan gives Bill a business card with the address of where to send his schedule. After lunch, the staff holds the final camp meeting where they hand out Notre Dame Camp attendance certificates. The certificates are impressive, formal, and suitable for framing. They are documents you want to display proudly, not just put in a drawer. After handing out the other awards, they give the final award for the best player in camp. There is no mystery or suspense regarding the expected award recipient. Coach Alan steps to the podium and makes the official announcement, "The award for outstanding player at the 1966 Notre Dame Quarterback camp goes to Bill Denton." The coach takes a trophy out of a box. It is beautiful, with a gold ND on top and inscribed in the base:

Outstanding Player 1966 Notre Dame Quarterback Camp

Everyone claps and shakes Bill's hand after the coach presents the award to him. A photographer takes a picture of Bill and Coach Alan with the trophy. Wearing his best "proved my point" smile, he thanks the coach and camp staff. He puts the trophy back in the box after everyone has a chance to see it, and then hurries back to his room to finish packing. He can feel Sarah's presence near to his heart and knows she is almost there.

Shortly thereafter, Sarah and her parents arrive at the camp to drive Bill back home. He carries his luggage from the dorm and puts it in the car. As they make final checks and begin to leave the room, Sarah sees the box and not wanting to leave anything, queries, "Hey Bill, does this box belong to you or does it stay in the room?"

He answers with a tease, "It's something I got for you." Carrying the box to the car, she opens it with great anticipation after they start back to Indianapolis.

With puzzlement on her face, she says, "Bill, this is a trophy from the camp. This isn't for me. It's yours that you earned with your hard work."

Seeing her confusion, he explains, "Really, you can have it. If I take it home, it will end up in my closet with some other things. You're my best friend and I want you to have it."

Sarah insists, "Bill, I did nothing to earn this. You need to display it proudly. When you're much older, you'll be happy to have this to show your kids. Besides, I wouldn't want to display it in my room. It'll always be more special to you than to me."

Deciding that now is the time for his other gift, Bill is disappointed that the trophy did not impress her as he hoped it would. Anticipating his other gift will reach her heart, he acquiesces, "Ok, I'll keep the trophy but only if you'll keep this." Pulling a small box from his pocket, he hands it to her.

"What's *this*," she queries as she opens the box. Suddenly, her scrutiny falls on the contents and astonishment leaps onto her face. With disbelief, she exclaims, "Bill, this is beautiful. You shouldn't have." A smile pours from his heart onto his face as Sarah continues to stare at the heart-shaped ruby necklace in her hand. Praying in her heart to hear the words for which she ached, Sarah requests bravely, "Why would you want to get this for me? *When* did you get this?"

Thinking rationally not emotionally, Bill explains, "Remember when I was injured and wanted to go to the mall? This is what I wanted to buy for you then. To me, you're the most special person I know. You mean more to me than the trophy ever will. I want you to remember how much I care for you, what great care you took with me when I was injured during the season, and our freshman year together. I want to remind you that you're the most wonderful person in my life." Thrilled with her response to his gift, he thinks, "I finally stepped up correctly like Uncle Bill said." Overjoyed with the gift, Sarah kisses him warmly on his cheek. After all, mom and dad are in the car too. While smiling broadly on the outside, her heart aches to hear him say he loves her. She loves him so much but she is afraid to say the words first and fears he may reject such an emotional advance. Not wanting their time together to end, she plans her next step mentally to bring Bill to realize he loves her and to verbalize it to her.

Taking the necklace out of the box, she says, "Bill, would you mind putting the necklace on me?" His hand trembles as he pushes the clasp together around her neck. Feeling his hands tremble, she inquires with curious joy, "Does it look ok on me?"

Overwhelmed by the vision in the seat next to him and longing to hold her in his arms, he replies, "Sarah, no one looks as beautiful as you do wearing the necklace."

Her parents notice all the movement in the back seat and ask, "Are you kids ok?"

Bill and Sarah reply simultaneously, "Yes, we're fine." Then, they both laugh together.

The laughter causes her parents to probe further, "Ok, what's *really* going on back there with you two?"

Wanting to lower their curiosity, Sarah adds, "Seriously, we're fine. We were just looking at Bill's camp trophy and oh, by the way, Bill bought me a heart-shaped ruby necklace."

As she leans forward for her mom to see it, her mom responds, "Sarah, it looks beautiful on you. Bill, you didn't have to do that."

Thrilled with her mom's reaction, Bill explains, "Yes ma'am. I really *did* have to do that. Sarah is my best friend and you all have taken such good care of me. I wanted to show you how much you, and especially Sarah, mean to me. When I was injured, I wanted to go to the mall and get this. I bought it later in the week and have been waiting for the right time to give it to Sarah."

Breaking the tender moment, her dad queries about the trophy, "Sarah, if there is an inscription on the trophy, would you please read it to us?"

From the trophy, Sarah reads, "**Outstanding Player 1966 Notre Dame Quarterback Camp.**"

Attempting to evoke a comment about Bill's performance, her dad probes, "Bill, *were you* the best player in camp *again?*"

Revealing more of himself, Bill answers, "Yes sir, I was. I had to prove a point because a couple of other players mocked me a little. Maybe there were trying to gain an edge or just see my character. It was one of those times I had to step up and be great."

With Bill finally talking about himself, her dad decides to have some fun and asks jokingly, "Aren't you always great Bill?"

Bill replies seriously, "No sir. Great players don't have to be great all the time. They just have to be great when the situation calls them to be great and this was one of those times. However, camp is over now and I can be just myself again."

Intrigued by his wordplay, her dad probes deeper, "I don't follow your meaning."

Then, the *Maestro* catches Sarah and her parents by surprise completely saying, "I like being *the* guy. I like walking onto the field and having everyone say, 'Is that him,' or 'There he is,' or that 'He's like a Broadway star on the field.' I liken the field to a stage. The bigger the stage, the more I like it. The whole atmosphere is exhilarating but here is the paradox. I like being in the spotlight but it's not who I am."

Surprised, her dad says, "I'm glad you see the person we have seen for the last year. I'm proud of you."

As Bill leans back into the seat, he says, "Thank you sir. It means so much to me to hear you say that."

Secretly, Sarah wishes, "Why can't he be more like that when we're together? If my plan goes well, I'll see more of that Bill in our relationship. I'll get him to see what a special person he is off the field now that he sees how special he is on the field. You know, it's really cool that he's fully aware of how good a player he is." Admiring the necklace again, Sarah puts Bill's arm around her and snuggles her cheek into his chest. While he hugs her gently in his arm, they both drift off to sleep for the remainder of the trip.

As the family arrives back in Indianapolis, her mom wakes them and inquires happily, "Bill, would you like to come to our house for dinner and relax?"

Speaking before he can answer, Sarah says, "Yes mom, he would."

With their eyes sparkling at each other, Bill gives her a kiss on her cheek whispering, "Thank you. I didn't want to end our time together either." After dinner and cleaning up the table, Bill and Sarah wash the dishes. Turning on the TV in their "special" room, they snuggle on the couch. Her parents go to another room to watch TV and leave Bill and Sarah to themselves. Sarah continues to admire the necklace while locked in Bill's embrace. Discussing plans for the rest of the summer, they describe how much fun they're going to have together. Looking forward to high school, they are especially excited about being in the same building. As their thoughts merge, Bill gives Sarah another hug but this time the hug is different from his usual hugs. It is a warm, loving, and extended embrace, an embrace that says, "Don't ever leave my arms. I love you." Unfortunately, Bill does not share the words hidden in his heart that match the blissful caress they share. Sensing the love in his embrace, Sarah still longs for the words she has yet to hear. The summer continues from the serenity of the couch to other venues. Excitement and adventure build for the Dirty Boys and FGS during several visits to Riverside Amusement park in Indianapolis while screaming together on the Thriller and Flash roller coasters. Being driven about an hour south of home, the same group strolls along the rolling hills of Brown County State Park and browses the shop windows around Nashville, Indiana. All told, they enjoy the summer fun with their friends and stolen moments alone together as a new school year approaches quickly.

A New Year

The summer fades as quickly as the memory of the fun times experienced then. It is time to return to business and stoke the competitive fires. Bill starts the year by getting the receivers together 3 days a week a month before the official workouts begin. Performing two hours of timing drills each day as a group, they progress to the point where they almost run them blindfolded. Creating impeccable timing, Bill's throws grow sharper with each practice. The *Wizard* weaves spells with the ball travelling to where the receivers run and it's there at the perfect time each time. As the official practice begins, optimism courses through the entire team about the season. By protecting Bill every play this season, the linemen know they have a great chance to make the state finals.

All the linemen pool their money and order t-shirts that simply say "*Protect The Man*" on the front. Displaying the t-shirts proudly, Bill shakes his head and smiles with embarrassment. After the linemen model the shirts for the team, they all want one. When the second batch of shirts arrives, everyone on the team has a "*Protect The Man*" t-shirt except Bill. With all the team wearing the shirts, they approach him as a group. Observing the stealth in their actions, Bill questions, "Ok guys, what are *you* up to?" With a stern look, the team's biggest offensive linemen steps forward and hands a special shirt to Bill. Confused by the gesture, Bill says, "Guys, I didn't order a shirt."

The team bursts into laughter and says, "That's ok. It's not *like* ours." Bill unfolds the shirt that reads simply, "*The Man*." Now, he is deeply embarrassed but his teammates make him put on the shirt. As he pulls down the shirt, the team erupts in cheers and starts chanting, "Protect the man, protect the man."

One of the players suggests, "Hey why don't we get one for Sarah that says '*Protect My Man*.'"

Shuffling his feet as he looks down at them, Bill shakes his head and says, "I'm not her man. I'm her friend. Please don't give her *that* shirt."

Some teammates insist, "What aren't you seeing that we are? We've seen her eyes when she's with you, man. This is high school and if you leave a beautiful girl like her alone, some dude will put a claim on her."

Though thinking back to his uncle's conversation with him, logic overrules his heart and he still replies, "Guys, we're just friends. Please don't give her the shirt." While the team agrees with him, they agree secretly to give Sarah a shirt that says "*Protect My Friend*."

One of the team takes it to her later. As he presents it to her, he asks anxiously, "Sarah, may I tell you something in strictest confidence?"

Thrilled with the shirt, she replies, "Ok, but what's so secret?"

He says, "We wanted to give you a shirt that said 'Protect My Man' but Bill wouldn't let us. He said you two were just friends. We can see you're more than that but what could we do?"

Appreciative of the information, she responds, "Thanks for letting me know. You secret is safe with me." Frustrated with his emotional reservations, she thinks, "Ok Mr. Denton, you keep telling people we're *only* friends. I guess I'll have to get desperate. I hoped it wouldn't come to this but you leave me no choice." Sarah displays for Bill how well the shirt fits her when he comes over for the weekend and performs her best super model poses for him.

Smiling with embarrassment, he stumbles verbally, "Thanks for wearing it." Most importantly, he mentions nothing about the shirt the team really wanted to give her.

Disappointed with Bill for not opening his heart to her about the other shirt, she reacts mentally, "That's it. What *do* I have to *do*, Bill Denton."

With summer ending and school beginning, the first football game is this coming Friday. Unfortunately, much to their disappointment, Bill and Sarah don't have any classes together. However, they *do* see each other during the day. The pre-game pep session Friday afternoon excites everyone about the game. By now, with her desperation plan in motion fully, Bill finds her wearing the ruby necklace when the pep session ends and asks excitedly, "Hi Sarah. Are you coming to warm-ups? Are we meeting at the same spot after the game? *Sarah?*"

As a serious expression slides over her face, she begins speaking slowly, "I'll be at warm ups and sit in the same spot as usual. However, I can't meet you after the game because I have a date with a junior who eats lunch when I do." Devastated by her words, he feels her emotional sucker-punch deep inside. Praying for the right words, she thinks, "Please Bill, tell me not to go because I'm your girl. You know I am. I'll cancel the date if you'll just say those words to me."

His thoughts flash to the words of his uncle Bill and his teammates, "I thought if I gave her the necklace it would be enough but I guess she needed to hear how I felt too. Well, I guess it's too late now and I've lost her to someone else." Failing to find the right words, finally, he says dejectedly, "Sarah, that's great. I hope you have a good time."

Of course, he doesn't really mean it and her heart breaks as she thinks, "No! Where is the Bill with whom I rode home from the football camp and spent the summer? I may *never* hear how he really feels now. I *know* he wants to go out with me. He's just afraid to ask but I can't wait forever for him to find his courage. I might as well go out with some other guys and enjoy high school. Maybe he'll *never* realize we *are* meant for each other. Why can't he *tell* me I'm his girlfriend?"

Again, Bill says, "I hope you have a good time. I'll look for you and your date. I have to go because I need to eat before the game. I have to focus on the game tonight. Bye Sarah." Turning his back to her, he walks away from her disconsolate. Watching him walk away, Sarah turns and begins to cry softly as their hearts ache and their minds lie to each other.

Bill determines to focus on the game because his teammates count on him to lead them. North Central is their opponent with South coming in as the 5th ranked team in the state. Showing no emotion in the locker room, his team knows he is ready. The team leaves the locker in its pre-game frenzy with the *Wizard* driving the whirlwind ahead of him onto the field. Refusing to think about Sarah at this moment, it is *show time.* The *Maestro* is ready and the stands are packed. As he swaggers onto his stage at a strolling pace, the stands erupt into a huge roar. Giving the crowd a fist pump as he saunters to get some water, he looks for Sarah and her date. Spotting them in the stands, he points and gives them a triumphant fist pump. Sarah's girls are dumbfounded and confused. Her date thinks, "I heard they are good friends. I guess that's true." While the *Maestro* plays to the crowd, Sarah's heart aches but she hides how deeply she cares for Bill from her date. Only the Dirty Boys, FGS, and his teammates know how deeply Bill cares for her despite his denials. No one in the stadium outside Bill and Sarah realize "the emotional play" occurring right in front of their eyes. While Sarah's FGS girls *do not* understand what's happening, they support her, as friends will do. Not knowing how or what to say to their dates, the Dirty Boys, they came together to watch their best friend play.

The *Wizard* whips his frustration and emotional hurt into a masterful spell that he invokes onto North Central. South wins 35 to 14 in a game where only the score was semi-close. Completely dominating, the first team defense gives up one touchdown in the 3rd quarter and the second team defense gives up a touchdown with less than two minutes to go. Bill's play never implied any heartbreak inside or emotional distress. In fact quite the opposite, he has a stellar game generating amazing stats, 27 for 32 passing, 4 touchdowns, and over 300 total yards. As Coach takes him out of the game with two minutes left, he receives a standing ovation from both school's fans.

With both hearts at an emotional precipice about to plunge into the abyss of loss, Bill does not look for Sarah during the game or after leaving it. She received only his triumphant fist pump before the game. While he considers, "After all, *she's* on a date and I've no business intruding on their fun. She needs room to be herself," her heart aches to meet Bill after the game.

She contemplates, "My heart hurts so deeply, but I can't show it. After all, *I'm* out with another guy and I don't want to hurt him." In the locker room, the team tells the reporters about their t-shirts worn under their jerseys during the game and that the shirts reflected their goal for the year. While he praises his teammates during his post-game interview, the press continues to probe him. His teammates are aware that Bill is spending much more time to answer all press questions. They sensed something wrong during the game, as he did not look for Sarah after warm-ups.

When he finishes with the press questions, Joey reminds, "Hey Bill, you need to hurry up or you'll miss Sarah. I'm sure she's waiting for you at your usual spot."

As dejection crawls over his face, he responds, "Sarah's not waiting for me tonight, Joey. She has a date and it's not me, man. I think I've lost her. Tonight, it's just you and me."

Momentarily stunned, Joey says, "I'm so sorry, man. If you want to talk, I'm here. Just let me know when you're ready." Deciding to meet the rest of the guys, Bill and Joey go to the Pizza Inn. As the two walk through the door, everyone begins a victory celebration with them and cheers wildly. Thanking each person individually as he moves past, he and Joey find a seat and place their order. After a few minutes, everyone realizes Bill isn't with Sarah and supposition takes a frenzied path through the patrons. *Bill and Sarah are always together.* The Dirty Boys, Pete, Jordon, D. J., and Andy sit at their usual table but they all have dates with Sarah's FGS girls. Sensing his loss, an awkward shroud hangs over all of them because Bill isn't with Sarah. Getting their pizza and drinks at the counter, Joey and Bill return to sit down.

Suddenly, Sarah and her date walk in the door and make eye contact with Bill and Joey as a deathly silence falls over the place. Everyone's eyes gravitate toward Sarah while she and her date feel the crush of their stares. Fixing their gaze on Bill and Joey's table, they walk to the guys where Sarah introduces her date to Bill. When he responds in his usual cordial manner, a gasp rushes from the patrons. Standing politely, Bill shakes her date's hand and says, "Man, you're the luckiest guy in the world."

Not certain of the words he hears yet expecting the worst, her date quizzes anxiously, "What do you mean?"

With a chuckle, Bill says, "That's easy. You're on a date with Sarah. That makes you the luckiest guy in the world." The silence breaks with whispers among the patrons after they had strain to hear Bill's every word. While Sarah's heart melts, she doesn't show it and just smiles from her heart at Bill. Missing her deeply but not wanting to offend, Bill says, "Thanks for stopping by to say hello. I always love to see you Sarah."

Sarah's heart leaps inside her and her mind races, "There still may be hope yet." However, Sarah and her date decide to get their pizza and drinks to go. The gossip fest and piercing stares are too much for both of them.

After the couple leaves, the guys stay a while still generating whispers from the other tables. Seeing the hurt on Bill's face, Joey says, "Hey man, you want to go. This place isn't as *friendly* as it used to be."

Still in emotional distress, Bill agrees, "Sure, I need to get outta here." Words fail both of them on the way home.

As they arrive at Bill's house, Joey says, "I'll pick you up for practice tomorrow morning."

With pain emanating from his face, Bill replies, "I'll see you then."

Suddenly, Joey verbalizes his thoughts, "Bill, I need to say something to you and I don't want you to be upset with me. I'm your good friend and I understand your insistence that you and Sarah are just friends. However man, I'm *not* buying it for one minute. You can sidestep all the rushers you want. You can weave all the spells you want. You can throw all the defenses at everyone you want. I can tell by your actions and I see your eyes go from steel to Jell-O when you're with Sarah or just see her. You're in *love* with her."

Attempting to hide his pain, Bill responds, "We're just friends and I'm happy for Sarah."

"That's bogus man," Joey retorts and continues, "I've seen the hurt in you all night and when Sarah walked in, your heart broke in front of me. I'll support whatever stance you want to take but you need to listen to one last thing. After that, I'll not say any more. Sarah is only gone if you want her gone. You open your heart, tell her your feelings, and she is yours. You keep your feelings to yourself, convince yourself you're not good enough, and she *will* find another guy. I'm telling you though. *She's* in love with *you* and it was written all over *her* face tonight, too. That's all, man. I'm done. Just remember, *I'm* your friend. You just needed to hear this."

Turning back as he saunters into his house, Bill says, "Thanks man. You're *still* my friend and more important, my *favorite* receiver. I appreciate your words and concern for both of us. Catch you tomorrow." As the door closes behind him, he contemplates, "Joey might be right. Maybe I still have a chance with Sarah. I'm so confused with her. I don't think I've ever hurt this bad even after the Luers game."

After practice Saturday, Joey asks, "Are you going to Sarah's house today?"

Rationalizing in his mind, Bill replies, "No, I'd like to hang out with you today if you're not busy. Maybe we can do something tonight."

Sarah wakes up with a hollow emptiness in her heart Saturday. Noticing the look on her face, her mom asks with concern, "How was your date, dear?"

Hiding her emotions, Sarah replies, "It was fine, mom. I had a good time."

However, her eyes and her soul could not lie to her mother. "You miss Bill don't you, dear," her mom probes with love in her heart.

"Yes mom, I do," she answers. By the middle of the afternoon, her heart sinks as her mind convinces her heart that *he* is *not* coming to her house today. Holding out hope that he will call, her mind realizes he won't be going to church with them Sunday. She ponders, "I really blew this big time. Is he mad at me, hurt, or both? I have to find a way out of this pit I put myself in. Will he *ever* forgive me?" She says, "Mom, I think I'll go lie down and take a nap." Shuffling to her room, she cries herself to sleep.

On Monday, Sarah hurries quickly to school early wearing the heart necklace Bill gave her. Her heart begged the entire weekend to speak with Bill and empty her soul to him. Finding him in the cafeteria before school, she inquires, "Would you mind speaking with me in private for a minute?" They locate a table with no one sitting near enough to hear them. She begins timidly, "Bill, are you angry with me?"

"No…. I'm not. You're my *friend*," he replies while hiding his true feelings.

"Are you hurt because I had a date," she inquires hoping to elicit a response that says her question touched him deeply and he really didn't want her to date other guys.

Hesitating with his response as she hits a nerve with her emotional blitz, his mind flashes, "Of course, I'm hurt. What do you think? No, I can't *say* that to her." Sidestepping her question, he says, "I care for you deeply."

"Well, if you care so much, why didn't you call me or come over Saturday? Did you think I *didn't* want to see you," she probes.

Fumbling for his response, he says finally, "Well I… I thought you would want to be with your date this weekend. I didn't want to intrude on your time together."

With those words, her heart breaks with his deference as she blurts, *"And what about us?* Why won't you tell me how you *really* feel? We spent last year and the whole summer together. We went to church together. I doctored your injuries and cared for you. You gave me this beautiful heart necklace that says you care deeply. Why won't you have the faith in me to give me your heart with your words?" Her face shows the distress in her heart awaiting the response from the person for whom she cares so deeply. "Please tell me. Please," her thoughts and heart beg.

Finally, Bill opens up, "I thought you must want some freedom to see other guys since you went out on a date with someone else. I didn't want to press you on the weekend *and yes,* it hurts deeply but I care enough to give you that freedom. However, I can never be angry with you. I pray you had a good time on your date…" The bell rings just as he is ready to say, "because I love you." Leaving their hearts in the cafeteria, a specter of hollow emptiness haunts them as they rush to their separate classes.

Even though it is only the second week of school, Bill's mind convinces him that Sarah wants to date other guys. His heart, though, heard her beg him to say the words that the bell stopped in his throat. The day passes with both of them in pain emotionally. Uncharacteristically, they don't see each other all day. His confusion drives him to contact the only person with whom he can confide. After school, he rushes to see Mr. Tibbs at East.

Bill catches Doug Tibbs completely by surprise. "Hello Bill. What brings you to my world today," Mr. Tibbs queries curiously given the expression on Bill's face.

"Mr. Tibbs, it's Sarah," Bill explodes.

"Bill, is she *ok*," Mr. Tibbs utters with concern.

"Yes…Yes, she is but I think I've lost her. She went on a date with another guy and I don't know what to do," Bill effuses.

Mr. Tibbs chuckles inside thinking, "Ahh, Teenage love," but he smiles at Bill. "Ok Bill. Let's analyze this like men," Mr. Tibbs opens and continues, "Did you tell her what she means to you?"

"Well, not in so many words," Bill responds timidly.

"Did you tell her that you want her as your girl," Mr. Tibbs quizzes.

"Well, not really but I gave her a heart-shaped ruby necklace," Bill adds as he examines his shuffling feet.

"Well, the necklace was a good start," Mr. Tibbs exclaims. "However, did you let her know how special she is to you with your words," Mr. Tibbs probes further.

"Well not really," Bill continues, "I thought my actions said the words."

"Big mistake son. Girls want to *hear* how much you care for them not just with gifts and helpful actions. Don't you think that she might have gone on the date to spur your heart to verbalize what you feel? Did you call her after the date or spend time with her," Mr. Tibbs counsels.

"I thought she wanted some space and wanted to date other guys," Bill explains.

Mr. Tibbs rolls his eyes in disbelief of what he heard. "Well, you certainly swan dived off *that* proverbial cliff. Ok, here is what I want you to do. Continue to be her friend. Don't be obvious in your actions, as you don't want to drive her away. If she gives you the opportunity, *tell* her how you *really* feel. Bring that on-field confidence into your relationship. You may have to go out with another girl and then come back to your relationship with Sarah. Support her when she needs support. *Always* be there for her. If she's your best friend as you say she is, let her know it in as many ways as you can without 'stalking' her. Be the gentleman with her that I know you are. Let time heal your relationship. If your love is meant to be, it *will* happen. I saw her eyes and her heart in her face when I gave her your note. Do you *want* her love? If so, you have to *win* her back. *This* is the game now. Now go do what you need to do with her and get ready for the game. Here is my phone number in case you need to speak with me. Life happens, Bill. Enjoy it," Mr. Tibbs finishes and gives Bill a head ruffling with his hand.

With mixed emotions, Bill replies, "Thanks Mr. Tibbs. I can always count on you to give me the fatherly advice that I need to hear. I'll try to use all that advice correctly. And yes, I *do* want her back and want to win her love." Bill walks away, mulling over the advice in his mind from his "father." Determined to be Sarah's best friend ever, he sets his heart to win her love back but knows he has to "let time heal their relationship." Ruminating mentally for a couple of weeks on Mr. Tibbs words, he plans, "If we have to be friends for life, then that's what we'll be. It'll cut deeply when she's out with another guy but I'll support her. I really love her and want her to be happy. Why couldn't I tell her? If I find another girl I want to go out with, I'll ask her out while I let time heal our hurt and emotions but I'm not accepting someone less. I'll allow Sarah time to heal and enjoy herself in the process."

Sarah's heart continues its proof of her depth of love for him, "He almost said what I hoped to hear. I just know it. However, I can't spend my whole life waiting on him to express his love for me. What if he never expresses his love? We may be best friends forever but then again, if I water it, the flower may bloom fully. Let's see how things progress." In the interim until the next game, they continue to grow their friendship. Continuing to support and encourage each other, both are available to each other emotionally. Not going to her house much and wanting to give her time to heal, Bill still calls and speaks with her more lovingly than ever. When he does go to Sarah's, they hug and snuggle as they did before Sarah started dating others. Both hearts reach out to the other and Bill is determined not to lose her to anyone ever. After all, he is the *Wizard* and thrives under competition. Happy together and always having fun, Sarah's girls and the Dirty Boys continue to date while the emotional play continues to unfold before them.

Maddie

The next game is at Warren, ranked 3rd in the state. South comes out of the locker room for warm ups in its normal frenzy being driven by the *Wizard*. As the team reaches the field with fire in its eyes, the *Maestro* swaggers onto his stage inducing wild cheers from the visiting South crowd. While the partisan Warren crowd thinks he is arrogant, he does not allow the crowd into his head. Sensing he is already in their heads, he continues to affect every team and crowd South plays. "After all, a star never runs onto the stage and yet performs great every time. Look out world, the *Maestro* is ready to conduct," he thinks to himself.

Not looking for Sarah or her date, he drinks his pre-game water from the fountain. It is his way of giving Sarah time to heal emotionally. Noticing this slight from him immediately, her empty yearning for Bill's love continues to grow. "I love being around him, his touch, and watching him play, but I need someone to quench this ache in my heart," she yearns silently.

Her date notices some distress in her expression and inquires, "Sarah, are you ok?"

Forcing the hurt inside with a smile, she replies, "Sure I'm fine. Why?"

"Well, the look on your face seemed to show some pain and I'm concerned," he explains.

"No, really, I'm fine but I appreciate your concern," as she veils the ache. Her heart knows for now she must be content with Bill's friendship while she dates others guys at school. As he puts his helmet on again, one of the South cheerleaders bumps into him after doing a back flip and falls down. Sarah gasps! Silently, she knows, "Oh no! That's *me* down there. I may just *have* lost him."

Helping the cheerleader to her feet, Bill notices she is a girl in three of his classes. He has never spoken with her but has noticed her in class. Suddenly as Mr. Tibbs words come to him, his heart opens his eyes and he remembers her name is Maddie Benn. Tall with blond hair, statuesque, and extremely gorgeous, she is the girl version of Bill. Every guy wants to date the beautiful cheerleader, not just Maddie Benn. Truly seeing him for the first time, she gushes, "I'm so sorry. It's my fault completely. I'm so clumsy and should have watched where I was going. I hope you can find it in your heart to forgive me." In her mind, Maddie knew exactly where to go and took one extra flip to reach him. Seeing him at the fountain and knowing if she hurried, she could arrive with perfect timing like a bolt from Zeus. It is an excellent way to meet him without raising suspicion.

Being Lancelot in a football uniform, Bill reacts graciously, "Are you ok? Please accept my apology. I should have paid more attention where I walked. It's entirely my fault. Are you *sure* you're ok?"

As their eyes meet and their hearts leap, their smiles show what they found. She answers, "Thank you so much Bill. I appreciate your concern for my welfare."

Her words lift his feet off the ground as the *Wizard* flies to the sideline. Turning back to Maddie, he says, "I'm happy you're ok and I'll see you in class." Exchanging heartfelt smiles again, he returns out to warm up. The drama unfolding before Sarah's eyes devastates her. Her heart sinks as she watches another steal Bill right in front of her.

As the game begins, Warren wins the coin toss and South kicks off. The Dragon's Teeth work their very best magic holding Warren to a three and out. As the South offense comes out, Bill and Maddie share long looks. Bill contemplates, "How did I miss seeing her in my classes? The Lord really blessed me when she crashed into me." Suddenly, making a bold move, he points to her and says, "Maddie, the first play is for you." She grins with embarrassment and nods excitedly at him. In the huddle, the *Maestro* orchestrates the play, "Guys, we're going deep on the first play. Let's see if we can catch them off-guard. Joey, I want you to run just as fast and deep as you can. The ball will be there."

Understanding the real implication of the play, Joey nods with a smile and jokes, "I'll be looking for it and oh by the way, nice catch at the water fountain."

Grinning red-faced, Bill says, "Thanks, now let's get that score." Starting from South's 20-yard line, Bill takes the snap and drops back. The *Wizard* begins weaving his spell while Warren tries hard to sack him. However, his offensive line turns to steel and follows their t-shirts, "*Protect the Man.*" Unleashing the ball deep, it travels 60 yards in the air in a perfect spiral where Joey snags it in full stride at the Warren 20-yard line sprinting in for a touchdown. The offense explodes with cheers and hustles off the field, one throw, and one touchdown. The *Maestro* jogs off the field after his performance for Maddie. Finding and pointing to her with a huge smile, Maddie melts with Bill's overture toward her while the other cheerleaders turn green with envy. At halftime, South leads 14-0. As the team hustles for the locker room, Bill runs by Maddie and jokes, "Don't you dare go anywhere. I'll be back."

Fawning back with a come-hither look, she says, "Don't *worry*, I'm *not* going anywhere that you're not there."

Hiding the hurt in her heart, Sarah watches Bill's actions with her from earlier games on display before everyone. However, another has replaced her as leading lady on his stage. Not believing what she has seen and heard, she tries to hold her emotions in check desperately. Turning to her date, she says, "Excuse me. I'll be back in a few minutes." Rushing to the restroom, she closes the stall door and cries softly. Her mind races, "I can't believe my eyes. Bill falls over another girl and suddenly performs for her the way he used to perform for me. Well, I'm not going away without a fight." Composing herself in time to catch Bill in private before he swaggers back to the field, she probes quickly and deeply, "Bill, I thought you cared deeply for me but you're performing for Maddie the way you did for me alone. Am I no longer the girl you want?"

Her words catch Bill off-guard and he replies, "Sarah, I *do* care deeply for you and I *do* want to be with you. But, you wanted to date other guys. I want to *allow* you the freedom you desire. I'm not trying to make you *jealous*. I *want* you to be happy. I thought you would want me to see other girls too. Are you *ok*?" While waiting for her answer, he notices people beginning to look toward him anxiously and he apologizes to her, "I'm *so sorry* Sarah but I have to get back to the game."

She says, "Ok, I guess I'll see you then. Call me sometime, please." The empty feeling in her heart deepens as she watches him rush to "his stage" and swagger out. Her heart urges, "Ok, game on then. Be his friend for now. It'll be tough watching him with Maddie. Your opening will come. You'll watch and wait for it while you go out with other guys. Enjoy yourself though, ok?"

As Sarah reaches her seat, her date sees her red eyes and asks anxiously, "Sarah, are you ok, really? With the pained look on your face earlier, I'm very concerned."

Hiding her feelings in her hear, she answers politely, "I got some grill smoke in my eyes. I'll be ok in a few minutes. Do you mind if I hold onto your arm? I'm a little chilly."

Meanwhile, Maddie finds Bill in mid-swagger back to "his

stage." Directing her smile at its target, she encourages, "Bill, that was a great performance in the first half. Go give 'em an even better one in the second half." Her body language speaks volumes to his heart. Warren feels the brunt of the *Maestro's* performance. The game ends in another win over a quality team, South 35 Warren 10.

The Dirty Boys and FGS see a completely different performance as Sarah and Bill engage in a two-stage play before their eyes. Paying for a different ticket totally, the crowd could not see the drama the friends saw. The group resolves to support their friends in any way possible short of breaking up themselves. Seeing another great game for South, the crowd watches Bill produce superior stats again. The media remains true to its natural curiosity aroused by Bill and Maddie tonight. Providing another circus of probing questions in the locker room, thankfully, they only ask a couple of the questions involving her. Bill answers with aplomb, "I bumped into her accidentally. I tried to do the chivalrous thing by checking on her during the game and wanted to make sure I didn't hurt her." His answer impresses and satisfies the usually probing media. The press asks their normal remaining questions about Bill and the team's performance, receiving the customary answers from everyone. South moves up to number three in the polls while their goal is to reach and maintain number one.

On Monday morning, Maddie and Bill share their first period class. While he doesn't sit close to her, class hasn't started yet nor has Bill. Waiting for the bell and the teacher, the two of them share longing looks at each other. The length of their gaze raises the curiosity in their classmates who watch with couched snickers of anticipation. Bill reasons, "I *have* to sit next to her. I had so much fun with her at the game and I want to spend as much time close to her as I can. I have to take a shot now."

Walking to John Bertolini in the assigned seat next to her, he whispers, "Do you mind if I trade seats with you. I'd like to sit next to Maddie. We bumped into each other at the game and made friends quickly. It'll make the class more fun if I can sit next to my new friend." Everyone in school knows Bill is a true friend to all. Therefore, John has no misgivings about exchanging seats and agrees with him with a big smile.

Besides, he thinks, "Oh, I *have* to do this. This should make class *imminently* more entertaining." Bill takes the seat next to Maddie as everyone in the room snickers and then breaks in to a quiet clapping. By the time the teacher, Mrs. Case, walks in for roll call, the class decorum restores.

Before the teacher calls roll, Bill walks up to her desk and requests, "Mrs. Case, I traded seats with John Bertolini. I hope you don't mind, do you?"

Before she responds, she glances toward Maddie and notices a big smile on her face begging, "Please let him sit here." Looking back at Bill's face for confirmation, the teacher smiles and replies, "I don't mind you sitting there as long as the arrangement *doesn't* disrupt the class. Remember, you're here to learn Mr. Denton." Everyone grins and then snickers at the situation while the teacher reasons, "Those smiles show there's something special between them. It's funny that the whole class sees it already. I wonder what changed suddenly with those two."

Bill whispers to Maddie, "I hope you recovered fully from me knocking you down." She replies, "I'm fine but it was my fault clearly." Suddenly, she reviews a mental picture, "And well executed if I must say so myself." Their faces erupt with big smiles.

After Mrs. Case imparts the day's lesson to the class, the students busy themselves with their assignment. Bill's normal lesson focus is intermittent today as he takes time to speak with Maddie while they work. He inquires intently, "Did you have a fun weekend?"

Considering his question in her mind, "He's really *interested* in me," she replies, "It was ok but I didn't do much. Simply, I stayed at home and helped my parents." After some problem solving, they continue their discussion.

Growing a bit bolder, he probes further, "I hope you don't mind my question but I'm truly interested. Did you go out with anybody this weekend?"

Hearing the deep intent in his words, she decides to have some fun with him and answers, "I went out to the backyard with my parents. Why do you ask?"

He whispers strongly, "*Very funny.* Really, it's so hard to believe as beautiful and bright as you are."

Maddie smiles and whispers back, "It *is* true. I *don't* date much." After few more problems, they return to their discussion.

Confused yet very curious, he asks, "Why not? Do you choose not to date?"

Slightly embarrassed, she states, "I enjoy dating but you'll think my reasoning is silly for not dating much."

Sensing her concern, he promises, "I won't think your reason is silly or strange. Please tell me."

Class work calls them to their assigned tasks again. Soon, she says, "Ok here goes. It's because I don't know if the guy wants to date Maddie, the cheerleader, or Maddie Benn."

Her response amazes Bill and sparks in his mind, "She's just like me." Smiling with empathy, he says, "Unbelievable, I understand completely."

Lightly probing his feelings, she asks, "Who do you go out with?"

Bill says frankly, "Well technically, I don't go out with anyone. I did hang out with one person though."

Probing deeper, she says, "Who is she and why don't you hang out anymore?" The ringing bell to dismiss class saves Bill to focus his answer.

As they walk out, he says, "Maddie, I think we need to talk. I'll see you 4th period. Let's talk at lunch."

His statement fills her with intrigue and she reflects, "I can't wait for 4th period. He's such a nice guy and never asked me one question about being a cheerleader. That's impressive."

Time drags on forever since they spoke in their first period class but finally, 4th period arrives. Lunch, friendship, and warm conversation await them. Scouring the room for a special table in the midst of the lunchtime crowd, the two locate a table and sit down where they can talk without being disturbed. Maddie probes further, "I hope you don't mind my questions but who is the girl you hung out with and why don't you hang out with her anymore?"

Having time to formulate the remaining words from their 1st period discussion, Bill begins speaking where he left off, "I have the same concerns that you have. *Most* girls want to go out with the quarterback. I have to be careful with whom I share my heart and emotions. I want to go out with someone who wants to date *me* and not necessarily, the quarterback. To answer your questions, the girl is Sarah Ormond. She's a very good friend of mine and we did a lot of things together."

She interrupts, "You said did?"

"Well… yes. She wants to date other guys and since we're very good friends, I didn't want to stand in her way. I *want* my friends to be happy," he continues.

Melted with his kindness and giving, Maddie responds, "Ok *then*, what do you think about *me*? Am *I* good enough to be your friend and hang out with you or am I just fawning over the quarterback?"

Caught off-guard a bit by her direct approach, he responds, "I think you can be a good friend. You seem to be speaking with *me* and not the quarterback. *I'd* like time to get to know you better since it *does* take time to build a friendship you know."

She inquires further, "I have plenty of time for you, but how can you be so *sure* about me?"

He replies quickly, "When I helped you up and you apologized, your *sincerity* spoke to my heart. It was like you bumped into a regular guy and you were truly sorry."

She responds with equal quickness, "For me, it started at the game, your apology and concern said you really cared about *me* and not the cheerleader. However, when we spoke in class, your sincere words said my feelings and ideas are special to you. You spoke with *me,* not some icon on a pedestal. You're very interested in what I say, do, and think. I'm a *real* person to you."

Lunch passes much too quickly for them to learn much about each other. On the way back to the room, he speaks with the person sitting near her and requests that they switch seats with him. Returning to his and Maddie's fourth period room, Bill pulls the same switch with another student as he did in first period. Their teacher informs them of a planned test on Thursday. Looking suddenly in each other's eyes and generating the same thought simultaneously, they ask in unison, "Do you want to study for the test together?"

Laughing quietly at the situation, Bill agrees, "Why don't I come to your house Wednesday after practice to study with you."

Maddie answers, "I'll look forward to seeing you then." Anticipating Wednesday, she reflects quickly, "He's probably the smartest guy in school. Besides, he wants time to build a friendship and I can't think of a better way to build it than helping *me* get ready for the test." Wanting to be close to her all day, he performs the same seating switch again in 6th period as each of his teachers has the same mindset about Bill. With his reputation as a good person and a model student throughout school preceding him, every teacher finds him to be an attentive, respectful leader in class. Leaders often receive some leeway and special treatment yet he accepts that graciously.

After practice, his favorite teammate and friend, Joey takes Bill home as usual. Before he gets out of the car, Bill says, "Can you get a date for Friday after the game? I'm going to have a date and I can't drive yet."

Joey practically explodes with excitement, "Wow, I'm glad you *did* it and got a date. I *knew* you'd listen to me and finally *ask* Sarah to go out with you. She's been waiting for you to ask her on a date for…"

With mixed emotions, Bill interrupts, "It's not Sarah, Joey."

Shocked, Joey retorts, "Are you *nuts*? Why in the world *not*?"

Verbally rationalizing, Bill replies, "Sarah is my best friend and said she wanted to go out with other guys. I didn't want to stand in her way and said it was ok."

Dumbfounded, Joey exclaims, "I've *never* seen such a smart quarterback be so *dumb* when it comes to her. Don't you *realize* she wants *more* of you not less? My money says she's trying to get you to *tell* her how much *you* need her. I can't *believe* you blew this and let her get away." The look on Bill's face speaks volumes to Joey. Replying to Bill's look, he says, "Ok man, you know both of you are my friends. I'll support you both in whatever way you need me too. I'm just sorry for you both because you care so much for each other. I'm going out on a limb here but your date wouldn't happen to be Maddie Benn would she? I saw her bump into you at the game and noticed your reactions afterward, like a lost puppy."

Reacting quickly, Bill says, "I didn't know *anyone* saw that but the two of us. Do the two of us a favor, please? Don't to say anything to anybody because I don't want us to become gossip fodder for the school."

Attempting to inject some reality, Joey answers, "Well, *I* won't say anything but the *entire* stadium saw you both. Didn't the questions from the press tell you *anything*? Even the *press* noticed. You have a *lot* to learn my friend. *Everyone* knows how close you and Sarah are, except you. This is going to shock some people but then again, Sarah *was* in the stands with another guy. Do you need anything else this week?"

Bill says sheepishly, "Well, I could use a ride to Maddie's on Wednesday. We're studying for a test on Thursday."

Chuckling, Joey says, "Of course, I can take you there and mum's the word," while thinking, "Wow, history repeats itself." Bill saunters for his house as Joey drives home.

Deciding to call Mr. Tibbs, Bill informs him about this change since their last conversation. "Hello Mr. Tibbs. This is Bill Denton," he says.

"Hi Bill. This must be important. What's up," Mr. Tibbs says.

Seeking fatherly wisdom, Bill begins, "Well, Mr. Tibbs. I tried to follow your recommendations regarding Sarah. Do you know Maddie Benn? Well, she was doing several back flips and bumped into me before the last game. Of course, she fell down and I had to help her up. I checked on her during the game to see if she was ok. I decided to go out on a limb and dedicated the first play to her. I have several classes with her including lunch. We talked about our lives and decided to study together Wednesday. I'm going to ask her out for Friday."

"Ok Bill, let me get this straight. At the game, she bumped into you as you had bumped into Sarah. You were your courteous self and helped her up. You have hit it off fairly well and you want to see more of each other, correct," Mr. Tibbs inquires.

"That's right," Bill responds.

Mr. Tibbs probes further, "My first question is have you spoken with Sarah? What's happening with the two of you?"

Jumping on the question, Bill replies, "Well, Joey thinks I'm nuts. He sees a great love between Sarah and me that I guess I'm too blind to see. Maybe I *have* put Sarah on a high pedestal. She went out on her date and I didn't want to bother her as you advised. It hurt me deeply to see her with another guy but I'm trying to give her the freedom to be herself but also be her friend. I wanted our relationship to heal but it's very difficult to let her explore other relationships.

She saw me during half time and asked me if I still wanted her for my girl. I didn't expect her to say that. I had to get back to the game before we finished our discussion but she *did* ask me to call her. I thought that she wanted to go out with other guys and I'm terribly confused. I still haven't told Sarah how I feel completely. I assumed she wanted me to go out with other girls. Why do I feel I made a *big* mistake?"

"Bill, life is complicated and so are relationships. I believe your mistake is *not* telling Sarah how you *really feel* completely. She needs that verbal reinforcement too. You're equals in this relationship no better no worse. You *must* remember that. When she asked if you still *wanted* her, she was reaching out to you. Maddie is now your friend too and you must balance the feelings of both. Can you *do* that? Do you want to go out with both Sarah and Maddie? You must eventually make a choice between them and it won't be easy. You must be a friend to both and probably go out with both to know the right choice. Remember, a cowboy can't ride two horses at the same time with one butt," Mr. Tibbs explains, providing his best counsel regarding relationships and choices.

"Thank you Mr. Tibbs, you continue to be like a father to me. I apologize for putting you in this difficult situation. I'm going to see how the relationship with Maddie progresses but I won't lose Sarah from my life either. I'll keep you apprised of important changes in my life. Good night Mr. Tibbs," Bill finishes.

"What a great kid? This is a tough road for him but a true learning situation," thinks Mr. Tibbs.

During school, Sarah speaks with Bill cordially whenever they pass each other in the halls between classes. For her though, the times when they see each other aren't frequent enough. Still, she struggles for the smile from her heart. Her heart aches less each time they meet and her legs strengthen more. The true friendship feeling returns slowly as it is hard to replace the love. She decides to go out with other guys but not date any of them seriously. Her heart harbors hope that Bill will come to his senses one day and realize they love each other. She reasons, "Maddie's not a bad person but I'm determined to win Bill back. This is *my* life and I *want* Bill in it if only as a friend for now. I'll let my love and kindness bring him back to me. I'll have to wait until later for him to be *more* than a friend." In the interim, her mind sets her course to become the best student she can be. Beginning to immerse herself in studies and school activities, she reasons further, "If he can be the best *quarterback* around, then I can be a *great* student." Setting sail toward her goals, she finds power in her determination and drive.

Study Time

C ontinuing to speak each day, Bill and Maddie wait anxiously for Wednesday night to drag itself to the present. Performing his duty as a friend, Joey delivers Bill to Maddie's house. As Bill walks up to her door, Joey calls to him, "Have fun, buddy. Don't forget to *call* me when you're ready to go home. Of course, *I* wouldn't *ever* call."

Bill glances back with a huge smile. "Maddie and I are studying physics together. We're going to have *so* much fun," he thinks as he strolls up to her door and knocks. Unlike his first visit to Sarah's house, his nerves create no imaginary obstacles to blind-side him this time and prevent him from reaching his goal.

Maddie answers his knock with an excited smile on her face and invites, "Please come in. I want you to meet my parents." Reaching out, she takes his hand and leads him through the living room. They walk past the study to the family room. "Mom and dad, this is Bill Denton. We have several classes together and he agreed to help me study for our Physics test tomorrow. Bill, these are my parents, Joe and Lori Benn," she explains.

"How do you do, Mr. and Mrs. Benn," Bill says respectfully. When Maddie makes no mention of him as quarterback, his heart warms to her immediately and he thinks, "Thank you Maddie for being so kind to me."

However, Maddie's dad recognizes him from a couple of the games and inquires, "You're the team's quarterback, aren't you son? I really enjoy watching you play. You keep up the good work."

Before Bill can respond, Maddie replies, "Dad, he is so much more than just a quarterback. Although he plays that position, he's a wonderful person and more interesting than just another athlete."

Not wanting to be rude, Bill answers, "Thank you sir for the compliments. I'll strive to do my best and bring that out in our team too." Her dad sees the look on Maddie's face and decides not to interrupt their study time with additional football talk. Inwardly, her quick response stuns Bill and leaves him wondering how she knows that about him.

Deciding to be bold, Bill asks, "How did you know that off the field I don't like to talk about football?"

Giggling, she says, "After seeing us talking at lunch on Monday, your interrogator, Andy Worley, cornered me after lunch Tuesday. By the way, is he some jealous closet stalker, if you don't mind my asking?"

Laughing at the situation, Bill replies, "Andy is my wingman, always has been since we were kids. He feels it's his job to make sure people want to be with me and not the quarterback. As you so aptly put it, *I'm* the quarterback but it doesn't define my personality or who I am."

"So, he gave you his approval to come over, *did he*," Maddie quizzes somewhat perturbed.

Answering quickly but with respect, Bill says, "No. I apologize if he was rude to you. He *means* well. I didn't even know he talked to you. If he believed you wanted to be with the quarterback not me, he would have told me not to come over. That's what he does."

Maddie states, "He's kind of…"

Knowing her next words instinctively, Bill interrupts, "a *big* jerk."

Maddie laughs, "Yeah that's it."

Providing assurance, Bill says, "As I said on Monday, I like you and want to get to know you better. I hope you still feel the same way. Surprisingly, Andy will be as protective of you as he is of me. A friend of mine and not the quarterback is a friend of his. I know that sounds extremely arrogant but if anyone can understand it, I know you can."

Intrigued, Maddie says, "I *do* understand and would like to get to know you better. I have a surprise for you. I planned for us to have dinner together before we study for the test. My parents ate dinner earlier."

Thrilled with her dinner offer, Bill says, "I'd enjoy that very much," as he reflects on her invitation, "Wow, I *sure* didn't expect that but I do enjoy spending time with her." When dinner ends, he starts to clean up the dishes as he used to do after meals at Sarah's house.

Maddie's mom says, "You kids need to study. I'll finish the dishes."

Courteously, Bill insists, "Please allow us to do the dishes, Mrs. Benn. After all, you prepared the dinner and the least we can do is the dishes to thank you." While enjoying each other's company, they finishing cleaning the table and doing the dishes. As they dry and put away the dishes, Bill ponders, "This isn't the same as with Sarah but it may never be with anybody. Still, I need to enjoy being with my new friend. She's *so* beautiful and very smart too. I can tell by the way she speaks and how she acts around me."

Maddie thinks dreamily, "What a great guy and those awesome looks too. I must be dreaming but don't wake me." After a short time of study, Bill's work convinces Maddie that he's the smartest kid in school. She cannot believe his level of understanding but more important, how he helps *her* understand it all. The physics study progresses quite well but time moves much too quickly and it is time for Bill to leave.

After he leaves, her mom has strong praise for him, "Maddie, Bill is *such* a polite young man. He's as good looking as you said he is."

Expounding on Bill's character, Maddie adds, *"He's* a nice guy and such a gentleman. I've never met *anyone* like him."

Picking up Bill at Maddie's house, Joey jokes, "You must not have had a very good time. It's still daylight. Oh, my mistake, that's just the light from your huge smile."

"Yes, I had a great time and she even had dinner for me. *Blew me away*! She's very bright and I enjoyed helping her repair a couple of tiny flaws in her thinking," Bill practically sings. He continues to relate his evening at Maddie's house with Joey graciously.

When test time rolls around the next day and despite a minor case of nervousness, Maddie gets an A. She is certain her grade is a direct result of Bill helping her study. Of course, Bill gets an A as well. After class, he walks with her and quietly inquires, "Would you like to go out with me after the game Friday?"

The excitement of his question overcomes Maddie's inhibitions of where she is and she screams, *"Yes,"* in the hallway. Everyone within earshot stares at her instantly and wonders what caused the commotion. The incongruity of the moment causes Bill and Maddie to burst out laughing. Before the day is over, every person in school including Sarah knows they are going on a date after the game.

At practice, Joey strolls up to Bill with a big smile on his face and exclaims, "You, *sir*, are my *hero*."

Confused with his words, Bill responds, "Huh? What in the *world* are you *talking* about?"

Praising his friend, Joey continues, "Any guy that gets a date with Maddie Benn is *every* guy's hero," and then he begins to dress for practice.

Embarrassed by Joey's explanation, Bill replies with a grin, "Ok, that's enough. She's a very nice girl and I'm fortunate enough to have a date with her." The thought of his impending date excites Bill but it *is* time to go to work. His stage calls.

A New Friday

riday arrives much later than Bill and Maddie cared to experience and it's pep session time. The team's success draws much of the community to the school and the pep sessions are social events demanding the people's attendance. If you don't want to go to the pep session, you're branded a heretic for your lack of belief. After all, it *is* the Friday night high school mass. Sessions are a place to see, to be seen, and to fire up the team, the school, and the public for the game. The student body and early people from the community enter the lower gym. Taking their seats as a group, the student body sits in the lower section while the early arriving public sits in a section across from them. The rest of the community sits in the upper section of South's gym. Holding over 7,000 people, it is full for every pep session. After an appropriate time of anticipation, the crowd demands the team's entrance with their cheering. Suddenly, the team makes its entrance with Bill trailing as usual. Swaggering into the gym, he trails the team by an appropriate number of steps to the roar of the crowd. When the team sits down, Coach Mulinaro steps to the mic and jokes, "Hey, you need to save some of that roar for the game. I want to thank everyone for coming. I'm going to turn this over to a few of the kids who will let you know how they feel." Performing some cheers, the cheerleaders display their gymnastic prowess followed by designated players speaking to the attendees. While the cheerleaders perform more cheers, the band plays the school song to the strains of the crowd. Since Bill is the chosen Captain, he gives the final remarks.

During the pep session, Bill and Maddie make eye contact multiple times generating huge smiles with each meeting. Continuing to build and strengthen their friendship daily in school, they enjoy this time and do not mind putting themselves on display. "After all, it is *our* stage," Maddie thinks.

As Bill comes up to speak, a small group of students start chanting, "Maddie, Maddie, Maddie." As the chant grows to a crescendo, Bill points at her and gives her his triumphant fist pump. The crowd becomes frenetic, thrilling Maddie immensely. The football team adds its approval with smiles, claps, and a standing ovation. Sarah and the FGS girls attended as well because it is *the place* to be. With the chanting, her friends look to gauge Sarah's reaction but she hides her true feelings by cheering the same as the rest of the crowd. While puzzled by her reaction, the girls say nothing to her. As Bill reaches the podium, the crowd falls silent immediately. Even though he is only a sophomore, his presence when rising to speak, entering a room, or taking *his* stage on the football field demands respect.

Responding to the anticipation, Bill says, "I'll make this short and to the point. It's a lack of faith in oneself that makes some people afraid of meeting challenges. God has given us the faith to believe and the talent to perform. We have faith in each other and ourselves. We will meet the challenge tonight. See you at the game."

As he gives the crowd his fist pump, they respond with a returned fist pump to him and start cheering loudly while the team hustles out of the gym. Once the team leaves the stage, school dismisses. As the team walks out, Bill lingers until he is the last of the team in the gym. Walking by the cheerleaders, he touches his heart and points to Maddie. Her face breaks into a huge smile and she invites, "My heart will wait for you here in the gym, Bill."

He nods, smiles, and says, "I hope so. My heart anticipates seeing you too. I'll be back to you quickly. I promise." Sarah observes the vignette while hidden from view by the crowd and the ache no longer lingers in her heart when Bill appears. She is happy Bill found someone with whom he feels comfortable dating but she hopes someday it will be her. From what she knows of Maddie, she thinks she is a good person. However, she cannot dwell on what might be as she has a date tonight for which to prepare herself and she leaves quickly with the rest of the crowd.

Returning to the gym quickly as promised, Bill finds it is empty except for Maddie and him. In the silent dimness that envelopes them, he reaches for her hand. Reaching back in anticipation of his touch, her hand meets his and they walk in shared bliss toward the exit. Reasoning in his heart, "Her hand feels so natural in mine. I want to wrap my hand around hers always." Her touch relaxes him instantly and his happiness seems boundless. As they near the exit door, he stops in front of her and turns face to face with her. Reaching out, he takes her other hand, holding both of them in his. Gazing into her eyes longingly, suddenly, he pulls her close and kisses her passionately on the lips. He feels her melt limply into his embrace and with his kiss feeling as if it will never end, she smiles from her heart at him. However, despite her smile, the kiss is over to quickly for Maddie leaving her heart desiring more. Laying her head on his chest, she hugs him tightly.

While hugging him, she contemplates, "He's a *god* under these clothes. I've never held anyone so muscular. Granted I have held almost no guys but he *is* amazing. Everyone sees Bill's strength in the games but he never wears clothes revealing his physique." Relaxing their embrace with each other, they begin to walk toward the car.

Continuing to hold hands while walking, the parking lot looms where Joey waits. When they reach Joey's car, he kisses her lightly on the lips again, thrilling her.

Anticipating their date after the game overwhelms her as he reminds, "Maddie, don't forget me between now and the game."

She replies quickly, "Not very likely considering our last few minutes."

He continues, "I'll see you at the game. Also, I have something for you after the game that I hope you like."

Excited by his surprise, she asks anxiously, "Could I have it now? I can't wait 'til the game is over to receive my surprise."

Replying in a teasing fashion, Bill says, "Sorry, you'll just have to wait until after the game."

As they drive off, Joey probes with curiosity, "What could you possibly have for Maddie? You have already hugged and kissed her and I *know* you. You don't have a lascivious thought in your mind." Reaching into his gym bag, Bill pulls out the surprise. While shaking his head, Joey inquires, "How in the world do you think of this stuff?" Stopping to get some fast food first, they hang out for a couple hours at Joey's house then head for the stadium to get dressed for the game. Bill likes to be the first player at the stadium on game day. On each game day, he greets his teammates individually as they walk into the dressing room. With each teammate, his greeting is different. For some, it's "hey man" or a fist bump. However, he saves a sarcastic remark to the ones who get there last. No one is immune to his humor and remarks.

After everyone arrives, Bill probes the last guys, "Do *I* need to get you guys a watch so you can get here on time?" The guys reply, "Hey, we're on time." Bill retorts, "Let me explain this once. There are two times to arrive, the regular time and *my* time. You need to learn *my* time." After all, this is *his* team and his words break up the room with laughter. Taking the good-natured ribbing, everyone expects this part of his normal pre-game routine. It's all in fun and Bill takes shots from his teammates as well as he gives them. His exhortations prod the team to do their best each game and they know it. Besides, he doesn't ask anything of them that he doesn't demand of himself. His teammates appreciate Bill and his leadership. They follow him wherever he leads, which so far has been wins over quality opponents. Arriving at his locker, Bill begins to get ready for the game. Putting on his pants, shoes, and a sweatshirt, he proceeds to get in some pre-game running to prepare his legs for game day. It's two hours before game time and one hour before official team warm ups. When he returns from his running, everyone knows it *is* serious pre-game time now.

Sarah is at home preparing for her date and is feeling happy. While she and Bill are still best friends, they go on dates with someone different. Putting on the heart-shaped ruby necklace Bill gave her, she quietly prays for God to keep them both safe tonight. Wearing the necklace keeps Bill close to her heart and in her mind. Her mom inquires lovingly, "Are you going to pre-game warm ups this week to watch Bill?"

Mulling over memories of him, she answers, "No mom. He has a date for tonight and so do I. We're still great friends though. I'm fine going at a regular time with my date." "But I still love him," she muses.

Empathizing, her mom poses, "You really miss the fun you have together and the attentiveness he shows you don't you, dear?"

Filling with warm thoughts, Sarah replies, "Yes I do, but our strong friendship still survives. Maybe Bill didn't ask me out because he didn't want to change our deep friendship. However, I think it will grow further yet."

Her mom replies, "I'm ok with that answer and can see it's something he would consider too. Enjoy your date and don't be out late."

Returning a beautiful smile to her mom Sarah promises, "I'll return on time." "This time in my life is so much fun," she muses to herself, "*I'm* happy that Bill is happy. However, I hope someday he'll be mine again and tell me how much I mean to him. Bill is happy now with his date and I have a date too. How could it get any better than this?"

Whipped to frenzy by the pep session and locker room speeches, the team prepares for its pre-game warm ups. As the Wizard swaggers out driving his team before him, he gazes at the cheerleaders. Pointing to Maddie, he smiles and adds a fist pump as usual. Looking back, Maddie turns towards him displaying a big red "10" in face paint on her cheek. Her spell reaches a hidden place deep in his heart. "That's my number and always has been. Wow, she did *that* for *me* and we have only known each other a week. How much better can this get," he ponders, swelling with pride. Swaggering for his usual pre-game water, he arrives at the water fountain and jokes, "Hey Maddie, don't bump into anyone while I'm on the field."

Laughing with him, she declares teasingly, "And why shouldn't I? It got me a date with the guy I wanted to go out with didn't it?"

Firing back quickly, he issues a mock order, "Just don't bump into anyone else during the game because you're my date tonight." Still under Maddie's spell, he enjoys the banter of the moment. As the spell disappears, his focus returns to the game and he's ready to step onto *his* stage again. It is *show time* and the audience awaits the *Maestro's* performance.

Eli

Tonight is a rematch of last year's Luers game. This time
Luers is ranked seventh in the state and South is still ranked
third. With a rock solid defense again and allowing only
10 points a game, it compliments their offense averaging 28 points
a game. South warms up on one end of the field while Luers warms
up on the other. While remembering fully the beating he received in
last year's game, Bill knows his line is another year older and better
than last year. As he throws practice tosses to his receivers, he notices
number 38 from Luers walking towards him. It's the guy who drilled
him in his ribs last year, Eli Kevlin. He is the kind of player that
can take over a game and has a goal of becoming a first team high
school All-American too. When Eli reaches Bill on the field, they
both extend their hands to each other, shaking hands as honored
opponents and warriors. Eli asks with a smile, "Hey Bill, you doin'
ok? I hope you've recovered fully from last year's game."

Pleased to see his old friend again, Bill replies, "100% You guys
have started the season pretty well. You look as tough as last year
and it should be another good game."

Agreeing with Bill, Eli bumps fists with him and then jokes,
"You know I'll be coming after you again."

Laughing, Bill replies, "I wouldn't expect anything less from a true warrior. Be safe." The conversation ends with each warrior returning to his warm-ups.

South kicks off to Luers and its vaunted Dragon's Teeth defense holds Luers to a three and out possession. The offense steps onto the *Maestro's* stage to roars from *his* audience. Receiving the play from the bench and glancing at Maddie, he says, "Your play's coming up." In the huddle, he calls "21 flash deep." Joey steels his nerve to fly down the field, as the play is a long pass to him. South worked their short then long passing game very well last year. With the coaches positive Luers remembers what happened also, the staff decides to mix it up and reverse the sequence in a huge chess match. Taking the snap, the *Wizard* drops back and sets up on his own 40-yard line. Checking his left, he sees Eli coming like a runaway diesel. As Eli roars toward him, the *Wizard* becomes smoke and disappears into the pocket leaving the warrior groping at air. The *Wizard* throws 60 yards to Joey in the end zone for a touchdown. Turning back to Eli, Bill reaches down to help him up.

As Eli extends his arm upward, he shakes his head and says with a smile, "We're off and running again, the battle is on, man." Bill returns a smile as they tap each other on the helmets and move toward their sidelines. Pointing to Maddie, Bill gives his fist pump to her as the student body chants her name thrice, leaving the rest of the spectators wondering at the meaning. Maddie directs a huge smile toward Bill while the chant turns her face scarlet. On Luers' first play of the next series, the defense covers them perfectly, coming in fast and hot like a top-fuel dragster. The Luers quarterback throws the ball out of bounds to avoid a sack. With the ball landing near the South cheerleaders and rolling over by Maddie, Bill rushes to her side quickly to get the ball, seizing an opportunity he may never have again. As Maddie hands him the ball, the *Maestro* leans close and kisses her on the cheek.

Exuberant with the moment, he whispers, "I'm really looking forward to our date tonight." After all, Bill reasons in his mind, "Would a rock star have performed any better for a group of screaming fans?" Viewing this vignette with amazement, the crowd cheers loudly as the students again chant Maddie's name three times.

While Bill hustles for the safety of his bench, the other cheerleaders rush to her, fawn over a superstar, and ask, "Do you realize how lucky you are that he kissed you?" She replies pragmatically, "Yes, I'm fully aware of that fact. Do *you* realize that he's a great guy, quarterback or not?"

The gun sounds for the half with the score South 21 Luers 7. As the team thunders for the locker room, Bill smiles at her but has a very serious look on his face, focusing strictly on the game now. Delivering the kiss was out of character for the *Maestro* even on his stage and his conscience makes certain he knows it. He allowed Maddie's spell to overcome his game focus yet he is a competitor and it *is game time*. Understanding his importance with the team, her heart wants this game to end quickly. She contemplates, "If I controlled time, this game would be over now." Bringing a change of clothes to the stadium, she doesn't plan to wear her cheerleader uniform for her date. Hiding her true intentions, she wants him to go out with her not the cheerleader. She calculates, "Besides, I'll look even better for him in those clothes than my uniform."

In the locker room, the coaches review what worked and did not work in the first half. Overall, the team's play pleases them but they want to know the mindset of the players. When the coaches ask them for input, their leader is ready with a response. Speaking up immediately, Bill says, "We have them coach. *We're* going to win this game. We have them doubting themselves and arguing with each other. They're beaten and the only question is by how much." No other teammate utters anything because the *Wizard* has spoken. The coaches hear the words they needed to hear. Putting on his helmet, Bill says, "Let's go take it to 'em." The team erupts in a thunderous roar in the locker room. Under the Wizard's spell, they run out with steely determination in silence. The team has a job to finish and the look on their faces says it all, "Luers, you are *ours*. We own you tonight."

The game ends to Maddie's satisfaction and now it's time to be herself. The final score is South 56 Luers 7 with South scoring 35 second-half points as Bill conducts the team like Stokowski tonight. While she rushes off to change her clothes, Bill and the team meet with the press corps. Mentally, Joey reflects, "It was a great show. We hit on all cylinders tonight." The game adds an exclamation on Bill's very short career, hinting of much more to come. In the locker room, Joey chuckles to himself, "This should be good." When Bill comes in the locker room, Joey looks at him and says, "Frank, you've got an *encore* to do so hurry up. What *took* you so long? You stop to kiss Maddie *again*?"

Chuckling, Bill says, "Nope. Some elementary kids from a little league football team wanted autographs."

Confused, Joey inquires, "You're a *sophomore* in high school and kids want your autograph. You should have told them no. Why didn't you?" The look on Bill's face speaks loudly to Joey. Before Bill can respond, Joey blurts, "Never mind, I know already. It's all part of being a role model and doing the right thing."

Bill exclaims, "Exactly! Those kids dream of being an elite football player in a few years. I want to help them realize that dream. By the way, we need to get out of here as soon as we can."

Again, the press corps readies its customary questions yet expects different answers. The team marvels weekly at how Bill handles all of the press commotion and determined probing with patience and aplomb. Knowing the probing will worsen as the team gets older and better but it will be much worse for him. Finally, Bill says to the press, "Can we wrap this up fellas? I have a date with the most beautiful girl on the planet and you can quote me on that." As stunned disbelief appears on the team's faces, his teammates reflect collectively, "In one evening, he kisses a cheerleader in public *during* a game, gives a stunning performance as the *Maestro and Wizard*, and now tells the press graciously he has to leave. He *must* be loosening up and enjoying this time in his life. After all, it only comes around once." Then, a few players yell at the reporters, "*He's Not Kidding Guys.*" The press corps laughs and responds to Bill, "Thanks for your time. Go enjoy yourself." Quickly, one of them inquires, "One last thing, what's the girl's name with whom you're going on a date tonight?" Bill replies, "Maybe another time guys." The team laughs and yells back, "**Maddie Benn!**"

A Special Evening

After Bill and Joey get dressed, they rush out of the locker room to meet their dates, Maddie Benn and McKenna Thompson, who is a cheerleader also. Joey and McKenna begin walking to the car while Bill takes up his "swagger" position behind everyone. Maddie grabs his hand and pulls him beside her as they start for Joey's car. Still trailing the other couple, Maddie gives Bill a "hey there" tug on his arm. Briefly startled, he looks concerned and inquires, "What's up? You haven't changed your mind have you?" Maddie's grin tilts to a smile as she stops and pulls him against her. Wrapping her arms around him, she resumes the passionate kiss she didn't want to end in the gym earlier.

In her deepest thoughts, she contemplates, "That's more like it." While Joey and McKenna speak with each other, they don't notice the passionate embrace behind them. Bill informed Joey earlier that he wanted to give Maddie her surprise but he didn't expect to *receive* one that passionately preempts his. "Would you like your surprise now," Bill inquires, gazing deeply into Maddie's eyes.

Filling with excitement after their kiss, Maddie answers, "Yes very much, please." Pulling her surprise out of his jacket, he hands an envelope to her, part of a set of fine personalized stationery.

Desiring this surprise to be very special for her, the look on her face assures him that he succeeded. Maddie opens the envelope slowly to maintain it as pristinely as she received it. Gazing at the hand-written note inside, she re-runs the movie of how she met him in her mind and reflects, "I feel so special with him. He took the time to write me a note personally on fine stationery and his thought process is amazing. Mom will be *very* impressed." Maddie starts reading the note.

> *Maddie,*
>
> *Thanks so much for helping me study for the Physics test. I'm sure I did so well because of your input. Thank you for going on a date with me tonight. This entire week has been wondrous fun speaking with you. I enjoyed coming to your house, doing the dishes with you, and sitting by you in our classes. I hope tonight is more of the same. I'm looking forward to having a great evening. I hope you are too.*
>
> *Your friend, Bill*

Tilting her head slightly, she shifts her gaze upward from the note and smiles toward him alluringly. She confesses, "This has been a great week for me too. I know tonight *will* be fun and very special." Resuming their stroll to Joey's car, Bill and Maddie hold hands. Considering the special nature of the evening, Bill and Joey decide their usual Friday night pizza or Kristen burgers are not good enough for this evening. Tonight requires food and atmosphere, a place more special. Thinking they are going for pizza, the girls are surprised when the four of them arrive at the TeePee restaurant. It is a modern one-story brown brick and glass building with a large stylized teepee on top. People come from all over Indianapolis to get one of their specialties, a Big Chief Burger or Strawberry pie. Flocking to the famous Midwest restaurant, people come seven days a week because of the food, service, and atmosphere. For more casual dining, there is in-car dining service behind the restaurant as well. Joey parks in a front parking space recently vacated by a family. Surveying the crowd through the restaurant's window, there does not appear to be an open table in view as usual. After all, it *is* Friday night and the game crowd has their food or waits patiently for it. The remaining people wait at the front for others to finish their food.

As they walk in, the host greets, "Good evening. The wait for a table is approximately 45-minutes. Is that ok?"

Discussing the wait length with Joey, Maddie, and McKenna, Bill turns to the host and agrees to that the wait time is satisfactory. As the host writes Bill's name down on the wait list, the manager reviews the list and inquires, "Are you the South quarterback, Bill Denton?"

Puzzled and concerned as to the reason the manager singled him out, Bill replies, "Yes sir, I am. Is something wrong?" While the manager smiles and extends his hand, Bill reaches toward him and shakes the man's hand.

The manager says, "I'm *so* glad to meet you. I really enjoy watching you play when I'm not on duty here. I'm *thrilled* you chose to dine with us tonight. I have our best table especially for you and your friends."

Even in the soft lighting, the other three could see Bill's face turn scarlet as he replies, "Thank you so much sir. I appreciate the kindness you are showing us tonight."

Then the manager surprises them all with his next statement, "Whenever you desire to visit us again, just tell me upon your arrival and I'll have this table for you. My name is Carl. Please follow me." Following the manager, they walk past the ornate wooden booths with black and tan vinyl backs and white tablecloths on their left. On their right, lush tan vinyl barstools swivel before the black and tan food service bar. Adorning the medium tan wall behind the bar were faux cave paintings of deer, warriors, and an Indian village. Continuing back to the romantically lit special dining area with more booths and tables, the manager stops in a corner at a crescent shaped wooden booth with a round table and the plushest seating with a rolled vertically tufted back. The tablecloth is white while the cloth napkins are deep red enveloping the silverware. While large enough for a family of eight, tonight it will seat these two couples comfortably. Suddenly, Carl inquires, "Does this table meet with your approval, Bill?"

Stunned by his kindness, Bill replies graciously, "You are too kind sir. Thank you very much."

Delighted, Carl says, "Please take your seats and your server will be with you shortly."

Bill knows they are getting special treatment because he is Bill Denton, the quarterback, and the manager told them that very fact. However, he knows it is a 45-minute wait for others. He doesn't like to be treated special ahead of others because he plays football well. While never trying to use "the Quarterback" to get anything, he also doesn't want to wait 45 minutes to eat tonight. Wanting to spend his evening with Maddie, he does not want to waste time waiting on their seating. Leaning toward Bill, Joey whispers, "It's good to be you," and laughs.

Embarrassed, Bill starts to apologize to Maddie but before he can say anything, she says, "It's ok, Bill. Sometimes you have to accept events graciously as they occur. You may not want someone to give the gifts to you. However, if the person gives them out of their joy, don't steal their joy by denying them the moment. It's all part of who and what you are." She kisses him on the cheek and continues, "I'm glad you're Bill and that I'm with you tonight."

Enlightened by her comment, he intones, "Maddie, thank you so much. That makes a lot of sense and means so much to me. I'm glad you understand so well. I never considered the other person's feelings or their desire to give and be part of the team's celebration in some manner. I did not realize how selfish I have been with these folks. I have been thinking only of myself. You have taught me a wonderful life lesson and for that, I will be grateful always." Then, leaning over, he kisses her on her cheek.

After sitting and perusing the menu, Bill asks, "Maddie, do you see something that you would like? Steak, seafood, burger whatever, tonight is for you. You can order anything you want."

She leans to his ear and whispers teasingly, "You sir. I want a large order please." Bill's face turns scarlet again. Sitting back up with a big smile, she says, "I think I'll have the Big Chief Burger with fries and a soft drink."

Recovering from her "large order" comment, he says, "That sounds good. I think I'll have the same thing."

After Joey and McKenna make their food decisions as well, their server arrives to take their orders and asks, "Will this be separate checks or one check?"

Taking charge of the evening financially, Bill answers quickly, "Please put it all on one check." As Joey starts to object, Bill smiles and explains, "Look, you haul my butt all over the place. It's the least I can do. This one is mine."

As Joey and McKenna place their orders, Maddie whispers timidly, "Bill, I don't mean to pry but are you rich? High school guys don't usually have money."

Replying simply, he says, "No I have a trust fund."

Puzzled at his response, Maddie says, "I don't understand."

Displaying a wry smile, he kisses her cheek and offers, "It's ok, Maddie. I'll tell you about it later." As the server turns to Maddie, Bill orders courteously for Maddie and himself.

Embarrassed at not doing the same for McKenna, Joey hides behind a chuckle, "Bill, Maddie is old enough to place her order. What's the matter? Don't you think she can order for herself?"

As Bill starts to explain his actions, Maddie interrupts to explain first, "Joey, Bill is just being a true gentleman. By ordering for me, he shows his interest in my welfare and my needs at this very moment. He shows the level of care he has for me. That's what gentlemen do." Surprised by her words and understanding, Bill smiles and gives Maddie a wink and a hug. She likes this part of Bill's character very much and learning about his personality, one step at a time. Tonight revealed to her what a caring person he is. Reflecting on the moment, she leans her head against his, "Most high school guys would not treat me as he does. They are only after one thing but I can be myself around him. I love being cared for and romanced like this."

Their food arrives and the aroma entices their senses. Beginning to indulge their taste buds with their orders, they allow their collective friendship to grow as well. Throughout the evening, McKenna sees the person about whom Maddie raves to her, the loving side of him, and reflects, "This is an impressive night. I understand what Maddie means when she says 'he's a great guy, quarterback or not.'" There is no talk about football or no talk about him. The *Wizard* only needs to make an appearance in tense situations. The *Maestro* only needs to appear when the audience demands a performance. However, this is not a game situation or his stage. Tonight is all about friends, Maddie, Joey, McKenna, and Bill.

All through the dinner, Bill and Maddie laugh and joke with each other. Their engaging looks to each other quietly say to Joey and McKenna to enjoy themselves too. This is a *very* special tonight. Their shared body language, leaning against each other, brief whispers, and chuckles all say there is more to come this evening. After finishing the excellent repast, they sit and converse a bit longer. Finally, Bill inquires, "Maddie, what would *you* like to do? How soon do you need to be home?"

After determined consideration, Maddie utters her thoughts, "What I'd really like to do is have Joey take us back to my house and talk some more. I want to listen to some music and curl up on the couch with you."

Excited by her words, Bill offers, "I'd like to share the time with you too." As the server walks by, Bill asks, "May we have our check, please!"

Shaking his head, Joey thinks to himself, "He *is* the man." McKenna does not believe the words she heard from Maddie. Motioning to her, the two girls excuse themselves to go "freshen up."

When they enter the restroom, McKenna checks to insure they are alone. Then, she glares at Maddie, "*Girl*, have you taken leave of your senses? Do you realize what you just offered to him? It's dinner and..."

Maddie interrupts and replies calmly, "McKenna, it's ok. I know exactly what I said and no, I did not offer *that* to him. I only want to curl up on the couch, speak with him, and have him hold me."

"Of *course*, that's *all* he will do," McKenna exclaims sarcastically!

Maddie replies softly, "Yes McKenna, that's all he *will* do. I know in my heart that *he's* different and won't try to take advantage of me or do anything disrespectful."

Responding to her quiet demeanor, McKenna says, "Well, I hope you're right." Maddie knows she is and they continue talking.

While the girls "powder their noses," a stunned Joey says, "Awesome *man*, you just had Maddie Benn tell you she wants to lie on the couch with you. That sounds like an open invitation if I ever heard one."

Bill explains quietly, "No Joey. It's *not* an open invitation to do more than she asked. She just wants us to hold each other, talk, and get to know each other better. Besides you know me, I'm not going to do anything disrespectful with her." The look in Bill's eyes confirms what Joey knows of Bill's character and that his word is golden. He'd never put pressure on her or put her in a compromising situation. While the girls are still away, they continue discussing how well the evening has progressed to this point.

Back in the restroom, Maddie continues, "Oh, I *am* looking forward to *something*. He's hugged me and I've hugged him back. Snuggling him will be ecstasy for me. If his body looks anything like it feels, it'll be indescribable but that's an entirely different conversation."

"*Maddie*," exclaims McKenna!

Verbalizing her thoughts, Maddie continues, "Ok, I can *dream* can't I? As I said, I believe in his character. He *won't* try anything."

"Please Maddie, tell me you're not going to do anything stupid," McKenna begs then laughs at the distorted look on Maddie's face, "By the way, I want full details Monday morning."

"You'll be the first to know anything," Maddie laughs then adds, "Any idea how I can get his shirt off?"

"Yes but neither of us would like the outcome," McKenna laughs.

Maddie answers quickly, "Let's get back to the guys. We're getting bad." Leaving the intimate cloister of the restroom, they continue their whispered discussion broken by moments of giggling. Arriving at the table again, they are still laughing quietly.

Noticing the laughter from the girls, the guys become suspicious and inquire teasingly, "Ok girls, what are *you* up to?"

Sheepishly, the girls giggle in reply, "Nothing, nothing at all."

Paying for the dinner, Bill tips the server well. As they reach the front entrance to leave, the four of them see Carl and say, "Thank you again for the great dinner and for the kindness to us tonight."

Happy to see both couples satisfied and smiling, Carl remarks with a smile, "You are quite welcome. See you next time."

At Maddie's

On the way to Maddie's house, Joey reminds, "Bill, don't forget to call me when you're ready to go home and I'll return for you like a bad penny."

Bill jokes, "Ok *mom*. I'll call if I *decide* to go home." Then, he queries, "Maddie, what time do you need me to leave? I don't want to upset your mom and dad on our first date."

They all laugh then Maddie reveals with a grin, "Well Bill, my first answer is *never*, but truly, I'm not really sure. I've never *had* a date come in the house. You're the only guy who has come over before." His kind look and warm smile says he understands her completely.

Realizing this is entirely new emotional terrain for her, he says to Joey, "I'll give you a call. I promise I won't be *too* late."

Maddie interjects, "You *wish*. *I'll* be the one to tell you when you can go home." After her comment, they all laugh again.

Bill knows Joey is his best friend on the team and will do whatever he can to help him. He tries not to take Joey's kindness for granted. After all, how often will a friend take you wherever you want to go whenever you need to do so? Planning ahead Bill inquires, "Maddie, when we arrive at your house, could we build a fire together in the fireplace and make some hot chocolate to share?"

McKenna muses to herself, "Maddie, tell me this guy is for real. That's *so* romantic. Does he have any brothers like him?"

Maddie teases him with a puzzled look then says, "Of course, we can. It sounds like great fun and so romantic but no marshmallows. I don't like them."

"Ok, one hot chocolate, hold the marshmallows please," Bill says as he gives her a hug. Sensing an excitement in Maddie, he mistakes her excitement for a case of nerves. She cannot wait to get home not just because of Bill but also because of his note to her. Barely able to contain her excitement about the note he wrote to her, she wants her mom to see it first. She hasn't told McKenna about it yet as the note is very special and she visualizes her mom's face when seeing it. Her mom has an overzealous sense of concern for her daughter and about how cautious she is when going on dates. She knows the note will help her mom relax a bit and not worry about Bill treating her properly and with respect.

After what seems to be an eternity to Maddie, they arrive at her house. McKenna is still concerned for her friend because of her statements earlier. Joey and McKenna say goodnight to them and Joey adds, "I'll see you later, Bill."

"Copy that," Bill answers. As she and Bill stroll toward the house holding hands, her parents wait for her inside. They are not upset with her. In fact, she is home well before mom and dad consider it a curfew violation. It is just true parental concern and after all, she *is* beautiful and her parents' only daughter. It is slightly after 11:00 PM and an acceptable time to them.

As they walk through the door to her mom's relief, she says, "Mom, Dad, Bill's with me. Is it ok to come in?" Her words surprise her mom as Maddie *never* brings home a date. With reintroductions complete, he shakes their hands pleasantly but firmly, Mrs. Benn first and then Mr. Benn. Maddie pulls her mom into the kitchen excitedly and shows her the note. As she reads the note, her mom's eyes fill with tears and Maddie inquires with concern, "Mom, are you ok? What's wrong?"

Overcome with joy for her daughter, she answers, "Sweetheart, the note is so kind and so special. You should keep that in a special place. He seems to be a very nice young man and I'm sure he'll treat you right. I'm so happy for you. What are you kids going to do?"

"Bill wants to build a fire and make some hot chocolate," Maddie replies. Putting her hand over her mouth, Mrs. Benn's eyes well up with a couple more tears and she says, "That's so romantic. Is he for real, hon?"

Excitedly, Maddie assures, "Yes mom. He's for real and he's treated me this way all evening."

Sensing Maddie's excitement, her mom hugs her and whispers in her ear, "Be careful, please."

Wanting to reassure her mom, she convinces, "I will be, mom. I'm sure you don't have to worry about me around him but I know what you mean. He's *not* like other guys in school. I've only known Bill since the beginning of school but I trust him totally. He's been perfect so far."

While Maddie and her mom are in the kitchen, Bill notices Mr. Benn looking at some blue prints and inquires with curiosity, "Are you planning on building this soon? It appears to be a deck."

Mr. Benn says, "That's a good read Bill. They are for a deck. I demolished the old one out last weekend and plan to try to build the new one tomorrow."

Curious about Mr. Benn's construction abilities, Bill inquires, "I don't mean to be disrespectful, but have you ever built one before?"

Mr. Benn chuckles, "No and I'm not sure what it will look like when I'm finished."

Reviewing the plans, Bill says, "Mr. Benn, it doesn't look too complicated. If you don't mind, I'd like come over tomorrow and help you with it."

"Do *you* know anything about carpentry or are you just being nice to impress Maddie," Mr. Benn queries.

Knowing Mr. Benn is unaware of the training from Bill's grandfather, Bill responds with a smile, "I've got a little game in that area too. However to be totally honest, I'd love to spend more time with Maddie as well."

"Bill, I'll take you up on your offer. When can I expect you tomorrow," asks Mr. Benn.

Bill answers, "I'll be over right after practice and will bring my tools."

Mr. Benn interjects, "I've a couple of hammers and a hand saw in the garage. You'll only need a tape measure."

"Sounds great, sir. I'll see you tomorrow. I plan to bring along another guy to help me if you don't mind," Bill inquires and shakes his hand to seal the deal. However, he still plans to ring his personal tools from home.

"It's fine with me, the more the merrier," Mr. Benn remarks.

As Maddie comes back from the kitchen with her mom, she queries curiously, "You two seem awfully chummy. What's going on here that *I* need to know about?"

Excited by his offer of help, Mr. Benn explains, "Bill is coming over tomorrow to help me build the deck. I'm eleated he offered to help me. I'm certain the deck will be much more solid now."

Maddie contemplates, "I can't believe it. My dreams are coming true. I'm still getting to know Bill and he'll be here all day. I wonder if he knows about building anything."

Suddenly, Mrs. Benn says, "C'mon hon, let's go to bed and give these two some privacy." Given his wife's overprotective nature, her words leave Mr. Benn confused totally. However, the look on his wife's face says Maddie is safe with this guy.

After her parents leave the room, Maddie says, "It was so nice of you to offer to help my dad. Since he doesn't know *anything* about carpentry, this should be very entertaining. Do you know what the best part will be?"

"Getting a new *deck*," Bill jokes.

"*Bill*," she exclaims then continues, "It's that you'll be here all day with *me*. I get to watch you *work*." With his face growing into a huge smile, he pulls her close and kisses her passionately.

When they relax their embrace, Bill looks deeply into her eyes and inquires, "Did you want to share that hot chocolate now or go build a fire in the fireplace?"

"Let's skip the hot chocolate right now and enjoy each other by the fire," Maddie recommends expectantly. Teasing each other all the way to the fireplace, their emotions are warm already.

"Do you have two sticks handy," Bill grins, "It's really the *only* way to start a fire."

"Bill," she mock scolds him as she slaps him lightly on his arm. Maddie gets the matches and they start the fire using a more modern method. Standing in front of the couch, she sizes up Bill and then the couch. She is taller than most girls are and Bill is a *large* athletic quarterback. "This isn't going to work," she says, contemplating for a minute, "What do you suggest?"

Grinning at her statement, he replies, "I recommend this recipe. Take two blankets and add two pillows. Fold the blankets in half like this. Add two kids who want to snuggle with each other. Mix well with flickering firelight. Add the warmth of the fire and two shared bodies by the fireplace." He puts the pillows at the end closest to the fire.

Tilting her head, she dons a tempting smile and says alluringly as she turns out the lights, "I like this recipe. Let's see how this simmers by the fire." Her words excite Bill but concern him also.

In the flickering firelight, he says, "Ok, pick your spot." Making her choice, she puts her knees on one of the blankets. Bracing herself on one hand, she slowly lowers her hip to the blanket. As she reclines on her elbow, she reaches up for Bill with her other hand. In the dim firelight, Maddie's face glows softly but he notices her hand trembling. He takes her hand gently without any words. Never allowing her heart to take her to this place before, the guy's intentions were always suspect. However, her heart keeps repeating, "Don't be nervous. He's not like everyone else." Still, her mind is still unsure as he lies next to her face to face and she smiles hesitatingly. As he wraps his arm around her, she reciprocates with her trembling arm. Drawing close to her, he feels her body become tense and trembling.

Looking at her with gentleness in the flickering glow, he whispers, "It's ok Maddie. You can relax. You're *safe* with me." While allowing herself to breathe again, her emotion trickles a tear down her cheek. He brushes her cheek softly with his hand as she whispers back, "I apologize that I'm nervous. I know I shouldn't be this way but this is my first time to do this. I've dreamt about this moment for a long time, a wonderful, caring guy, a cozy fire in the fireplace, and being held like this. I never dreamed I could be here with you." Hugging her tenderly, he kisses her softly and they continue to share each other's touch, kisses, words, and gentle passion.

As they intermittently probe each other verbally about anything and everything between kisses, finally Maddie quizzes emphatically, "Do you *really* know anything about building a deck? Are you being super nice *or* do you just want to be with *me* tomorrow?"

Laughing at her questions, Bill replies, "Guilty as charged. All of the above, my grandfather is a carpenter. I've been building projects with him since the second grade. So, I *do* know a little bit about carpentry. What are *you* going to do while I'm helping your dad?"

"Watch you bend over," she quips. They continue to talk and quietly laugh between shared embraces and kisses. Maddie's excitement grows during the evening but her expectations for tomorrow are astronomical. Her mind quizzes her heart, "Have I found the guy I've been looking for, the perfect gentleman and a really great guy?"

Suddenly, Bill says quietly, "Maddie, I should probably go home. I have practice tomorrow and a deck to build with your dad. I'd better get some rest."

Wanting to extend the evening's fun, she begs, "Can't you stay longer with *me*? I'm having so much fun and I don't want it to end."

Feeling the same desire, he says, "You know I'd like to do so but I don't want to upset your parents on our first date. Remember, I'll be back in the morning. Who knows, I may be here all day. We'll have plenty of time together."

Reluctantly, Maddie acquiesces as he calls Joey and she responds, "I guess if I can't entice you to stay, I'll *have* to let you go." Disappointed, she walks him to the door. At the door, she perks up suddenly and wraps her arms around his neck. She plants a warm, wet, passionate kiss on his lips that seems to last forever and begs him to stay.

Looking into her eyes deeply after the kiss, he jokes, "Would you please stop begging? I'll be back tomorrow." As he leaves, he relates, "Oh I almost forgot. Please call McKenna and have her come over for the day too."

Annoyed at a rival for his time, she quips, "No way. I refuse to share you with *anyone*. Your time is *mine* tomorrow. McKenna will not have any chance to get your attention."

Recognizing the incongruity in her statement, Bill retorts, "Not for me goofy, for Joey, he's going to help build the deck even though he doesn't know it yet. Besides, Joey likes her a lot. Don't worry about anyone else getting my attention because I'm your guy." He kisses her goodbye again softly as Joey pulls into the driveway. While watching them drive away, her excitement about tomorrow knows no bounds. Gliding back to the house, she dreams about having him near her all day tomorrow.

As she floats into the living room, her mom appears suddenly to inquire with concern, "Maddie, are you *ok*? Was he *upset* with you or something?"

Glowing, Maddie answers dreamily, "No mom, he's fine. He's just that kind of guy. He went home because it's our first date and he didn't want to upset you and dad by staying too long."

Relieved by her words, her mom asks rhetorically, "He is very special, isn't he?"

Maddie replies anyway, "I *think* he is. He knows what to say and what to do at the opportune time, like the note he wrote and ordering for me at the TeePee. He likes to share the romance of the moment with a girl, not just take her out. He's the dream guy of every girl at South and he's with *me*. That's hard for me to fathom." Her mind replays her words, "He could have any girl he wants at South and he wants to be with *me*. *Amazing*! Lots of guys want to be with the 'cheerleader' and he doesn't care about that. He wants to be with *me*."

Seeing and sensing Maddie's excitement about the evening and hearing her words, she and her mom sit down to talk. Being just as excited as Maddie, Mrs. Benn says, "Sweetheart, I want to hear *everything* about your date. It sounds like the two of you had a *lot* of fun."

Maddie's mind unleashes a joyous memory dump of their relationship on her mother. Starting with a small fib, she says, "We bumped into each other at the game." She does not inform her mom that she planned to bump into Bill. However, she *does* relate *everything* about her week with Bill including the kiss during the game in front of everyone. She finishes with her date tonight.

"We saw that kiss at the game, dear. It was very special, don't you think," her mom inquires with excitement in her voice.

"Yes it was. It was like performing on stage with *him* as my leading man. While that was fun, *tonight* is the best night of my life," Maddie says with a big smile.

"Ok, what are you hiding behind that grin," her mom probes lovingly.

Responding to her mom, Maddie continues, "Joey is coming to help tomorrow too and Bill wants me to have McKenna come over. You see Joey likes her. Originally, I told him I didn't want anyone else here trying to get his attention. I didn't realize she was for Joey until he laughed about it. Then, he told me not to worry about that because he was *my* guy. I'm not sure what he means totally by that but I sure liked hearing it."

On the way home, Bill says, "I had a great time with her tonight and we're going back tomorrow with your dad's truck."

Looking puzzled, Joey says, "Huh? *We* are going back?"

Mentally reviewing his plan, Bill answers excitedly, "You bet *we* are. *We* are building a deck for Maddie's parents. We'll need to bring my tools too."

With no carpentry experience, Joey retorts, "What have you gotten me into? I don't know *anything* about building a deck. Besides, she's going out with *you* not me."

Laughing at Joey's statement, Bill remarks, "Have I ever led you wrong? I've seen the plans and it's a piece of cake. Just do what I tell you and you'll be fine. Oh by the way, I've got you covered too. I told Maddie to have McKenna come over."

"*Sweet*," Joey exclaims, "*I'm in.*"

Sarah's Date

arlier, while the four are at the TeePee, Steve Powell, a South junior, knocks on Sarah's door to pick her up for their date. Going on several fun dates together, she enjoyed his company each time. Two other nice things about him, he has a new, candy-apple red Pontiac GTO convertible and he has always been courteous with her. As Sarah and Steve walk out to his car, she rubs the ruby heart on the necklace Bill gave her. Her way of thinking about Bill has become a reflex action for her. Things begin well as they go out to dinner at Pete Steffey's, one of those ideal restaurants to begin a special evening. Expecting a good time again, she did not anticipate going to such a nice dinner. After enjoying the repast of filet mignon, baked potato, salad, green beans, and rolls, Sarah declines dessert. Still, her intuition tells her something about tonight is different. As they drive to a movie after dinner, Steve asks, "Sarah, have you enjoyed the evening so far?"

"It's been wonderful. Thank you," she bubbles.

With such a positive response, he explains, "I have an even more magical evening planned." After dinner, he did not take her home as she expected. Instead, he drives out to Lake Road where they stop, watch the stars with the top down, and exchange kisses.

Although enjoying the time, Sarah senses something different from their previous dates and inquires, "Steve, I've had a great time but can you please take me home now?"

Not appreciating her request, he replies curtly, "*Sure, we can go home now.*" His mind schemes on the drive to her house, "I spent all this money on you this evening. I'm going to get more out of this than a few kisses." As they arrive at her house, he suggests, "Sarah, it's not past curfew. Would you like to sit in the back seat where we have more room to look at the stars?"

While being a bit apprehensive, Sarah agrees, "That's ok, but I'll have to go inside soon." When they get into the back seat, Steve puts his arm around her and pulls her close to him gently. While sharing kisses in his embrace, the kisses begin to turn from soft to strong and pressured. Sarah interrupts, "Steve, I think I should go in now." Ignoring her wishes, he tightens his embrace with his one arm and his hands begin moving toward areas that make Sarah very uncomfortable. As she begins to resist, he fights to gain an advantage, putting his hands on her forcefully. Thinking this has to stop now, she demands, "Steve, please stop this and let me go. This is *not* fun for me."

Persisting with his intentions, he retorts, "I paid for a great dinner and movie. We have gone on several dates and you owe me. You're in high school now. *Everybody* does it. So what's the problem?"

As her inhibitions scream, Sarah exclaims, "I don't *care* about everybody. I don't do those things." With those words, he tries more desperately, grabbing at her clothes. Filled with fear for her safety, she envisions, "Where's Bill when I need him. If only I was *his* now, this would *not* be happening. Still, I won't give in and be a victim." Grabbing her left arm again forcibly, Steve leaves her right arm free. Sensing an opening, she flips her right hand back and stiffens her wrist into a battering ram. Mustering all her energy and will in the moment, she drives her ramrod right palm into his left cheekbone.

Stunned by the blow, he falls backward and loses his grip on her left arm. The suddenness of her counter-attack disrupts his defenses, as his stomach is unprotected. Quickly, Sarah stiffens and aims her freed left arm, her left hand in a fist. Driving her stiff right palm into her left hand, she pile-drives her left elbow into Steve's solar plexus. With Steve stunned and doubled over, Sarah grabs the door handle, kicks open the door, and rushes out to freedom and safety. Running at full speed and without looking back, she reaches the safety of her porch and grabs the door. Holding her heart necklace against her pounding heart, she closes her eyes for a moment and ponders, "Oh Bill! Why? Why?"

With the sentinel trees providing safety again, Steve yells at her from his now started car, "See if I ask you out again, bitch." As he speeds off, Sarah rushes into the house from her "date" and moves quickly to her room without speaking to her parents.

Sensing anxiety in Sarah's actions, her mom knocks on her door and questions, "Dear, was your date a good one?"

Struggling with her answer, Sarah mutters, "Sure mom, it was fine but I'm tired and I'm going to bed." Although detecting something wrong in Sarah's tone, her mom does not pursue the questioning further. However, Sarah *wasn't* fine and neither was her date.

Building the Deck

Bill and Joey arrive at Maddie's house mid-morning with Bill's tools. Hearing the truck pull into the driveway, Maddie and McKenna rush to greet them before they open their doors. "Hey guys," Maddie says with a huge smile.

McKenna adds flirtatiously, *"Hi Joey. It's nice to see you."*

With her words making him *very* happy, he echoes, "It's *very* nice to see you too." Maddie hurries to Bill's side, giving him a big hug and a kiss.

"How's *my* girl today," he inquires sincerely.

A bit perplexed, she replies, "Well, if you mean *me*, then *your* girl's fine"

"Who *else* would I mean," Bill says with a smile and gives her another hug. His words thrill Maddie's heart and she smiles at McKenna.

Shifting her growing smile back to him, she quizzes, "Did you happen to read the paper this morning? They quoted you in one of the stories."

Indifferent to the story, he responds, "That's nice I guess but I never read the paper. I don't like to read the sports clippings about me."

"No, no it wasn't about the game," she replies with a big grin.

With his curiosity aroused, he probes, "What was it then?"

Smiling broadly again, she asks, "They quoted you about *me* I *think*? Did you *really* say that? You wanted to wrap up the questions because you had a date with the most beautiful girl on the *planet*?"

As a smile leaps onto his face, Bill replies, "I sure did and they got the message. We were finished talking. I wanted to get out of there and be with you." Maddie's excitement and joy overcome her inhibitions as she giggles and jumps into Bill's arms.

Trying to become his new skin with her hug, she whispers in his ear, "I can't believe you said that about *me*."

While kissing her cheek, he whispers back his reply, "I did and I meant every word."

Mr. Benn and the guys review the blueprints and start constructing the deck. After about an hour, Bill says, "Mr. Benn, thank you for all your guidance today. Joey and I can finish the deck from this point." It is a nice way of asking him to stay out of the way. The day provided evidence Mr. Benn really doesn't know how to hammer a nail.

Hoping to provide assistance, he queries, "Are you sure you don't need me to help, Bill."

Responding politely, Bill answers, "We're doing fine. I'm sure Joey and I can finish the deck from here."

"Thanks Bill. It *is* looking great," Mr. Benn exclaims. Two hours into the deck, Maddie and McKenna bring the guys some food and sodas. While sitting on the completed part of the deck, they enjoy lunch together. After finishing lunch, the guys get back to work immediately. As it is a warm day, the guys are hot and sweating but don't make any complaints about the work or the company. They both decide to take a break for some water due to the heat. Bill begins to pull off his soaked t-shirt to wipe the sweat from his face with it. As he pulls it off, Maddie and McKenna gaze at the sweat beads on his athletic physique while Maddie analyzes mentally, *"Hello Zeus! Command me now!"* Glancing quickly at each other, the girls exclaim simultaneously, *"Oh My!"* Seizing the moment, Maddie takes Bill a towel as McKenna takes one to Joey. "Thought you could use this," Maddie tells Bill.

As he dries his face, he says, "Thanks sweetheart." Puzzled somewhat by his words, Maddie has never heard this term of endearment from a guy when referring to her. However, reflecting over the last few days and what she has heard, the words thrill her nonetheless. Finishing the main project, the guys proclaim the job magnificent from all angles. Suddenly, Bill notices one small problem. Mr. Benn ordered too much wood for the project. So, he decides to add some accessories on the deck. He builds benches all the way around, a large deck chair for two, and a picnic table for outside dining.

Shaking his head, Joey says, "Great show Frank." Leaning into McKenna, he whispers, "There isn't anything he can't do."

"What's the Frank stuff mean," Maddie probes curiously.

Checking first before explaining its true meaning, Joey answers, "Well Bill…"

"That's enough Joey," Bill interrupts and continues, "Maddie, I'll explain it to you later." Walking up to the guys, Mr. Benn surprises both of them with $50 each.

After thanking Mr. Benn, the guys gather their tools together, put them in the truck, and prepare to leave. Concerned by these actions, Maddie and McKenna walk over to the truck. It's only about 6:00 PM and Maddie quizzes, "Bill, are you guys leaving so soon?"

Sensing her concern, he teases, "Yes. We *have* to go. You really don't like us right now."

Taking the bait completely, Maddie responds, "What do you *mean*? *Why*? It's early yet and we *do* like you."

Ignoring Maddie's questions, he requests, "Would you like to go to a movie tonight and grab a pizza?"

"Huh, sure, I'm confused," she says.

Smiling at McKenna, Joey inquires, "Would you like to go too?"

Fearing emotional rejection, she answers emphatically, "*I* still like you and I like your offer *very much.*"

Interrupting quickly, Bill says with a laugh, "Then, we have to go and take showers. We stink after working all day in this heat. You wouldn't like us very much in this condition."

Maddie slaps him lightly and says, "*Bill!*" Then, she leans over, kisses him, and laughs, "Oooh, salty kisses."

Knowing the ruse worked perfectly, he laughs too, "Ok, that says it all. We'll be right back after we shower."

Together on the Deck

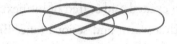

Returning from the movie and pizza, the slight breeze and warm evening air make it a perfect night to try out the new deck. Maddie inquires with hope, "Can you stay for a while, Bill?"

Warming to her sincere words, he replies, "As long as you want me here."

Deciding to christen the cozy new deck chair with him, she proposes flirtatiously, "Would you hold me? I want to burrow down in your arms and look at the stars."

With a wry smile, he responds in his best stage voice, "Lean back, my love, and let my arms envelope you gently. The stars await us."

Laughing at his words and accent, she answers, "How can I resist such a welcome invitation?" Snuggling down into his arms, she lays her head against his shoulder softly.

Gazing at Bill's face and the sky behind him, she says, "I could stay here with you forever. I feel so safe in your arms."

Recognizing a perfect opening for tease, he chuckles, "That's me good ol' safe Bill."

Slapping his stomach lightly, she says, "*Bill!* You know what I mean."

"Yes I do, hon, and I'm glad that you feel that way with me," he says.

His words embolden Maddie to ask what her heart is afraid to hear. With hesitation, she begins, "Bill, I have to know something. I hope I don't upset you. You told me yesterday you were my guy. Today you called me your girl, your sweetheart, and just now hon. Are those just words you're saying to me or do you really mean them?" She is both excited and scared of his next words.

Beginning with a warm and serious tone, Bill responds softly, "Maddie, sit up for a minute." Turning to face her, he gazes into her eyes and takes her hands, "I owe you an apology."

As she begins to tremble, her heart is sure he'll say his words mean nothing. "An apology for what," she struggles to ask.

Struggling to get the words out, he continues, "I know we have only known each other since the first week of school. We only spoke briefly until this week. I owe you an apology for never looking into your eyes and saying how I felt. You should know what you mean to me and that I want to be with you. I should have explained."

Her heart aches as her mind joins in, "Here it comes just like other guys and what he wants." The throbbing anticipation reaches Maddie's eyes and a tear trickles down her cheek. Breaking her gaze with Bill, she lowers her head.

"Please don't cry or I won't be able to get this out. You'll make me cry too," Bill urges.

Her hearts leaps as she contemplates, "No guy has ever said anything like this to me." Lifting her chin gently, he brushes the tear from her cheek softly.

Then, brushing back her long, blond hair from her face, he holds both of her hands again and continues, "I want you to be my girl and I want to be your guy. I want us to date each other exclusively. I don't want to share you with anyone. I love you Maddie. I'm sure that sounds strange since we've only known each other a short time. That's how I feel and I pray you feel the same too."

Relief and shock overcome her as the realization hits, "Bill Denton wants me to be his girlfriend. He can have any girl he wants and he wants me." She gushes, "Really, I didn't *mis-hear* you did I? It *is* me, right? *I'm* your girl and you're *my* guy, really?"

Reeling from her reaction, he utters, "Yes, *really*. Is that ok?"

Elated, she continues, "It's more than *ok*. It's *awesome*. I love you too. This happened so fast it's like a dream." Falling back in the deck chair, Maddie wraps her arms around him tightly and they kiss passionately for a young eternity. Blissfully, they caress each other and enjoy each other's touch in the starlight. Her mind floods with reflection, "I'm so lucky. He's had every opportunity to do something disrespectful and he hasn't even attempted anything. What a wonderful guy."

At the same time, Bill's thoughts reflect as well, "I'm the luckiest guy in the world! If only I could have opened my heart this way to Sarah, imagine what might have happened."

With the tension released, her muscles relax completely and she remembers to ask, "What's this Frank thing? Why does Joey call you Frank when no one else does?"

Laughing as his thoughts turn back to Maddie, Bill answers, "Ok, I promised to tell you about who I am. Ready? Hang on! When I'm on the field, it's show time. I want to entertain everyone at the game. It's the big stage and the bigger the stage the more I like it. I want to be *the guy*. He calls me Frank because I like Frank Sinatra and the presence he has on stage that says, 'I'm the man.' I like to walk out and to have people say, 'There he is.' I love the spotlight and it *is addictive*. I know there's nothing I can't accomplish on the football field. God gave me the tools and the faith to believe in my teammates and myself. Building the deck today was another stage and I think the performance was very good. Again, God gave me the tools to do it. So, Joey said, 'nice show Frank.' However, when I leave the field, I'm just Bill Denton, great student and good guy. I have that same faith in God and a quiet confidence in myself. I'm not arrogant and off the field, I don't like to talk about myself. In fact, it took more courage to look into your eyes and open my heart to you than anything I've done on the field. I just want to be a regular guy. I asked you out because you never said anything to me about football. You seemed to be interested in Bill and not the quarterback."

With his words taking her completely by surprise, she exclaims, "And you never asked me anything about cheerleading. You asked about my weekend and *me*. That's why I said yes. I understood completely and knew how you felt. Guys want to go out with the cheerleader but I'm never sure if they want to go out with me."

Tickled with her explanation, he says with a laugh, "I do want to be with you. Being a cheerleader is a bonus because you're always close to the field."

Without waiting for a response, she interjects, "And you can kiss me during the game. Maybe it's not the kind of kiss I want but I'll take what I can get. You spoke of God blessing you with faith, wisdom, and tools. Would you mind going with my parents and me to church tomorrow? I'd like you to come to a cookout at my house tomorrow too. My parents are having some friends over to enjoy the new deck. Are you available?"

Yearning to be the object of *her* hearts desires, Bill answers with a chuckle, "Yes, I'd love to go to church with you and yes, I want to come over after church for the cookout."

On Sunday, they attend church together with her parents but the scene is like a play. Bill stuns everyone with his handsomeness in his tailored suits and elegant manners. Playing the leading lady and man on *this* stage, all her friends are awestruck at their presence. Each of the Benn's friends at church experiences the story of Bill's excellent treatment of their daughter. Bill brings a spare change of clothes for Maddie's house and the cookout. At the cookout, some of her parent's friends have kids at South and they try to talk football with him. Maddie will have none of it, telling them politely, "It's Sunday not Friday night. Just let him relax and be himself."

Bill is very thankful for her intervention and as the day progresses, she remarks, "I really thought your suit looked great on you today."

"Thank you so much. I'm glad you liked it. Because of my build, the suits have to be tailor-made," he replies gratefully.

Disbelieving what she heard, she inquires, "You said suits. How *many* do you *have?*"

He replies, "I have five other ones. I bought six of them so I wouldn't have to go back."

"Wow, that's a lot of suits for a guy to have. What did your parents say when you ordered six suits," she exclaims.

Quickly adding the facts surrounding his trust, he replies, "My parents died in a car wreck when I was 10."

Believing him to be joking, she thinks, "He must be kidding." When she looks deeply into his eyes, she realizes he's not and the tears begin to flow down her cheeks.

Filled with sadness and anxiety over her question, she begs, "Bill, can you ever forgive me? I'm so sorry for asking about your parents and bringing back sad memories."

Reassuring her in his arms, he whispers, "Maddie, it's all right. How could you have known? It's not something I talk about much. I've learned to adjust and accept it."

Concerned about his welfare, she inquires, "With whom do you live?"

Captivated by her concern, he replies, "I've lived with my grandparents since my parent's died. That's how I received my trust fund." He explains further, how he can use the trust fund.

She continues crying softly as he says, "Maddie, it's really ok, I love you. You're the most important part of my life now." His words touch her deepest emotions and her crying becomes more intense. Holding her close, he comforts her, "It's all right. You've not hurt me. Just rest yourself against me until you feel better. You know if you continue crying, then I'll have to join in. I'm ready to cry myself."

She ponders, "I can't believe how sensitive he is. No high school guy would admit to crying or potentially crying. Amazing." His comforting and teasing soon turn her sorrow to joy. The rest of Sunday's cookout is a delightful time for the Bill and Maddie as he impresses all of the Benn's friends with his character. Finally, he calls Joey to take him home and McKenna rides with him to Maddie's house.

Chivalry Lives!

Monday morning as Bill finishes his workout and proceeds to his locker, Steve Powell arrives at school with a shiner below his left eye from Sarah's blow. Steve is *not* happy as speculation runs rampant and word spreads rapidly regarding the injury and its cause. Everyone knows he was on a date with Sarah over the weekend. As Sarah arrives at school, the pain of facing everyone with what she went through overcomes her will. She rushes to the cafeteria, finds a secluded table, and begins to cry.

Seeing his boys coming toward him quickly, Bill inquires with a smile, "What's up guys?"

With distress in his voice, Pete responds, "Sarah's in the cafeteria crying. She needs to talk to you *now*."

"*Crying*," Bill exclaims, "and she wants to talk to me? I can't imagine why. We spoke recently but very briefly."

"Yep," Pete says, "and she's pretty upset. She needs to see you *right now*." Grabbing his books, he rushes to the cafeteria with anxiety and concern coursing through his thoughts.

While rushing, his mind blurs, "Sarah. Is she hurt? Something must be deeply wrong for her to be crying at school. *She's* my best friend but if she's *asking* for *me*....I love Maddie but I love Sarah too. I have to help her, whatever it is." As he walks in briskly, he sees Andy sitting with her. While Bill makes his way to her table, a crowd gathers around Sarah's table. Andy and the boys keep the crowd back to give Bill and Sarah some space and privacy. The room turns electric with rumors pulsating through the crowd at lightning speed, centering on Steve and Sarah.

Although Maddie is in the cafeteria too, Bill never sees her but speeds straight to Sarah. Not looking for Maddie or any other person, his focus is solely on Sarah's pain. Trusting him totally, Maddie received his pledge of love to her only yesterday. Not upset with his slight, she hurries to them to comfort Sarah. "If Sarah is hurt then so is Bill and he needs me with him," she reasons. Sitting with D. J., she inquires, "Do you know what's wrong with Sarah *for sure*? I heard the rumors as I came over and I pray they're not true."

D. J. responds, "What *are* the rumors? Sarah said she wanted to talk *only* to Bill. So, I'm not sure either but I know she's pretty upset." Maddie contemplates what she heard and fears the worst seeing Sarah sobbing. Hugging Bill, Sarah lays her head on his chest as she composes herself tucked safely in his arms. Detailing her date to him, she explains how it started so well and ended in such fear.

Leaning over to her ear, he whispers, "Everything will be fine, hon. Steve won't bother you ever again."

With his words filling her with anxiety, she whispers back, "Bill, I'm worried, that sounds like a threat. Please don't do anything to harm him. I love you too much for this to ruin your life. He isn't worth it."

Responding calmly to her concern, he says, "You're my best friend and I need to protect you from guys like him. I'll not do anything rash."

With a loving look to Maddie, he motions for her to come to Sarah and him. Seeing the tracks of Sarah's tears on her face, she says, "Come with me Sarah. Let's get you ready to face the world again. I'll help you freshen up." Turning to Bill, Maddie says, "Don't worry, I'll take good care of her. I'll have her ready for class in no time. See you in first period."

Gathering his friends together, Bill explains, "Steve Powell assaulted Sarah on their date Friday. If it had not been for God's grace and her strong will, the result would have been far worse. I can't let this go unpunished."

Ever the vigilant guard of the Dirty Boys and their closest friends, Andy interrupts, "Leave Powell to me, Bill. I'll take care of it."

With eyes of flaming steel, he responds calmly, "No Andy. Powell is mine. I'm going to take care of this personally." His words stun the Dirty Boys and they gasp, "You can't."

"Yes guys, I can and I will. I wasn't there for her on Friday. Nobody else is going to avenge her honor but *me*," he explains as calmly as a hurricane eye. As the bell rings, they all rush for class. However, his friends sense something dire about to happen despite Bill's cool calmness. He'd *never* utter, "taking care of this personally." With Sarah's reputation at stake, the *Assassin* arises from the football field as a stealthy ninja waiting to strike.

Taking his seat in class next to Maddie, Bill starts to explain his earlier actions. Before he utters a word, she assures, "Bill, everything is fine with me. I understand you and Sarah are best friends. I know you're the kind of friends who are there for each other and trust each other. Everyone needs friends like you two. That said, I know I'm your girl and you're my guy and I trust you in every way."

Amazed, Bill inquires, "How do *you* know that Sarah and I are best friends?"

Maddie laughs softly, "We go to South High School. Everyone knows everything you and I do immediately. The U.S. should have a communication network so good. Today's event was in the cafeteria not in some parked car on Lake Road. Even if it was on Lake Road, I'd let you explain the circumstances first. It's faith, hope, and trust that defines the love between a couple." A tear runs down Bill's face and he smiles as her words put him at ease. She holds his hand and whispers, "I love you." Mrs. Case starts the lesson and the class proceeds at its usual pace.

Maddie and Bill have lunch during the first lunch period. After the class arrives again at their room, Bill asks the teacher, "May I return to the lunchroom because I left something there." The unsuspecting teacher says, "Hurry there and back. I don't want you to miss any part of the lesson." Steve and Sarah's lunch is during the second lunch period. Making his presence known through Bill's nerve, the *Assassin* slips with stealth to the cafeteria, drawing no suspicion. Steve will soon feel the ice in Bill's words.

Walking into the cafeteria, Bill enters with his game time swagger where everyone sits in silent anticipation. The crowd roar is ominously absent as one of Sarah's friends questions, "Sarah, why is Bill here now? This *isn't* his *normal* lunch period."

Knowing the real reason for his appearance, still Sarah responds, "He's probably coming to talk to me." Yet, her heart screams, "My knight in shining armor is here to avenge my honor but I'm terrified at what these next few minutes may hold." The *Assassin* surveys the room for his target and finds Steve.

Moving straight to Steve's table with ice in his veins, not even glancing at Sarah, he probes, "Mind if *I* sit down?"

As Bill takes a seat, Steve lifts his gaze from the table and asks sarcastically, "What do *you* want?"

Leaning over the table, Bill confronts, "You *assaulted* Sarah last Friday. *That's* a crime but I'm *not* going to the police myself. I'm not *even* going to the teachers or administration. Someone else can do that. My business is with *you and you alone.* You *injured* Sarah's emotion *and* her honor. If you *ever* approach her, attempt to *speak* to her or *touch* her again, *you'll* answer to me. *You understand meathead?*" Numbers give cowards backbone and Steve had plenty around his friends at lunch.

Emboldened by his minions, he challenges with an arrogant attitude, "Why *wait*? Let's get it on *now*." Expecting that Bill's words carry no weight, Steve stands up, miscalculating the depth of Bill's protective nature and feelings for Sarah. Much to his surprise and chagrin, Bill stands to meet his challenge.

Bill flips both hands at him twice quickly to lure him in and says, "*Bring it, clown.*" Taking a fearfully weak swing at Bill, Steve misses wide when Bill dodges it as deftly as a blitzing safety. His swing leaves Steve's midsection unprotected again and the *Ninja* takes advantage of the opening. With his hands stiffened at the knuckles into blade-like weapons, he drives his left weapon powerfully against Steve's stomach, bruised already from Sarah's second blow on Friday. As Steve begins to double over in severe pain, Bill's right hand flips backward and his wrist stiffens. Delivering a ramrod blow with his right palm against Steve's right cheek, he uses all his will and strength. The ferocity and power of the strike lifts Steve off his feet, flying backwards onto the cafeteria floor as his supporters scurry for cover. Leaning over his vanquished, moaning foe, Bill says in an icy, calm voice, "*Never again!*"

The suddenness, speed, and power of the battle leave everyone in the cafeteria as stunned spectators. No one has seen or anticipated this side of Bill Denton. Sarah's friends are as dumbfounded as the other spectators but Sarah knows in her heart what occurred and why. Injuring both her emotions and her honor, Steve had become an immediate threat to her well-being as a student and more importantly, a person. Bill performed his valiant service to eliminate the threat and to restore Sarah's honor for her. While she smiles silently, her friends look at her in amazement and the teachers on lunch duty rush over expecting additional blows but the battle needs none. It is over in an instant and the teachers cannot believe what they witnessed either. Ordering Bill to the principal's office, two of them accompany him.

Vindication and Exoneration

I n the principal's office, Bill waits as Coach Mulinaro comes in to meet with him and Mr. Cole, the principal. "My first question, Bill, is why? What in the world prompted this reaction from you," Coach inquires.

Looking in the coach's eyes, Bill responds calmly, "It's a personal matter. I did what I did and I'll accept the consequences of my actions."

"But why did you do it," Coach Mulinaro asks again.

Continuing to protect Sarah's honor with his silence, Bill says, "Coach, this really is a very personal matter to me. I can't explain it further."

A stunned Mr. Cole speaks, "You have two things going for you. You have been a model student until today and he swung at you first."

"Thank you sir," Bill replies respectfully. Mr. Cole and Coach Mulinaro look at each other in disbelief.

With no open recourse, Mr. Cole orders, "Bill, go back to class and I'll know your punishment by the end of the day." After Bill leaves, the two men discuss, "There has to be more to this. We need to determine why this occurred."

Coming to Bill's last period class, Coach Mulinaro motions him into the hallway and says, "We considered the fact that you're a model student. We *never* considered the fact that you're the quarterback. We know there is more to this incident but no one wants to talk about it. There has to be atonement for this transgression."

"I appreciate that Coach. What's my reparation," Bill inquires anxiously.

Coach addresses him further, "You're suspended from playing in the game this Friday. *You'll* practice this week and do everything else as normal but you won't play."

"I understand Coach," Bill laments.

Attempting to evoke an answer from Bill, Coach probes deeply, "Are you sure you don't want to tell me why? There has to be an overwhelming reason for you to react this way."

"There is a strong reason for my actions but I must maintain my silence sir," Bill replies.

"Ok Bill, I have no choice. We'll leave it at that. I'm sure you have your reasons. I hope they're worth it," Coach finishes with regret. Knowing his star player will not be available, he needs a plan B for Friday unless information appears to exonerate him. Bill returns to class and most of his boys are in there. Making eye contact with them, he shakes his head no. They understand Friday's game is out of reach unless someone comes forward with information.

Arriving at home, Bill calls Mr. Tibbs to relate his transgression. After Mr. Tibbs answers, Bill begins, "Mr. Tibbs, I've always come to you for advice and tried to follow your directions. I fear I've made a huge mistake for the right reasons."

"What's wrong, Bill," Mr. Tibbs inquires fearing an ominous response.

"Well, Sarah and I are best friends but are dating other people," Bill replies.

"I'm sorry to hear that didn't work out for you. She's a wonderful girl," Mr. Tibbs empathizes.

Bill replies excitedly, "It *is* about Sarah, Mr. Tibbs. She was on a date last Friday with Steve Powell. He assaulted her outside her house and it was only by God's grace and her strong will that it was not something worse. She was crying today before school and told me what happened."

Mr. Tibbs gasps, "Bill, this is serious. Is she all right? Do her parent's know yet?"

Anxious to provide more information, Bill continues quickly, "She's ok physically but not emotionally. However, she did inflict some damage on him. Steve came to school with a shiner under his left eye. I don't think her parents know or she'd have told me so. Mr. Tibbs, I could not let her honor remain unrestored."

Fearing the worst, Mr. Tibbs interrupts, "Bill, I pray you did nothing illegal or harmful."

With a nervous chuckle, Bill responds, "Well, it wasn't illegal but I won't say my actions were completely harmless either. I confronted Steve at lunch about assaulting Sarah and warned him never to come near her again. Choosing to ignore my warning, he took a swing at me instead. I reminded him that my words carried some force behind them. I only swung twice. My left fist caught his stomach where Sarah bruised him Friday. My stiffened right palm caught his right cheek and sent him flying backwards to the floor and his minions scurrying. I'm sure he'll have a second shiner tomorrow. However, I'm suspended for Friday's game. Did I do the right thing?"

Mr. Tibbs ponders for a few moments then responds, "Bill, I *am* proud of you for defending Sarah's honor. I'm proud too that she defended herself and escaped from him. However, this may not stop him from trying the same thing again with another girl. Let me reiterate that violence does not solve anything. You both should have reported this to the authorities. I assume that you did not tell any teachers or Coach?"

Embarrassed at his lack of foresight, Bill hesitates, "Well, uh, no I didn't."

Wanting to impart a life lesson, Mr. Tibbs adds, "You should trust the staff at school, Bill. You may have gotten off with no punishment. You have a strong protective instinct being the leader that you are. Sometimes, you have to defer that protection/retribution to higher authority. One last thing, I want to emphasize again that I'm very proud of you, son."

His words bring tears to Bill's eyes as he says, "Thank you Mr. Tibbs. I'll have to tell you about Maddie Benn sometime."

Mr. Tibbs interjects, "Oh, you mean the cheerleader who bumped into you during the game. I saw that myself. Anything more, Bill?"

From his heart, he responds, "Yes. Thanks dad. I can always count on you."

Practice progresses normally during the week and only Joey and the Dirty Boys know why he did what he did. After Thursday's practice, Bill leaves the locker room and Joey locks the door. With the Bill and the staff gone, Joey relates the cause of Bill's ire and actions toward Steve to the team. Breaking into spontaneous cheers, a few teammates yell, "Yeah. The dude deserved what he got. Righteous! Amazing!"

While the team plans to clear their leader's reputation as well, Coach Mulinaro comes from the coach's office to the locker room door, finds it locked, and questions, "What in the world is going on here?"

After Joey unlocks the door, the coach comes in somewhat perturbed. Joey steps up as leader in absentia and explains, "Coach we all understand why Bill isn't playing Friday. It's your decision and we support you. However, there *is* a good reason for Bill's actions. We know you've tried to find out what happened. As a team, we can tell you because we know. Bill probably wouldn't be happy if he knew but we want you to know why he did it. He's a great friend to all of us and our leader *and* he's very protective of his friends also. In many ways, he is an anachronism, a Knight seeking to restore his friend's damaged honor. You know Sarah Ormond, the redhead he hung out with all last year?"

"Yes, I know who she is," Coach replies.

Desiring to finish his defense quickly, Joey continues, "She had a date with Steve Powell last Friday. He assaulted her, coach, ripping at her clothes, and trying to get her to do things she refused to do. She begged him to stop repeatedly. Finally, she escaped from his car by inflicting some damage on him. She gave him that shiner and for that, he shouted obscenities at her as she ran for the safety of her house. Because they talk about everything and anything, Bill and Sarah are *best* friends in the truest sense. When one of them has a problem, the other one helps."

"Isn't he dating Maddie Benn," the coach probes with confusion.

Feeling an urgency to exonerate his friend, Joey continues, "Yes he is but she understands Bill and Sarah are best friends and friends only. Coach, Sarah is helping Bill keep track of his recruitment letters. This started before he met Maddie. She recognizes the special nature of Bill and Sarah's friendship and accepts that. He knows Bill loves her but he had to defend Sarah's honor against Steve. It's a chivalrous duty he performed. Like I said, it's like a Knight would do."

Shaking his head in amazement, Coach Mulinaro says, "Thanks guys, I appreciate that."

Hoping to close the sale on Bill's exoneration, Joey finishes, "Like I said coach we support your decision and we aren't trying to change your mind. We just wanted you to know." Coach ponders his next move. Still, he needs to report this to the school and the authorities.

It's game time Friday and the team runs out, pumped as usual. Bill swaggers out as usual and gives the crowd his fist pump. However, the *Maestro* or the *Wizard* need not appear, as he is not playing tonight. Gazing at Maddie with a smile, he walks over to her and gives her a hug and a kiss on the cheek. He reiterates, "I love you Maddie. I want to be sure you know," and rejoins the team. Understanding why he is not playing, Bill accepts his punishment. He and Maddie have had another great week together and he feels confident that Sarah is safe tonight. All is well in his world tonight and he can be calm. During the first quarter since he can't play, he becomes the teams head cheerleader stealing Maddie's stage. Unable to be an uninvolved person, he continues to encourage his team. He gives the starting quarterback as much advice as he can. Still, despite of his best coaching efforts, the first quarter ends with the score South 3 and Seymour 10.

Calling a team huddle, Coach Mulinaro attempts to fire up everyone. However, his efforts are in vain and the look on everyone's faces reveals a problem. Finishing his pep talk, the look from the team begs the coach to insert Bill into the game. Bill's defense of Sarah's honor fills them with pride. Coach Mulinaro mulls the team input as the offense hustles back to the field and he sends the play in with Joey. As Joey turns to go in with the play, he says to the coach, "Chivalry and honor, Coach, there has to be something good about that." However, while mulling over Joey's words, the coach's silence is deafening. South runs the play, option left, and only gains 2 yards.

Standing next to Coach now, Bill looks to the field while the coach turns to him and says, "Get in there and protect our honor."

Putting on his helmet, Bill turns and says, "On my way coach," as the coach grabs his jersey.

Pulling him back, Coach gets in his face, "Denton, I'm proud of you and what you did. Now get out there and show 'em *why* you're playing tonight." Bill's heart swells in his chest. Running out to a huge roar, he gives a fist pump to the crowd. The *Maestro* is in the stadium and he has just entered the stage, calling his favorite play, Z 21 flash, for Joey. The possession clock is at 5 seconds and the *Maestro* takes the snap as the clock expires. Joey flies deep into his pattern and the ball is right on target, touchdown. It is another great performance by Bill and he runs to the end zone pumping his fist all the way. Picking up Joey, they fist pump the crowd together.

As they run off the field, Bill tells Joey, "Thanks man, I know what you did for me. You're a very special friend indeed." With the Wizard driving the offense, Eli urges the Dragon's Teeth to stiffen and counter-attack the opposing offense. The final score is South 38 Seymour 10. Chivalry and honor do count for something and vindication is sweet!

After the game, Bill and Joey want to finish the interviews quickly and go on their dates. The press interview process has begun to wear on them too. The questions are always the same. Joey receives scholarship offers from colleges now for his receiving prowess and the reporters want more of his time too. However, it is nothing like the questions they direct toward Bill. Uniquely, tonight they ask why Bill did not start the game. Bill deflects the questions to Coach who says, "It was a question of Chivalry and Honor. Bill did the right thing but we needed to keep him out for a quarter. That's enough questions along this line. In fact, let's end the questions altogether for this night."

Testing the Waters

B ill, Maddie, Joey, and McKenna go to Kristen's Burgers on their date. The atmosphere is electric as usual with kids fueling the excitement. The four of them make their way through the crowd and to a table in the back and sit with the boys and their dates. After they sit down, Maddie gazes at Bill intently and comments, "How do you handle all this? I understand the personal side of it but how do you handle all the hype and stuff? What's it like to be Bill Denton? I really want to know. I want to understand what you have to go through because I love you and care about you."

Smiling back, Bill replies, "I'll tell you later when we're alone." Maddie agrees and they continue enjoying the food and friends during the evening.

After the evening with friends ends well, Joey takes Bill and Maddie to her house and says, "Give me a call whenever you're ready to leave."

Giving a thought to future events, Bill exclaims expectantly, "Only two more weeks Joey."

Concerned by his meaning, Maddie asks intently, "Two more weeks for what?"

With a light-hearted tone, he replies, "Until I get my driver's license."

"When was your birthday," she inquires.

He answers, "My birthday was just before school started."

"So *before* we knew each other," she probes.

The tone in her question made him concerned and he reacts in kind, "*Yeah why?*" After all, this week had a very difficult beginning. The end seemed to be turning as well.

Speaking a bit sharply, she responds, "Because *if* you had a birthday *after* we met, I *wouldn't be* very happy that you *didn't* tell *me.*"

Becoming perturbed by her probing, he responds, "*Why* would you be unhappy about *that?*"

Deciding to push a little harder, she responds quickly, "Because I'd have wanted to do something *special* for you on your birthday."

Reflecting quickly on the conversation, dialing his concern back and adding restraint, he says, "No problem. I'll keep that in mind for next year."

Maddie contemplates the exchange also, "He responded better than I thought he would. Just had to push him a bit and see. He's definitely my guy. He even plans to be with me next year at this time. That's cool." Joey senses a tension in the conversation but decides it is only a battle of wits and drives off in a daze of thought.

Extending her hand for Bill, Maddie leads him into the house near the fireplace. The two of them prepare their favorite spot and curl up on the floor as usual. Breaking the tension by tickling and wrestling with him, they relax into shared kisses, hugs, and warm words for each other. Suddenly, Maddie's boldness surfaces again, "Please tell me what it's like to be you, both of you, the quarterback and the regular guy."

"Are you sure you want to hear this? It's very boring," he states.

Listening with anticipation, she responds, "Yes please."

Starting at the beginning of his day, Bill explains his daily routine in detail. "You do that *every* day," she asks disbelievingly.

Remembering another point, he continues, "Yes, that's my daily schedule, Monday through Friday except in the summer when I work out at Nalley's Extreme Fitness too."

"Ok," she says, "that all sounds like just the personal side. What about the quarterback side?"

Somewhat frustrated with her simplistic comprehension, he explains, "Maddie, you don't understand. Just as you practice your cheerleading moves and gymnastics, I have to work hard or there is no quarterback on Friday. Those morning workouts are the quarterback too."

"Wow, I didn't realize. And show time Frank," she queries with a chuckle.

Responding to the understanding light in her eyes, Bill explains with his wry smile, "That's right, it's Friday night and I have a show to put on for the paying public. Granted they do not pay me but it's my stage, my team, my game. I owe it to everyone to bring the best I have every Friday. When I step onto the field, the *Maestro* is in the building. When the game calls for it, I step to a higher level and call the *Wizard* to make an appearance. However, on the rarest of occasions, the ice-cold *Assassin* comes out to pull our butts out of the fire. Then, the game is over."

Maddie's jaw drops as she reflects quickly, "I have seen all these sides of Bill in action and not just on the field. He didn't even mention the romantic *Buccaneer* sweeping *me* off my feet or the *Knight* rushing to a friend's honor. I didn't realize he could call on so many facets of one character. He *is* Zeus."

As Maddie contemplates his words, Bill continues, "It's pretty simple really. I don't like the football side interfering with my personal side. Fortunately, it's there to call on when I need it, like Monday. I'm very protective of my friends. I don't like all the non-team stuff with reporters from all over the Midwest now. There are more and more of them weekly like sharks to a feeding frenzy. Coaches are coming to visit me and talk to me about their school. Each one tells me how much attending their school would benefit me. Then, there's the recruiting letters. I get about one a week during the season. I imagine after this season is over I'll get about 25 more during the rest of the school year."

Gaining more understanding with his words, she deduces, "*That's* what Sarah helps you track? Who they're from and what they *want?*"

Recalling memories of Sarah fondly, Bill replies proudly, "*Yes she* does. I'd throw them in a box and tell myself I'll look at them later and never would. She helped me put together a 'gracious refusal' letter and tracks the schools to which I send them."

"Is there more to your football side," she inquires.

Having so much more of his life to reveal, he responds, "Yes, there is. Television people want interviews for their sports cast. With all that, I got a letter from the country's premier sports magazine asking if I would agree to an interview providing they decide to do an article about me."

"*You have to be kidding,*" she interrupts excitedly and contemplates, "Here's *my* chance to be seen nationally. Wow, what a boost to *my* goals."

"Yeah, it sounds silly to me but I told them I would. Put all that together with the visits and meetings with little league football teams and that's the football side," Bill explains.

"Oh my gosh, I had no idea," she exclaims, "People have no clue what you go through either, how do you do it?"

Revealing his coping structure, Bill confirms, "I have good friends who are always there for me. I have grandparents and Mr. Tibbs who guide me and best of all, I have a girlfriend that I can turn to with my love and comfort and receive the same back."

Finishing their evening together in each other's arms, Bill says, "Maddie, I'd better go now. You have a competition tomorrow and you need your rest."

Ecstatic over his concern for her, she responds, "Ok, you're right. I do need my rest to give my best performance."

After Bill's phone call, Joey comes to pick him up at Maddie's house. They kiss each other goodnight while Joey waits in her driveway. After their passionate goodnight adieu, he wishes, "Good luck at the cheerleading competition tomorrow. I know you'll do very well."

Overjoyed with his confidence in her abilities, she replies, "Thanks Bill. I get to perform on *my* stage for *my* public tomorrow." South's cheerleaders are competitive cheerleaders and their next competition is in Terre Haute, Indiana all day Saturday. The site is about an hour and fifteen minutes southwest of Indianapolis.

Terre Haute

O
n the way home, Bill proposes a road trip to Joey for them both tomorrow then he asks excitedly, "What time do we leave tomorrow?"

Laughing at the thought, Joey replies, "As soon as practice is over, we're on our way. The girls have no idea we're coming." Bill and Joey plan to drive to the competition and surprise the girls Saturday.

"Yeah, I can't wait. I hope our visit doesn't throw the girls off their game," Bill says, envisioning Maddie's performance and her surprise at seeing them tomorrow. The guys show up in Terre Haute and enter the Gerstmeyer gym to view the competition. Fortunately, the girls don't see them come in. They are too busy with warm up and competition focus to be aware of who enters and leaves. The guys don't want to affect the girls' performance and plan to surprise them during the lunch break. At the break, the guys have to maneuver through the crowd leaving the gym deftly to arrive at the girls' location. No one pays any attention to the guys inching through the crowd toward the girls and Maddie and McKenna don't see Bill or Joey. The guys glide up right behind them as the girls walk out to find some food. Bill comments, "I'd sure like to eat lunch with some hot cheerleader."

"Me too," Joey chimes in.

While the girls talk with each other about the competition so far, they don't recognize the guys' voices. In response to the droning in their ears from the crowd, they turn around to tell these two guys to mind their own business. As soon as the two girls recognize Bill and Joey, their eyes open in exclamation. Running to the guys, they nearly tackle them with huge hugs while the boys throw in a couple of kisses. "What are you guys *doing* here," McKenna asks them excitedly.

"Just coming to surprise you two and support the team," Joey replies.

With her hands on her hips, Maddie warns jokingly, "That's fine as long as it's just *two* members of the team. No really, I'm just kidding. It's great of you guys to drive all the way here to watch us but then again, it's easier than flapping your arms and trying to fly here." Everyone laughs while walking out to join Maddie's parents for food in the parking lot.

Seeing the two couples walking toward them, Mr. Benn concludes, "Well, I guess you're not eating with us?"

"We can all go to the same place," Bill offers, not wanting to offend.

Catching Maddie's glare, Mr. Benn smiles and says, "Thanks but you kids go enjoy lunch. We'll meet you back here."

"Sounds good," Joey responds. The guys plus the cheerleaders find some food they all like and eat quickly. The team discusses their next routines as the guys listen intently. After lunch, the group returns to the gym to watch the remainder of the competition. Bill and Joey sit with the Benn's but are distracted constantly by people realizing who he is. Introducing themselves without hesitation, the populace wants to meet Bill or get his autograph. As the competition ends, it seems like everyone wants to talk to the quarterback. Cordially and politely, Bill moves through the crowd. Introducing Joey to everyone along the way, they juke step their way to meet Maddie and McKenna. In the throng of people, Joey ponders with awe, "Unbelievable! How bad is this going to get in the next few years? How does he deal with all this every day?"

McKenna watches the scene of the guys encircled by the seething mass with shock. "I had no idea how big a deal Bill is all over the Midwest," she contemplates.

Shifting her gaze to Joey for verification, he explains, "It's like this everywhere we go."

"Wow, how does he do it," she quizzes, amazed at the words she's heard and the things she's witnessed.

Unhappy with the situation, Maddie has seen enough and steps into the middle of the crowd. After all, this is *her* show and Bill is upstaging her in front of *her* audience. Taking his hand, she pulls him away while taking over the situation. Joey and McKenna follow her but are very confused by her actions. Was she performing a heroic rescue or upset with Bill and the crowd for upstaging *her* with *her* public? While they can't discern her intentions, they provide the trailing guard to prevent bothersome access to Bill from behind him. "He *is The Maestro*," Joey mulls again. Quickly fleeing from the crowd, Bill thanks the others outside and they get into the Benn's car with Maddie.

"See you guys after a while," he relays to Joey and McKenna.

"All right man, I'm sorry about the crowd," Joey replies. On the drive back to Indianapolis, he and McKenna discuss the events after the competition ended. They talk about Bill's adoring public and speculate the effect on his life by the time they get out of high school.

"Are you ok, Bill," Mr. Benn inquires.

Knowing this is part of his life now, Bill answers, "Yes sir, I'm fine. I'm used to the public demands for the most part. I've learned to adjust to it getting more invasive as I get older."

Looking at him with sadness, Maddie says, "You warned me about this side of your life but I had no idea the public is so frenzied."

Pondering the interruptions from the public, Bill explains, "I feel bad for those with me when the public demands my time. I don't mean for it to interrupt their lives too as their time is as precious as mine is. Maddie, you know these demands will certainly get worse as time passes. I hope you'll be all right with this." He perceives her protective nature with him as taking over each situation and that impresses him. It adds to why he loves her.

However, Maddie muses to herself, "I didn't realize I was going to have to pull him away from a horde of groupies of all ages. Today was *my show*." The Benn's take Bill to his house and wait while Bill and Maddie kiss and hug each other goodbye.

The Mustang

Hearing a deep rumbling in her driveway, the sound begs Maddie to look out the window, finding Bill with his new car. After getting his license, he used some trust fund money to get a car. It is a new 1966 Shelby Mustang GT 350H, Jet Black with two big gold stripes from front to back and a gold stripe on each rocker panel. Having five-spoke magnesium wheels, the car's drive system consists of a four-speed transmission, 289 cubic inch engine with a Holley four-barrel carburetor and a Paxton Supercharger. That configuration generates 400 horsepower and a top speed over 140 miles per hour with a deep-throated rumble heard only from a Shelby Mustang. At $5,000, it is rather expensive and soon to be a coveted classic. However, it is one awesome car for a high school quarterback. When Bill is behind the wheel, the *Maestro* in him appears and it *is* show time.

Running out quickly, Maddie shouts, "Oh my gosh! Oh my gosh! It's unbelievable."

Thrilled with her reaction, Bill entreats, "Come on and get in. We'll go to Joey's and show him the car."

As Maddie gets in but before Bill starts the engine, she probes keenly, "What does Sarah think about it?"

Confused as to whether she is "checking up" on him or is displaying a jealous streak, Bill replies with a puzzled look, "Well, she hasn't seen it yet. My plan was to show you my car."

Completely unexpected, Maddie's next words leave him dumbfounded, "She's your best friend. Why not show her the car and take her on the first ride? You and I will have a lot of riding time in this car together."

Contemplating with great confusion, he reflects mentally, "Are you *kidding* me? I can't believe what I just *heard*. My girlfriend just told me to take *another girl* for a ride in my new car. Is this *amazing or what*? Wait a minute. This makes no sense. I wonder what her *real motive* is for this move."

Although, her gesture appears genuine, she reasons, "Can I put on a show or what? After his defense of Sarah, I need him to get this out of his system and join me on *this* stage. We're a star-power couple and he needs to realize it."

Still confused, Bill probes, "Are you *sure?*"

"Yes, very sure," she clarifies, "She's special to you and I understand that. Go take her for the first ride and then you and I will go to Joey's together. Don't tell her I told you to go see her. It's *our* secret."

Napping softly, Sarah is in her room when a pleasant rumble gently wakens her as Bill pulls in the driveway. When he knocks on the door, her mom opens it. The sight of Bill fills her with surprise and she remarks, "Hello Bill, it's great to see you. What brings you by?"

Happy to be in familiar surroundings, he replies, "It is good to see you too. I have something special to show Sarah. Is she here?"

Mrs. Ormond answers, "Yes she is. Please come in and I'll get her."

As Bill enters the house, his Notre Dame Camp trophy on their mantle catches his eye. The fact that she still displays it prominently thrills him and touches his heart unexpectedly. Walking into her room, her mom says, "Wake up sleepy head. There is someone special here to see you." Strolling into the living room, Sarah glimpses him through the sleep in her eyes. Her mind drifts back to better days with him, to all those Saturdays they spent together. With her steps frozen by her thoughts, she stumbles momentarily. Seeing her halting steps, Bill inquires gently, "Sarah, are you ok?"

Reacting with muted joy, she says, "Yes, I'm fine. My feet don't appear to be awake yet. What brings you by my house? Not that I mind, but what's up?"

Pondering her muted reaction, Bill replies sheepishly, "Uh, I have a surprise in your driveway. I wanted you to see it first."

With her curiosity piquing, she inquires with a smile, "What are you up to now?" As they walk out the door, she exclaims, "Wow, I *love* the color. It's *very* sexy. Whose car is it?"

Shuffling his feet, Bill looks down and says, "Well uh, it's mine. I wanted you to be the first person to go for a ride in it." Shaking her head in disbelief, her mom smiles, remembering how good he is for Sarah and how much she misses him.

Knowing he still is dating someone else, Sarah questions, "*Me? What about Maddie?*"

"You're still my best friend, Sarah. I want *you* to be the first one to ride in it," Bill confesses his heart's true feelings. Moved by his words, she decides to let him know what he is *missing*. Jumping into his arms, she wraps herself around him. As Bill's emotions overcome his love for Maddie, he returns her embrace. Recalling what they mean to each other, they kiss each other passionately while the passion burns another impression into their minds. Their hearts miss each other so much and Sarah still loves him deep in her soul. Finally, she relaxes her full body embrace and says teasingly, "*What about a ride now?*" Unfortunately, his heart is now deeply torn.

Professing his love to Maddie yet his heart says silently, "Sarah, I love you." As he recovers his emotions, he says, "I'm so *glad* you *asked*."

As Bill and Sarah cruise the Southside, they have great time laughing and teasing with each other. Making several passes through the restaurant parking lots of the TeePee, White Castle, and Steak 'n Shake down through Jerry's restaurant in Greenwood and back, they reminisce about Saturdays and fun times together. Waving to friends who have puzzled looks at seeing them together, they relish being seen as a couple again. However, their shared time passes much too quickly and their ride has to eventually end. Expecting him to return soon, Maddie waits for him to take her with him to Joey's house to show off his car. Struggling in his heart with leaving Sarah, his mind recognizes a tear in his love between two strong girls. Reluctantly, Bill takes her home and walks her to the door. Starting through the door, Sarah turns around, pulls him close, and kisses him again passionately on his lips as they did earlier. Then, stopping suddenly and leaving him begging for more emotionally, she says, "I've wanted to do that for a long time." Rushing inside before he can say anything, she glances back at him with sparkling eyes leaving an indelible memory in his mind.

Her memory deepens the tear in his love but he cannot go back on his word. His profession of love for Maddie holds its sway over him for now and he knows she expects him to return. Leaving for Maddie's house to pick her up, his heart is now an emotional wreck. At her house, he says, "Thank you so much for allowing me to take Sarah on the first drive." Riding with Bill to Joey's house to show him the car, she doesn't ask any questions, assured that her performance around Bill will keep him with her.

Believing her plan to be successful, she reasons smugly, "After all, why would he give his love to Sarah when he has me. He said I'm the most beautiful girl on the planet. The newspaper quoted him on that and I've no competition from her, as they are only best friends. I trust him completely and know he loves me and only me. There's no room in his life for another girlfriend."

Dissonance

The season completes and is very successful. South is among the final four teams in the state football tournament but loses the championship game on a fumble at St. Joseph's two-yard line. Bill took them 88 yards in 1:54 but the fullback fumbled and South lost the ball with three seconds left. The team finishes the season 11-2 but the championship loss carves a deep impression in Bill's psyche. Purposing to avoid being in that position again, he plots his course for the future whatever the cost. He receives first team all-state honors and second team high school All-American honors, an amazing feat for a sophomore.

Maddie and Bill are fast becoming *the* couple at South and emerging as student leaders of the school. On the social side, if Bill and Maddie don't come to your party, it isn't considered a successful party. Loving this part of their relationship, she now has her stage and he makes great eye candy. Not truly caring for this aspect of their relationship, Bill wants to spend time with Maddie privately. He begins to feel that show time is not *only* on the field but anytime he is with her. In the community, they visit the elementary schools and the little leagues like a royal couple. While Bill is the quarterback, all the kids tell Maddie how pretty she is and she *craves* the attention. Although they go to church every Sunday, he feels he is there for show and not to worship. This is very troublesome, as he has never taken the praise away from God intentionally. Now he believes when he is with her at church, he is doing that very thing. In spite of his misgivings and his tugging conscience, he remains with her and they are happy outwardly to be with each other. Being role models for everyone, they carry that role in exemplary fashion. All the parents want their kids to be like Bill and Maddie.

Attempting to catch a glimpse of the couple, the crowds grow almost exponentially around them at the games while the request for Bill's time increases daily. Maddie appears very protective of him at all times but strives to receive her share of the spotlight with him. While he wants to be just a regular guy, she steers his schedule to the important things as *she* views them. Although he is happy to be with her, he would like more time away from the parties and the glitz and needs some personal downtime to recharge his emotional batteries. Refreshingly, Bill attends four camps in the summer, Texas, Notre Dame, Purdue, and Michigan. He *is* the best player at each camp and the country's premier sports magazine has a writer following him doing research. Maddie is proud of him as he shows her each of his trophies after the camp. However, remembering Sarah's wise words, he decides to keep these trophies rather than giving them to Maddie. He has no faith that she treasures them as much as Sarah did. Understanding how special he is to other people, he vows to remain humble despite the glitz and glamour clamoring around him now.

The Chosen One

About three weeks before school starts, the country's premier sports magazine contacts Bill at *Maddie's* house. Filled with excitement, Maddie listens on another phone. The representative says, "We want to do a preseason article on you for the football preview issue. We will arrange for a writer to come to Indianapolis the week before school starts. The writer will stay until after the first game during the first week of school. We plan to hold the preview issue until the writer has his article ready to print."

The first game of the new season could not have gone better if someone scripted every play and his *stage* is bigger than ever. With a responsive, highly charged audience, the *Maestro* comes to perform accordingly. The stadium roars its frenzied approval throughout the game and rises to its feet in thunderous applause for him at the end. Bill has a monster game, five touchdowns, over 400 yards passing on 28 for 30 throws. After the game, the locker room is complete chaos with local writers and now national magazine writers probing him with question after question.

When the writer finishes the article, the country's premier sports magazine publishes the story. The magazine sends the school 100 copies arriving special delivery on the next Monday. Coach Mulinaro takes a copy to Bill in his first period class. As he hands it to him, the anticipation of the moment nearly overcomes Maddie. *Expecting* to be in the same article, she *does* share the same field with him after all. Then, seeing the cover, she cannot believe her eyes that *she* is *not* on it. The cover is a full picture of Bill throwing the football. However, the caption has her in near shock saying in large print capital letters, "THE CHOOSEN ONE." In smaller letters, it says, "Bill Denton of South High School in Indianapolis *is* the best football player in the country high school or college."

"*Oh my gosh*," Maddie exclaims aloud. Shaking his head at her exclamation, he chuckles at the situation and hands the magazine to her.

Another staff member comes in and asks, "Bill, would you like the rest of the copies brought here?"

Thinking of others, he replies humbly, "I recommend that you put them in the guidance office but leave me five copies. That way other people can have their own copy. I don't want to hog them myself." However, he makes sure he saves signed copies for Mr. Tibbs, for Sarah and her family, and for Maddie.

Coach Mulinaro shakes his hand and says, "I couldn't be more proud if you were my own son. You're growing into a wonderful person not just a star athlete. It's your character of which I'm most proud."

Touched deeply by his coach's words, Bill replies respectfully, "Coach, that means so much to me coming from you. I always want to make you proud of me. I hope to never let you down even after I graduate."

The article amazes Bill with its coverage depth of him, highlighting the camps and his camp performances. It details the week of practice and the unusual occurrence if more than three throws a day hit the ground. Unlocking Bill's understanding of the game, the piece shows his ability to analyze the game in progress. Revealing the kind of person he is, it discusses his intelligence in depth. Disclosing how respected and liked he is by everyone at school and in the community, the commentary speaks of his winning smile and personality. It is a well-written article about a fine young man. With all the great personal information, the main portion of the piece will have people all over the country talking. Its headline reads like the magazine cover, "BILL DENTON: HE IS THE CHOOSEN ONE."

The article reads, "Once in a while, an athlete or an individual comes along who makes a difference in the world immediately. Something happens about which generations will talk after seeing the person in action. We are witnessing that action right now in Indianapolis Indiana. Bill Denton of South High School is the best football player in the country, high school or college. He could start for every college football team and play any position. He is 6 feet 6 inches tall, weighs 245 pounds, is fast, strong, with a great arm, and completes 77% of his passes. He breaks tackles and he *will* play professional football. Amazingly, he is only a high school junior. The football gods chose him to be the one, the one to bring glory back to any tradition rich college program that may have been down on its luck for a while. They chose him to be the one who could bring a championship trophy to a town that's never had one. I am writing this article with 25 years of sports journalism knowledge and I am 100% certain that Bill Denton is the *Chosen One*. I have *never* seen a player like him in all my years of writing. I have *never* met a finer young man off the field in my 25 years and never met anyone in any sport like him." Then the article continues to describe many other positive aspects of Bill's character, game, and intelligence.

After reading the article, Bill turns to Maddie and says with a wry smile, "I hope you can hang onto your hat. It's really going to get crazy now."

"I can only imagine," she replies with a smile, thinking, "And I'll be there on stage with you enjoying the spotlight."

By the end of the day, word spreads through the high school and community like a wildfire. In his last period class, the school secretary brings him fifteen requests for interviews from around the country.

Giving them to Maddie, he inquires, "Would you mind reviewing these. I want to know if any of them are worth the time. We can go to the TeePee tonight and decide which ones you think I should accept."

Surprisingly, Maddie isn't happy, "Why can't they let you be yourself? Everything is about the quarterback."

In reality, it is about Bill, the player and not the young man or student. They are not news but neither is Maddie, the Cheerleader, and the media does not want her on this stage. Picking her up after practice, he drives her to the TeePee in his new Mustang. When they walk into the busy restaurant, everybody wants some of his time for autographs and questions. Three reporters see him and spring to reach him like blitzing safeties ready with question after question.

Seeing his friend Carl, the manager, Bill motions him over and requests, "Can you get us a seat out of the way with some privacy please?"

Taking them back to their familiar secluded table near the romantically lit back of the restaurant, Carl requests a couple of the bulkier employees to stop anyone attempting to reach the couple. Maddie likes the throng when they *include* her in or *exclude* Bill from the spotlight. However, this evening was about Bill keeping the quarterback *and* the cheerleader from the spotlight to enjoy a quiet evening with his girl.

When they leave, Bill finds a busy Carl and says, "Thanks so much for your care of us and being so nice to us. I'll leave four tickets at the 'Will Call' window for you for Friday's game. If you want to wait after the game, I'd love to meet your family."

Graciously, Carl says, "Thank you so much for dining with us again and allowing me to serve you. I'll see you next time and thank you for the tickets."

Announcement

After the fourth game, South is steam rolling through the season. With his thoughts focused on his future, Bill strolls into the locker room to find the place a frantic madhouse. The crowd is so huge, he can hardly move and claustrophobia runs rampant. The scene is becoming dangerous for all as the public and the journalists alike crowd his teammates while they attempt to dress. Gazing at this scene, Bill decides to end the chaos before they injure one of his teammates.

Determined to be heard above the din, he shouts, "*Excuse me. Listen up. I need everybody to come into the meeting room now.*" He informs his teammates, "Don't answer any more questions for now." With everyone staring at him, he walks into the team meeting room, steps up to Coach Mulinaro's podium, and speaks, "First of all, if you're not on the team or a journalist, I must ask you to leave. The situation is becoming dangerous for all involved. We have lives other than football and want to enjoy our time as teammates and high school students. Finally this, I have an announcement to make about my future. I'm committing verbally to the University of Notre Dame and Coach Alan. The recruiting and intrusions into my personal time and my teammate's personal time has to end. By announcing now where I plan to attend, I hope it'll cut back on the pressure that all of the team feels. I want my teammates to enjoy their own college plans. I want my coaches to be able to help them without detriment from me. I don't want the students at South High School bothered as all of you try to obtain a different story angle or scoop. Please make your interview requests through the athletic office and *we'll* call you back if we want to do the story. I want to be able to relax and just play football. You can come at me with everything you've got but leave my teammates alone *unless* you want to speak with them about their play. Gentleman, we're done here tonight."

Bill's speech amazes the team. They experience one thought, "He's our leader and still he's putting our welfare before his own. We wouldn't want to get in front of those reporters and utter those demands. Certainly, we wouldn't want to be him."

After Bill dresses, he addresses the reporters one last time, "One more thing guys, Joey Sanders is one of the finest receivers in the country, honorable mention high school All-American as a sophomore. Fellas, it's not because I throw to him. It's because he's that good and I predict he'll be a first team high school All-American after this season. You guys should be writing about *him*. He leads the country in receiving yards and touchdowns. *There* is your story, fellas, not me, but him. Sure, I throw the ball but someone has to catch it and he does it better than anyone."

As Joey and Bill leave the stadium, Joey says, "Thanks for trying to help me out with college publicity."

Knowing his words to be heartfelt, Bill replies, "I wasn't trying to do you a favor. I meant every word. You *are* that good. If you continue to play the way you are now, *you'll* be first team high school All-American after this season, D 1 football all the way. I told the reporters I committed verbally to Notre Dame. I wanted to get it over with so that we all can enjoy the next two years. I don't want to have the team deal with the media pressure. By the way, do you want to go to Notre Dame with me?"

Filled with gratitude, Joey replies, "Thanks man. It's certainly something for me to think about." Laughing at the thought of four more years together, they leave with Maddie and McKenna.

The season and the team march onward relentlessly. At season's end, South wins the state championship with an undefeated record of 13-0 repairing the hole in Bill's psyche left by last season's championship loss. However, his podium experience inflames his desire for one more championship drive next year. Averaging 38 points a game, they allowed only 9 points a game on defense. Without question, they are the best team in Indiana.

Sarah's Year

With the lighting flash of Bill's announcement racing through school, Sarah receives word of his verbal commitment to Notre Dame too. Knowing Notre Dame is the only school he really wanted to attend leaves her extremely happy and proud of him. At the same time, deep sadness permeates her thoughts and emotions, "I'll no longer be helping him track his recruiting letters. At least, I'd have him at my house as a friend to help him. I've tried everything possible for a Christian young woman to try to get him to open his eyes and realize how much I love him. I should have been his girl not Maddie. I'll have to dream about what might have been. I'll dream about being by his side to protect and shield him from all the hype, media, and public requests for his time as Maddie has done. I'll always love him and want to be with him. My dating others has not been all that successful and that should tell me something. There are too many Steve Powell's and no Bill Denton's. What am I thinking! There is only *one* Bill Denton and *for now*, she has him. While Maddie and I have become good friends, there *is* something wrong with how she treats Bill. She keeps taking control when she's with him. That's not right but I can't tell him that. He wouldn't believe me anyway and it would hurt our friendship if I did. Well, God, I'll have to put him in your hands. You tell me what I need to do with him. I tried on my own and what happened? *She's* in his arms and I'm not."

Sarah's junior year is one of patience building. She plans, dates, and waits for her opening. With God working on her, she knows He will provide and her time will come. Like a female lioness, she prowls the corridors on the hunt for the right time and the right words to say to bring Bill back. While waiting for her opening, she enjoys herself with a steady guy every now and then. Dedicating herself to her schoolwork and activities, her academic goal is to be among the top ten students in school. She reasons, "I'm as much a leader as Maddie and I don't need Bill to do that. I'm strong enough on my own. I'm as pretty as she is and I'll show everyone humbly, not flaunting it. I'll bet I can be homecoming queen my senior year. In fact, I *will* be that but it'll be an uphill fight without Bill as my manager."

Enjoying hanging out with her girls, the Dirty Boys are still among her friends. She *is* that model person and student and enjoys making her final college selections. Yet unlike every other girl in school, *she* sees Maddie's relationship growing shakier the more Maddie tries to control Bill. Great memories with him flood her mind continually, hardening her desires in their emotional forge. Her most poignant memory is Bill riding into the cafeteria on his white charger, protecting her honor from Steve Powell's evil intentions toward her. Never forgetting that day, Bill's chivalry, or the two-punch thrashing Steve received, Bill remains her "knight in shining armor." Knowing that constant prayer works wonders for her inner beauty, outwardly the other kids and Bill consider her the prettiest girl in school without question. Maddie lost that title due to her demanding nature. It's only a matter of time before Bill realizes that too.

South Bend Visit

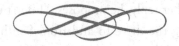

D ecember arrives very soon and Bill reveals to Maddie excitedly, "I have to go to Notre Dame next Saturday for an interview with some South Bend reporters. Would you like to go with me?"

Realizing she will not be in the spotlight, she replies indifferently, "I'm not sure I want to drive that far. I'll let you know."

Replying to her cool response, he pleads, "You won't need to drive there yourself. You can ride in *my* car."

Answering with apparent disinterest, she, "As I said I'll let you know." She contemplates, "After all, what is there for me? It's his interview not mine."

Her cool reception to his invitation puzzles Bill but he says, "Ok, that's fine. Let me know your decision early this week." Pondering her lack of interest, he considers, "I'd never have to beg Sarah to go with me." During the season, he began noticing Maddie's growing apathy and tiredness with all the requests for his time where she isn't the center of attention. He reasons, "Certainly, it's not easy to being my girlfriend but at least she could show interest in the same things I do. I try to include her as much as possible. I thought she'd be happy about a trip together."

Reflecting on future possibilities and interrupting his thought processes, Maddie probes, "How long do you think this will take?"

Believing he knows the interview parameters, Bill answers, "It is only two reporters. So it shouldn't take too long."

Indifferent to his desire, she replies somewhat sarcastically, "I don't mind if *I'm* in the interview too. Remember, I want *my* time with you too."

Confused by her reply, he proposes, "I don't understand. We'll be together during the drive to and from South Bend. I thought we'd have lunch and dinner together too. It'll be a nice day together except for the interview process. I'm sure we'll have a good time. Don't you think so?"

Not happy with the impending process, she replies curtly, "*Yes. Sure.* Whatever *you'd* like."

Unhappy with her tone, Bill adds, "After we get back, I thought I'd spend some time with my guys I haven't been out with them in a while and they plan to do something next Saturday night." Agreeing reluctantly to his pleas and offers, she believes she will be on the interview stage with him in South Bend.

Andy Opens Eyes

ndy is in bed and hears the sound of a basketball bouncing outside next door. It is 40 degrees outside and he ponders intensely, "Why in the world is someone playing basketball at 11 o'clock at night?" Peering out the window and finding *Bill* shooting hoops, he puts on a sweatshirt and ambles over to Bill's driveway.

Confused at Bill's nocturnal activity, Andy probes, "Well, what the heck are you doing out here?"

"Contemplating," Bill answers.

"I'll bite. What about," Andy inquires and prepares for the worst.

Deciding to air his emotions, Bill opens up, "I feel bad for Maddie. She puts up with all the requests for my time knowing it takes away from our time together. She's always there and always tries to shield me as much as she can. She steps in and answers many of the questions herself. Now, it's more than the local media. Next Saturday, I have to go to Notre Dame to speak with a couple of South Bend reporters. She isn't happy that it'll take up our entire day. I told her we'd have fun and be together all day. I told her that when we return, I was going to hang with you guys. It's just hard on her being my girlfriend."

Hearing enough unwarranted self-deprecation, Andy begins to reply, "Bill, you know that I've always been straight with you. I don't think that's it at all."

Puzzled, Bill inquires, "Go on. I trust what you have to say. Tell me what you think it is."

Taking a deep breath, Andy says, "The boys and I have talked about Maddie's odd behavior as of late. From our point of view, it has nothing to do with her protecting you. You like the stage and being the headliner on that stage, like *Broadway*. Maddie likes the stage too. Though you both have that in common, she wants to be the center of attention and gets that attention in *your* spotlight. However, when the game is over, you're done or so you think. Whether you like it or not, the show is nearly 24 hours a day now and it's nationwide as well. The country's premier sports magazine articles saw to that. My friend you *are* the chosen one. Every guy in America wants to be you but few can ever approach where you are or going. Maddie realizes that too. For her though, the show's always been 24 hours a day. For Maddie Benn, everywhere she is *the performance is also*, drawing all eyes to *her* and you're the *operator* that shines the spotlight on her. When you go out with her, you're the *eye candy* for her arm because you're the *quarterback*. However, I know you like Maddie sharing your stage with you."

As Bill starts to interrupt, Andy says, "Wait, just listen and let me finish. When you two started to date, the show was for the most part just around you. She enjoyed being with Bill. Then, people noticed who *she* was because of being with the *quarterback*. She *craved* the part as the star quarterback's girlfriend. As time went on, she made the show about *her* when you thought she was looking out for *you*. Her performance was as Bill's girl taking care of him. So, it was about *her* and being center stage. It *was* all about Maddie Benn. Now that the show has become all about *you* due to the national attention, we certain she doesn't like that at all. She's trying to control *you and her stage too*. In her mind, the question is, 'What about *me*?' You *know*. Look at *me. I'm Maddie Benn*. She can't handle the spotlight and national news all being about you not *her*. Simply put, I apologize for my next statements. We think she's self-centered, controlling, demanding, and high-maintenance. She wants to be with the *quarterback* not Bill Denton and make the show revolve around *her*. It's only *our* opinion and observations. You should do what you think is right but from what we can see, she's going to get *much* worse. We're all here for you and we'll support you in any way possible. You're a great friend and we all feel it's our place to take care of each other. We know *when* your plans succeed, you won't forget about us. We know you'll be there for us regardless of how famous you get."

Saddened but understanding of his friend's genuineness, Bill says, "Thanks for being straight with me as always. I value your friendships and observations. Your words explain many things I've had concerns about with Maddie lately. For now, I'll still be with her but we'll see what happens with the Notre Dame visit. She wasn't thrilled at all about going there or with me spending next Saturday with you guys."

Concerned for Bill's emotional well-being, Andy says, "Please don't lie to yourself and everyone else. You know she'll not change. I'm going to tell you something we all have held back until now."

Expecting worse news, Bill quizzes with hesitation, "Ok, what's that?"

Andy continues, "We know you love Sarah but you're afraid you *lost* her. This is why you try to be friends just to keep her in your life. However, she never had a problem being the supportive friend for you. You think about the two girls. Which one is beautiful, inside and outside? Which one gave you a full body hug and kiss when you took her for a ride in your car? Which one shows you love in so many different ways and never asks anything for herself? We know this because she told us. She still talks to us all the time about *you*. She asks how everything is going for *you* and she tells us how much she misses *you*. One last thing that you'll not here from anyone but us, *she still loves you. Her kisses should have said it all.*"

Notre Dame Press Conference

addie decides it is a good idea to go with Bill to South Bend. Saturday is a beautiful December day in Indiana. The snow has disappeared from the roads, making the trip relatively safe. Brushstrokes of white blanket the ground and trees lightly. The Master Painter provides scenes of joy that bring thoughts of Christmas and love to the travelers. The view transforms Maddie back to her previously happy self, smiling, laughing, and telling Bill how much she loves him. Upon their arrival at Notre Dame, the beautiful campus and their wonderful treatment by everyone impress Maddie. Even after Andy's revelation, still Bill makes it a point to introduce her as his girlfriend to everyone they meet.

Walking together to the coach's office, they proceed to the Irish team meeting room to talk to the perceived two reporters. Upon entering the room, near shock fills them both as seventy-five reporters from all over the country wait to interrogate them. The coach escorts Bill to the podium and has Maddie take a seat on the side of the room. To her chagrin and frustration, she becomes a wallflower not the center stage attraction in this testosterone-charged environment. The interview process takes an hour and a half, simmering her to a full, irritated boil. Bill finishes, "Thank you for the opportunity to represent Notre Dame and play for such a great university. We appreciate how nice everyone has treated us today." Maddie remains silent as the snow outside but her look shouts her exasperation.

As Bill walks, Maddie pouts her way back to the car. When they get inside, he asks with concern, "Maddie, is something wrong? Are you ok?"

Pouting over not being center stage, she replies curtly, *"I'm fine."*

Thinking that she is hungry from the trip and the probing, he inquires warmly, "Would you like to stop at a restaurant and have a nice meal before we leave?"

With the same curtness, she answers, *"I'm not hungry."* The scenery turns ominously dark in the roar of her silence on the drive back.

When Bill pulls into her driveway, he stares and probes, "Ok, you gave me the silent treatment all the way home and I did nothing to deserve that. You refused my offer to take you to a nice restaurant near campus also. What in the world is wrong?" His mind flashes, "Sarah never treated me like this."

With growing perturbation, Maddie answers again curtly, *"Nothing is wrong."*

He probes with anxiety, "Please tell me what's wrong? We should not leave things unsaid tonight. Besides, I still want to meet with the Dirty Boys later."

With anger overflowing, Maddie explodes, *"After what happened today, are you really going to meet the guys tonight?"*

Using great restraint, he replies calmly, "Yes I am. I've not spent any time with them in quite a while."

With exasperation flowing strongly, she erupts further, *"You've not spent time with them, what about me? When do I get my time with you?"*

Adding more conviction to his arguments, Bill replies more

strongly, "Maddie, we spent the *entire* day together. However, you chose to act the way you did and *spoil* that time."

Reacting to but ignoring his chastisement, she vents, *"I didn't like sitting on the wall through that long news conference. There were only supposed to be two reporters there and I should have been on the stage with you."*

Detailing the situation, he describes, "They informed me that only two would be there. However, I don't have any control over that. Notre Dame set up the news conference and I have to do things the university's way."

Centering on her needs only, Maddie reacts abruptly, *"What about what I want? What about me?"* Finally, he sees the person about whom Andy warned him. This entire conversation has been about her and nobody else.

Astounded with her reaction, he explains, "Of all people, I'd have thought you would be the one who knows what it's like being in the spotlight."

Focusing her tirade, Maddie's anger reaches critical mass and triggers, *"I know. It isn't about me. It's all about you."*

Employing a highly restrained nature, he explains again calmly, "Maddie, it's through the efforts of my team and me that I won a scholarship to Notre Dame. The reporters didn't come to interview you because you'll not be playing quarterback at Notre Dame. For the same reason, I wouldn't presume to be the cheerleader that you are on this stage here. You'll be the great college cheerleader that I cannot be. My stage is at that university and because of that, nationwide. People all over the country want my time. I need you to understand the magnitude of that."

Demanding, Maddie hears enough and yells, *"I understand it's all about you. When does it get to be about me?"*

"That tears it. Sarah would never treat me this way," he reasons. Tiring quickly of her tirade because of what he is and what he does, he understands that the quarterback and Bill Denton are one in the same. Having to do everything the right way, he speaks calmly, "Maddie, you have no idea what my life is like now or is going to become. I thought you did and I thought you could handle it. As time progressed during this last year and a half, it's become clear that you need the spotlight to shine on you at all times. I can't survive in that glare. I expected you to be a more supportive and protective person."

Suddenly, Maddie realizes what she has done and asks him fearfully, "Bill, what are you saying?"

Realizing their relationship is broken, he explains its status calmly, "I need someone who is more supportive and unselfish. I didn't want to do this because of my love for you. However, I see we have come to view life differently than at first and have grown apart. We need go our separate ways. I can't go out with you anymore. We can end this as friends if you'd like. I still love you but we'll only end up hurting each other and resenting it."

Shock and realization overcome Maddie as the tears begin to stream down her cheeks and she says, "You're *right*, Bill. *I'm not* happy in your shadow. I *thought* we'd always *share* the spotlight but I see that *can't* happen. Since I can't *share* your spotlight, I'll *continue* to have a problem with this until we *hurt* each other. So, we *can't* stay together but I still love you too." The anger gives way to heartache and regret. Saying tearfully, "Goodbye, Bill," she bolts out of his car and rushes into her house.

Pizza Night with the Boys

Sadness grips Bill as he drives to D. J.'s to meet with his friends and dull his pain. At D. J.'s house, he strolls up the drive to meet the guys and tell them what happened. After explaining the problems of the day, he tells the guys they were right. He comments on the situation, "She's all about herself and kept saying 'me, me, me,' throughout our conversation. I noticed changes in our relationship some time ago but I didn't want it to be true. So, it took me by surprise and she's no longer part of our circle of friends." Not discussing anything more about her, Bill turns to Pete and D.J. and says, "You're the good time guys. So what are we going to do tonight to have some fun?" Earlier in the evening, Sarah called D. J. to invite the guys to the Pizza Inn and then to catch a movie with them. All the guys know about this except Bill.

Completing his thoughts verbally, D. J. says, "Let's get a pizza and then go to the movies. It'll be a great time and you need it after today." Everyone agrees that it sounds like fun. With impish glee, D. J. hides the fact that Sarah and the girls will be there. Sarah expects the five of them only, which includes Joey now and believes Bill is on a date with Maddie.

As the group walks into the Pizza Inn, the counter hides the back tables from view. Walking to the counter, the boys place their orders and make their way to the back tables as usual. Sarah and the five girls are sitting where the Dirty Boys usually sit. Bill is the last one past the counter as he pays the bill. While the other guys hide him from Sarah's view, they also hide her from his view. With an obscured view, she thinks it is only the five guys and invites the group to join the girls. Halfway to the table, Bill almost comes into view, as it is hard to hide his physique for long. Looking past them toward the counter again, her eyes meet his eyes. Fresh from the pain of the day, Bill's heart melts at seeing her again and he whispers, "Sarah," as his face bursts into a huge smile. "And she's still wearing the ruby necklace," his mind marvels! Sarah's heart leaps and urges her body to run to meet him as her smile echoes his. Listening to her heart, she rushes with joy to his open arms. With their arms longing for the other's touch, they hug each other tightly.

Suddenly, realizing she is *not* the girl that should be in his arms right now, Sarah questions, "Why are you here without Maddie?" Hesitating with his response, Bill continues to hold her desperately.

Finally, he says, "I'm glad you're here instead. I've missed you so much."

His words raise her curiosity and she probes more deeply, "Bill, where's Maddie?"

Realizing that his caress is *not* enough to satiate her concern, he shuffles his feet and explains, "Maddie and I had a talk today. We both agreed we view life differently and because of our differences, we both thought it best if we stopped seeing each other."

Concerned with his next answer but inwardly elated, Sarah probes, "Are you ok with that?"

With his wry smile popping on his face, he answers boldly, "It turns out she really wasn't the girl for me. I know there is only one girl for me." Knowing by his look that he means her, Sarah holds her ruby necklace close to her heart. No one mentions Maddie's name again the remainder of the evening.

The evening is only just beginning. The Dirty Boys including Joey each pair up with one of the FGS girls. Joey figures when McKenna gets the story from Maddie and he tells her Bill was right, he won't be dating a cheerleader either. Besides, he *is* one of the boys now and the boys stick together. Not wanting to stop dating McKenna, however, Joey knows she *is* one of Maddie's girls and she probably won't want to continue dating him for that reason alone. Sarah and Bill have melded their minds and hearts once again. The scene around them fades as their eyes fixate on each other. The joy of the slightest touch sends waves of bliss sweeping over them both. Their rapture sweeps them to a different time, not so long ago and everyone else knows not to disturb their euphoria. Back together again, they hang out and enjoy each moment of the evening. The scene convinces everyone that time *does* indeed stand still.

Movie Night

The spectators to this blissfulness interrupt with laughter, "Hey, you two want us to leave you here or do want to go the movie. We need to leave or we're going to be late." Strolling to the cars while enjoying each other, the group leaves for the movies. The car arrangement plan is to let Bill and Sarah make up for lost time. The two of them drive to the theatre alone in his car. The other ten of them jam into two cars and follow, discussing the implications of events occurring in the lead car. Upon arrival at the theater and almost as they enter, the other patrons recognize Bill and Sarah. People come over for autographs, talking football, and Notre Dame. While Bill is cordial to everyone and thanks each person, he walks unceasingly to the ticket counter with Sarah. The others in the group purchased their tickets earlier during the delay and await the two at the entry doors.

Arriving at the ticket counter, Bill requests, "Two tickets, please."

The manager says, "I know you kids. Thanks for the great football season. Give them both a pass. They don't need a ticket."

Immediately, Bill responds, "Thank you sir. That means a lot."

Taking Sarah's hand again, he notices her face register the shock that he didn't *insist* on paying. "Is this the same Bill that I knew or has Maddie corrupted him?" she ponders.

While walking into the theatre, Sarah gently probes, "The Bill I knew wouldn't have accepted those tickets without paying. You've *changed* a little bit from the Bill I love."

Hearing her words in his heart, he asks softly, "Have I *really* changed that much?"

Sarah says, "Well, there was a time when you'd insist on paying for the tickets."

Chuckling, he says, "Don't worry Sarah. I've not gone materialistic on you. I realize that these folks are genuinely doing this out of the goodness of their hearts. It's their way of connecting to the game. Besides, I realize that I'm hurting them by refusing their gestures. I began to notice the hurt and embarrassment in their faces. It's not worth that hurt to argue about whatever someone is doing for me. I hope that not paying for the tickets doesn't upset you."

His words assure her he has changed very little. Sarah responds, "No at all. I've kept tabs on you. I watched you slowly bring your football side together with your personal side. It's making you more wonderful than you were already."

Suddenly filled with concern, he inquires playfully, "What do you mean you keep *tabs* on me?"

Chuckling, she says, "At least one of your Dirty Boys is in every class I have and I keep asking them how you are doing."

With her words breaking his heart, the tears start to trickle down his cheeks in the darkened theatre. "You're still taking care of me aren't you," Bill asks with fond memories of earlier days with her.

Sarah's love beams from her face and she responds, "Yes I am because I want to do so and I understand who and what you are. I want you to be the best you can be as I'm trying to be that too. I want to be the loving and supportive girl you need." Her words swell his heart with emotion and he knows why she *is* his best friend.

Overcome by the moment, he says, "You are and always have been." In his heart, he knows she is and always will be the one he wants by his side. Amazed by his words, she envisions, "This night just keeps getting better. I'm sure glad I invited the guys for pizza and a movie with the girls and me tonight."

After Bill and Sarah select their seats, the rest of their friends give them some space, sitting a few rows away. Nervously, he stretches his arm around her shoulder and draws her next to him. As the love in her heart urges her on, she rests her head on his shoulder and sighs with relief. Feeling the love in the moment, he reveals softly, "I miss holding you, talking with you personally, and spending time with you." The emotion of having her so close again draws out his love for her. As he leans over to give her a kiss, she still does not trust her emotions and turns her cheek to him. Seeking to dispel her emotional concerns, he whispers, "My heart longs to be with you and you need to be with me." Gently caressing her face with his hand, he turns her face towards him and kisses her warmly on her lips, savoring her touch in his yearning heart. Sarah gives way to her heart and presses his lips gently in return. An eternity of waiting ends in that moment as time stretches for them alone. To their friends, however, the scene is much too brief as the love overflows to them as well.

Flooded with her heart's joy, she seizes the momentary break and kisses him again as her mind wanders, "Wow. Maybe, just maybe, I'll get to hear more of his love for me but this was great. I'm going to enjoy this now." His mind wanders as well, "*She's* really mine and not just as a friend. Andy was right. *Her kisses do say it all.*"

While leaving the theatre, Jordon, the self-charging battery of the group, asks eagerly, "What are we going to do now. It's only 10:30 and there's still plenty of time to do stuff." Jordon *always* wants to go all night, every night.

Interjecting her own ideas, Sarah answers, "I don't know what the rest of you have planned, but Bill and I are going back to my house to do some heart mending."

Turning to Bill with a huge smile, Jordon exclaims, "You sir *are* the man!" Everyone laughs while Bill and Sarah drive off to her house.

As the couple walks into her house, Sarah calls, "Mom, Dad, I've brought someone to see you." Bill and Sarah stand next to each other in the living room holding hands. Walking into the living room, her parent's faces break into smiles.

Knowing how much Sarah missed not being with him, they each give him a hug and relate, "It's great to see you, Bill." Additionally, her mom whispers, "You know we both miss having you here, Bill, but Sarah has missed you terribly."

"Ok mom, what did you say to Bill," Sarah questions.

"Nothing dear, you two have fun," her mom grins as she walks away. Then, the two parents walk back down the hall arm in arm leaving Bill and Sarah alone again in the living room. Holding Sarah close, he loses himself again as he looks in her twinkling eyes.

While under her spell, he intones, "I couldn't be happier than right here. I missed you so much. I'm exactly where I need to be, next to you."

Responding in kind, she whispers, "I've missed you beside me and here at the house too." Their hearts quickly long for the sanctuary of the couch. There is no need for shared words, as their hearts know what to do. Glancing at her with a warm smile, Bill moves toward the couch as Sarah gets their blanket with a grin. They snuggle in perfect harmony on the couch while their hearts bask in love's emotional glow. Sarah shares, "At the concession stand, Andy revealed to me your real discussion with Maddie. I'm sorry that you both had to go through that. However, I'm happy for myself that it led you back to me. Thank you for respecting her feelings too and not discussing your conversation with her. It makes me love you even more." The words flowed from her heart but her mind is still unsure.

As they lie on the couch, Sarah adjusts her body from snuggling to facing Bill. She has a bold thought that causes her to probe.

"I guess you aren't going to the Christmas dance at school now, are you," she inquires.

"You know that's a funny thought but I guess not. Really, I *was* hoping to go," he reveals.

"Because it's another stage for you," Sarah jokes.

Opening his heart to her, Bill says, "No honestly, I pictured how beautiful you'd be in my mind. I wanted to see the reality of your beauty in your Christmas dress for myself."

Stunned by his words, a disbelieving Sarah responds, "Yeah right. You're just teasing me."

"Really Sarah, I'm *very serious*," he replies, "I was going to be with Maddie but I expected to see *you*."

Somewhat embarrassed by his admission, Sarah chuckles, "I'm sorry but you would have wasted your time because I wasn't going."

"Why not," he questions considering her beauty, grace, and popularity.

"I didn't want my parents to spend so much money on a dress and accessories for a one-time date with a guy," Sarah explains.

"You're still beautiful whether you were at the dance or not," he clarifies. Suddenly formulating a plan, he smiles wryly, and halts any further conversation about it. With the dance being next Saturday, they decide to hang out at her house as popcorn and TV sound so much better than a stuffy, old dance. While Sarah agrees with that assessment, Bill has an alternate reality in mind.

The Christmas Dance

Sarah arrives home from school late Friday afternoon. Hearing the door open, her mom says, "Sarah, a package arrived for you today but it doesn't say who sent it. Were you expecting something?"

Answering quickly, she replies, "No mom, I have no clue who sent it." Entering into the kitchen, she and her mom begin to open the package. As they open the lid, a hand-written note appears inside. Grabbing it excitedly, Sarah begins to read.

> *Sarah,*
>
> *This is for you to wear to the dance tomorrow night. I will pick you up at 7:00 pm. After the dance, we will go to the same steakhouse we went to the first Sunday we went to church together. I made an appointment for you to get your hair done at 2:00 pm at the salon in the mall. I chose the dress and shoes for you myself. I know you will be the most beautiful girl there. Don't bother trying to find me to*

tell me we aren't going. We are going to the dance!

Love, Bill

As she unwraps the package, she removes the box lid carefully. Suddenly, Sarah bursts into an astonished smile and exclaims, "Oh mom! Look!" The outfit is a spectacular, deep indigo designer dress with matching high-heel shoes. The cut and color say expensive to Sarah and her mom and its beauty stuns them both. As she slips on the dress and shoes in her room, she assesses her look in the mirror with amazement as the clothes fit perfectly. Gliding into the kitchen, she models the outfit for her mom.

The vision of Sarah's beauty amazes even her mom and radiates on her face as she exclaims, "Sarah, you're so beautiful in that dress and it fits you perfectly." Seeing the perfect cut of the dress on Sarah, her mom wonders, "How did Bill know what sizes to buy? Wait, it's Bill and he always seems to know what to do."

At exactly 7:00 pm, Bill knocks on the door, wearing a dark blue suit, crisp white shirt and a power tie. As always, he looks like a movie star walking off the pages of a fashion magazine. Opening the door, her parent's stand speechless looking at this sharply dressed young man coming for their daughter. "Hello Mr. and Mrs. Ormond, is Sarah ready," he inquires as they invite him into the living room. While her parents remain in the room to watch his face, Sarah makes her entrance. The vision of her beauty melts his heart as time slows dramatically. As his knees weaken, he loses his grip on the small box in his hand. Fumbling to catch it before it falls to the floor, he chuckles. Regaining his strength and nerve, he confesses, "This is the *other* gift I've wanted to give you for so long. It seemed to be perfect for a certain beautiful *doctor* who cared so much for me all this time."

Opening the box he handed to her, tears begin to trickle down her cheeks and she regrets, "Bill, it's beautiful but I can't accept this. It is too much money to spend."

Responding quickly, he says, "Sure you can. You're worth every bit of this. I won't take it back." Sarah shows the 2-karat diamond necklace to her mom.

Insisting, her mom explains, "Bill, you need to take this back. It's too much for you to spend."

Gathering his courage, he explains, "Mrs. Ormond, I can't take this back. It explains to you and Sarah everything that she means to me and has done for me. Most important it expresses how I feel about her. Besides, it compliments her dress beautifully." His words cause Sarah and her parents to acquiesce finally and Bill helps her put it on. Reveling in the vision before him, he says, "I thought you were beautiful before but my eyes deceived me. My heart convinces me that I never saw your real beauty until today." As he dries her tears gently, Sarah illuminates the room with her incredible smile. After she freshens her makeup lightly with her mom's help, Bill takes her hand and they leave for the dance.

Rather than driving to the dance, Bill seems to be driving elsewhere. Her mind races to an earlier difficult date, "The direction isn't right and he's making all the wrong turns. I've been here before but never with Bill." Apprehensively, Sarah finally speaks up and questions, "Are we going someplace before the dance?"

With his plan working to perfection, he answers with a big smile, "Nope, we're on our way to the dance."

Looking with concern at her watch, she urges, "Well, if we don't hurry soon, we're going to be late and it's not fun to walk in late."

Finally revealing his plan with a smile, he explains, "Being late is all part of my plan. I want us to be late."

Befuddled by his response, she probes, "Why in the world do you want us to be late?

"Because I like the stage," he responds in a joking fashion.

"Okay, I *know* that but I thought your stage was just for football," she responds with exasperation.

Full of love and wonder for the beauty sitting next to him, he reveals everything, "It's not my stage tonight. It's yours."

Slightly confused but seeing the love in his face, Sarah exclaims, "Say what? I don't think I heard you. Repeat that one more time but slowly so my ears can catch up."

Laughing and shaking his head, "Yes, you heard me right. The stage is all yours tonight and no one will even see me because you're so beautiful. When we stroll into the dance, everyone will stop what they're doing and gaze in your direction. Your face and smile will illuminate the room, as people stare in awe at your beauty. All of your girlfriends will come up to you and fawn over your dress and your great look. Their boyfriends will not be able to keep their eyes off you and no one will even know I'm there. Your presence and aura will flow throughout the room and electrify everyone. You won't need a spotlight because your beauty will radiate light to the darkest corners of the room. Tonight the stage and the show are one in the same and they are you."

Red-faced by Bill's love and adoring words, she blushes as she inquires, "Do you really mean those words or are you just being nice?"

"From the innermost corners of my heart, I mean those words sincerely. You watch when we go in. It's what will happen. Really," he convinces.

Everyone has been at the dance for at least ten minutes, enjoying the mastery of the set decorators. Red candy-cane stripes encircle the white doorpost of the entry welcoming visitors to an enchanted village, a forest of lighted evergreens, and billows of angel hair snow. Overhead, layers of streaming clouds dance above the couples on the floor. A full moon created by a golden-filtered spotlight glows above a painted mural from the book, The Night Before Christmas, gives a warm glow to the dancers and settings around them. Other painted murals adorning the walls mirror the story from the book and delight dancers throughout the evening. A large lighted and fragrant balsam fir decorates the center of the floor around which the couples dance. Bathed in spotlights, the dance band emanates familiar tunes from one corner of the winter wonderland. Yet all this delight is soon to become awe-inspiring.

As the couple enters the Christmas Village like royalty, they are fashionably late by design. Seeing Sarah walking through the door, one of the spotlight operators swings his filtered beam onto them. Suddenly, everyone in the place stops mid-action and gazes with awe at the couple captured in its glow. Basking in the attention, Sarah glides radiantly into the room with Bill attending her every move. He whispers while smiling from ear to ear, "I told you this would happen." Seizing the moment, he steps slightly aside and with a gesture of his arm, presents her to the adoring throng gathering just outside the light. For the next, fifteen minutes they graciously ease their way to their table through the onlookers. Finally, the spotlight leaves its object of desire and returns to its banal existence illuminating the band. Tonight, all creation wants to stand with Sarah. Contented with the unfolding play before him, Bill is enraptured to be with and yet protect her from the well-wishers. Whispering within the din, he inquires, "Would you like some refreshments, my queen?" She giggles affirmatively. Obedient to her request, he excuses himself from the group.

Once he is out of view, Jordon hurries over to Sarah and whispers, "I'll have the band play some slow dance music. You need to get him on the dance floor or he's going to be a wallflower all night. He really can dance but he needs to be on stage to start him up."

Looking at the normal jokester in disbelief, Sarah questions, "Are you *kidding* me?"

Jordan replies, "Really, I'm very serious this time." Bill returns to the table with the refreshments. As he sets the sodas on the table, the slow dance music starts to play.

Before he can sit down, Sarah grabs his hand and pulls him to the dance floor. Grumbling all the way, he protests, "I don't dance. I just shuffle my feet until I slowly lose my rhythm."

Seeing through his objections, Sarah retorts, "Yes *you do* because Jordon told me." Finally, seeing his protests are in vain, he shakes his head and follows her lead. Secretly, he has taken dance lessons for many years because he wanted to learn to dance and to help with his on-field coordination. Finding an open spot on the floor, like Fred and Ginger, the couple takes the proper starting dance position for the strains echoed by the band. The stage calls Bill to display his prowess and he takes the lead for Sarah graciously. As the pair on the floor stuns everyone with their graceful moves and fluid lines, no other couple can believe their eyes. Sarah and Bill appear as one while they execute move after move and lose each other in the joy of the moment. While gliding around the floor, their hearts fix their eyes lovingly on each other. Their smiles bear witness to their enjoyment of the other's touch and nearness as the room disappears in clouds of adoration. The other dance couples cease their shallow imitation and begin clearing the dance floor to view the magical scene. Quickly, everyone surrounds the dance floor and watches the royal couple with amazement. When the music ends, Bill and Sarah look around to find everyone clapping for them with huge smiles.

Suddenly, the band strikes up the opening notes of the Tango as Jordon rushes from the bandstand. A spotlight operator swings his light around to present the couple to the adoring fans. Bill smiles, nods toward Sarah, and whispers, "I'm going to kick Jordon's butt."

With a puzzled look, Sarah questions, "*Why?* I'm *enjoying* this."

Responding to the music and the crowd's anticipation, he utters, "I hope you know how to Tango." Hugely surprised, Sarah shakes her head in a negative response. Bill instructs, "Just follow my lead. I'll tell you what to do and when. Just let go and have fun." Catching up to the music, he holds her in the Tango's opening position. Suddenly on cue, they begin their moves again. Fluidly and in perfect harmony with the band's sounds, the pair moves around the empty dance floor as the spotlight traces their form. Again, they lose themselves in each other's gaze and touch as the room fades around them. Near the end of the dance, he tutors, "Sarah, I'm going to spin you out to the right. When I spin you back in, jump into my arms, ok?" With sheer enjoyment on her face, she nods yes and executes the move with perfection. The surrounding couples erupt in frenzied cheers and joyous clapping for the witnessed performance. "Go with me on this encore," Bill whispers. As he spins Sarah her out to the left, he stops, bows, and presents her to others at arm's length. The crowd's roar increases mightily. While everyone continues to clap, Bill steps back again and points to her. Not wanting to receive these accolades alone, Sarah glides next to him and embraces him lovingly. At her heart's urging, she gives him a long, passionate kiss on the lips to the delight and awe of those viewing the scene. Because of the crowd's joy and it's Bill and Sarah, the dance chaperones leave them alone. When the shared kiss ends finally, her emotions overflow with joy at the unbelievable events of the evening and how he made her feel that she ruled at the center of this wondrous hamlet. Everyone runs to them. Eventually making their way back to their table through the enrapt throng, they sit with their friends and enjoy their praise. The evening passes too quickly after transitory words and more dancing while Bill and Sarah browse through the village, hold hands, and catch stolen kisses in the forest.

After the dance ends, they eat a late dinner at the steakhouse. Driving back to Sarah's house, she confesses with a smile, "Now it's your turn. When we get to my house it's going to be all about you." At her heart's demand, she kisses him on his cheek and continues with a tease, "There's more where that one came from."

Having a good idea of her meaning, Bill replies, "I'm looking forward to that." After this wonderful evening, he will be very gentle with her psyche and continue to treat her like a queen. After the bad date earlier this year and even though she's with Bill, her parents wait for the couple to arrive home.

Seeing the joy on their faces, her mom asks excitedly, "How was your date, dear? I want to know everything about the evening." Starting with their drive to the dance and ending with their trip home, Sarah details the evening's events and her heart's deepest desires. Finally, seeing the love emanating from his face, her mom questions, "Bill, did you have a good time too?"

With a huge smile, he says, "I truly did Mrs. Ormond but Sarah was the star tonight. I wish you could have seen her dance. She was the perfect partner, like Fred and Ginger. Everyone will remember how she ruled tonight. My queen was *so* beautiful."

Her parents leave the room with great joy flooding their hearts for their daughter. While she holds her diamond necklace near her heart, she muses, "My happiness has returned." Bill and Sarah make it a perfect evening together on their couch wrapped in each other's love.

The Buzz

Bill and Sarah's performance at the dance has the cafeteria electrified with amazement Monday morning. Everyone sitting with her praises how great she looked while others randomly interrupt those at the table with additional acclaim. When Sarah responds to the inquiries about the dress, the inquiring girls can't believe Bill chose the outfit himself and bought it for her. The envy among the other girls at South for her grows rapidly. The girls' awareness of Bill's special qualities spreads like a firestorm reaching even Maddie. One of Sarah's friends inquires with a smile, "Do you know of any more like him?"

Responding to the question with a huge smile she says, "As far as I know, there isn't anyone. He's one of a kind." Looking for Sarah this morning, Bill walks into the cafeteria to the applause of all the girls as Sarah's embarrassment and love for him grows. While sitting with several of the cheerleaders, Maddie gets up suddenly to talk to him. As Sarah's friends watch with apprehension, Maddie stops Bill to make a last attempt to win him back.

Fearing the worst for Sarah, they warn, "Maddie stopped *Bill* and she's *talking* to him. You need to get over there and *rescue* him." With a loving, knowing smile, she responds, "Girls, you don't have to worry for me because I'm not worried at all. Watch how real love handles itself." Sarah's heart knows he's coming to be with her and Maddie hasn't a ghost of an opportunity. They watch the play unfold before them as Maddie, having heard about the dress and the dance, makes her plea to Bill.

Attempting to reach his forgiving heart, she says, "Bill, I'm so sorry. I've had a lot of time to think about us. I really want to be the girl you want me to be. I can be everything you want. I miss you terribly. Can we still be together?"

After listening to her pleas, he says, "Maddie, I want you to be yourself. I don't want you to change for me because I'm not the person you want in your life as we see life differently. I love Sarah and always have. I love seeing you cheer at our games for us and I'm still your friend. However, we cannot date each other again." Sarah's friends watch Maddie begin to cry and walk away but their mouth's drop at Bill's words.

Relaying the words they read from Bill's lips to Sarah, she treasures six of those in her heart, "I love Sarah and always have." Overjoyed that her heart heard the words she longed for, her mind is in a blissful mood. She flashes a loving smile to him and stands while he strolls over to her. He gives her a little peck on the cheek and asks with a tease, "Did I miss anything?"

Not satisfied with Sarah's earlier answer, her friend inquires again, "Bill, are there any more like you?"

Smiling back at Sarah, he says, "Sorry, I'm the only one because there's only one of Sarah." Smiling with overwhelming joy, Sarah hugs him tight as the bell rings and they rush to class.

As he walks into his first class, Mrs. Case stops him and says, "Bill, word spreads fast around here. I heard about the Christmas Dance and your amazing devotion to Sarah. That's the most romantic thing I've ever heard, especially for a student. I've never had such a fine young man in my class in all my years of teaching. By the way,

I moved you back to your original seat. I thought it would be less awkward for you both this way."

Embarrassed by her words and sensitivity, he replies, "Thank you, Mrs. Case. I appreciate that very much." Finally, when Maddie comes in the room and he doesn't sit by her, everyone knows their relationship has ended for sure. Meanwhile, Bill and Sarah's friendship continues to deepen in wonderful ways as they do everything together. They both remain comfortable with the growth of their relationship. However, neither wants to push the other into a premature commitment.

Winter Love

Seeds planted during the Christmas Dance blossom into full flower. The royal couple enjoys the leadership positions shared in school but treasure their times out of the spotlight. Trying different venues in nature, they visit Nashville, Indiana to see how the winter changes the village. Each lamppost along Van Buren Street wears its finest 19th Century garland and décor transporting the regal pair to glimpses of Charles Dickens time. Twinkling stars of light peaking amidst the garland spread generously around every shop post and sill breathe an air of old-world gaiety into the trip. Bathing all grounds from each shop window, light paints each rustic shop liberally beckoning the shoppers to enter and sample the warmth and wares. Even the Christmas Store dresses more resplendent than ever. Avoiding the cold, the couple flits from shop to shop laughing and teasing each other along the way. After lunch at the Ordinary, they drive to the open areas of Brown County State Park. Snow falls softly on the trees and vistas within the park while the couple shuffles through tufts of white cotton gently kissing the meadow and hills. Stopping for a brief respite to enjoy the winter scenes, the two barrage each other playfully with snowballs and finish their park visit making snow angels. Before driving back home, they stop in Nashville for hot chocolate and warm apple dumplings for dessert spiced with warm glances and enveloping hugs.

The Camp

Early in February, the royal couple are together in the cafeteria in the morning talking. Looking for Bill, Coach Mulinaro comes into the cafeteria and finds him with Sarah, the Dirty Boys, and the FGS girls. As he walks up, everyone s their attention to listen to him, "Bill, I have a Professional Football letter for you."

"What's in the letter," Bill questions expectantly.

Replying with a smile, the coach says, "I didn't open it because it's for you." Everyone surrounds Bill waiting in silent anticipation as he opens the letter. As he reads it, Sarah snuggles close and does the same.

Looking up from the letter with amazement, Sarah says, "I can't believe it."

With the looks on the readers' faces filling everyone with expectation to learn the letter's content, Bill divulges casually, "It's just about a football camp." Laughing in her heart, Sarah shakes her head and smiles at his humbleness.

Emboldened by her love, she proclaims to everyone, "It is an invitation only elite quarterback camp hosted by professional football and held in Pittsburg this year. Only the top twenty *college* quarterbacks in the country are invited but they want Bill to be there too." All the guys congratulate him on such a great honor. Sarah's girls all hug Sarah and congratulate Bill as well.

Stepping up, Andy remarks, "You my friend are on the way to greatness."

Embarrassed by all the clamor, Bill thrills to Sarah's words, "I'm so proud of you." As the embarrassment rushes off, Bill's smile appears for Sarah's presence next to him.

They hug each other and exchange warm kisses as he gushes, "You mean so much more to me than the invitation ever will." As the bell rings bidding them to start for class, Sarah and Bill leave the cafeteria holding each other's hand.

Desiring to spend time with him, Sarah inquires, "Bill would you mind coming over tonight and showing the letter to my parents."

"Okay, I agree but it's really not that big of a deal," he responds nonchalantly.

"I love how humble you are about the invitation but I think you'll find this is really something special. Whether you want to admit it or not, you *are* a big deal now. I understand that fully and I'm fine with that," Sarah explains with a loving smile.

Elated with her words, Bill replies, "Thanks hon but I only want to be a big deal for you."

Something Special

With Spring Break only eight weeks away, Bill decides to put a bold move into action and asks eagerly, "Sarah, what are you doing for spring break?"

Thinking for a moment, she replies, "Really, I don't know yet. My parents and I might stay home and then go on a big family spring break next year. What are you doing? If you don't go anywhere, we can hang out all week."

Smiling broadly, Bill offers, "Wow that sounds good to me. Could I come over and have dinner on Wednesday like I used to do?"

Exhilarated at spending more time with him, Sarah answers excitedly, "Sure, I'll tell mom you're coming."

With a plan in mind, he responds eagerly, "I'm really excited because I want to speak with you and your parents about something special."

"*Oh*, you *have* to tell me now. I'll burst with anticipation before then," she exclaims.

With a wry smile, Bill retorts, "*Sorry, you'll* have to wait until Wednesday to find out."

Trying to wrest the truth from him, Sarah pleads, "Please, please, please tell me so I can give them a heads up."

Recognizing her ploy, he teases with a big smile, "*Sarah Ormond*, you can't get the truth out of me that easily. I'm not telling you until Wednesday."

Bill arrives at Sarah's house at exactly six o'clock. Anticipating his punctuality, her mom has dinner ready and waiting for everyone on the table. After sitting down and offering a prayer, they begin to enjoy the meal. In a few minutes, Sarah overflows with excitement and exclaims, "I can't wait any longer. You have to tell me what the big secret is."

Chuckling, Bill declares, "Okay before you burst, I don't want to go to Florida with the Dirty Boys. I just want to get away and relax. Last year, I went with them before the country's premier sports magazine article and the demand on me was bad enough. I anticipate this year will be a lot worse."

"Is that all? You just want to relax and don't want every girl in a bikini chasing after you," Sarah teases.

Continuing her teasing, Bill returns the tease with a smile, "No I don't. I only want *you* chasing after me."

With a big grin, she answers, "That's fine with me. You need to run fast because I'll be supercharged."

Sensing that the discussion is off-target, Bill continues to explain, "Okay, enough teasing, I don't want to deal with the media finding me after going out *one* time. I just want to relax."

Her dad says, "I can understand that. So what's your plan?"

Outlining his plan, he says, "I'm sure you have heard of Mackinac Island in Michigan. You can rent cabins with fireplaces, shop for groceries for the week into town, and visit the numerous shops and activities. By the fire, you can make hot chocolate, roast marshmallows, and enjoy s'mores. It sounds very relaxing to me."

"And romantic," Sarah chimes in.

Puzzled, her mom questions, "Bill, you paint a great mental picture but what does it have to do with us?"

His expression turns serious and he clarifies, "I want all of you to come with me as my guest."

Probing further, her dad inquires, "I'm not certain I heard you correctly. What did you mean when you said as guests?"

As his face grows red, Bill forces a smile and he says, "I want you all to come and I'll take care of everything."

Concerned, her parents respond immediately, "Bill, we can't let you do that. We can't let you shoulder all that expense. It all sounds wonderful but it's too expensive."

Emboldened, Bill doesn't blink an eye and explains, "Well, I look at it this way. I can never repay you for all you've done for me, for all Sarah has done for me. You know I care for her dearly and you both are very special to me. I already made reservations for the four of us."

Responding to his heartfelt words, her parents say, "You're very special to us and we know how special you are to Sarah. However, we wouldn't feel right to have you spend so much."

Deciding to inject a little humor into the conversation, Bill snickers, "Well, you can hang out with me in Michigan or have me hang out here all week with you. Either way, Sarah and I want to spend the entire week doing things together. Personally, I'd rather do things in Michigan where we won't be bothered. Here, Spring Break week will be like every other week."

Finally, Sarah interrupts and pleads, "Please, please say yes. I want to go and it sounds like so much fun."

Her parents silently communicate to each other with their eyes. Her dad concedes and says, "Okay, we'll all go but we'll at least pay for our half."

Smiling at their words, Bill says, "Thank you for deciding to go. I know we'll have a great time together. We'll discuss who pays later." After finishing dinner, Bill and Sarah start cleaning the table as they used to do together when he'd visit for dinner. The two of them sneak loving glances and expressions as they too communicate silently to each other with their eyes.

As her mom starts to speak while walking into the kitchen, Bill says, "You don't have to say anything. Sarah and I will wash the dishes and then do our homework." Smiling at them both, her mom shakes her head, turns around, and walks out of the kitchen. Walking toward the family room smiling and discussing Bill's offer, her mom and dad leave the living room to Bill and Sarah.

While walking to the family room, her dad glances toward her mom and says, "He's an unbelievable young man and so good for our Sarah. She really cares for him so much. Did you see the sparkle in her eyes when she looks at him? It's so cute how she teases with him."

"I know," her mom replies. As the dish washing ends, Bill and Sarah continue their emotional exchange of love begun while cleaning the dishes from the table. The living room's familiar environs beckon them.

Arriving in the living room, Bill admits, "Really I don't have any homework. I just wanted the room for the two of us alone. This is a very special evening for me. I'm so excited to spend Spring Break with you. I can't think of anything better." As the couch begs them to share its caress together, he confesses, "Sarah, I have a big favor to ask of you."

Filled with love and excitement, she sparkles, "Yes, whatever it is, I'm yours."

Sensing the love in her heart and seeing the expectation in her eyes, Bill blushes, "No Sarah, that's not what I'm asking of you." As Sarah blushes at *his* words, he assures, "Don't be embarrassed. It doesn't bother me when you say those things. I feel your love for me and want to return it too. However, I don't feel any pressure to do something. I have too much respect for you to compromise your love and trust in me." His love for her appears in so many ways including his character strength and the way he cares for her, making *her* the queen of his heart. Her love for him grows daily as their emotions, thoughts, and spirits blend easily. Continuing, he explains, "Here is my request. Please don't tell people that I'm paying for the trip. I don't want it to become a big deal or be a negative reflection on you or your family. I'm just trying to do something special for you and your parents who have been so good to me."

Comprehending his meaning, Sarah agrees, "I understand. We don't want to become fodder for the rumor mill at South." They continue to enjoy each other and to blend their spirits in their favorite setting as the room fades around them. Allowing their eyes to caress the other's face, they continue holding each other spicing the mix with frequent gentle kisses.

Spring Break

D ue to their shared anticipation, the time between the decision to go and Spring Break passes much too slowly for Bill and Sarah. The week in Michigan is an enjoyable time of sharing, blending their hearts and spirits in the natural setting. They relax in each other's arms, take long nature walks holding hands, and share warm embraces and gentle kisses surrounded by God's creation. While they find time to wander through the shops in town, the sports reporting hounds still encounter them and beg for Bill's time. Making an agreement with them, Bill schedules a Q&A session with all the reporters on one day. Since the reporters let the information slip about Bill being in town, well-wishers and football groupies caressing the premier sports magazine story want him to autograph it. Suddenly, people appear in front of Bill and Sarah or call to him from behind and ask, "Are you The Chosen One?" or "Are you Bill Denton, the quarterback?" With each request, he is gracious, treating each person respectfully while Sarah stands by his side every minute. Her support for Bill makes them the perfect couple to everyone, as Maddie's discord is a distant memory. On the last night together in Michigan, everyone sits around the fireplace with Sarah resting her head on Bill's shoulder and her mom and dad holding hands. The setting is idyllic and they share the love in the room.

Wanting to learn more of Bill's character, her dad inquires, "Bill, I know you don't like to talk about football or yourself but how do you handle all of this. How do you do it, being a high school junior and how much worse do you think it's going to get?"

Surprised at his sincerity, Bill answers, "Well, I have a great support system with my grandparents, my closest friends, teachers, and coaches. Most importantly, I have Sarah to keep everything perfect." As Sarah becomes embarrassed at his admission, he continues, "How much worse do I think it's going to *get*? Much, much worse, I have something to share that I have not even let Sarah until now. I found out about this just before spring break and I didn't want to start our trip on a down note. South high school and our opponent schools have agreed that the crowd size and control will be difficult this season because of my popularity at South and the potential ire of opposing fans. For away games, they are assigning a deputy sheriff to guard me from the time we leave school until we get back. At South home games, the protection would be from the time I arrive at the stadium until the deputy tells me it's ok for me to leave. They're doing this because so many people want to get close enough to see me and ask for autographs. The anticipated crowds are so large I could get hurt and potentially ruin my season and my future. Unfortunately, some people don't like me just because of who and what I am. They might even try to hurt me intentionally. There has been discussion about the deputy picking me up at my house and taking me back after home games."

"Oh my goodness Bill, are you serious," Sarah exclaims.

"Unfortunately Sarah, I *am* serious. This thing grows bigger by the day. I'm so glad we have each other to get through this together."

His announcement stuns Sarah's parents. They knew he was a big deal but they had no idea the situation had become that serious.

Interjecting a dose of reality into Bill's mind, Sarah says, "You have always said you didn't think you were a big celebrity. Do you realize *now* that you *are* that celebrity? Has it hit you yet and do you really understand how good you are?"

In a very serious tone, he replies, "Yes Sarah, I understand fully now that God has blessed me with some very special tools. It may sound silly but yes I'm very special." Looking deeply into Sarah's eyes and heart, he says, "I'm the best football player in America. I know that and I have to handle that in a positive way because everyone in the country is watching. More importantly, I need you to help me maintain my focus. I need your strength and love."

Realizing his commitment to Sarah, her mom and dad commit to Bill, "We'll always be here for you too as you have been here for Sarah. We're going to leave you two to discuss your futures." As her parents leave the room, Bill and Sarah cuddle up on the floor with pillows and a blanket.

Looking with love into his face, she notices tears running down his cheeks. "Bill, are you okay," she questions with concern. With equal love in his heart, he replies, "Dear heart, there is nothing wrong in my world tonight. I'm so happy you're in my life. You make my whole crazy life worth living. How could I live it without you?"

Uneasy Signs

U nfortunately, the remaining school year fulfills Bill and Sarah's concerned expectations of time demands consisting of increasing requests for interviews, pictures, and articles about him. Even South HS put strains on their time together, scheduling him to speak with groups of elementary kids. Usually, he does not mind the requests but at often twice a week, he and Sarah have to devise a way to spend time together. He informs school administrators, "I need Sarah Ormond to help me. When I'm with the students, I lose track of time and spend too *much* time with them. Keeping me on time, she takes notes of what I say and offers improvements for my next visit. I really can't do this well without her." While all this is true, he really enjoys having her with him during these visits. Quickly, she is becoming his other half and the mirror of his life. He wants to spend as much time with her as possible. These time demands give them both an ominous prophetic view of their future. Despite these demands, they battle together against anything that threatens to separate them.

South High School remains Bill's comfort zone. He and Sarah are friends with everyone there. Since their performance at the Christmas Dance, everyone respects and supports them. This has been his dream, to be a great football player and yet accepted as just another student by his classmates. However, it is a difficult high-wire act of a lifestyle without a *personal* safety net. Knowing that Sarah is his safety net, she provides reality and stability in his life. Loving to play football, he knows he's the best player today. Although he knows God gave him the tools to be that player, he still needs someone in some *place* with whom he can be himself. Being that person for him, Sarah is his world. South is the larger world in which his world with her exists. Outside its familiar confines, another world clamors for his full time and threatens to destroy the joy and love they share together. It is a different world than he ever imagined including the one he shares with Sarah. Attending Notre Dame, Bill will be on the national stage where every game is a big televised game. The demands will increase even further with press conferences after every game and requests for his time all week. Practices and class work leave little time for anything else, as it is the job of a stellar college athlete. Racing through his mind, these thoughts require him to seek sanctuary in Sarah arms. Attending Purdue, she will live a more relaxed college life with classes, a social life, and weekends free of public demands. Most students expect this of college life, a preparation for their future. Although certain she will see him only on TV instead of in the stadiums, she fights her own thoughts of this time line. She dreams of a college life where she spends frequent time with him. However, she knows this will be difficult while attending different schools a couple of hours apart. She fears that though they are best friends who love each other deeply, even best friends can drift apart. Just over the horizon, two different worlds beckon them strongly as they fight to resist the siren call.

Deputy John Layton

In early May, Bill meets Sarah apprehensively at her locker after school and says, "I'll have a deputy sheriff with me at all the games in the fall. As we feared in Michigan, the anticipated crowds *are* large enough that schools have concerns for my safety. I don't know how it's all going to work out for us. I'll know more when they select a deputy and the two of us talk. As soon as I have the details, I'll let you know. I wanted you with me at the meeting to meet the deputy for the protocol but the administration told me that they would allow only Coach Mulinaro, the deputy, and me." Unfortunately, the tug of war between their two different futures begins and threatens slowly to tear them apart. Remaining silent about the situation, the concern over time spent together shows on their faces as they embrace.

In mid-May, Bill receives a message to come to the main office during second period. The message doesn't tell him why but he knows already. As he walks to the office like one condemned, his mind races with thoughts of protection, snuggling with Sarah by the fireplace, warm evening walks in the neighborhood, and concern it is ending in a few minutes. The deputy sheriff waits to protect him from potential harm. As Bill walks in the main office conference room, Deputy John Layton stands and they shake hands firmly and business-like while Mr. Cole introduces the two of them. Visually, Deputy Layton's uniform impresses Bill. It is crisp, clean, and all the metal shines brightly. His ribbons and other uniform items are perfectly straight as is his stance commanding respect with his presence. Those in the room know he is in charge of this meeting and the events will unfold with the utmost professionalism. "This man will be Marion County Sheriff someday," Bill muses to himself at the entire visual presence.

With the formalities out of the way, Bill inquires, "Sir, what are the details and what do you expect of me?"

Deputy Layton explains, "First, for home games, I'll pick you up at home and return you there after the game. For away games, I'll escort the team busses to the games. I'll be with you from the time you step off the bus until you get back on it for the ride home. Then, I'll escort the busses home. Once at the stadium before all games, I'll station myself outside the locker room door and will not allow anyone but team personnel inside." Once Bill explains his pre-game jogging routine to him, Deputy Layton says, "Ok, I'll be on the field with you as you warm up. When the team comes out for the official team warm up, I'll go out right beside you. I'll be on the sideline watching during warm-ups and the game. After the game, I'll be in the locker room to insure the crowd does not overwhelm you and the team and there'll be a deputy outside the door with other deputies at the games for crowd control. I've heard stories about your 'swagger' and that you're always the last one on the field. I assure you I'll be right with you going onto the field and coming off it. Being last, I'll have a better view of the surroundings. I've been on VIP details before and I understand what to look for and how to keep you safe." Then with a serious, commanding tone, he orders, "Bill, this is extremely important. You follow my instructions to the letter and don't ask questions. I'm not here to change any part of your routine. I'm here to protect you while you do the things the way you've always done them. I'll make changes only on as needed basis. As far as access to you during these times, absolutely no one will have it unless you acknowledge it's ok. Bill, is there anyone who you want to have total access to you? This should be a very short list and don't put football players on the list because they're already cleared."

"Sarah, my best friend, only Sarah will have complete access," Bill replies quickly, "Everyone else on the list will need my ok."

"Girlfriends usually have complete access," the Deputy says with a smile. In return, Bill smiles and gives Deputy Layton a picture of her so he can identify her when he sees her. Agreeing with Bill and thanking him for the photo, Deputy Layton explains, "She'll have a designated place to wait for us until you come out of the locker room."

"Ok, that sounds good but how can I be sure Sarah will be safe waiting by herself. Everyone knows her, who she is, and what she is to me. I'm very concerned," Bill inquires from his heart.

Deputy Layton explains further, "The other deputies are under orders to assist me when I deem it necessary. She'll have a deputy with her from the time she arrives until the team comes out of the locker room." With relief, Bill says, "Thanks very much for protecting her. She's very special to me."

The only people with access to him before, during, and after games are on the list he hands Deputy Layton. The access list includes the Dirty Boys, Sarah's mom and dad, Mr. Tibbs, and the manager from the TeePee. No one else need ask, as it's a very exclusive club. Bill queries with concern, "Will you protect Sarah as you do me? She is with me at all times and I don't want her to get hurt because of me. Can Sarah ride with me when you drive me to the home games?"

Hearing Bill's deep concern for her safety, Deputy Layton informs with a smile, "Ok, I sense your concern for her safety and

I can tell Sarah is very special to you. Let me assure you. I'll make certain she's safe and will let nothing happen to her. It'll be fine for her to ride with us. Bill, you don't need to worry at all. You go out and play football to the best of your ability. The department and I will do what we do to the best of our ability and everything else will go like clockwork." The meeting ends as the two shake hands. Bill knows in his mind this is a lot to expect of Sarah and he has much to tell her. However, his heart assures him that their love will carry them both.

Changing Worlds

Bill leaves the meeting with his thoughts ablaze visualizing his world's continuing changes with Sarah. Despite the winds of change blowing a hurricane around them, they have one more year together at South. Striving to fight the change side by side, they keep their world together intact and unbowed. Best friends always pull together in stressful times. After his lunch period, he asks his teacher, "May I go back to the cafeteria to talk with Sarah?"

His teacher replies with a smile, "Yes, as long as you promise one thing. Don't hit anybody." They both laugh at the recent event involving Bill, Sarah, and her honor.

As Bill walks into the cafeteria, everyone in the room stares at him as he moves quickly to Sarah's side. Sitting with her and the FGS girls, he outlines the protection plan for the two of them during the next season. He expounds, "You and I can ride together while the deputy drives us to all the home games. You'll have a deputy assigned to you at the games also. The deputy will stay with you from the moment we arrive until Deputy Layton and I come out of the locker room. There is a designated area for you to wait for us. I gave the deputy a list of people with access to me at the games. It includes your mom and dad, the Dirty Boys, Mr. Tibbs, and because he's been so great to us, the manager from the TeePee. No one else will have access to me unless I say it's ok."

Puzzled and clutching her ruby necklace over her heart with her hand, Sarah inquires, "Why do I have a deputy with me?"

Clarifying, he answers, "It's because everyone knows who you are and how special you are to me. I spoke with Deputy Layton about you. He had to assure me that you would receive protection at all the games. I told him that you mean the world to me."

She hugs him and gushes, "You always think about me and my welfare. You have no idea how deeply your words of concern for me touch my heart. I've tried to convey to my girls how big a celebrity you are. I think your statement about police protection for me because I'm your best friend makes them understand fully."

Their junior year ends well despite the ominous note sounded earlier and the warm summer break beckons. The old senior class is gone as their world welcomes them as the newly christened senior class. Meeting together on their last school day before summer, they reminisce in amazement over how their relationship came into being and flowered while three years flew past them. Memories bring mingled joy and sadness causing them to hug each other desperately. For all too soon, the best time of their lives will pass in one short year. As reality breaks their embrace, they walk out of the building hand in hand casting loving glances at each other. While they discuss their special bond, Bill allows Sarah to drive to her house in his car.

The Party

arah's girls, the Dirty Boys, and Bill and Sarah all receive invitations to an end of the year pool party at Debbie's, another friend of Sarah's. The party starts in the late afternoon on the first Saturday of summer break. Quivering with excitement, Sarah thinks, "Wait 'til all my friends see Bill in a swimsuit. Check that. Wait 'til *I* see him in it. I told them about his physique all through high school but guess what, finally, he's mine."

Bill's thoughts race on the same track as her thoughts, "Finally, I'm with Sarah. It seems like I've waited an eternity and a half for this moment. My friends are here too with no outside distractions. Wow, this couldn't be better." As they arrive at the party, Bill whispers, "Sarah, you'll steal the show today when you walk out in your two piece swimsuit."

Laughing at his comment, she says quietly, "No one will even notice me. There are plenty of other girls here better looking than me."

Disagreeing with love in his heart, he whispers the quick response of one in love, "I disagree completely. No one here is prettier than you are." Stopping suddenly, she hugs him tightly. Sharing some joyous moments, he teases, "I could hug you here all night or we could go to the party." After entering the party and changing clothes, they walk out while everyone stops what they're doing to gaze at them. It is the Christmas dance all over again as everyone runs to Sarah and Bill steps back. She glances at him presenting her to everyone as her heart overflows with love and smiles. All through the afternoon, the girls melt over Bill but no one does more than look. Sarah's watchful eye of love shouts, "He's mine." The guys are intoxicated with the vision of Sarah. However, the tiger's eyes keep vigil for anyone daring enough to challenge him for the love of his mate.

Suddenly from the shadows, a challenger crashes the party deciding to break from his self-created prison. After all, Steve Powell has been in social solitary confinement since his encounter in the cafeteria with Bill earlier in the year. Steve has not had a date at South since then but he does not dare come near Sarah again until today. While speaking with others, Bill hears her let out a little scream, "*Steve*, please leave me alone." As Steve reaches for Sarah, Bill moves like lightning, grabs him, and throws him in the pool.

While everyone laughs, Steve gets out of the pool and moves quickly toward Bill and Sarah again saying, "This is between Sarah and me. Butt out." As Steve races toward them, Bill steps in front of Sarah to protect her and flips both hands at him twice in glaring challenge. Once again, Steve underestimates his opponent's strong protective nature for his love greatly. As Steve arrives where Bill waits, Andy and the boys step in to protect Sarah and leave Bill to the challenge. The *Assassin* arises again in full defense of Sarah waiting to spring with the strength, focus, and power of a tiger on his unwary and naive foe. With his hands already flipped back into steel ramrods, Bill unleashes a lightning fury of blows culminating in two rocketing off Steve's cheekbones again. The blows' ferocity stuns Steve and knocks him off his feet. Lying on his face, Steve struggles to rise and falls flat again.

Delivering his warning with its results, Bill leans over him and says, "You should have listened in the cafeteria. It's time for you to go." Andy and the boys come over, lift Steve up, and escort him out. They make sure he is ok but that he *leaves* also. Back at the party, Bill and Sarah cling tightly to each other with relief while he whispers, "I'm here this time. My love will *never* let any harm come to you."

With those words, she relaxes her embrace to give him a passionate kiss. Her mind could no longer restrain the words in her heart, "My knight in shining armor has come to my defense again. I love you so much."

Affirming his role as her safeguard and fortress, Bill whispers softly from his heart, "I'll be here for you always to protect you with my strength and love." As everyone rushes to see if the two are ok, the collective thoughts are that these two belong to each other.

A Visitor in South Bend

During the second week of summer, Bill drives to Notre Dame for two camps back to back, a basic quarterback camp and a seniors only camp. Again, Bill is the best at both of them while everyone else watches him in amazement. The Notre Dame receivers serving as camp assistants fill with anticipation for his arrival after his senior year. Surprising Bill, Sarah drives South Bend on the Friday afternoon of the first camp. With Sarah planning to stay the weekend to be with Bill, the two arrange a hotel room for her. After she settles into her room, they locate a restaurant for dinner. Walking into the restaurant, everyone recognizes him immediately. The two cannot find a place where a horde of groupies and autograph seekers do not appear. Finally, after requesting a booth in a corner to obtain some privacy, everyone respects the couple's request as the restaurant does its best to accommodate.

After the dinner privacy allows them to relax, they decide to return to the hotel rather than face the prying glare of further public scrutiny. Not wanting the night to end and with her heart filled with love, Sarah states boldly, "Bill, I don't want to be alone tonight. Please stay with me and hold me close."

Honored by her request but still cautious, he replies, "Sarah, are you *sure* you're ok with this."

Listening to her heart, she clarifies, "I've never been more certain of anything in my life. I'm completely safe in your arms. Your protection of me from Steve Powell and the love you professed that night said everything to me. Would you please stay with me tonight?" Immediately, his mind tears between his respect for her and his desire to be with her.

Nervously but with Sarah's words filling him with warmth and elation, he answers, "Yes Sarah, I'd love to stay with you to caress, protect, and keep you safe in my arms tonight." With Bill in his sweats and Sarah in a Notre Dame Football t-shirt and gym shorts, they snuggle next to each other. As he pulls her close to him, he whispers, "I've never been happier in my entire life. I want you next to me like this forever. I'm so glad you came here this weekend." They share gentle kisses and embraces.

Answering with the love in her heart, she says, "Bill, I'd love for you to hold me like this for the rest of my life. This night is so special for both of us." She understands his level of respect for her and that respect reinforces her love for him. Relaxing in the enchantment they share, they release their emotions to the call of the Sandman and fall asleep in each other's arms.

On Saturday morning, they wake with surprise and delight to find each other still there. Running her fingers lightly through his hair, Sarah voices gently, "Good morning, sleepy head."

Brushing the sleep from his eyes and caressing her face gently with his hand, Bill says softly, "Good morning, Princess." Looking longingly at each other, they discuss what to do with the day after gently kissing good morning with delight several times. With so much of Notre Dame that Sarah has not seen, they decide to go on a personal walking tour of the campus, making a game of avoiding prying eyes. After getting ready with the excitement of the new day together, they explore the Grotto where they lite candles and pray. Walking hand-in-hand, they view the Basilica of the Sacred Heart, which is the big Catholic Church on campus, the Golden Dome, and the large mosaic mural of the resurrected Jesus on the Hesburgh library. Students know the mural affectionately as Touchdown Jesus because of its unique visibility from the football stadium. Along the way, they sneak with laughter into wooded venues to catch loving kisses and hugs. Finding a restaurant out of the public eye, they enjoy a late lunch in relative obscurity. After the dinner difficulty on Friday night, they decide to drive away from campus later for dinner and a movie to avoid prying eyes and autograph seekers. Returning to the hotel room in secrecy, they snuggle together in laughter for memories of the day. As they relax from the day's clandestine activities of hiding from the press and fans, they lose their game with the Sandman in each other's arms again.

Sunday morning arrives while they kiss each other awake in joyous rapture and decide to attend a local campus church. After all, it is a college campus and they *don't* have to dress to impress anyone. God understands it is *not* clothes but the heart that matters. After lunch, Sarah begins packing to return home. The wonderment of his weekend with her in his arms and the bliss of waking to find her beside him blazes through his mind. Suddenly filled with anxiety at the thought that this will never happen again, Bill takes a deep breath and timidly inquires, "Sarah, would you like to stay this week and watch me in camp? We can spend our evenings together then we can drive back together on Friday. I can follow you home to make sure you arrive safely."

Thrilled at the prospect of a week with him alone, Sarah gushes, "Yes, of course I will." and leaps into his arms again.

Overcome with dread that he may have unlocked an emotional Pandora's Box, Bill insists, "You need to call your parents and ask them if it's ok with them. I don't want them to worry or be upset with us." Sarah calls her parents and waits anxiously for their response. After what seems an eternity, her parents finish their discussion with them both and then agree after assurances from Bill and Sarah. Filled with elation, they return to the hotel desk and Sarah starts to get her dad's credit card. Before she can pull out the card, Bill puts his card on the counter and says, "This one is on me. It was my idea and I won't have your parents paying for your room."

Amazement reaches her heart as her mind races, "Wow, this is our *first* vacation together alone. I'm going to *enjoy* this time with him. Food, fun, his arms around me for a week and no intrusions, what more could a girl want." Any thoughts of protest melt in this ecstasy of anticipation. She smiles and teases, "You always take good care of me. Of course, you realize you'll be worthless this week with me here."

"That's what you think. Now I have to impress you and the college players too," he retorts.

"Not really, I have always been impressed by you," she returns. With that thought, they hug each other joyously.

When Sarah arrives at the camp with Bill, a guard stops them at the gate and says, "I'm sorry. There are no spectators allowed at this camp."

Not satisfied with the guard's response, Bill says, "Please wait here a minute Sarah. I'll be right back."

In a few minutes, Coach Alan walks to the guard with Bill. Since he and Sarah met earlier, he says, "Sarah, would you please come with me. I'm giving you full access to the camp and you can go anywhere you want. Please make sure you wear this tag to prevent any questions." As he finishes, he hangs the all-access pass around her neck and shows her where to stand to see everything. After introducing her to the other Notre Dame personnel on the sideline, Coach Alan turns to the staff and says, "Gentlemen, whatever this young woman wants make sure that she gets it."

As he promised her, Bill has another superb week of camp at Notre Dame and impresses everyone including Sarah, who simply bursts with pride all week. After Bill gets his MVP award at this camp Friday as he had during the first camp a week earlier, the two drive home under Bill's watchful eyes. When they arrive at her house, hurricane Sarah blows through the front door quite literally.

With so many emotions overflowing her heart, she cannot contain her excitement, "Mom, dad, you'll never believe the treatment I received from the people at Notre Dame. I felt like royalty and they let me stand on the sideline with the coaching staff. They were all extremely nice to me. Bill spoke to the coach on the first day of the camp and Coach Alan even spoke with me, giving me an all-access pass. I know Bill did this to show me how special I am to him. Are you sure I can't go to Notre Dame? If that's how they treat people, it would seem to me there's no place like Notre Dame."

Concerned about education financing, her parents respond, "That sounds wonderful Sarah. Why don't we discuss this a bit later."

Pittsburgh

Two weeks later, it's time for the weeklong Elite College Quarterback camp for which he received an exclusive invitation in February. A local newscast sends a reporter and cameraman to document his success or failure against the best college seniors in the country. While they try to make a story of him, Sarah brings him to the airport and her heart misses him already. As they wait at the gate for his boarding call, she reveals, "I miss you *so* much and you haven't even left yet. A week away from you will be an eternity to me. I hope you do so well that the TV crew puts you on TV every night."

With his heart aching already, Bill replies, "I miss you deeply too. You mean the world to me and I don't want to leave. Just knowing you're waiting for me makes my heart long to stay here. Unfortunately, I have to go to this camp to show others how I compare to the top players." As the airline announces boarding, they hug and kiss each other repeatedly.

Realizing time is short, she says quickly, "My heart is going to burst without you here."

Walking toward the ramp door, Bill adds, "Mine too." With his heart aching already, he stops just past the door, turns to look back, and mouths to her, "I miss you and I love you." Reading his lips, her heart leaps as she frantically waves goodbye. Seeing her waving, he throws her a kiss and walks down the ramp to board the plane. Knowing he has to focus on the upcoming camp, his heart fights his mind on the flight to remind him continually of the beauty he left at home.

When he disembarks the plane, the media circus begins. Twenty-five reporters rush him at the airport sticking microphones in his face and shouting questions at him. Wishing Sarah was with him, Bill stops to answer their questions for thirty minutes. Finally, the camp officials come to his rescue and take him to the hotel where all participants are staying. The intensity of the week begins. By the meeting the next morning, Bill has regained his swagger and the college quarterbacks don't like him being there. They think he's just window dressing to publicize the camp.

The week is a whirlwind of activity and triumph for Bill as Sarah catches glimpses of his performance on TV. In the 40-yard trial, he runs a 4.5 beating his nearest competitor by half a second. In the arm strength test, he uses only one of his five possible throws for 80 yards and still beats the others' longest throw by 10 yards. Of the 20 plays to memorize, he runs his ten plays selected by the staff perfectly making all throws on target and with strength. Anticipating the coming tests the next camp day, the professional scouts suddenly appear from everywhere with great interest. When the tests come against professional defensive players, he is the last to perform and puts on an unbelievable show running eighteen of his twenty plays and no interceptions. No other QB has more than twelve completions, as everyone is awe-struck by his prowess. This drill is the most important one of the entire week as it tests the quarterback's decision-making skills and accuracy. The stage is his and the *Maestro* does not disappoint anyone. Celebrating his performance, the professional defensive players congratulate him personally. As the media begins their blitz again, the premier sports magazine decides to put him on the cover again with the caption in capital letters "THE CHOOSEN ONE IS READY FOR PROFESSIONAL FOOTBALL NOW." Watching the updates nightly, Sarah receives calls from all her friends about how wonderful she must feel to be his girlfriend. Bursting with pride and love, she does not deny their assessments and Sarah's parents share in her happiness.

Bill arrives back in Indianapolis on Saturday afternoon with his Professional Football Elite Quarterback Camp MVP award, which he eventually gives to Sarah. Coming off the plane, a media frenzy mobs him at the gate exit. With reporters shouting questions from every direction, it is a madhouse. Unable to get through the media crush and excited people trying to get to him, Sarah yells from the back, "*Bill, Bill,*" as he looks up to see her getting pushed and jostled. Suddenly, Deputy Layton appears and breaks through the crowd to take Sarah to Bill.

Sensing the situation is tenuous, he orders, "Sorry folks, show time is over. Bill, it's not safe for either of you here. You two need to follow me now." Quickly guiding them safely to the Sarah's car, he keeps the crush of reporters away from them. Then, he provides them a police escort to Sarah's home.

Arriving at Sarah's, Bill says, "Thanks for the rescue. How did you know we would be in trouble?"

Deputy Layton answers, "I saw all the news broadcasts. At that point, I rushed to the airport because it wouldn't be safe for either of you. If you're going anywhere football related, you need to call me and I'll be there with you."

Again expressing his debt of gratitude, Bill says, "Thanks so much." As Deputy Layton drives away, the realization strikes them that their world has changed in the blink of an eye. Fighting back the future dread with the shared joy of South Bend, they plan to spend the rest of the summer together. Walking into her house, they curl up on their couch in a loving embrace and hold each other tightly for a brief eternity. Their eyes convey their hearts' desires for the days ahead without the confusion and difficulty of exchanging words.

Senior Summer

Blossoming emotions drive them to each other almost daily. It is common to find them walking hand-in-hand around the neighborhood in the evenings, enjoying God's creation and each other. If not walking, they often sit on a blanket under the trees or hide in the woods behind Sarah's house sharing nature with the local wildlife. They spend so much time at Sarah's house that her mom jokingly suggests, "Why don't you kids go to Nashville, Brown County, or go see a movie. You kids need to get out and do more."

Her words tap them on the head to open their tiny world. "Why don't we go to Nashville for lunch and walk around town like we did last winter," Bill recommends.

Quickly, Sarah replies, "That sound like a lot of fun. I'll bring a blanket for later."

Working up an appetite on the drive, they decide to eat at the historic Nashville House restaurant. Walking up the rustic brick walk and into the Old Country Store, they survey the cookies, candy, and cooking items before turning left across the dark wooden floor and moving up the wooden stairs to the restaurant. While marveling at the exposed wooden beams and dark oak paneling providing a warm, natural setting, they request seating near the large stone fireplace.

Sitting in the rustic wooden chairs at a table covered with a "country checkered" tablecloth, Bill orders the turkey dinner with all the trimmings for himself and the baked Hoosier ham dinner for Sarah. With all the wonderful food comprising the main course, they enjoy the fried biscuits and apple butter even more. Finishing lunch, they browse the wares in the store and in the different shops around town. Laughing about planning culinary delights, trying on clothes, studying artists' works, and buying small memories, they stop their meandering just long enough to steal private kisses and longing gazes at each other.

Suddenly an idea strikes her, "Bill, let's go to Brown County State Park. I want to curl up with you at a vista and watch the clouds change shape."

Envisioning quiet time with her, Bill gushes, "Oh yeah. You lead and I'll follow anywhere. Pick your spot while we drive and we can claim it for ourselves." Sarah finds a lovely vista from which they gaze at the horizon, scan the trees for wildlife, and dream among the clouds. Hiding behind the car on the spread blanket, they try to discern the cloud designs that God painted. Between their analyses of formations floating across the sky, they caress and kiss each other gently, sharing the warmth of love in their hearts. While enjoying the kisses in the warm sun, they decide to walk around Lake Strahl and find some privacy in the trees. Caught in the rapture of bird songs and soft breezes, they steal kisses and hugs periodically from each other while wandering the trail. Laughing at the infrequent people going by, they hide in the trees from the "spies following them to obtain their secrets."

As the summer progresses, they travel to the South 31 Drive-In several times to see "Doctor Zhivago," "The Graduate," "Where Eagles Dare," a Doris Day movie marathon, and a Frankie and Annette beach movie marathon. While they enjoy the movies, they enjoy the time alone together more as the school year approaches quickly. The Pizza Inn and Kristen's Burgers become frequent haunts for them when they desire time with their friends. Still, while the conversations rage around them, the room and sounds fade while gazing into each other's eyes longingly. One of the girls, Karen Anderson, suggests, "Hey, anyone up for going to my Uncle Bill and Aunt Lillian Cheever's house near Columbus this weekend?"

Wanting to be with Sarah, Bill questions indifferently, "That sounds kind of boring. What's so special there?"

Knowing the fun awaiting them, Karen replies, "Well, they live on Grandview Lake where we can all go swimming and waterskiing."

Jumping at the chance to be on a lake with Bill, Sarah says, "Let's go. *We're* ready."

On the weekend, they all drive to Karen's Aunt and Uncle's house on the lake. The Cheever's live in a two story, mid-century modern home nestled into the side of a thirty-five or so degree sloped, wooded hill on the lake. Wrapping-around the upper story is a balcony with glass walls and sliding glass doors on both stories providing generous, idyllic lake views year-round. After changing in the house, most of the group runs down the long hill and jumps in the lake off the boat dock. As Karen brings the wake board from the house, Bill inquires, "Do you mind if Sarah and I borrow it?"

Karen responds, "No problem. I brought it down in case anyone wanted to use it." Paddling out onto the lake, Bill and Sarah float together while holding onto opposite sides of the board. While talking about the upcoming school year, she wraps her legs around his waist with a big smile and refuses to relax her hug. Eventually, he wriggles free and dunks her teasingly. Surfacing behind him, she hugs and kisses him on the neck. Spending the rest of the day with the board and each other, they share more hugs and kisses in the water. However, the day ends much too soon for them. Shortly after leaving the lake, the group stops at the Grandview Grocery to get bags of chocolate chip cookies and soft drinks to share on the trip home. Returning home, they all mull over thoughts of the coming school year.

Senior Year

I t is opening night of the new football season for the *Maestro*. The 9,000-seat stadium at South overflows with 12,000 people. Deputy Layton picks up Bill and Sarah at Bill's house and introduces her to her bodyguard when they arrive at the stadium. Constantly by her side, the deputy even sits with Sarah and her parents. Surrounding the playing field, people are stacked like cord wood craning to get a view of the game. Telling Bill not to stop to talk with anyone, Deputy Layton and Bill wade through the crowd to rush him into the locker room. Quickly, he changes into his pre-game warm up gear to return to the field. Being the only one on the field except for his guardian, the crowd erupts in frenzied cheers watching him warm up. As the remainder of the team joins him, they finish their regular warm ups together with the *Maestro* leading and return to the locker room.

Coach Mulinaro delivers and concludes his pre-game speech to the thunder of the team's storm, sending them to challenge the opponent. The *Wizard* again drives *his* storm to the field accompanied by Deputy Layton as the attendant throng explodes with cheers. While moving to the field, Maddie and Bill make eye contact as Bill requests, "May I have a moment alone with Maddie? I won't be long."

Deputy Layton replies, "Yes but it really can't be long. Too many people will view it as an open invitation for your time."

Bill says, "Thanks. I'll be back quickly," and moves in Maddie's direction. Walking toward her, she displays a red "10" on her cheek again. While they exchange smiles, he gives her a hug and queries, "How have you been? Are you doing ok?"

She assures, "Yes I'm fine. I hope we can at least be friends?"

Happy to see she remains a friend, he assures, "We'll always be friends. The time we spent together will always be very special to me." Before returning to the field, he gives her another hug and they both smile.

Showing great concern at seeing Bill speaking with Maddie, Sarah's friends ask, "Why would Bill stop to see Maddie? What's up with that?"

Experiencing Bill's love for her in her heart and mind, Sarah replies with confidence, "Trust me when I tell you he's just saying hello to a friend. He is *all mine.*" She muses in her heart, "Besides, there is only one person he loves. *It's me.*" Her friends all know she is right because whether admitted or not, Bill and Sarah *are* in love with each other.

As the game ends, the defending state champions show they are better than last year winning 42-0 with Bill having his usual, terrific game. After getting dressed, Deputy Layton escorts him to Sarah and her parents. Still, the crowd remains relentless in their pursuit of autographs and personal well wishes. After the family greetings, Deputy Layton says, "We need to get you and Sarah home as soon as possible." Listening to the deputy's instruction, the three of them move quickly to the sheriff's car.

As he drops them off at Bill's house, he says, "Please keep in touch. Remember, next week is an away game at Luers."

As they enter his car, Bill inquires eagerly, "Sarah, where would like to go somewhere to eat?"

Having experienced enough of the public demands for this night, she replies boldly, "All I want to do is go to my house. We can find something to eat there. We need to go where we can be alone and no one can bother us. You've had enough public crush for one day. By the way, can I drive home? I love this car."

Loving her mothering, he answers, "That sounds great, but Hannah Nuckolls is having a party. We ought to go there first."

Exercising her strong-will, Sarah says, "No sir, we *aren't* going to the party. *We* are going to my house. You know how the crowds have been tonight. Do you think it will be any less hectic at the party?" Having seen that look for her before, he understands what she is doing.

Finally, he concedes, "Okay, you can drive the car home. Just don't stick your foot too far into it. You know I'm grateful I have a friend like you who has such concern for my welfare." When they arrive at her house, they surprise her parents by not going back out.

Responding to their questions, Sarah answers, "We decided to spend the evening at home. The crowds were too much for us to attempt to fight them at a restaurant. We want some peace and quiet." Her parents understand why they're staying home.

Finding some roast beef in the refrigerator, they make a couple of sandwiches then stroll toward their favorite couch. Their eyes convey a special bond between them and the communication tonight is very strong. When they get to the couch, Sarah gives Bill's her sandwich and orders, "Come with me. I have an idea." As she picks up two blankets, they hurry into the backyard to eat under the stars. Hidden in the darkness from prying eyes, they enjoy their sandwiches while watching the stars and discussing the evenings' events. Unexpectedly, she proposes with excitement, "Let's stay here all night, count the stars, and wait together for the sun to come up."

"Sounds like fun to me. You count the blue ones and I'll count the red ones. First one to see a shooting star wins," he offers as their game begins. Exchanging glances, they start to count interspersed with long, soft kisses. Soon the silent communication gives way to gentle caresses beneath the blanket. Holding each other in the dew and shared warmth, they begin to kiss each other very passionately. Suddenly, Bill's conscience overcomes his desires as he says, "Sarah, let's stop for now. I really love being here with you. However, you mean too much to me and I'm afraid of where this will lead if we continue tonight."

Reluctantly, Sarah inquires, "Do we really have to stop? I really care *so* much for you and..." The look on his face confirms her conscience too and she concedes, "Okay, if I must. Besides, the greatest guy in the world owns my heart. The passion will takes care of itself and I know how much you love me. Just hold me close." As the dew falls around them in the trees and on the ground, she lays her head on his chest and listens to the heart *she* owns.

Monday at school, Sarah relates Friday night's events to her friends. During the discussion, Karen says, "You're so lucky to have a guy that loves you that much."

Sarah says, "I know I'm really blessed. However, I wish he would have the courage to tell me more often."

"He'll tell you more openly when he thinks the time is right," Karen responds. Suddenly, Bill comes into the cafeteria and sits next to Sarah.

Whispering in her ear, he speaks from his heart, "Friday with you was so special to me. I loved your idea to go outside under the stars and you too," and then kisses her on her cheek. Her friends ask again, "Are there any more guys like you out there?"

Chuckling at their question, he says, "No there isn't because there's only one Sarah. Our hearts beat as one."

Karen says jokingly, "If you ever get tired of Sarah, I'll be right there waiting for you." As Bill teases with hesitation, Sarah waits breathlessly for his response.

Finally, Bill replies, "*Gotcha*. Sorry, that will *never* happen. Sarah means the world to me and my feelings for her run too deep in my heart." With his words, Sarah's heart melts and she knows her friends' hearts are melting too. As the bell rings, Bill and Sarah rush off to class. Fawning at Bill while they walk away, her friends glance suddenly at each other saying, "Don't you wish Bill had spilled a soft drink on you instead of Sarah?"

Final Luers Game

Friday night rushes the week to the eternal time line and the ride to Luers in Ft. Wayne looms. Bill looks forward to seeing his rival, Eli Kevlin, and to a challenging opponent. Deputy Layton picks up Bill and Sarah for the ride to the stadium and the buses. As Bill boards the team bus, he gazes at Sarah boarding the fan bus. Deputy Layton escorts the bus convoy and Sarah's deputy follows it as the convoy travels to Fort Wayne.

During warm ups, Bill strolls across the field to say hello to his rival and friend, Eli Kevlin. A great friendship and mutual respect developed between them during their games against each other. As they shake hands and pat each other on the back, Bill cracks a wry smile at Eli and says, "I hope we have a good game and put on a show for the fans. You know I'll miss our annual battles. It's been great fun if not sometimes painful."

"Well, if you like the rivalry that much, you'll really love it as my teammate. I decided to go to Notre Dame with you and will announce it after the season," Eli informs him.

Elated to be teammates, Bill says, "Man that's great. Wanna be roommates?"

Warming rapidly to the idea, Eli responds, "I think that's a great idea. Keep an eye out for my announcement." They shake hands again and return to their teams to finish the warm-up routine. Both teams complete their routines and depart the field for pre-game coaching.

When they return to the field for the game, an overflow crowd of 11,000 people packs Luers stadium. As Bill swaggers out with Deputy Layton, the South crowd erupts in cheers while the Luers' fans boo loudly. Bill reacts with a wry smile again, as he knows what to unleash and gives the crowd a fist pump to show he's ready to play. Bill calls Z-21 deep for Joey on the first play amid the smiles from his teammates and Joey nods he is ready to go. As the *Wizard* takes the snap and drops back, one of his linemen slips and falls. Eli blitzes in the hole left by the fallen lineman and nails Bill in the ribs again. As Sarah cringes, Eli helps Bill to his feet. Smiling, the two tap each other on their helmets while the Luers crowd roars with frenzy.

Bill signals Coach Mulinaro to run the same play and coach nods in agreement. In the huddle, the lineman who fell apologizes. With everyone in the huddle laughing, the lineman understands Bill is not upset at all. Again, the *Wizard* takes the snap and this time the lineman lays *Eli* out. Joey grasps the lightning launched from the Wizard's hand resulting in a 72-yard touchdown. Bill fist pumps and points to Sarah as he runs down to celebrate with Joey. Filled with the love sent her way, Sarah's heart returns the love in her radiant smile. Bill has an extraordinary game as South wins 35-7. After the game, Bill meets his friend and future teammate, Eli, at midfield again. As they discuss being roommates at Notre Dame, some of the Luers crowd reaches the edge of the field. Noticing the crowd, Deputy Layton motions it is time to go and quickly escorts Bill to the locker room.

Homecoming

With autumn in the air and football season well underway, it must be Homecoming time at South. The History club decorates and sells hundreds of colorful mums for sweethearts to wear at the game. Six senior girls receive nominations for queen while only one wins and the rest become the court. Being run like an election, each girl has a senior guy as their campaign manager who attempts to garner votes among the student body. Of course, Maddie and Sarah are in the running for queen. The principal reveals the contestants' names during the afternoon announcements the week before homecoming. Acceding to Sarah's wishes, her teacher allows her to leave class a couple of minutes early. Running on Mercury's wings from her class in the opposite end of the building, she reaches Bill at the other end before the other candidates can reach him. While Bill and Sarah don't have any classes together this semester, Bill takes three steps out of his classroom as soon as the bell rings only to find Sarah waiting there for him. Filled with excitement and anticipation, Sarah asks, "Bill, will you please be my manager for Homecoming Queen?"

Elated to be her choice, he responds warmly, "Yes I would be honored to do it."

Finally, in an emotional release, Sarah exhales deeply in a huge sigh and says, "*Thank you so much.* I wouldn't want anyone else to run my campaign." Silently, she considers, "I just might *be* the queen with Bill as my manager."

Verbalizing his feelings, he replies, "There isn't anyone else for whom I would consider doing this." After hugging each other and starting to their next classes, three other girls including Maddie ask Bill to manage their campaigns. To each request, he answers cordially, "Thank you for asking. I'm honored that you considered me. However, I apologize that I can't be your manager because Sarah Ormond asked me already and I accepted her offer."

After he denies Maddie's request to manage her, she says to one of her friends, "Well, it is going to be very difficult to win now without Bill as my manager. Sarah is so lucky to have him manage her."

Dumbfounded, Bill considers silently, "Wow, I never imagined Sarah asking me let alone so many other girls. Maybe I *can* help Sarah win as queen." With so many requests for him to manage queen campaigns, the guys with him start joking, "Hey, can you manage *our campaign* for queen? We're a cinch to get elected. We'll even wear dresses and wigs *just* for you." "Enough already guys. I'm as surprised as you are," Bill retorts.

Hitting the ground running during that day, Bill begins to ask others that day to help with Sarah's campaign. She offers to have everyone meet at her house to build a float and make campaign signs. The sign making is in her parent's basement while others build the float in the driveway. Arriving at her house early, Bill finds an anxious Sarah sitting nervously on the porch steps near the driveway. As he walks to the steps to sit beside her, she says, "Hardly anyone has arrived and those who have are all milling around. No one knows what to do. I'm not sure myself and need some guidance from someone." Looking deeply in her eyes, her concern and plea for help are as evident as her love. As he sits next to her on the steps, his heart swells with the love emanating from those beautiful eyes. Seeing the concern on her face and the love and trust in her eyes, he vows in his heart to do everything possible to fulfill her dreams.

"Don't worry Sarah," he answers as he hugs her, "I'll organize them into several work teams. We'll have you elected by the end of the week. Just leave it to me. I'll have one team make yard signs using yardsticks I obtained. Another team will make car signs. Others can work on the float. I'm excited about this. With your beauty and grace, you'll have no problem being elected queen. Trust me on this fact."

Relieved with his words, she hugs him again and hurries into the house while more people arrive. All the while, the sentinel trees gently wave in approval. Bill hurries to the back yard to organize the swelling crowd of helpers into the work teams he outlined to her. The sign making teams walk into Sarah's house while her mom directs them to the basement. She comments, "Sarah dear, I'm concerned about getting the work done in time for you. I know how much being homecoming queen means to you. I'm so nervous that you might not get elected."

Confidently, Sarah responds, "Don't worry mom. Bill has everything under control. He's doing an amazing job of organizing kids to do the work. We'll be fine now. I can see how much he loves me with his leadership and the work he's doing." After getting the float builders moving full bore on creation, he walks into the basement and past the full bar to check the sign work for himself. The *Maestro* takes the stage and orchestrates sign creation. While work develops smoothly, he plans to market "Sarah for Queen" carefully but visibly over the Indianapolis south side with as many yard signs as they can distribute. The local ice cream shop agrees to display "Vote Sarah for Homecoming Queen" on its marquee. Presenting her as a well-known name for whom any student will want to vote, he manages the campaign plan for her very well. Meanwhile,

Sarah dreams of how important it is to be a model representative of the school and muses, "I really want to be the queen, but I don't want people thinking I'm arrogant. I just want them to see me as a normal person. However, I want to represent the school and students wherever I am. After all, *I'll* be the Homecoming Queen and part of its tradition for the rest of my life."

Friday's pep session is the day of the vote. Each manager dresses in a white tuxedo jacket, black bow tie, and formal black pants gives a speech about their candidate and introduces her. When Bill's turn to speak arrives, he swaggers boldly to the microphone and delivers his oratory, "The office of homecoming queen is a huge responsibility carrying with it the weight of generations of young women who proudly bore the title before this year's queen. You as a student body want a person who is not only beautiful to the eye but who has beauty in her spirit as well. You want to elect a young woman who represents the entire student population with grace and respect. You want to elect a model student and a leader who exemplifies that tradition for another year. You want to elect a young woman who will carry that title into your hearts and make you proud you voted for her. For your careful consideration, may I present the embodiment of those characteristics, Sarah Ormond." The crowd roars its approval as she glides into the gym wearing a floor-length, aqua-blue formal with short cap sleeves, long line white gloves, and white pumps shoes.

After her manager announces her to the students, Maddie walks in wearing white shoes and a floor-length, low-cut, empire waist formal with thin straps and deep red bodice, while the lower portion of the dress is bright white. As her campaign plan utilizes every possibility, Maddie hopes to entice student votes by wearing a dress with colors nearly matching the school colors. To the approving student body, the other girls enter into the gym in floor-length formals individually after their introductions with each candidate receiving a single, white rose. Promenading the length of the gym, each girl stands next to their manager for group pictures. All the girls are beautiful in their formals but three girls stand apart from the others. However, one of the three is amazing with luscious, flowing red hair and a quiet spirit of confidence and leadership worthy of a queen. During the pictures, the peering camera eye catches a nervous Bill glancing in the opposite direction of the others and to the gym floor. As the photographer completes the pictures, the group takes their seats for the remainder of the pep session. After a few additional speeches about the importance of the game and the moment, the pep session ends. While the student body returns to their rooms to vote, the anxious candidates await the school's announcement of this year's queen at halftime of tonight's game.

The few hours until game time drag by slowly. Finally, the prayers and nerves of the candidates force the sun from the sky. In an open field near the school, the student body gathers around a huge stack of wood that will soon become a blazing bonfire. The faculty cheerleading sponsor pins homecoming corsages carefully on all the cheerleaders. Meanwhile, the candidates have changed from their formals into business attire more suited to the bonfire. Sarah is stunning in a camel color Pendleton blazer, a gold and brown plaid Pendleton skirt, and a dark, old gold polyester blouse with a button-down collar. Maddie is resplendent also in a grey, herringbone plaid suit and a white ruffled blouse with a closed neck. They wait together for the results announcement at halftime. As the bonfire starts and grows quickly, the fire department is on hand to prevent any accidents. During the next half hour, the crowd whips to frenzied levels before moving to the stadium across the street as the fire department extinguishes the remains of the bonfire. While the candidates move to a seat of honor on a platform near the field, the previous year's queen waits in attendance to crown her successor after the halftime announcement.

South moves swiftly to control the game well by the half. The Wizard drives the team to his best half of football in anticipation of what is to come. At halftime, the floats created by various clubs and student groups parade around the stadium interspersed with convertibles carrying the queen candidates. One unique float has a student dressed in a cardinal costume in a chariot drawn by a donkey under control of a student in a sombrero and serape. Others carry various cardinals and designs unique to the imaginations of their creators and clubs. As each car reaches a designated spot on the track, the young woman inside departs her coach and waits for the others. Once all candidates arrive at the gathering, they promenade onto the field for their introductions with their managers. All the managers are in suits except for Bill who is in his uniform, sweaty from a half of combat. Great anticipation and excitement runs through the crowd as the candidates shift their stances nervously. Suddenly, the announcer proclaims, "Ladies and gentlemen, we have tallied your votes for your Homecoming Queen. Without further delay, here are the results. She's an outstanding student. She has style. She has grace. You love her as a leader and will love her as your Queen. She has luscious, long red hair. I present your new Homecoming Queen, Sarah Ormond."

With the long, red hair proclamation, Sarah screams and gives Bill a huge hug. While hugging him, she whispers in his ear, "I wouldn't have won if it wasn't for you."

Overjoyed and emphasizing her inner and outer beauty, he whispers back with a big smile, "You would have won no matter who your manager was. Didn't you hear the announcer? Sarah, I have never loved you more than I love you right now." Her heart cannot believe what her ears just heard as Bill wipes his sweat off his queen's arms and face with a clean towel. Still reeling from his words, Sarah receives a bouquet of a dozen red roses as last year's queen places a silver tiara on her head. Dreaming of what might have been, Maddie urges a queen's court smile of support. While Sarah's mind takes in the whirlpool of activity around her, she replays the moment of Bill's expressed love repeatedly. As the newly crowned queen and her court move back to the viewing platform, the crowd cheers enthusiastically with approval for their choice. A beaming Sarah takes her seat as queen on the newly placed throne in the center of the platform with her court on either side.

South demonstrates its mastery again in the second half and continues its march towards another state championship. After the game, Bill changes quickly into the suit he had Joey bring to the game for him. Rushing out of the media room, he relays to the reporters, "I'm sorry guys no questions tonight. I'm going to meet my Queen."

Floating out on love's wings with Deputy Layton close to him, he meets Sarah and her parents, surprising them totally with the suit. She chuckles, "I guess we're not going for pizza tonight."

Revealing a wonderful surprise, Bill replies, "This night is too special for just pizza. We're going out to dinner at a steak house that Deputy Layton recommended to me. He called the owner already and asked that we not be bothered during our dinner."

After parking Bill's car, they walk into the St. Elmo's restaurant where the manager greets them as old friends. Yet, this was their first time there. He says, "Please follow me. We have a special place waiting for you already." As the royal couple walks through the restaurant, they catch the eye of everyone they pass. The manager gives them a booth off in a corner away from prying public eyes. The evening is perfect as the staff is very attentive. They enjoy sharing their loving glances and warm touches together in this special place.

After the wonderful dinner, they return to Sarah's where her parents wait for them. She bubbles about the evening, the restaurant, and Deputy Layton's care of them. Sarah's parents say, "We're thrilled for you both. We're glad you didn't have anyone bother you. Although, we know you don't like being given special treatment."

With joy overflowing his heart, Bill answers, "On special evenings like this one, it's good to be treated with extra care. Tonight was about treating Sarah like the queen she is."

As Sarah walks to her room to change clothes, Bill says, "I have some clothes in my car. Is there somewhere that I can change?"

With a smile, her mom answers, "Your room is still in the same place." Quickly, Sarah changes into her pajamas with a surprise in mind as Bill changes into his sweats and a Notre Dame Football t-shirt.

Coming out of their rooms, Bill says, "Sarah, I have one more surprise for the night for you to put on," as he hands her a Notre Dame Football t-shirt. Coyly, Sarah pulls her pajama top off in front of Bill to try on the shirt. He is embarrassed but relieved she wore her bikini top underneath and one other item as she puts on the t-shirt. "*Sarah*, you still wear the heart necklace I gave you." he exclaims.

"Why *wouldn't* I wear it? It is a very special part of me and of the love we have for each other." she responds. Buoyed by that love engulfing the moment, they walk hand-in-hand to their couch and cuddle under their blanket. Discussing the special night they shared and their love for each other, they drift into the arms of the Sandman. Suddenly, Bill awakens, confused where he is. It is 2:00 AM and Sarah is sound asleep safely in his arms. Slowly, he works his way off the couch trying ever so hard not to awaken his sleeping queen. Picking her up tenderly, he lovingly carries her to her room. Lowering her gently into her bed, he tucks her in softly and slips to his room quietly. It is a moment in which most guys would attempt to press an advantage. However, he loves her too much to entertain such ideas.

Waking up first, Sarah notices Bill's door remains shut. As she opens the door stealthily, he lies sleeping in his sweatpants and without a t-shirt. Feeling the love welling in her heart, she sits next to him gently and softly kisses him until he wakes up. The love in his heart surges as he smiles and says tenderly, "Wow that was nice. Can you arrange to wake me up like that every day?" His words of love evoke a passionate response from Sarah as they hug and kiss for a while longer. As Sarah's parents come out of their room, Bill and Sarah saunter into the kitchen. Bill offers, "Sarah and I will fix breakfast."

Her mom jokes, "All this time we thought you were only a football player. Now besides everything else you can do, we find you're a chef too."

Having cooked at home for several years, Bill replies with a chuckle, "Well, I do know a little bit about cooking." He and Sarah start to work on some omelets, toast, and juice.

Bill fixes a fresh spinach, ham, mushroom and shredded white cheddar cheese omelet with toast and fresh squeezed orange juice. It is a breakfast soon to become of note for him at Notre Dame and everyone marvels how good the breakfast is. After breakfast, Bill and Sarah clean up the dishes together. Sarah says, "I'm going to take a shower and get ready for this *wonderful* day."

Not wanting to inconvenience the Ormonds, Bill explains, "I want to shower as well and will return as soon as possible."

With excitement, Sarah says, "You can shower *here*. You have some clothes in a gym bag you left a while back." A bit uneasy with her offer, Bill looks to her parents for approval.

As everyone laughs, her parents reply, "We give you our approval on one condition. You both have to promise not to shower with your steady."

Sarah takes her shower first after saying, "Bill, while you shower, I'll get your clothes from your bag and lay them on the bed." Expecting no subterfuge, Bill begins to shower in the bathroom.

Finishing his shower, he calls down the hall to the family room, "Sarah, I'll be ready in a little while." Going into his room with just a towel around him, he finds Sarah sitting on his bed with a huge smile. Surprised and red-faced, he asks, "Would you *please* excuse me for a minute?"

With a wistful tease, she replies, "I'm not going anywhere." Shaking his head, he smiles, grabs his underwear and pants, and returns to the bathroom to change.

On the way, he warns her jokingly, "Sarah Ormond, you had better not be here when I get back."

Having a different idea in mind, she agrees, "Ok. I'll be out in the family room."

Putting on his underwear and pants, he returns to his room and knocks on the door asking, "Sarah, are you in here?" Hearing no answer and feeling somewhat safe, Bill opens the door slowly. Peeking through the opening expectantly, he spies Sarah still sitting on the bed and decides to walk in anyway. Speechless, Sarah smiles at him, gazing longingly into his eyes. She saw him in his swimsuit at the pool party and the lake but his finely sculptured body still mesmerizes her. Thinking to himself, "Ok if that's what you want to do," he shrugs his shoulders and attempts to finish dressing. After watching him stand shirtless while time stands still, Sarah's emotions break free from her mind's logical confines. Attacking him with delight, she showers him with passionate kisses and full body hugs as the joy of the moment with her overcomes his inhibitions.

Signing Day

As the season ends, South has another perfect record, 13-0 and another state championship. Finishing his high school football career, Bill has two state championships, a twenty-six game winning streak, and his team ranked number one nationally. The second championship expunges the pain of the championship game loss two years ago from his emotions completely. It is only a catalyst memory that fired his drive to carry to team to greater achievements. Ruminating football memories in his mind, his thoughts of Sarah intertwine with those memories inexorably. Anticipating an exciting future with Notre Dame, his emotions drift with increasing sadness at closing his high school career and camaraderie with current teammates. However, the media continues a watchful eye with many strongly speculating about his college career potential. The excitement builds regarding his national signing to fulfill his verbal commitment to Notre Dame. After all, he is the greatest quarterback prospect to appear in quite some time and he will play on a national stage against the weight of tradition and media scrutiny.

Not to be outdone, Sarah climbs academically into the middle of the top ten in the senior class. She *is* that leader she purposed to be as homecoming queen. Very active in South academics, she is a National Honor Society member, a candidate for Hoosier Girl's State legislative experience, an academic letter recipient, a yearbook staff member, and an Art Club member. With each new goal she achieves, Bill praises her intelligence and wisdom. Inside, he explodes with pride watching her successes. Knowing the future will take them to separate schools and life paths, they revel in every moment and joy they share now. Together, Sarah and Bill *are* the royal couple at South.

Their senior year advances like a freight train running downhill without brakes. Adhering to each other as time struggles to separate them, they spend time at the Pizza Inn and Kristen's Burgers with friends, enjoy movie nights together and sometimes with friends, but most often, private walks in the neighborhood, in Brown County, and in the woods behind her house. Snow carpets their paths during the winter painting special scenes as they open their eyes and hearts to each other, to snow angels, and to God's creation. Bill takes special care to present Sarah at the Christmas dance as he did last year only this time he presents *his* queen to everyone. The senior prom beckons them as a couple to share this special time with each other and with friends in sartorial splendor. With February's arrival, National Signing Day approaches quickly. That's the day Bill will sign his Letter of Intent to attend Notre Dame on a football scholarship. Sarah emphasizes, "Bill, this is the biggest day in your life to date. The media coverage will be crushing."

Mentally reviewing his time with her quickly, Bill contradicts, "Sarah, the biggest days in my life are with you, the soft drink incident, your honor in the cafeteria, the Christmas Dances, and especially Homecoming. This pales in comparison. I'll just sign it in Coach Mulinaro's office and be done with it."

Hearing his love and praise but adding her special dose of reality, Sarah states, "Bill Denton, that's not how it's going to be done."

Seeing that determined look and hearing her strong willed tone, Bill questions, "What do you mean? I don't understand."

Sarah explains, "You have so many supporters in this community. They spent their hard-earned money watching all your games and your career and you owe it to them to include them in your process. You need to be attentive to their feelings about you. You have to make the signing an event in the gym so everyone in the school and community gets to see you. Besides, you're at your best when the stage is immense and the event is extremely important."

Finishing her comments, a big smile bursts on her face. Bill considers openly, "I *do* know who and what I am. Although I'd rather the event be a small quiet one, you're absolutely right. I need to share this last event in my high school career with you and your parents, Mr. Tibbs, my friends, Deputy Layton, and all the folks who supported the team and me in my career. We'll do it together."

Ten thousand people pack the seven-thousand-seat gym at South. Joey, who as Bill predicted, is a first team high school All-American and plans to sign his letter first to attend the University of Texas. Bill handpicks the persons to join him on the podium. Coach Mulinaro, Deputy Layton, Bill's grandparents, Mr. Tibbs, Notre Dame's Coach Alan, Ted Davidson, the Notre Dame Athletic Director, and of course, Sarah will sit beside him and share in the special moment. Awaiting their entrance to the gym with Bill, Sarah says, "I shouldn't be up there because I don't have anything to do with the team."

Knowing her importance to him, Bill insists, "If you're not there, the whole deal is off. The gym may be packed but I need you there with me. You've always been by my side and I want you to sit next to me. Sarah, you're the one who's the most special of all." With her love in full display, she agrees with a big smile and an embarrassed foot shuffle. Walking into the gym together, the applause and cheers begin to build as a storm surge. When Bill steps to the podium with Sarah at his side, the surge erupts in a thunderous standing ovation lasting fifteen minutes. Finally, he gives them a fist pump and after additional thundering from the audience, motions for them to be quiet. Holding Sarah's chair for her as she sits, he continues his courteous ways to the approving roar of the crowd. Again, he quiets those in attendance respectfully. After a few remarks to the crowd regarding his strong appreciation of their team support and coming along for a great ride, he receives his official form from AD Davidson and signs his name. Holding the signed form up to another thunderous standing ovation, he hands it to Coach Alan. Overflowing with pride for Bill, Sarah stands with applause yet witnessing the tear in their world begin.

The writer from the premier sports magazine, now a good friend and confidant, approaches as Bill and Sarah leave the gym to another standing ovation. Ever vigilant, Deputy Layton steps between Bill and the writer quickly. Recognizing his friend, Bill tells Deputy Layton, "He's ok sir. However, he is the only writer with whom I wish to speak."

Deputy Layton takes the writer with him outside the gym in the hallway. The writer explains, "Bill, my magazine wants you on their cover again for the College Preview issue."

Bill replies, "Now that I'm a Notre Dame signee, you'll need to acquire permission for the article through the Notre Dame Athletic Department. That said however, I'm looking forward to working with you again as always." Walking in convoy to Bill's car, Bill and Sarah get in and drive to Sarah's house with Deputy Layton's escort.

With his arm around Sarah's shoulder, they walk into the dimly lit house. Since Sarah's parents didn't have a police escort like Bill and Sarah, they have yet to arrive at home. The South post-event parking lot malaise has them still searching for an opening, waiting for time to extract their car. Arriving at their couch and sitting down, he says, "Thank you *so* much for making me see the right way to approach the signing. You always have great insight and vision regarding others. May I be completely open with you?"

"Of course, you can always be open with me," Sarah responds warmly.

With anxiety in his voice, he says, "Okay, you know I'm deeply in love with you but I'm concerned about our future. I don't want to lose you but I'm afraid. With us going to different schools and my time commitments with practice and schoolwork, will we have time for each other?"

Sarah opens her heart too, "I love you so very much. Let's not talk about the future and enjoy the time we have together *now*. We *still* have four months before you go to Notre Dame. We have *so much* we can do together." As the reality of the futures weighs on their hearts, Sarah rests her head on Bill's chest while he holds her tightly. While neither utters any further word, the tears running down their cheeks speaks volumes about the pain in their hearts. Suddenly, he gently rests her backward in his arms and kisses her passionately as if he will never feel her touch in his arms or the press of his lips against hers again. Sarah responds passionately as though she will never feel his warm caress again.

Time Running Short

During the next four months, Bill and Sarah spend as much quality time together as possible with schoolwork. On the weekends, he stays at her house often while they share their love with cozy evenings on the couch or on blankets in the back yard in each other's arms. While in the back yard, they snuggle under the watchful eyes of the stars and the sentinel trees. The Meridian and South 31 Drive-Ins give them time alone to be entertained yet time to talk about their futures and plan their prom attire. At the senior prom, they are the royal couple again. Knowing how special they are, everyone allows them to dance, laugh, and best of all hang out with their most special friends without distractions. At the after-prom party, they have even more fun finding empty corners in which to engage their hearts with stealthy kisses and warm caresses. Eventually, they arrive at Sarah's house around 3:00 AM.

Her parents are fast asleep while Bill and Sarah change quietly into their sleeping attire. They both come out of their rooms at the same time and as Sarah moves toward to his room, Bill takes her hand to stop her. Gently and with love pouring from his heart, he explains, "This is a very special night for us. Tonight will be perfect if we fall asleep in each other's arms but we should fall asleep on the couch. Your parents wouldn't ever let me stay again if we fell asleep together in either of our rooms."

Reluctantly, she agrees, "I'd love to spend the night together with you. I just wanted to spend it somewhere besides the couch but it *has* been our special place. Hey, maybe we could sleep outside under a couple of blankets and wait for the sun."

At first enamored with her idea, Bill replies quickly with a huge smile, "Are you sure you weren't thinking *love's dew* and not *the dew*? We'd get *soaked*." As they laugh and move quickly to the living room couch, they begin to kiss each other passionately and caress each other warmly but Sarah's wish doesn't happen. Again, he whispers, "I love you Sarah." She echoes back her love for him as they cuddle closely and fall asleep.

In a couple of weeks, they walk together at graduation as their high school world concludes. Graduation pictures, awkward final goodbyes, and parties finish the day, as some old friends part ways forever. Sarah garnishes her excellent high school career with an academic scholarship. Back at her house together, they discuss how to do what they want yet avoid the prying public eyes until Bill leaves for Notre Dame. With voluntary workouts just three weeks away, the first week of July, they plan to spend every minute they can together. He explains, "Since the workouts are voluntary, I can come home on weekends. Let's keep this to ourselves so it can be just our time together." When they enjoy a movie or dinner, they make it a late one to avoid the big crowds. Having gained the friendship of Karen Anderson's aunt and uncle, Bill and Sarah drive to Grandview Lake several times during the next few weeks to spend time alone together. Swimming in the lake sharing kisses and hugs, the sun warms their hearts and the water. On other occasions, they sit on the balcony in solitude sharing their hearts verbally while blending with nature and the view of the lake. Often they share their hearts and minds with Karen's aunt and uncle in friendly discussions. Returning home through Brown County and Nashville, they enjoy blankets together in the park, solitary nature walks through the forests, and food while shopping in the town.

One of the biggest events of the summer is "JudeFest," a fundraiser for St. Jude Catholic School. The school is located on the campus of Roncalli Catholic High School, one of the finest high schools in Indianapolis. The FGS girls and Dirty Boys along with Sarah and Bill go to "JudeFest" every year. In previous years, it has been great fun, always drawing a huge crowd of people. This year, Sarah and Bill walk in and the crowd swarms them immediately to meet and greet Bill and obtain autographs and pictures from him. Wanting to spend time with him, the crowd engulfs Sarah as she disappears within it. Fearing for her safety, Bill locates and spirits her away after they make concerned eye contact. Their hearts know what their eyes convey that their world has changed rapidly in a few short weeks. As they arrive safely away from the crowd, Sarah whispers to him, "Bill, can we leave, please. I want to be alone with you and not share you with this crowd. They aren't going to allow us to be together and just have fun."

Agreeing with her assessment, he says, "That's a great idea," as they leave for Sarah's house. Arriving at her house and parking themselves on their couch, they hold each other fearfully knowing the coming future and watch TV for solace. Both their eyes are red with tears with the knowledge they gained today. Speaking no words, they exchange long kisses that express their innermost fears to each other silently.

While Bill and Sarah savor every moment they have, July rushes upon them quickly. With Saturday being the final night before their future arrives tomorrow afternoon, he spends the night at Sarah's, each in their separate rooms. After catching a late movie and grabbing a pizza to go, they head back to her house. None of their friends expects to see them tonight, as they all know that tonight is just for Bill and Sarah. Their friends are aware that tonight is very special for the two and they need solitude. As she listens to his heart beating while resting her head on his chest, the tears begin to flow silently down her cheeks. He protects her in his arms for now but misses her touch in his heart already. His tears track silently down his cheeks for her as well. Sunday morning, they recover old memories by repeating familiar activities together, attending church, and eating at the same steak house as they did their first Sunday together. Returning to Sarah's house, Bill packs his remaining items, changes into traveling clothes, and bids goodbye to her parents. Adding their best wishes, the Ormonds convey, "Good luck Bill. We look forward to watching you on TV on Saturdays this fall."

As Bill and Sarah walk to his car, they wear their emotions on their sleeves and their cheeks without reservation. He clarifies, "Sarah, please don't cry. I'll be back on the weekends. Besides, it makes this that much harder on us both. We have such great memories together and we can draw on that for now, the Christmas dances, the prom, the lake, and especially Homecoming. Wear the heart necklace to keep me near *your* heart and in your thoughts always." With that review, they both stop crying. Finally, after more discussion, hugs and kisses, he gets in his car reluctantly and she watches him drive off. Bill watches his world fade in his rear-view mirror while Sarah watches her world disappear down the street. New journeys begin for them too soon.

After arriving at Notre Dame, Bill unpacks and mentally prepares for his future. Eli Kevlin arrives and unpacks in the room as well. The next day involves time spent meeting with the coaches, receiving instructions, and getting acclimated to life as a major college athlete. When Bill meets with Coach Alan, his time is cordial as expected from his Notre Dame camps and recruitment process. They discuss plans for his workouts and team activities. Suddenly, the coach makes a proposal to him. "Bill, in looking at our personnel, we would like to add a couple of talented people in critical positions for you," Coach expounds.

Excited with the proposal, Bill says, "Coach, I'm a bit confused. I thought all the scholarships were given for this year?"

Coach explains in detail, "Yes Bill, you're correct. Here is what I'm asking. With another couple of critical additions to the roster, we'll have the group we want for you and the program to compete for the national championship during your years with us. You're very important to this program and I wouldn't ask this unless I was confident building the program around you. I'd like for you to red-shirt your freshman year and then experience the full four years of our building for you. You don't have to answer now but I would like an answer before mandatory practice starts."

Overwhelmed at the coach's request to build the ND program around him completely, Bill considers for a moment and inquires intently, "Coach, I *do* have a couple of questions. Will I still have a full scholarship? Can I practice with the team in the interim? Finally, can Eli Kevlin and I still be roommates?"

"Good questions, Bill. Your scholarship remains in force, as we *have* to protect your relationship with us. You'll do everything as you normally would regarding practice, schoolwork, and roommates. The only difference is that you'll not play this year. I know this is a lot to ask a young man to consider. However, I have not seen anyone who performs as you do in my tenure as coach. Think of how much you can learn during this year while studying defenses and plays. Now, I'm sure the media will be relentless but if any person can handle the pressure, I know you can," Coach Alan explains. With his questions answered by the coach, Bill agrees to forego playing for one year.

On his first weekend back home in July, Bill informs Sarah, "I have some interesting news for us. I'll not be playing for one year. Coach Alan is building the team around me and needs a couple of critical recruits to complete his process."

Excited at the prospect of more time with him, she bubbles, "That's great news, right? We'll have more time together on the weekends." Apprehensively, he explains, "Well, not really, I still practice and do all the things I normally would with the team except I don't get to play."

Disappointed, she answers, "Ok, we'll find a way to work all this out. I still miss you more than you can ever know and *now* I won't even get to see you on TV for a year."

"Oh, I think I have a clue. I miss you deeply in my heart too," he returns. They continue enjoying the time shared together. After several wonderful July weekends together, August 1 arrives and with it, the official practice time for the season.

Redshirt

W ord spreads like a raging wildfire among the media that their hailed champion at Notre Dame will not play this year. The premier sports magazine cover regales, ND COACH ALAN: CRAZY OR CRAZY LIKE A FOX. Directing all media requests with aplomb to the Athletic Department, Bill is content in the knowledge of the team building around him. The Coach and the Athletic Department continue to ply their plans in secret from the media. Recognizing the stealth exhibited by the school, Bill accepts his part in this spy novel with relish. Secretly, he always wanted to keep the media guessing in high school but never wanted to offend. Now with the blessing of the school, he has a newly found freedom from the media. Still the media searches for meaning to the fact that THE CHOSEN ONE has yet to appear on the playing field. Anticipation and curiosity grow steadily since he is *not* suspended or academically ineligible.

All the while, Sarah and Bill continue to pursue their love for each other mostly from afar. He schedules time on Sundays to see her at Purdue but the five-hour round trip leaves precious little time together with schoolwork. In the brief times they share at Purdue, they spend time sharing blankets and kisses on Slater Hill. They visit

Chauncey Hill and surrounding areas and eat at the Triple XXX, Arni's, and other restaurants in the Purdue West area. They stroll along the Wabash River in the park, Purdue's Memorial Mall, and window shop at the Mall a few miles from campus. Their flame of love burns steadily although each has developed new friendships at their particular schools and the dampening pull from the new friends grows steadily. Calling Sarah as frequently during the week as his practice time and schoolwork permits, Bill doesn't expect her to sit and wait for his calls. However, the times when he actually reaches her grow less frequent as the year progresses and her social groups grow steadily wider. While absence makes the heart grow fonder, total lack dampens even the most ardent fire as Sarah begins to enjoy her time with her new friends immensely. As the season progresses, he gains a strong knowledge of college defenses from sheer observation and memory retention. Helping direct signals to the current quarterbacks, he observes coaching patterns in the staff. The year proves he is as much of a coach as anyone on the staff is. Excitement builds quietly among coaches in anticipation of what Bill brings to the program in the coming year.

Continuing his correspondence with Sarah, Bill's love burns brightly for her as the summer approaches. Excitement builds as he can barely wait to see her again. The first college year ends successfully for them both and they arrive back at their homes. He contacts Sarah excitedly, "Hi Sarah. Are you free this afternoon? I would love to come by to see you."

"Oh Bill. It's good to hear from you again. I missed talking with you but the year has been so busy. You're welcome to come by at… say 1:30," she responds. He agrees on the time but notices a difference in her voice. Passing it off as a growing sophistication from college, he readies himself for their agreed time together again. Arriving at her house, she greets him warmly at the door.

Missing her touch more as the year progressed, he offers, "Why don't we sit on our couch and pick up where we left off? I missed you immensely."

With a different thought in mind, Sarah counters, "That definitely sounds inviting but why don't we go to a movie and pizza instead?" Puzzled at her response but wanting to be with her nonetheless, he agrees to her suggestion. At the movie, he snuggles next to her with his arm around her shoulders. Surprisingly, she does not lay her head on his shoulder as usual. However, by the end of the movie, they laugh quietly and converse warmly as they once did. At the Pizza Inn, they saunter back to their usual table and snuggle next to each other while feeding each other slices of pizza. After enjoying the pizza and each other, he lets her drive his car back to her house, much to her delight. Exchanging gentle kisses in the car, she offers, "Bill, would you like to come in for a bit?" Agreeing excitedly, he spies the heart-shaped ruby necklace still gracing her neck. Slowly on the couch as his heart warms to the reminiscence, they reacquaint themselves with each other's touch.

During the summer, they spend as much time together as they can. The media crush begins again as they know he will play this fall. Bill and Sarah begin their game of spy versus spy to elude the throng and the most elite of reporters. Not having seen Karen's aunt and uncle for a while, they contact them to inquire about spending some time at the lake with them. Again, Bill and Sarah drive to Grandview Lake a few times during the summer to spend time with Karen's relatives and be alone together. Each time they return home through Brown County and Nashville to eat dinner. During the summer, they drive to other Indiana State Park getaways like Turkey Run, Spring Mill, and Clifty Falls, enjoying picnics and blankets together under the clouds and exploring nature's solitude. However, Brown County remains their favorite. Despite all the fun, Bill senses an emotional change in Sarah that he cannot pinpoint and which they don't discuss. Being happy to experience her kisses and caresses again, he does not want to spoil his time with her as July's workouts rush at them again. On the last weekend before mandatory workouts begin, Bill is at Sarah's house and says, "Our second game is home against Purdue this year and I'll leave you two tickets to the game in case you want to bring a friend. I'll call you the week before the game and tell you where and how to get to the locker room. I want to see you before the game. Would you please come?"

Remembering their games together at South, Sarah thinks, "That sounds wonderful" and says, "I'll be waiting for your call."

The Fighting Irish

In the weeks leading up to the game, Bill notices coolness in Sarah's voice when he calls. It is *not* as if she doesn't care about speaking with him. Her words are still warm and caring. Nevertheless, the *Wizard* senses a difference there. Before the Purdue game in Notre Dame's season, Bill appears on the cover of the premier sports magazine again. This time the caption reads, FINALLY, THE CHOSEN ONE LEADS THE IRISH. Stating Bill will lead the Irish back to glory again, the article fills the faithful with great anticipation. The magazine bases its premise on his performances at South and the first game of the season. After the first game against Northwestern, which ND won 35-14, his teammates know he *is* the guy who can do it. In recognition of that fact, they copy the South t-shirts using Notre Dame colors of navy blue with Notre Dame gold lettering. All of them wear shirts under their uniforms that say "PROTECT THE MAN" and they toss Bill his t-shirt reading "THE MAN." While he really does not want to wear it, the upper classmen remind him with glee, "Hey Bill, you may be *the* quarterback but you're still a red-shirt freshman to us and you have to wear it." As he smiles and shakes his head, he slips on the shirt. The team erupts in thunderous approval, stoked, and ready to unleash its fury on Purdue. Bill completes his pre-game warm ups and walks out of the locker room while everyone finishes getting ready.

A Tearful Meeting

eaving the locker room, Bill walks to the barricades to talk to Trooper Larry Ted, his state police bodyguard at all the games. He relates to the trooper, "There will be a beautiful, petite, redhead who will come up to you and ask to see me. You'll have no problem recognizing the girl about who I'm talking. If anyone else is with her, please keep them at the barricade. This is very important to me. She's the only one with whom I want to speak. I'll be sitting on the chair by the entrance to the field."

Trooper Ted says, "It's ok Bill. I understand and that's how it will be."

Strolling over to the media throng, Bill inquires, "Guys, I need you to give me and my friend I'm expecting to see some privacy. I've never once asked for a favor from any of you and I've always tried to be cordial. I have always answered your questions and requests for photos. I never questioned any article or photo you folks have put out about me. I understand who I am and what you expect of me. I always try to accommodate all of your requests."

The media throng agrees with all his statements. However, one curious reporter smells a great story brewing and asks, "Hey Bill, what's going on? This must be something very special."

Not wanting to divulge his true feelings to the world, he explains with a twinge of sadness in his voice, "My best friend in high school is coming to the game today and I may not get to see the person again for a long time. I would really appreciate it if you don't write or photograph anything about our visit. This is very personal to me and I trust you to honor my request."

They press corps shakes their heads in agreement and reply, "Bill, we're all human. Don't worry. You've been good to us and we'll honor your request."

A few minutes later to the surprise of the press corps Sarah and her date come to the barricade and she calls out, "Bill, Bill."

The trooper calls aloud, "Bill, over here. There is someone here to speak with you." As his eyes make contact with hers, a huge smile engulfs his face and he nods his head in affirmation. Trooper Ted opens the barricade to allow Sarah through and her date starts to follow. As the trooper steps in front of her date, he informs, "Sorry son, only Sarah is allowed to speak with Bill."

Putting up a typical college protest, he says smartly, "Hey you can't do that. I'm with her and she's my date to this game."

Trooper Ted replies, "Sir, you need to step back behind the barricade. This is a private conversation between two old friends." While he isn't happy about it, he complies with the trooper's directive.

As Sarah nears him, Bill strolls up to greet her with a hug. He positions himself with his back to the media and other prying eyes as she stands facing him. Ever vigilant regarding her care and protection, he wants to be the only one to see her face. Making deep eye contact, they hug tightly and start crying uncontrollably. Regaining his composure first, reluctantly Bill says "I can tell we both know what today is, right?"

His statement ceases Sarah's crying and she responds, "Yes, I know. Today is our last day together. We love each other so much but it's not enough."

Agreeing with her, Bill adds, "You're right as always. I don't want to let you go because I love you so but this isn't fair to either of us. I *have* to let you go *because* I love you."

Hearing his expression of love again, Sarah explains through her tears, "Our world has split into two different worlds. We've tried to keep in touch but we're both busy in our two worlds, prisoners of the immediate. Our letters will become almost non-existent and the phone calls will become fewer and fewer. The tyranny of our daily lives will become our task master and jailer."

Hearing the words he feared most, Bill continues to explain his heart, "I understand completely. You'll do what your new world demands of you. It's a new social world and you'll become a strong businesswoman. If you are very fortunate, God may allow you that time to be the artist your talent demands. Whatever your future brings, I know you'll be successful and I'll always be proud of you. I'll be the *Maestro* on the biggest stage of which I ever dreamed. The media will analyze and scrutinize everything I do and the persons with me. We'll be the same loving, caring people we are but in two different worlds now."

Expressing the pain in her heart, Sarah opens, "I miss you already, your touch, your kisses, your protection, and most of all your love."

Sharing the pain in his heart, Bill adds, "I started missing you at the end of our junior year. I knew this was coming and I savored every moment of every day with you when we were seniors, the Christmas Dance and Homecoming when South crowned my Queen. I fought this day's arrival, the day we say goodbye to each other, the day I say goodbye to my best friend. Please tell your parents how much I love them and you."

Overcome with the pain, Sarah says, "This is so hard I wanted our love and us to last forever." Suddenly, she reaches back with both hands and unclasps her heart-shaped ruby necklace. Taking his hand, she places the necklace in it then says, "This has always been next to my heart to remind me of you. You *are* forever in my heart but let it remind you now of the love we share apart from each other."

As tears begin to flow down his cheeks, Bill quietly exclaims, "We'll last forever and so will our love, just from different places now. Goodbye Sarah, I love you more than my feeble words can express."

Adding a note of finality to the moment, Sarah says, "Goodbye Bill, I love you so deeply. There is a special place in my heart where you will always stay."

Returning to the press line, they give each other a hug to burn in their memories forever. Relaxing her hug, she queries, "Would you like to meet my date?"

With the pain still fresh in his heart, Bill replies, "No, not really. I hope you understand." Understanding his reasoning fully, she decides against adding to the pain that both hearts felt.

Giving each other one last "memory" hug and kisses on the cheeks, both express how much they will miss each other again. She hopes one last time to hear his voice express the love he has for her. Her heart aches and her mind echoes a prayer, "Please God, let him say it. Please tell me you love me one more time." Feeling God tug at his heart, he whispers, "I'll miss you more than you'll ever know. I'll always love you." Sarah whispers another prayer, "Thank you God." To Bill she whispers, "I'll always love you too."

Sarah dries her tears and walks to her date. When Bill is within hearing range, her date says smugly, "Hey Denton, Purdue's gonna kick your butt today." Breaking the sadness of Bill's moment with his challenge, Sarah and Bill make eye contact with each other and his wry smile tells her Bill has a point to prove now. Unfortunately for Purdue, the *Wizard* awakens from his painful slumber. Seeing this smile many times before a big game, Sarah's face bursts forth with a huge smile and she shakes her head. Exasperated by the mental and emotional connection between Sarah and Bill, her date quizzes, "Ok, what is it with you two and why are you smiling so big?"

Sensing her date's distrust, she replies with a raised eyebrow, "Wait until the game and *you'll* find out." Hurrying into the locker room, Bill places the treasured necklace carefully into his gym bag. Sarah's and his new worlds apart from each other have begun.

Game Time

G ame time quickly approaches and Coach Alan has the Irish
fired up. Purdue is their in-state rival and it's always a big
game. As the Irish head out of the tunnel, a TV employee
stops Bill. As Bill questions, "Hey, why did you stop me," the TV
crewperson directs, "We saw the entrances you made in high school.
We want the same thing from you right now. We want the world to
see the 'swagger' right in that cameraman's lens. Can you do this?"

Laughing at the statement, Bill shakes his head and says, "No
problem! Let's do this." As the TV crewperson holds up his hand in
count down, 3-2-1 point, the *Maestro* takes his stage and swaggers
out. The Irish crowd goes wild as the attending Purdue faithful boos
him. A small group of the visiting Purdue students yells some very
uncomplimentary words and phrases but the Irish crowd quickly
drowns them out. Having experienced this before during his senior
year at South, he knows to expect this now and during his entire
career. Knowing where Sarah is supposed to sit, Bill searches the
stands in her vicinity but there are 80,000 people in the stadium.
Seeing him search in vain in her direction, the love in Sarah's heart
moves her to stand on her seat and wave wildly. Seeing her beautiful
red hair flowing in the breeze, Bill recognizes Sarah waving her

arms among the stadium patrons. She is a lasting vision that burns in his heart and mind. Pointing to her, he gives her a fist pump, as they perform in their own play oblivious to the tumultuous roar. It is their farewell performance and the last time he will ever look for Sarah at one of his games.

Before the first play, Coach Alan quizzes, "Are you ready, Bill?"

Having that wry smile burst on his face again, he replies, "I *am*, Coach. Let's do this. People in the stands had better be ready because 'Here come the Irish.' Coach, I want to go deep on the first play."

Missing Bill's initiative and drive, Coach Alan replies, "I prefer to *work* you up to game speed, to run some simple plays, and to get you into the flow."

With his wry smile climbing across his face again, Bill reiterates, "Coach, I *really* want to go deep on the first play. After that, I'll run whatever plays you call."

Agreeing as the team rushes onto the field, Coach Alan turns to Eli and questions, "What's that funny smile of Denton's all about?"

Reflectively, Eli explains, "Unfortunately for me, I've seen it many times before as an opponent and it means he has a point to prove. When he has a point to prove, the other team had better look out because no one can stop him."

Coach Alan says, "Well Eli, I guess we'll *all* find out."

The TV commentators have poured out their hype on the game for 60 minutes. They all agree, "This is a high pressure setting for a 19 year old quarterback. It's the most intense setting he has ever seen. Coach Alan will run some simple plays and short passes to get Denton used to the speed of the college game. He will want Denton to work out his jitters first in this high profile rivalry before attempting riskier passes. Welcome to the college game at Notre Dame, Mr. Denton. It's game time."

Winning the coin toss, Notre Dame elects to receive the kick off. Purdue's kicker puts the ball through the end zone and the Irish start at their 20-yard line. Bill spent extra time with the receivers during every practice in preparation for this moment. Taking charge in the huddle, he calls "Irish Streak Post" with authority, the Notre Dame version of Joey's 21 Z flash. The *Wizard* takes the snap and drops back into the pocket. As the Purdue safety blitzes, All-American lineman Conner Seligman pancakes him hard, giving Bill plenty of time. While Bill looks the defense off to the left, Purdue takes the bait. Coming back right, the *Wizard* throws the ball 75 yards in the air to Ryan William, a pre-season All-American receiver. Making the catch in perfect stride, he strolls the last five yards into the end zone. The TV commentators exclaim with amazement, "Did you see that throw? How many quarterbacks do you that can make a 75 yard throw like that, let alone a red-shirt freshman? Hello Purdue, welcome to the Notre Dame game with Bill Denton at the helm. If he continues to direct Notre Dame *this way*, it's going to be a long day for you. This guy bears watching for the next four years."

Silently Sarah smiles from deep in her heart as her date says, "Did he do that because of what I said?"

"What do you think," she chuckles.

"Dang, I unleashed a monster," he verbalizes and mulls in his mind preparing for a long day at *this* stadium.

"Well, that you did! He only needed a point to prove to unleash the talent God gave him," Sarah laughs. William finishes the game with 10 catches for 186 yards and three touchdowns. The relentless Irish defense makes a huge statement with middle linebacker Kyle Andrew having 9 tackles including 2 sacks. Bill has a superior game for a freshman, 30-35 passing, 384 yards, and no interceptions. The Irish roll to a 48-0 win.

As the on-field TV announcer interviews him immediately after the game, the co-eds in the national audience take notice suddenly of the TV and Bill without his helmet during his close-up. His first home post-game news conference proceeds briskly with Bill praising how well his teammates played especially Ryan and Kyle and continually referring to the total team effort. Not satisfied with his responses, the press becomes more aggressive demanding his thoughts about *his* performance. With a calm demeanor, Bill says, "Guys, it's this simple. I take the snaps, hand it off or throw it, and the rest of the team wins the game.

The reporters who covered him for the last couple of years have heard this response before from the humble young man. Chuckling at the scene, these reporters inform the others, "Friends, that's about as much as you're going to get him to say about himself. He lets his *game* do the talking." After the game, Bill and Eli stop at the barricade to sign a couple of autographs for some kids. As Bill glances up, Sarah smiles from her heart one last time and waves goodbye as she and her date walk past. He smiles broadly and waves at her as she disappears into the crowd with another. With his one world fading in the distance, he returns to signing autographs for the crowd in his new world. Everyone continues talking about the game as the trooper escorts Bill and Eli to the locker room. Changing to street clothes, the pair saunters back to the dorm together, talk about classes, and their plans outside of football.

School has been in session for about a month and the Irish are undefeated. Knowing it's not high school, Bill is elated to be making a run for the National Championship as a freshman and is ecstatic with his team's performance. Personally, he is having an All-American year with Eli and him becoming great friends, doing everything together. They go to a few parties, study sessions in the Father Hesburgh Library, and in other words, enjoy being at Notre Dame. There is no place like it in Bill's mind, except where Sarah is.

Eye Catching

With his heart pained but mending, a girl in Bill's Calculus class catches his eye. She is beautiful with sandy blond hair, gorgeous eyes, and very curvaceous. Simply put, she is extremely good looking, turning guys' heads wherever she is. However, she always seems to be alone despite her beauty. With his class schedule allowing a couple hours between classes, he stops by the student union often during the intervening time to study. He always notices her studying alone at the student union yet the guys continue to stare even there. Finding her alone again today, his heart refuses wait any longer to meet her. Strolling to where she sits, he decides to ask bravely, "Is this seat taken? I would like to sit here with you."

She replies with cautious sarcasm, "Well let's consider. It's a public place and no one else has occupied the seat. You don't *appear* to be dangerous. So, I might as well offer you a seat." As He starts to introduce himself, she interrupts him and says, "I know who you are and I don't date football players."

Taking a slightly different approach, Bill responds, "Ok, I can accept that. Most of us are a bit dense anyway." His candid response takes her by surprise. Observing the surprise on her face, he asks respectfully, "Would it be ok with you if we start over? My name is Bill Denton."

Pleased with his candid, friendly manner, she answers, "Hi. My name is Kathy Adams."

With a pleasant smile on his face, he adds, "I'm pleased to meet you officially. We have Calculus class together."

Deciding to lower her emotional shield somewhat, she replies in kind, "I noticed you in the class too."

While working through introductory topics with each other, he inquires with interest, "Where do you live when you're not here at school?"

She replies, "I live with my parents in San Diego."

Impressed that she's a California girl, he inquires, "What do your parents do for a living?"

Impressed by his interest, she explains, "Well, my dad works in the shipyard and my mom works on the Naval base. Truly, I'm blessed by their sacrifice for me to attend here. My parents are such hard workers and they instilled that strong work ethic in me. They are doing everything they can to make sure I can stay at Saint Mary's, Notre Dames sister school." It will be two more years before Notre Dame becomes a co-ed school but current Saint Mary's students have full access to Notre Dame facilities. Curious about his life, Kathy inquires, "What do your parents do for a living?"

Reluctantly, he explains with sadness, "They died in a car accident when I was 10. I've lived with my grandparents since then and they instilled that same strong belief system and work ethic in me too."

Filled with deep empathy for his hurt, Kathy says, "Bill, I'm so sorry. You must feel very alone at times. I'm glad you're good enough as a football player to get a full scholarship."

Surprised at her depth of concern, he says, "Yes, I worked very hard as a football player to get where I am. However, I'm not here on an athletic scholarship. My scholarship is a full academic one. I chose an academic scholarship to allow the football team to give another player the chance to come to Notre Dame." Impressed by his concern for others' welfare, she makes no more comments about football through the remainder of lunch. On the other hand, Bill makes the whole conversation about her.

Not wanting to believe her heart, Kathy ponders, "He *is* very impressive and great looking too. He's not like the other players I've met because he's so genuine and caring. Maybe, I *can* let my hair down around him and get to know him better."

Party Time

During the week, Eli learns of a party after the game Saturday through an invitation he receives. Watching out for Bill's welfare since Sarah's departure, Eli quizzes, "Would it be ok if I bring a friend with me?"

The hosts reply, "Sure as long as you bring only one person and not the entire football team."

Later, while with Bill, Eli informs, "Since Sarah left, you've done almost nothing socially, including parties since we've been here. You're coming with me to this party."

Stunned by his friend's candid observation, Bill agrees, "Ok, I'll admit I've been a bit unsociable lately since Sarah and I broke up. Maybe I do need to get out of my self-imposed solitude. Let's go to the party Saturday."

After their Calculus class on Wednesday, Bill requests, "Kathy, would you like to come to the game Saturday? I don't have any ulterior motive or hidden agenda. I have tickets each game to give away and I wanted to know if you would like to use them with a friend."

Impressed by his sincerity, Kathy lowers her guard a bit more and says, "Yes Bill that sounds like fun to me."

Excited by her answer, he responds, "Ok, just go to the 'Will Call' window and ask for the two tickets from me. Oh, I almost forgot. You'll need to show your ID to get them. I apologize for leaving so quickly. I have to go to a team meeting but I'll see you in class tomorrow, ok?"

Replying in a teasing manner with a big smile, she says, "Of course you can. Where else would you be?"

On Saturday, Kathy and her roommate arrive at the "Will Call" window. Asking for the two tickets from Bill, she shows her ID to the person in the booth. After checking her ID, the attendant in the ticket office gives her the tickets and says, "So, *you're* the one!"

Confused by the statement, Kathy looks puzzled. While walking away from the ticket window, she overhears people whispering, "Wow, she's the one who picked up tickets from *him*." Unknowingly, she has just entered the demanding, public world of Bill Denton. Determined to find out the meaning of the scene just played, she plans to ask Bill about their whispers in class on Monday. Game time is 1:00 PM on national TV as it is every week. The Irish have a tremendous day beating Army easily 51-10 and Bill has another superior game. Again, the on-field announcer interviews Bill to the delight of the growing number of co-eds watching nationally to catch a glimpse of him. During the interview, he praises his teammates' game performance and downplays his role in the victory again.

Eli and Bill treat this Saturday night like other Irish victory post-game night. Keeping it low key, they are the only two players attending the party as requested. Arriving at the party and entering with Eli, Bill's eyes sweep the room and merge excitedly with Kathy's probing gaze immediately. Curious about her afternoon experience, he strolls through the crowd and asks, "I hope you enjoyed the game as much I did."

Impressed with his *human* response, she replies, "I enjoyed watching your performance immensely. However, I do have a question for you. When Debbie and I picked up my tickets, the attendant said that I was the one. What did he mean by that remark?"

Laughing at the statement, Bill explains, "The attendants are always asking me when my girlfriend is coming to a game. I keep them guessing, saying I don't have a girlfriend but they just won't believe me. So, when you got the tickets, they figured you were *that* girl. I'm sure they didn't mean anything by it. They're always joking around with me about a girlfriend they haven't seen. With whom did you come to the party?"

Her laugh at his statement draws a puzzled look on his face. Seeing the puzzlement, she explains with a huge smile, "Silly, you should know better. I didn't come with *anyone*. The apartment is my roommate's and mine and it's *our* party. Eli is in Debbie's Physics class and she invited him."

Knowing she fooled him completely, Bill offers with a respectful smile, "Thanks for letting me come too. I'll just mingle about the room. I want you to have fun because it's your party."

Turning with the smile still on his face, he walks toward the kitchen to get a soda. On the way, a party-crasher hands him a BYO beer as Kathy hears him say, "No thanks. I don't drink. Can't afford to and be in *this* shape."

She thinks, "I can't *believe* he said that. He's not a bad person at all. Maybe, just maybe he *is* for real." After the BYOB offer and as the evening progresses, Bill keeps a watchful eye on Kathy. His protective instincts activate due to the guys he saw showing their true character. Smitten by her beauty, character, and gentleness, he understands why she says she does not date stereotypical guys.

Suddenly, his eyes catch a drunken guy who has Kathy cornered in the kitchen. While she tries to get away from him, he sloshes some of his beer on her yet he refuses to relinquish his pressure on her. Remembering Steve Powell's attack on Sarah, Bill rushes over and interrupts, "Hey, what do you think you're doing with my girl?"

The guy slurs in his stupor, "I don't care if she's your girl. She'll be mine 'cause I'm irresistible. So move on." The helpless look on Kathy's face is all he needs to see. Inserting himself quickly between the drunk and Kathy, Bill protects her from the guy's advances. Suddenly, clarity of mind and Bill's size react together to drive the guy off and Bill takes her hand quickly.

Maintaining his protective attitude, he warns, "Don't forget she's *my* girl. I don't want to see you near her again," and takes her into the front room.

Greatly moved by his protection of her, Kathy says, "Thank you so much Bill. I was scared what might have happened to me if you hadn't been here." They both enjoy the rest of the party with each other.

As the party starts to clear out, Kathy feels a bit sick from the smell of the drunk's attack on her and rushes to the bathroom. Seeing her quick exit, Bill gets the attention of her roommate, Debbie. While they both hurry to check on her to make certain she is ok, Debbie walks in alone to help. Finding Kathy's clothes are wet from the attack earlier, Debbie suggests, "Kathy, I think you would feel better if you change your clothes and get into some dry ones."

As Eli arrives shortly thereafter, Bill requests, "Eli, would you go to my car and get the t-shirt and shorts out of the back seat. They're size medium so they'll fit Kathy." While Eli rushes to get the change of clothes, Bill substitutes for Debbie as the smell of Kathy's soaked clothes begins to make her sick also. Cleaning up Kathy tenderly, he wipes the results of the earlier attack off her face and hands gently.

As he steps out of the bathroom, Eli gives him the clothes from the car. Thanking Eli for the help, he hands Debbie the t-shirt and shorts. Wearing concern for Kathy deeply on his face, he asks, "Debbie, would you mind putting these on Kathy? I'm certain she'll feel better wearing different clothes." After Debbie dresses Kathy in the clean clothes, Bill returns to scoop her up gently in his arms and carries her to her bedroom. Overcome with his tenderness, Eli and Debbie gaze at him as he puts her in bed gently and tucks her in softly. Memories flood Bill's mind as he recalls the very special evening with Sarah after the prom. With a tear trickling down his cheek, the *Prince* leans delicately over his suffering friend, gives her a kiss on her forehead, and whispers, "Goodnight, my sweet one."

Debbie turns to Eli in amazement and whispers, "He barely knows her yet look at how lovingly he cares for her. Is he always this caring?"

Breaking into a big grin, Eli shrugs his shoulders and responds, "You're seeing the *real* man. This is very much his true character."

Feeling queasy from the evening too, Debbie says, "I need to go to bed too. I know I'm asking a lot but would you mind locking the door when you leave?"

Bill and Eli clear out the remaining partyers informing, "Ok folks, the party's over. It's time to leave." Despite objections from several people, they manage to usher everyone out of the apartment. With the apartment cleared of revelers, Bill recommends, "Eli, we need to clean up the remnants of this party for the girls. They won't feel like doing it when they wake up Sunday. Let's make it spotless. What do you think?" Eli agrees and they clean the apartment quickly and quietly, even taking all the trash out when they leave.

Getting up Sunday, the girls walk into the living room and kitchen, finding the rooms in immaculate condition. Expecting the dregs from last night's party, the sight of their apartment in such amazing condition leaves the girls speechless and pondering, "Who would have been so nice?"

As Kathy turns to make coffee, Debbie points at her, exclaiming, "Oh my."

Surprised by her roommate's outburst, Kathy jerks back toward her and asks, "What's *wrong Debbie*?"

Not believing her eyes, she bursts a response, "You have *his* shirt and shorts on."

Exasperated by the obvious, Kathy says, "Of *course* I'm wearing a Notre Dame Football shirt, silly."

Debbie explains, "It's not *just a* football shirt and shorts. The shirt and the shorts have *his* number on it. They *have* to be his." Reviewing the prior night's events with her, Debbie explains Bill's kindness last night, "After spiriting you away from that drunken guy, he cleaned you up when you lost it in the bathroom. Carrying you to your bed, he tucked you in so gently. Finally, he kissed you on your forehead and whispered, 'Goodnight, my sweet one.'" Her friend's revelation leaves Kathy speechless.

"Physician" Visit

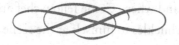

About 1:00 PM, the girl's receive an unexpected knock on their door. Cautiously, Debbie looks through the security lens in the door to find Bill and Eli standing there with anxious smiles on their faces. With a puzzled smile on her face, she opens the door enough for Kathy to see them as well. A huge smile grows on Kathy's face and she says, "Hi guys. We weren't expecting a visit from anyone today." Nervously the guys reply in unison, "We apologize for stopping by unannounced, but we wanted to make sure you both were doing ok after last night's party."

Deciding to be a bit bolder, Bill continues, "We were going for some lunch and wanted to know if you both would like to join us."

Still cautious regarding the guys' intentions, Debbie declines and explains, "After last night's troubles, we probably shouldn't. It's nothing you two have or haven't done. You guys were perfect gentlemen. However, we would rather stay home and rest."

Catching Eli's vibes regarding his feelings for Debbie, Bill inquires, "Okay, are you girls at least hungry?" The girls reply, "Yes we are but we're determined not to go anywhere." Taking the conversation lead, Bill says with his wry smile, "That's ok. Eli and I will fix all of us a late brunch here. How does that sound?"

The girl's mouths are agape and they tease with elation, "That's a wonderful idea! Just a thought, can either of you cook without burning the water?"

With his back to the girls, Eli has surprised dread resting on his face and mouth and mouths to Bill, "Are you crazy? I don't know anything about cooking."

With his smile still radiating, Bill says, "Just follow my lead. I know what to do and when. Come fellow chef and let's prepare the repast." Then, he chuckles to himself at the scene unfolding around them.

Concerned about his friends' possible queasiness from last night, Bill inquires, "Do you girls feel healthy enough for a killer Southwestern omelet?"

"Not really, last night was a real drain on us both," they reply.

"Okay, what about an omelet that's a bit blander? How about fresh spinach, ham, mushroom, and shredded white cheddar cheese blended in an omelet with toast and fresh squeezed orange juice?"

Intrigued by the menu, Kathy clarifies, "The omelet and toast sound delightful. As long as the OJ is from sweet navel oranges, I think I will be ok. Tart orange juice and I just don't get along too well."

As the girls start to set the table excitedly, Bill says playfully, "Eli and I will take care of everything. Your doctors prescribe that both of you rest. Shoo! Today is all about you and Debbie. Think of it as a thank you for inviting us to the party."

Glancing at each other, parallel thoughts stream into the girls' minds, "What are these guys up to? No football player *or guy* for that matter can be this nice." As the preparation ceases and serving time arrives, the girls' excitement builds while Eli and Bill present an excellent table. The breakfast is a big hit with Kathy and Debbie who begin to clear the table.

Wanting to leave a lasting impression for Debbie, Eli stops them and explains, "You need to rest and take it easy. Bill and I will take care of the dishes."

"Oh my gosh! You're kidding right," the girls exclaim and ponder, "How can we be so blessed to find two wonderful guys like these two."

Eli and Bill clean the kitchen and dishes and put the dishes away. Unexpectedly, after finishing the cleanup, Bill comments, "You both need your rest. We thought we would go now that we're sure you're ok. We'll see you in class tomorrow."

Looking at Debbie with surprise, Kathy inquires curiously, "Were you the ones we should thank for cleaning up after the party?"

"We have to confess. We cleaned up for you after the party. Neither of you were feeling well last night. That said, we just couldn't leave the mess for you if you were both sick," Eli admits. His admission of care was all the girls needed to hear. These two guys are the most amazing people they have ever met and extremely kind-hearted and courteous.

As the guys walk toward the door, Kathy quizzes expectantly, "Would you two mind staying here with us for a while? We can hang out and watch TV. There's a chick flick on and a football game."

Sensing the girls' anticipation and taking a considered approach, Bill interrupts quickly, "We don't need to watch football. We would rather watch the movie with you."

"Pinch us. We must be dreaming," the girls wonder mentally. Debbie sits on the love seat with Eli while Kathy lies on the couch.

Bill decides to sit on the floor and Kathy says, "Bill, are you *sure* you want to sit on the floor when I have a *comfortable* couch here with me?" Not one to refuse such an offer from such a beauty, Bill grabs a pillow and sits on the couch.

Preparing a comfortable spot, he offers, "Kathy, you can lie down and put your head on the pillow." He has one arm on the end of the couch and his other arm along the top of the couch. Lying on the couch with her head on the pillow, Kathy takes his arm from the top of the couch and pulls it around her snugly.

Looking up at Bill, she says, "Thanks for everything, last night at the party, cleaning up, and then cooking brunch for us. Oh, before you go, if you'll give me a couple of minutes, I'll change and give you back your t-shirt and shorts."

Wanting to add to their growing friendship, Bill responds quickly, "You don't have to change. You can keep them. They are the wrong size but they sure look good on you."

Kathy smiles broadly and thinks, "How could God bless me with such a terrific guy?" Unfortunately, their Sunday night team meeting beckons and the guys are forced to cut short their enjoyable time with Kathy and Debbie. The girls walk them to the door and thank them again verbally and with hugs. Returning the hugs tenderly, Bill and Eli remain perfect gentlemen and don't try to kiss them goodbye. The hugs build a desire for both couples to experience each other's touch and more. The guys have barely gone when the girls begin discussing the weekend events and the anticipation of class tomorrow. "Can you believe it? They fixed us brunch, spent the afternoon with us watching a movie, and didn't even attempt to steal a kiss when we hugged them." Excitement fills them because they found two guys who aren't just nice guys, they are *awesome* guys.

"Me, Are You Sure?"

For a nearly two weeks, Bill and Kathy sit in Calculus class together and study together at the student center. Taking time to become friends, he enjoys being with her daily. Once they sit down to study, he asks with hope, "Kathy, would you reconsider dating a football player?"

Deciding to have some fun with him, she teases, "Well, I have to think really hard. Hmmm... Yes, as long as it's only you."

Relieved with her answer, he inquires, "Would you like to see a movie Thursday night?"

A bit puzzled, she says, "Yes but why Thursday and not Friday or Saturday?"

Seeing her confusion, he explains, "Well, we have an away game at Navy in Philadelphia on Saturday. The team flies out on Friday and gets back late Saturday night."

As the revelation sinks in, she agrees, "I understand completely why you said Thursday now. Can you come over Sunday and explain how a relationship with you and football works, especially given what you are?"

Blending his thoughts with hers, he exclaims, "That's a great idea. If we're going to spend lots of time together, assuming you decide to go on a date with me more than once, you should know what to expect in our relationship."

Confused and suddenly concerned, she says, "I don't understand what you mean by 'expect in our relationship.' I think you're a great guy but you have me a bit concerned."

Wanting to alleviate her concern, he says, "Don't worry. Everything is just fine. I'll fill in the blanks for you on Sunday. Let's enjoy the rest of this week together."

Walking into the movie Thursday night, Bill reaches his hand boldly for Kathy's hand. Cautiously, she gives her hand until they reach their chosen row. When she chooses her seat, she turns and smiles expectantly at Bill. Returning her invitation, he places his arm gently around her shoulder and draws her close. Enjoying the warmth of his touch, Kathy lays her head on his shoulder. As "Airport" progresses, she snuggles her head on the edge of his chest. Contented ardently, Bill enjoys her warm touch, the fragrance of her hair, and her snuggling on his chest throughout the movie. The only respite from this collective bliss was for soft drinks and shared popcorn. On the way back to her apartment, Kathy considers, "And I get to watch him on TV Saturday."

On Saturday, Kathy, Debbie, and some other girls from Saint Mary's watch the game on TV. The announcers' statements about Bill to a national audience amaze all of them. Reality hits Kathy in her heart as she melts at the thought of going out with Bill's persona off the field. Watching the *Maestro* swagger onto the field, Kathy believes she has an idea about his mega-star performance world but reality is often more forbidding than appearance presents. Truly, she has no idea *what* his world is like. As they watch the game, Debbie and all the girls tease her each time they show Bill on camera saying, "There's her guy," to giggles and laughter. They exclaim on several close-ups, "Wow, he looks good. Are you *sure* you want to go out with *him*?" Kathy returns as good as she receives when they show Eli but Bill is on-camera much of the time.

The Irish win again in a cakewalk, 56-7. Drawing more praise with each game, Bill is outstanding again. The obligatory post-game TV interview with him occurs before he runs to the locker room. As the interview nears its end, the reporter asks, "Any additional comments you want to share, Bill?"

Looking straight through the camera to Kathy's heart, he says, "See ya Sunday, Kathy." The girls scream wildly at his words and Kathy falls back in a mock feint because she can't believe what she just heard. Watching the game with friends, Sarah's heart sinks with Bill's words.

Welcome to My World

Time cannot deliver Sunday fast enough to satisfy Debbie and Kathy. As the day progresses to afternoon, a sudden knock on their apartment door sends them both rushing to answer it with great anticipation. Peering through the security lens, Kathy spies *two* familiar faces not one, much to her delight. Opening the door, Bill and Eli's big smiles greet them excitedly. Kathy's joy at seeing Bill floods her face as she leaps to hug him and whispers, "I can't believe you mentioned me on TV. That was very special and I loved hearing you say it."

With his face growing into a huge smile, Bill returns her hug with equal elation and says, "I hope that said how much I wanted to be with you and I wanted everyone to know. This was only part of what I go through in my life."

Seeing Eli appear with Bill, Debbie's heart leaps with excitement and the glow on her face reveals her heart. She considers, "Amazing. He's here for *me*. I certainly didn't expect this but I really like his idea to drop by spontaneously with Bill."

From the look on Eli's face, he feels the same euphoria at seeing her. Eli says, "Debbie, I couldn't wait to see you again. It felt like the flight would never arrive back home. I came to see you as soon as we arrived and I wanted to help Kathy understand what Bill is going to tell her too."

With Eli's statement, Bill begins to explain, "I want to be open with you regarding what the media attention of being with me can mean in your life. You saw the national attention the media pours on me because God gave me the tools he did and the fact I use them to the best of my ability. Everything I do, everything I say, and how I say it is on the national news. If I say or do the wrong thing, it's on the national news. The media spies track me constantly during football. If someone sees me out very late at night or coming out of the wrong place, it makes the news and it could damage my reputation. The media hype has built a national following around me. People who are fans and people who want me to fail follow my world. It's a world that's controlled by Notre Dame and the media. I have to steal any quiet time I get, for the most part. Kathy, I apologize for being so frank with you but it wouldn't be fair to you if I wasn't. If you choose to continue to do things with me, you need to know *that* part of my world will become your world too. People will want to be your friend for their own popularity and may not really care about you. Writers and photographers will want to talk to you and take your picture alone and with me. Everything you do will become news also. I know that's harsh and I apologize again. I care for you deeply or I wouldn't say anything."

Wanting to elaborate further on Bill's life, Eli says, "Kathy, I have known him through high school rivalries and as a roommate. If you and Bill become serious and he *is* a genuine guy, you have to understand and accept one fact. There'll be times when you're with him that the media will make you invisible while trying to get Bill's attention or an interview. Bill would never say this to you because he's too nice of a guy. If you're going to be his girlfriend, you'll need to be by his side and supportive of him regardless of the situation. I've watched him become a national icon playing on one of sport's biggest stages. I just wanted you to understand fully who he is and what he is. Basically, your life, your world will not be the same. Your picture will be in newspapers and magazines. The TV cameras will find you and put your face on national TV. It's a good bet you won't be able to sit in the student section at any games. You'll become a rock-star celebrity with the crowd wanting to see and meet you constantly. It'll be that bad."

The look on Kathy's face appeals to Bill to interrupt Eli's observation. Sensing her concern, he offers, "Kathy, if you don't want to be part of this lifestyle but just to be friends, I'll understand. Conversely, if you *want* to be part of it and at some point, the lifestyle becomes too much, you can change your mind about this world and I'll understand that too. However, if you want to be the woman in my world knowing what it's like and share the special moments with me, it would make me ecstatic."

The joy of their earlier meeting gives way to relief and exasperation simultaneously. Kathy says, "I feel like I just had a job interview and now you want me to decide if I want the job."

Bill apologizes, "I wanted you to know what would happen if we became serious about our dating relationship. I understand it's a pretty cold way to explain it but you wanted to know what my world was really like."

Responding to his care and concern for her feelings, Kathy expounds, "Well Bill, I can see we have a problem now because I fell in love with you. As far as I'm concerned I'm your girlfriend. You're a great guy and very respectful of me. You never put me in an uncomfortable situation. You took special care of me when I needed it and even cooked for me as well. You treat me better than any guy has ever treated me. I fell in love with *that* person not the larger than life persona I saw on TV." Hesitating for a moment, she continues with a teasing laugh and flirting tilt to her head, "Well *that* and the fact you happen to be a *gorgeous* hunk."

Her confession of love draws relief across Bill's face and he says, "I *want* you to be my love. I fell in love with you the first day we had lunch at the Student Union. I knew the moment you said you didn't date football players that I just couldn't stay away. I was lost in the depth of those gorgeous eyes of yours." Kathy grabs his face in both hands, sits on his lap facing him, and starts kissing him passionately. What an amazing beginning to their afternoon!

Not wanting to interrupt Bill and Kathy's time together, Eli suggests, "Debbie, why don't we go grab a something to eat and leave the two of them alone."

Providing an alternative, Debbie says suggestively, "Well, that's fine but wouldn't you rather stay here at the apartment with *me?*" Expressing great elation and affirmation on his face, Eli gives Debbie a huge hug. After the emotional release, she continues, "I know your world isn't as hectic as Bill's world but whatever it holds for *us*, I want to be the love in *your* world. My heart *melted* the first day I saw you in class. Then, you captured my heart with Bill when you cared for Kathy and me so *wonderfully* after the party."

Barely able to contain his joy, Eli is ecstatic as he tenderly holds Debbie's hands in his and says lovingly, "I hoped you felt the same way I did. I'm deeply in love with you too. You swept me off my feet with your first words to me. I was just afraid to say anything for fear of pushing you away with my depth of feeling. I apologize for not revealing earlier how I felt."

"No apology needed. All you had to do was ask, your eyes had me at our first meeting," Debbie confesses. Meanwhile, Bill and Kathy continue enjoying their newly discovered devotion to each other on the couch.

Maintaining Perfection

otre Dame continues rolling through opponents at South Bend with the *Maestro* at the offensive helm and Eli keying the defense. Pittsburgh succumbs to the juggernaut by the score of 46-14. However, two opponents come into South Bend to throw challenging defenses at the team's perfection. The first opponent smothers the ND receivers and stifles the running game. Responding in kind, Eli fires the defense to match Georgia Tech blow for blow and give the offense a chance. Kathy and Debbie cheer their guys to ultimate on-field performances with their great mental support. With the receivers covered for much of the game and the ground game having to grind out yardage, GT forces the *Wizard* to use most of the magic in his book of football spells to conjure a victory, 10-7. Eli has the defense playing at extraordinary levels.

While Georgia Tech was extremely difficult, LSU was even more so. As two heavyweight fighters buffet each other's mid-sections with repeated body blows, the defenses rail on their combatants while each team's offense struggles mightily. With Eli whipping the defense into a performance worthy of a Patton command, Kathy and Debbie cringe with the home fans in the stands at each blow yet urging their offense onward. Responding to the demands of the crowd, the

Wizard drives the ND offense to a field goal. Unfortunately, Bill goes down with a high ankle sprain in the next series as the crowd gasps and Kathy buries her head in her hands. Watching the game on TV at Purdue with friends, his old love, Sarah, cringes and closes her eyes remembering how she nursed him back to health in high school as the staff helps Bill off the field. Eli drives his command to even higher performance levels to protect his fallen friend and the team's perfect season. With LSU's last-gasp drive on fourth down and out of field goal range, Eli stuffs an LSU runner short of a first down but drags himself out of bounds with the same injury as Bill. The Notre Dame offense runs out the clock to maintain their perfect season, 3-0, but it is a costly one. Neither Bill nor Eli is available for the Southern California game Thanksgiving weekend. As a precaution, both guys will remain home to rest their injuries before a possible bowl game to the delight of Kathy and Debbie.

Thanksgiving Plans

After a visit to the training facility, attending church, and while spending a very restful Sunday afternoon at the girls' apartment, Eli asks, "Bill, are you still planning to go with me to Ft. Wayne for Thanksgiving?"

With visions of the feast dancing through his mind, Bill answers, "Sure. I wouldn't miss it."

Noticing the expression on Debbie's face, Eli questions with hope, "Would you want to come home with me for the holiday too? Since your parents live so close to school, I thought you might spend it with them." She lives just about an hour south on highway US 31 in Peru.

With a huge smile on her face, Debbie replies, "I'd love to spend the holiday with you. I can't think of anything more special. However, I'd better check with mom first. I'm sure it will be alright though."

With one couple nearly confirmed, Bill inquires, "Kathy, are you going to San Diego for Thanksgiving?"

With sadness in her eyes, she says, "No, I can't afford to go. My parents are saving money for me to come home for Christmas break."

Suddenly thinking about Kathy being alone during Thanksgiving, Bill offers, "Well, I could cook a little dinner just for two and stay at the apartment with you if you would like. You *shouldn't* spend Thanksgiving alone. If you *are* spending it with someone, it should be your guy, right?"

Probing teasingly, Kathy asks, "Well yes, I *would* rather spend it with you but can you *really* cook a Thanksgiving dinner too? I thought you were just a *breakfast* chef."

Displaying mock offense, he responds, "I can cook about anything you want to eat. My grandmother taught me to cook and my grandfather taught me to be a carpenter."

As they both laugh, she inquires, "You're a carpenter too?"

Wanting to show her more of his character, he explains, "Yes, I can build most anything. I helped a friend's dad build a deck a couple of years ago."

Leaning over to Debbie, she whispers, "He keeps getting better and better. It's no wonder I fell in love with him."

Wanting both couples to spend the holiday together, Eli assures, "Kathy, it will be ok if you and Bill come to my house in Ft. Wayne for Thanksgiving. When I asked my mom, she said it was ok as long as I let her know how many people were coming." As everyone agrees going to Eli's will be fun, he continues, "Since it's also the weekend of the USC game, we can all watch the game on TV. We're ineligible for the game because of our injuries anyway. So, it'll be fun to watch the game together."

Wanting to assure her parents, Kathy says, "I like the sound of that. I'll let my mom and dad know I won't be alone for Thanksgiving."

Before she can call them, Bill inquires, "What if they come out here with us? Eli, call your mom and see if Kathy's parents can come too."

Suddenly confused, Kathy objects strenuously, "Bill, didn't I *just say* that they can't afford to fly *me* home? Then, how are they supposed to come *here* for Thanksgiving?"

As Eli calls his mom, he says, "Kathy, don't worry Bill is the guy who can make these things happen." After discussing two more people for dinner, Eli confirms, "Mom approves. She looks forward to meeting Bill's girlfriend and her parents."

With her thoughts now jumbled, Kathy says, "Wait a minute, you said *me and my parents*. Do your parents *know* Bill?"

To reduce her confusion, Eli explains, "Yes they do from back in high school. We were the two best players on the field. We would meet and talk after games until it was time to go."

Thinking about warm family gatherings, Bill adds, "They sort of adopted me since I don't have any parents and treat me just like their second son." Mentally changing direction, Bill inquires expectantly, "Kathy, do you think your parents can get the whole week off?"

Surprised by his request, she answers, "I really don't know but I'll have to call them and see."

With a huge smile on his face, he hands her the phone and says, "Please call them and check. It will mean so much to you *and to me.*"

When her mom answers, Kathy inquires with hope, "Would you be able to get the week off? Bill wants you to fly to South Bend and spend Thanksgiving with us here. I know you can't afford it and I told Bill but he insisted I call you anyway."

Seeing her difficulty, Bill says, "Hey Kathy, why don't you let me explain my idea to your parents." With phone in hand, he begins to explain to her mom, "Mrs. Adams, this Bill Denton." Before he can begin his explanation, he starts answering her questions as if dodging a blitzing safety, "Yes, I'm the quarterback at Notre Dame. Yes, I'm the guy that's been on the premier sports magazine cover. Yes ma'am, I'm the guy they interview after the Notre Dame games on TV. Okay, yes, the same guy people say has movie star looks. Well, thank you ma'am but the pleasure is all mine. Yes, I *am* the guy that can make this all happen." Red-faced by her mom's accolades, he continues, "I want you and Mr. Adams to come to South Bend and spend Thanksgiving week with Kathy. We'll all have Thanksgiving dinner at Eli Kevlin's house in Ft. Wayne and drive back to South Bend after dinner. With our injuries, Eli and I won't have to practice or fly with the team to the game. Yes ma'am, Eli is the guy that plays a corner spot and has five interceptions. I can tell you watch the games too. With all due respect, Mrs. Adams, you won't need to discuss this with Mr. Adams. I want you both to come to South Bend for the week and then watch the Notre Dame-USC game on TV Saturday afternoon with us. I'll take care of everything and Kathy will call you with the details tomorrow. All you have to do is get the week off." Excited with her mom's response, he says, "You *will*? That's fantastic. I'm really looking forward to meeting you. Yes ma'am Kathy *is* my girlfriend. I'm going to put Kathy back on the phone now."

Amazed at the conversation she heard in part, Kathy says, "Mom, I'm so excited you and dad will come. Yes mom, he is very special to me. I'll call you tomorrow with the details. Bye mom." As she hangs up the phone, Kathy continues probing Bill, "Ok, it's not that I don't have faith in your abilities but we have my parents all excited to come here. How do you plan to pull this off?"

With his face growing into his wry smile, he says, "Stand back and watch the *Wizard* work."

Picking up the phone and calling his travel agent, Brett Andrews, Bill says, "Brett, I need a favor." He is the guy who sets up Bill's flights to all the football camps and his special trip to Michigan with Sarah's family.

Knowing Bill's needs are always "special," Brett replies with a chuckle, "I can provide anything *you* need."

Receiving his desired affirmation, Bill requests in detail, "I need round trip first class tickets for Ruey and Rosy Adams from San Diego to Indianapolis. I need them to leave on the Sunday before Thanksgiving about 10:00 AM. They'll need a rental car for the week and will fly to San Diego the Sunday after Thanksgiving from Indianapolis early in the afternoon. I'd like them to stay in the hotel just off the Notre Dame campus. When you complete the particulars, please call this number." As he gives Kathy's number to Brett, he says, "Ask for Kathy and provide the details to her. She can relay the details to her parents."

Curious about the plans, Brett asks one more question, "Ok Bill, I have to ask…"

Before he can finish the question, Bill interrupts with a laugh, "Yes Brett, she's my girlfriend and yes, she's *awesomely* beautiful. If you'd ever come up for a game, you could see for yourself." That ends the conversation, as Brett isn't a Notre Dame fan and refuses to come to a game.

Having seen the *Wizard* work before, Eli shakes his head and smiles. Debbie is speechless while Kathy stares in utter disbelief at his conjured spell. Regaining her senses, Kathy shows her appreciation giving Bill a huge hug and probes, "How in the world can you do all this?"

Bill laughs and with a teasing tone, says, "Sometimes, it's good to be me."

Amazed at what she has heard, Kathy exclaims, "I guess it is. I knew you could get game tickets but this is beyond amazing." Mulling what she has just seen and heard in her mind, she ponders, "Did I find an amazing guy or has he done something illegal to afford this?"

Seeing the concern grow on her face from her pondering, he says, "You don't have to worry. It's really not important. I just want you to be happy that your mom and dad can share Thanksgiving with you and me." As her eyes start to get teary, he takes her hand

and gives her an affectionate kiss on the cheek while they sit on the couch. Holding her tightly, he whispers, "Kathy, I love you. That's how important you are to me."

Concerned about his finances, Kathy replies, "I love you too but I'm concerned about the money you're spending though. It's a lot and you're in college."

Feeling her pain for him, Bill finally relents and explains, "When my parents died, they left me a trust fund that I can use for anything I want as long as I stay in school. You three can't tell anybody because it would be all over the news. If that happened, I'd be bombarded by people I don't know asking me for money."

Thanksgiving Week

After church on the Sunday before Thanksgiving, Bill, Kathy, Eli, and Debbie wait anxiously at the girls' apartment for Kathy's parents. With a sudden knock on the door, Kathy rushes to answer it. Peering through the security lens, she begins to cry as she opens the door. Plenty of tears flow with joy and happiness. While Bill remains in the background, Kathy and her parents enjoy the reunion with lots of hugs and kisses. Finally remembering Bill, Kathy introduces him, "Mom and dad, this is my boyfriend, Bill Denton. Bill, these are my parents, Ruey and Rosy Adams."

Polite as usual, he says, "I'm very pleased to meet you both."

Filled with joy at meeting their daughter's special friend in person, they reply, "Bill, with all we have heard about you from our daughter, the pleasure is all ours. It's an honor to meet the best player in America especially one who treats us and Kathy so well."

Embarrassed by their praise, Bill fumbles for the words, "Thank you so much but it's the Lord who gave me the tools to play and the wherewithal to help others. I'd like to introduce Kathy's roommate Debbie Aleman, and my friend and teammate, Eli Kevlin. Now that everyone is acquainted, I'm sure you'd like to check into your hotel room and freshen up. Once you're ready, I have a room reserved for us to have dinner."

Impressed with his planning detail, Kathy inquires, "Are you sure you want to go out to a restaurant?"

Smiling with satisfaction, Bill whispers, "Kathy, it's ok. I really appreciate your loving concern but I planned this for your parents and you. I wanted you to enjoy being with each other again."

After checking the Adams' into their room and helping them unpack, the group walks to the car to drive to dinner. On the way to the car, Kathy pulls her mom and dad aside and explains, "Bill doesn't talk about himself or football very much. He doesn't think he's all that special even though he's the most recognized athlete in America." When they arrive at the restaurant, a large crowd packs the seats even though it's Sunday night. With no classes this week at Notre Dame, the normal team meeting is re-scheduled until tomorrow morning giving the couples more time tonight.

Walking into the restaurant, everyone recognizes Bill instantly. People begin to walk up and ask him for autographs. The host says, "There's a 30 minute wait. Will this be okay?"

"Yes," Bill answers. Kathy is used to being by his side while autograph seekers engage them almost everywhere.

After a few moments, the manager walks up to their party and requests, "Would you please follow me?" Taking the group to two tables out of most of the patrons' view, he assigns a staff member to prevent public intrusions during their dinner.

With an amazed expression covering her face, Kathy asks, "How in the world did you arrange for us to be out of the way and not bothered?"

Chuckling with a wry smile, Bill explains jovially, "Well, sometimes it's *good* to be me." Pausing for effect, he continues, "Actually, I came in earlier today and requested the manager to seat us where we wouldn't be bothered during dinner. While agreeing to seat us privately, the manager asked, 'Would mind doing me a favor?' Intrigued by his request, I replied, 'Certainly, what is the favor?' The manager went into his office and brought out two of the premier sports magazines with my picture on them. He told me his two kids were big fans and if I would sign the covers for them, they'd be thrilled. So, I signed them, personalized each one using his kid's first names, and telling them to never give up on their dreams. It's a fair trade don't you think?"

As the group enjoys dinner, Debbie leans over to Eli and inquires in a whisper, "How does Bill do the things he does?"

A smile crawls across Eli's face as he whispers back, "He's not the kind of guy who expects people to do things for him and give him free things. However, he does know when and how to use his celebrity status to benefit others fully. He is very selective when he does use it and it's usually small stuff like this."

Amazed at Bill's care for all of them, Debbie says, "It's a wonderful thing he did for Kathy and her parents. I'm happy he chose to include us in his provision for them."

On Thanksgiving morning, the group drives to Eli's house together. Eli and Debbie take his car while Kathy and her parents ride in Bill's Mustang to keep the Adams' rental car cost as low as possible. Leaving around 7:00 AM, the group expects to arrive at Ft. Wayne around 9:00 AM. This allows them to maximize the time that Eli and Debbie get to spend with his family. During the drive to Eli's, they enjoy the scenery while Bill keeps the conversation focused on Kathy and her parents, not wanting to venture into football and his game performances. Despite his reserved discussions, her parents *are* very impressed with their daughter's new boyfriend and his kindness toward Kathy and them.

As they walk into Eli's house, his parents greet Bill as if he is their own son. Over the past short years, the family has grown very fond of him and his friendship with Eli. Mr. Kevlin is trying to install a new door between the house and garage. As Bill strolls over and offers to help, Mr. Kevlin says, "You know me Bill. I'll take all the help I can get." Bill stays with Eli's dad to help with the door while the others meander to the living room to wait for dinner and become acquainted better. After some interesting family discussions, Kathy, Debbie, and Eli go to watch the construction. In the interim, Bill has once again become the project manager as he did at Maddie's several years ago. His skills as a carpenter amaze everyone and after about an hour and a half, he finishes the project complete with perfectly cut trim molding. Astounded at his woodworking prowess, they all chuckle and shake their heads.

After watching with delight while Bill finishes, Kathy quizzes with surprise, "Eli, is there anything Bill can't do?"

Quite literally, Eli replies, "I haven't seen anything yet that he can't do. When he puts his mind to something, it gets done." Shortly after Bill finishes the door, Eli announces that dinner is ready and everyone finds a seat at the holiday table. Proceeding noisily, the meal features timely banter and joyous discussion after a prayer of generous thanks for the blessings received during the previous year and the bounty before them. After cleaning the table, washing the dishes, and an appropriate time of visiting, the group starts back for South Bend satiated physically and emotionally.

On Friday, after the early morning walk through, Eli and Bill drive to the girls' apartment for breakfast while the remainder of the team boards the flight to Southern Cal. Having required time scheduled at the training facility, the guys continue their injury rehab. Working hard during their rehab activities, their goal is to be ready for the post-season national championship game. On Saturday afternoon, they plan to watch the ND/USC game on TV. Until that time, the guys hope that two beautiful "nurses" will manage their recovery. Since the guys cooked breakfast last time and offered to do so again, the girls plan to cook breakfast and order the guys to rest their injuries. Not wanting to be the cause of the guys' injuries not healing in time, the girls ignore the guys' pleadings to be in the kitchen with them while they cook. After some minor objections, the guys realize their pleas are in vain and take their rehab spots around the apartment.

Kathy and Debbie begin to fix breakfast with their backs to the guys. While the guys' bodies are injured, their hearts are full of love watching the girls at work on the food. Suddenly grabbing Eli's attention, Bill says, "Let's sneak into the kitchen anyway and give the girls a hug. Are you game?" Quietly hobbling into the kitchen, the guys put their arms around the girls' waists to squeals of surprise and delight.

Snuggling Kathy in his gentle caress, Bill kisses her softly on the nape of her neck. "How do you expect me to make breakfast with you doing that, silly," Kathy says responding to the tantalizing sensation of his touch. Then, turning around quickly, she wraps her arms around his neck and gives him a warm, passionate kiss. For a brief time, breakfast preparation comes to a halt as kisses and hugs abound.

Finally, Debbie says, "We'll never finish breakfast before lunchtime if we don't get back to preparing breakfast. You guys need to go back and rest if you expect to heal anytime soon, not that we didn't enjoy the surprises."

As everyone laughs, Bill whispers to Kathy, "I have some bad news. Your days of sitting in the student section at the football games are over."

Confused at his meaning, she probes, "Why would you say that?"

He continues his explanation, "I saw the picture of us walking on campus together on the front page of the South Bend paper this morning. Now the public will clamor to be with you and the remaining media will surely find you. Sitting in the crowd won't be safe for you. I have seen this media blitz before and I'm concerned for you."

Impressed by his love and concern, Kathy says, "Bill, I know that this will become part of our relationship. However, I'm willing to make that personal sacrifice to share your love." With her words of love, Bill's heart melts.

USC Game Time

As everyone gathers at the apartment to watch the game, Kathy shares Bill's concern for her welfare with her parents. Sensing the growing anxiety from Kathy and her parents for her safety at the games, Bill reveals, "I have a wonderful surprise for you all. The Notre Dame Athletic Director, Ted Davidson, agreed to provide seats for you and Debbie in the guest suite for all home and away games. Due to my concern about your safety at games, he made all the arrangements at the other schools left on the schedule." Mr. and Mrs. Adams are impressed again with his level of concern and love for their daughter. As Notre Dame warms up, the group settles into their seats with snacks and soft drinks listening to the announcers talk about the problems Notre Dame faces without Bill and Eli in the lineup. The guys express their displeasure with the statements to the others in the room, "We are not the entire team and have great players to take our place while we heal." As the team leaves the field after warm ups, Bill says, "Mr. and Mrs. Adams, thanks again for accepting my offer to spend Thanksgiving with Kathy and me. I know that Kathy has enjoyed spending time with you so much but I have enjoyed the time with you as well." After he leans over and gives Kathy a kiss, he whispers, "I'm glad I could bring your parents here for you. Enjoy the game as it should be a good one."

With a huge smile growing on her face, Kathy responds, "I have a surprise for you." She takes off her jacket and reveals a t-shirt Eli gave her that says "PROTECT MY MAN." Embarrassed, Bill smiles and gives Eli one of his "I owe you" looks. Remembering his huge mistake with Sarah and a similar shirt in high school, Bill determines not to fumble this opportunity verbally as he did not so long ago. With a loving smile on his face, he declares, "Kathy, that shirt looks great on you! Thanks for modeling it so *well* for me. I will make *certain* the line follows your orders." The "PROTECT *THE* MAN" t-shirts are the hottest selling t-shirt in the Notre Dame bookstore and gift shops. It seems like everyone on campus has one. Amazed at the response to the shirts, Bill shakes his head and chuckles when he sees one on campus. He is proud yet humbled that God uses him as a tool to unify the Notre Dame family.

The famed Irish Guard high steps in their kilts leading the band out of the tunnel and onto the field. The band forms a big ND and plays its opening number representing the visiting team on the field in a battle of the bands. Then, the band breaks into the Notre Dame Victory March and the TV announcer says, *"Here come The Irish."* With that statement, the Irish team runs out of the tunnel and onto the opposition's field all fired up. Notre Dame is 9-0 and ranked No. 2 while USC is 5-4-1. The Irish get the ball first and call the Irish Streak Post. With the Senior ND quarterback taking the snap, wide receiver, William, breaks deep. While the Notre Dame QB overthrows on that play, he drives ND 80 yards for a touchdown on the opening series. The group stands and applauds. Kathy's "Protect My Man" t-shirt is in full view of everyone as she cheers for the team.

Teasing, Bill chides, "Hey, you're supposed to reserve those kinds of cheers for me." However, after the opposition drives the field in response, their tailback scores to knot the game at 7 each. USC takes the lead after stopping the Irish next drive. The USC quarterback connects with his running back for a 45-yard touchdown. The Southern Cal defense stifles the Notre Dame offense for much of the first half. It is a hard fought ball game with Southern Cal holding a halftime lead over Notre Dame, 24-14. In the second half, momentum turns against Notre Dame as the Irish fumble away the game by losing the ball twice, once in their own end zone. Much to the extreme disappointment of the group, Notre Dame cannot overcome their mistakes. However, the Senior Notre Dame QB sets a school record of 526 passing yards in the losing effort, but he has four interceptions and loses a fumble in the end zone. The Irish lose the game 38-28 and really miss Bill and Eli on the field. It is a great loss for the team and kills their chance at the National Championship. However, they still receive an invitation to play the number one-ranked Texas in a bowl game on New Year's Day.

After the game ends with the result to Bill and Eli's chagrin, Kathy's parents offer, "Bill, thank you for such a great time this week. Everyone here at Notre Dame treated us wonderfully this week. It has been great to see Kathy much earlier than we expected."

Humbly, Bill responds, "It has been my pleasure to do this for you. I do have something to explain to you all. Kathy, the press has found you and they all will want a story. The newspaper photo and article yesterday proves that. The media will find your phone number and call you. They'll take even more pictures of you everywhere, just like a movie starlet. They'll want to write more articles about you and will ask your opinion about everything but especially about being my girlfriend. In essence, your normal life as a student is changing dramatically. The events we talked about earlier are beginning to occur." Looking deeply into her eyes, he continues, "I love you so very much. However, this is a lot to ask of you and if you don't want any of this media blitz in your life, I understand."

Moved by his love and concern, she takes his hand. With her parents observing expressions and listening to her answer, she replies, "I want to be more than just your girlfriend because I love you so much. I can endure the media blitz because the prize is worth the effort. You need me with you and I want to be there for you." Her parents nod their approval as they can see the depth of love in her heart for him. During their week with Kathy, she discussed with them that no one has ever treated her as wonderfully as he does.

Debbie and Eli excuse themselves to go to a local restaurant and carve out their own time together. With the Kathy's parents leaving tomorrow morning, Debbie and Eli want to give the Bill, Kathy, and her family as much time together as possible. During the evening, her parents discuss what they have seen and experienced in the area and how much fun it was. They gush about how much appreciation they have for Bill, his care of them, and his love for Kathy. After a farewell dinner together at a restaurant out of the public view, her parents leave for the hotel to pack. As they are leaving, Bill reminds, "We'll come over to the hotel and see you off in the morning."

On the following morning, Bill and Kathy drive to her parents' hotel to say goodbye. Knowing that she will see her parents at Christmas does not dull the pain of saying goodbye for Kathy. Seeing her life is changing, she has concerns without her parents near for a support system. It is a time of joy being with Bill, apprehension of the media unknown, and sadness of watching her parents leave again. Hugging each of her parents, she gives them warm farewell kisses. As Kathy's parents step into their car to drive back to the Indianapolis airport, Bill promises, "Please don't worry. I'll take special care of Kathy and will do whatever it takes to make sure she is safe."

Shaking Bill's hand, Mr. Adams says, "We won't worry. I know you will worry enough for both of us."

Missing her mom and dad already, Kathy bids them good-bye,

"It was so great to have you here this week. I don't know how I would have made it through the holiday without you and Bill to celebrate it with me. He's been a real blessing in my life and now yours too. Christmas will not come fast enough for me. I can hardly wait to spend time with you again."

Bowl Time

New Year's Day arrives and the team is in Dallas in pregame warm-ups against number one-ranked, undefeated Texas. Notre Dame's opponent rides in on a 30-game winning streak. The bitter taste of last year's 27-17 bowl loss to this same opponent burns in the minds of the Notre Dame players and coaching staff. Unfortunately, after their loss to USC, Notre Dame is *not* favored. Tucked safely in one of the stadium suites, Kathy and Debbie anticipate seeing Bill and Eli play again. After all, they worked hard to nurse the guys back to health from their injuries. Today is the unveiling of their efforts and the excitement has them on edge.

After the pre-game festivities and introductions end, it is game time. The two heavyweights come out delivering blow upon blow toward each other. Texas strikes first with a field goal. As the defenses continue to battle it out, Bill untracks the Notre Dame offense on the following possession. Determined not to let the team finish the season with back-to-back losses, he drives the offense with great purpose. The *Maestro* performs a monster concert during the first two quarters. Moving the team 80 yards in 10 plays with perfection, he caps the drive with a 26-yard bullet to William, 7-3 Notre Dame.

In celebration, he fist pumps the air and points to Kathy in the suite. Meanwhile, Eli receives instructions to unleash a brand new defensive scheme designed by the coaching staff to look similar to the Texas' Wishbone offensive set and frustrate their players.

In the suite, Kathy jumps up and down revealing her "PROTECT MY MAN" t-shirt to everyone watching. Suddenly, the TV cameras follow Bill's point, catching her celebration as she sees herself on the TV monitor in the suite. Caught up in the moment, Kathy holds her shirt with both hands for everyone to see the words on it. The TV cameras show her excitement several more times during the game. Finally, one of the TV commentators says on air, "Did you catch the beautiful co-ed in the suites? Her touchdown pass celebration says quite a bit to everyone, such youthful exuberance and displaying that special shirt for all to see. Her t-shirt says to me that she just might be the Notre Dame quarterback's girlfriend. If she *is* Bill Denton's girlfriend, there are lots of co-ed hearts breaking all over the country at this moment." As Kathy becomes an instant celebrity, Sarah's heart breaks while she watches the game with friends. The cameras bring the new desire of Bill's heart right before her eyes. However, she is happy that Bill has found someone very special and hides her emotions with her smile.

On the ensuing kickoff, the cover team pops the ball free during Texas' return and recovers the ball at the Texas 10-yard line. Bill cuts sharply off right tackle for a three-yard touchdown to make the score 14-3. Eli has the defense humming, continuing to hold Texas' fearsome running game in check. After an exchange of possessions and a change of quarters, the *Maestro* again orchestrates a concerto down the field. He saunters the final 15 yards of the drive for 21-3 lead. Reacting to the ease of Bill's trip to the end zone, the Irish defense, and its own ineffective running game, Texas changes its offensive philosophy in favor of a passing attack infrequently seen during their regular season games. Texas moves the ball sharply down the field in an 84-yard drive capped by a two-yard run. After the Texas defense stiffens, Notre Dame struggles but manages a field goal, the halftime score remains at 24-11. Following strong direction and encouragement at halftime, both defensive units develop fierce responses to each other's offense during the second half. While both offenses moving the ball around the field, the defenses keep both teams out of the end zones. With Texas driving well into Notre Dame territory in the third period, Eli energizes the defense to make a huge stop on 4th and 1 and return the ball to the Irish. As a result of the second-half defensive war, the final score remains the same as it was at the half. Notre Dame wins the game breaking the Texas 30-game winning streak and ending their National Championship bid. Due to the quality of the Texas defense, Bill has an uncharacteristic game for him, 9 for 16 passing for 176 yards and 22 yards rushing. However, his sole concern was the win the team garnered with their efforts. As the season ends, the Irish finish 10-1.

As the post-game press conference ends, the press is still searching for answers to their questions. Bill and Eli leave the pressroom to locate Kathy and Debbie. As Bill finds Kathy and greets her with a huge hug, a reporter in the press corps shouts, "There she is." The cameras whir with the snapping shutters capturing various images of Bill and Kathy together. As their police escort leads them through the crush, the press shouts questions at Bill and Kathy. "Are you two dating?" and "Is she the girl with the 'Protect My Man' t-shirt?"

After getting into the trooper's car, Kathy exclaims, "That was amazing. I never realized what Hollywood types have to go through. I certainly have a new appreciation for their off-screen lives. I see what you meant at Thanksgiving."

Concerned about the media pressure, Bill replies, "Well hon, the press found you for certain."

Breakfast Celebration

B ack at South Bend, they plan to go out to breakfast the next day. On following morning, Bill arrives at the girls' apartment to pick Kathy. While walking to the car, the two of them discuss the game, her performance, and the love they share. After they step into his car, they continue their discussion of love and relationship. Driving to the restaurant, he decides to ask again fearfully, "With yesterday's events, I want to make sure of your feelings because I love you so much. Are you sure you want to be part of all this?"

Replying from her heart, she says, "Yes Bill, I really love you. I can accept whatever the media throws at me to remain by your side. Our love together is worth the effort and sacrifice." Arriving at the restaurant, a national newspaper in the paper stand contains their picture on the paper's front page with a caption reading, "*She's the One.*" Spying it at the same time with Bill, Kathy exclaims, "I can't believe it. They printed that picture so fast. I didn't expect to be so newsworthy. How do you deal with all of this?"

He assures, "It gets easier with time. I'm sure you'll get used to it." The picture accompanies a short paragraph stating the photo caught Notre Dame Quarterback Bill Denton and his girlfriend Kathy

Adams leaving the stadium together. The article continues that they are the new royal couple of America, America's new sweethearts.

It further states how beautiful she is and how much in love they are. Somewhat exasperated as the tone of the article strikes a nerve, Kathy questions, "I realize they can determine my looks from the photo and TV shots. The problem I have is this. How do they know how much in love we are?"

Hearing her frustration, Bill answers, "They don't know hon. They often speculate and write their speculations as fact. However, in this case, they *are* right on target. We *do* love each other deeply and you *are* beautiful."

Spending quality time together, Kathy and Bill blend their lives interspersed with classes, homework, church, and friends. They devise places to meet to stay out of the public eye as their hearts entwine more deeply. On weekends, Bill and Kathy travel around northern Indiana's state parks when schoolwork permits. While the Dunes beckon along Lake Michigan's shoreline, Potato Creek State Park becomes their favorite idyllic getaway to shut out the world with shared blankets, bundled walks in the cold, and many warm hugs and kisses. During the remainder of the winter, Kathy, Debbie, Bill, and Eli spend several weekends at Pokagon State Park's refrigerated toboggan run. It is a bigger rush than dodging a blitzing safety and no reporter would dare venture down the run just for a quote. A couple of school dances bring memories of Christmastime at South not long ago as Bill and Kathy display their fluid mastery together. The group builds snow angels when walking through the cotton-covered fields and warms themselves with hot chocolate by the fire at the Inn. Winter slips into spring as their love intensifies to the awakening blossoms around them. Scenic getaways now include secluded picnics while evading the probing media and paparazzi. Spring football interrupts their fire for each other and spurs the media further with little success. As spring warms toward summer, their school year ends more rapid than both of them desire. Kathy gives voice to her thoughts, "Bill, it'll be a long summer in San Diego without you there. I miss you already. I don't know how my heart will survive without you near me there."

As her heartache appears on her face, Bill says, "Don't worry hon. I *have* to fly out to see you. My heart can't bear three months without you in my life. Letters and phone calls alone won't replace you near me." As Bill takes her to the Weir Cook Airport in Indianapolis, they make plans on what they will do when he visits.

Visiting San Diego

During the early summer, Bill's grandparents went home to the Lord suddenly. During his discussion with God to get him through this time, suddenly Bill decides to call his mentor and surrogate father, Doug Tibbs again. Explaining his loss with a heavy heart, Bill requests, "Mr. Tibbs, my grandparents were the only family I had left. I need someone to help me through this. Would you mind being my father again?"

With a smile, Mr. Tibbs answers, "Bill, I never stopped being here as a father for you. I'm glad you still believe you can call on me. Thank you for allowing me to support you when you needed me in this difficult time. Let's get through this together." As they plan the funerals and the announcements, Bill empties his emotions while relating the story of Sarah, Kathy, football, and himself. Meeting together at Doug's house over the next several days, Bill enjoys the pleasure of family meals and care again. After the funerals, Doug invites Bill back to the house to clear his head and release his emotions. While there, Mr. Tibbs offers, "You spoke about selling your grandparent's house. Why don't you let me take care of that for you? I know a couple of people who care and would sell the house for you fairly. I'll help you close out the estate as well. What else could a father do for his son?"

Opening his heart, Bill says, "Mr. Tibbs, you have been there for me through the most difficult issues in my life with the right direction always. You accepted me into your family without hesitation. I can't find the right words to express what you mean to me and always have meant. So I'll just say thank you, dad. I love you."

After settling the estate and selling the house, Bill makes plans to live in South Bend. He and Eli move into their own apartment with Bill getting all the furniture for them. Once they settle into the apartment, Eli returns to Ft. Wayne and visits South Bend periodically, staying in the apartment when he visits. During that time, Bill finishes plans to go to San Diego and visit Kathy for two weeks. Disembarking the plane and walking toward baggage pickup, he sees Kathy rushing toward him with the intent in her eyes of a blitzing safety. Before he can say anything, Kathy smothers him with hugs and kisses as if they have been apart for years. Her heart confirms the love she expected to find in him still burns brightly as he returns her affections equally. Finally, they exchange verbally how much they miss each other. However, their reunion arouses some of the local media to their presence and the paparazzi begin taking their pictures and stalking. After the public photo demands subside, Bill questions with deep concern, "Has the press been very difficult for you here?"

Mulling the media pressure in her mind, Kathy explains, "It's as bad here as it was for us at school and the places around South Bend. My picture is in the paper quite often and the reporters call the house constantly, wanting interviews." She continues with a big smile, "It's all worth the sacrifice to be with you." As they continue walking to her car, they cuddle each other's hands and take brief respites for warm embraces and ardent kisses. The next morning, the San Diego paper's front page has one picture of them kissing and one picture of them walking holding hands with a caption reading, "America's Royal Couple visits San Diego."

Bringing the paper into the kitchen as they all sit down for breakfast, Kathy's dad says with a laugh, "I hope you two weren't expecting any time alone. With the pictures in today's paper, good luck having any private time here."

Looking at the picture together and smiling, Bill and Kathy say, "It's really no big deal. We'll be fine as we're used to it now." For the two weeks he spends with Kathy in San Diego, the media stalks them relentlessly. They attend church with her parents by hiding in the back seat of the car while her parent's drive. Finally, they lift their heads up from hiding when the car clears the media siege line. Their picture is in the paper every other day from different locales and tourist areas around the city. The couple tries to see as much of the city as time and the media allow. Visiting Coronado Island beach, they catch some quality time in the surf and on a shared beach towel. Beach sunsets are especially pleasing to their eyes and hearts, enhancing the love they share. Evenings along the Gaslight Quarter provide some spots to steal kisses while shopping. While there, they sneak off into Bread on Market, the Tin Fish, and the Field, an Irish restaurant, of course. While at Balboa Park, they manage to lose their media stalkers for a time at the botanical gardens and sneak more hugs and kisses. Patronizing several of the museums there, they evade the paparazzi while doing so. Their game of spy and counter-spy is just beginning to get interesting. However, regardless of their location, they are news. Yet whenever cornered, they handle every situation with class being cordial and polite to everyone. The last picture printed is of them kissing goodbye at the airport as Bill leaves for home. This time the article makes the paper's front page reiterating they are America's Sweethearts. The article also states that they are the two nicest, most polite people the writer has ever interviewed. Kathy's parents decide to save that article.

Not satisfied with just one visit, his heart tugs at him to make several, long weekend visits during voluntary workouts. Before he makes his last visit, he inquires hopefully, "Kathy, would you like to come back with me and stay in South Bend just before school starts?"

After discussing the subject at length with her parents, they inform them both, "We trust you two. If it were anyone other than Bill, we'd probably not allow you to do this. However, we've gotten to know him very well and we agree to let you go." Since there are no classes to attend, they will get to spend lots of time together and be themselves, blending their lives further. Of course, they are still America's Sweethearts with the media blitz continuing to grow. With the two of them, it's *always* show time now.

Back in South Bend

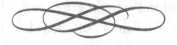

At the apartment, they enjoy spending time with each other and visit their favorite hideaways frequently. They attend church weekly and even manage to hide in plain sight shopping the Miracle Mile in Chicago. Exploring nature's secrets, they share special emotions at their favorite hideout from the media, Potato Creek State Park. One evening while enjoying hot chocolate at Bill's apartment, Kathy inquires curiously, "What it's like when you're on the field. What do you feel like? What are you thinking?"

Explaining the different facets of his character as he did with Maddie, he expounds with a laugh, "I'm very protective of my friends. My high school friends claim that I'm like a *Knight* of antiquity because I'll do almost anything to protect and restore a friend's honor and emotional well-being. I protected one friend in particular from harm a couple of times in high school. The first time, I wasn't there when my friend needed me the most. It affected me so much that I had to restore their honor. The second time, I *was* there when the same foe thought my warning to him could go unheeded. He found quickly that my words still carried a force behind them. I *did* learn an important lesson regarding that protective instinct though. 'There are times when you have to relinquish that protective instinct to higher authority.' Mr. Tibbs, my surrogate father, taught me that important distinction." While continuing, he includes the *Maestro* and the big stage, his Broadway scenario, "I didn't realize until this season how much I enjoy hearing people say 'there he is' when I walk on the field. I really enjoy the looks from opposing team players when I swagger out and the intimidation I see. However, I'm only that way when I'm in the game. To me, football has always been what I do not who I am. I really don't like the other stuff but I know the media crush is part of this. I guess I didn't anticipate the levels to which it would go. In spite of all that on field stuff, I found the perfect girl with whom to make the journey. I like snuggling with you, caressing your face, getting lost in your eyes, and even watching romantic movies with you. Your touch is warm, soft, and amazing. Time slows to a crawl when we hold each other. Most of all, wherever I am with you is heaven for me and fills my heart with elation and love." His words overflow Kathy's heart with love meeting her deepest desires. Bill and his perfect girl enjoy the rest of the evening together thoroughly.

Their school year progresses well but the other teams have their young guns trained on Bill. The team finishes the season 8-2 eking out a one-point win at Purdue but losing to LSU and USC. Watching excitedly from the Purdue stands, his previous love Sarah's heart leaped for joy while Bill directed the Irish victory over Purdue but she kept her emotions hidden deep inside. Receiving first team All-American honors, he still maintains a 4.0 grade point average academically. Requests for Bill and Kathy's time keeps growing and forces her to sit in the guest suite at every game she attends as the Notre Dame AD had arraigned. Just like Sarah in high school, Kathy receives her own assigned State Trooper. She still wears her "Protect My Man" t-shirt with Bill's number on the back during every game. The TV cameras paint her image across the ether and the stadium screens liberally during every game. Sharing Bill's celebrity status, she has become almost as much of a celebrity as he has become. Bill's friend at the premier sports magazine has an idea and requests, "Do you mind if I write an article on you as I did with Bill in high school." After discussing the article together, they agree to it with Notre Dame approval but only with him privately. The article appears in print with Kathy and Bill walking through campus pictured on the cover with the big caption, "They Are America's Sweethearts." The article centers on them together and is painless, relatively speaking, with nothing about football or Bill's on-field performance. The article speaks to their character, maturity, cordiality, politeness, and positive Christian worldview. They are intelligent young people, who know where they are going and who they are. Bill, Kathy, and her parents are very happy with the article's tone.

College Junior Year

Their new year ends almost as well as the previous season. In the first four games, Bill, Eli, and the team pitch two shutouts and two other wins including a big win against Purdue. However, in game five, they lose a heartbreaker to Missouri at South Bend. After the Missouri loss, the team responds with four wins including another shutout. The final regular season game is at USC against Bill's nemesis. Unfortunately, the Trojans pound the Irish 45-23. Although receiving an invitation to the Bowl game, the team did not respond well to the USC loss or the month layoff between games. The team loses it focus and poise as Nebraska pummels them 40-6 while the Nebraska defense throttles the Irish receivers and runners. In spite of the losses, Bill receives first team All-American honors as well as Academic All-American for the second year in a row.

Media demands on Bill and Kathy are beginning to wear on them both. Kathy intimates, "Bill, I'm feeling like a prisoner at the games. While I have a great seat and I'm treated excellently, the constant guardian makes me uneasy. I love you so much and don't want to leave. I just wish we had more time together without the press pursuing us everywhere."

Remembering similar circumstances with Sarah, Bill empathizes, "I agree. For the first time in my life, I feel encroached on too. We need to find some better hiding places from them. I have an idea. Why don't we disguise ourselves when we go out? Let's improve our game with them and see who is better. I think we can be great at this. It'll be like Halloween every night." The both laugh and make their plans. As the year progresses, they become adept at avoiding the press while maintaining their privacy. Even long-time members at their church barely recognize them. When they are alone, they spend time planning evasive tactics for their next day's movements. After planning and homework, their minds and hearts give in to each other. They exchange caresses, warm snuggles, and heartfelt kisses. While preparing dinner in the apartment, they enjoy teasing each other while cooking and even wash dishes together. Interspersed within their mealtime laughter, they gently feed each other finger food. The depth of their love overcomes the siege mentality of the season and blazes to life again.

College Senior Year

From a media standpoint, their senior year starts just like their junior year ended with the "circus" still in town. The Irish receive the number one ranking in the preseason polls and are favorites to win the National Championship. When cornered by the media, Kathy and Bill still answer all questions with patience, graciousness, class. During the regular season, they had three close games, two were at South Bend, and one was at Purdue, 20-7. During the win at Purdue, Sarah sat in the stands for her last glimpse of Bill in person. After the game, she stayed in the stands watching him walk off the field after his post-game interview. Her heart sank, her emotional limits were eclipsed, and the tears flowed as he disappeared into the tunnel for the final time and out of her life. The Irish struggled next in a hard fought win against Michigan State, 14-10, but finally, Bill and the team beat USC, 23-14, for the first and final time during his career. As the juggernaut steamrolls onward, they pound their opponents and finish the regular season 10-0. The team receives an invitation to play in the bowl game on New Year's Eve for the National Championship.

Christmas Break

During the two-week Christmas break, Bill and Kathy fly to San Diego to spend the holiday with her parents. The only anticipated problem is Bill's availability for the bowl game practices. However, instead of the holiday period being the expected family Christmas, the national media turns the time into a frenzied circus. Still, managing to sneak through the media siege line, the family attends Christmas Eve services at church. Deploying reporters outside the Adams' home on Christmas morning, the media attempts to catch a glimpse of the family opening presents. Peeking through the curtains to glimpse the day's beauty, Kathy shrieks in horror at finding an unknown face peering back at her through the window. Bill is *not* pleased with the media intrusions into the family but chooses to represent the university in a positive, courteous manner. Walking outside to confront the sports hounds, he says, "Guys, I'd love to interview with you but we need some peace this Christmas Day. Please go home to your families and leave us alone today." Walking back in the house, he finds the constant media blitz straining Kathy and her family emotionally. This celebrity treatment from the media has grown more intrusive each year for almost four years. The media reduced Kathy and Bill's time away from them to solitary confinement in their separate apartments. To venture outside even for class or church is to invite a media assault. It is very difficult to visit each other, go to dinner, or even grocery shop without media chaperones. It feels like house arrest to them both. Finally, with only the bowl game left, Bill capitulates to media pressure and enlists the aid of the university athletic director rather than continuing his solitary effort to keep the media at bay.

With the media intrusions building to a crescendo, Kathy decides to discuss their coming life together with Bill. Because of his superb skills and immense potential, she knows he will be an elite pro football player. After speaking for a while, they agree that the media will be as relentless, at the very least, and could be even more so. Putting that conversation on hold for now, they strive to enjoy the remainder of their Christmas break together. However, the tension is obviously present in spite of their warm emotions, snuggling, and teasing. As Bill readies to leave for the bowl game on New Year's Eve, Kathy calmly renews their discussion about their future. She probes deeply, "Will we spend holidays together without the press or can I expect to be alone at Christmas like the last four years?"

Hoping to avoid the subject, she catches him completely by surprise. Hesitatingly, he answers, "I'm sorry, Kathy. I really don't know with any certainty. It all depends on how the team performs." The indecision in his voice dampens her heart's enthusiasm for their time together. She hoped to hear some encouraging words that included them as a couple together.

Her parents take Bill to the airport accompanied by Kathy. To spend more time with her parents, she is leaving on a different flight for the bowl game. When they arrive at the airport, Kathy's heart fills with tears that she hides but her face show the sadness. "I wish our time together has lasted longer. I will miss you so much until we see each other again. Look for me at the game but remember I *am* in your heart," Kathy adds voice to her emotions.

    His leaving saddens his heart deeply as well and Bill says, "Kathy, I miss you already. This bowl game will be an eternity away from you. We can arrange our flights from the bowl game to arrive at Indianapolis airport near the same time. Let Andy know when to pick you up at the airport and we can meet there. Just drop me off at the airport departure area. There is no need to breach the frenzy that will erupt when I go to board their plane." Arriving at the airport, the anticipated chaos waits and the media throng presses around him as he attempts to make his way through the crowd. Two San Diego police officers recognize him in the midst of the crowd. They push through to reach Bill, take him by the arm, and wedge their way through the crowd to reach the gate and get him onto the plane. As he reaches the plane's entrance ramp, Bill thanks the officers repeatedly and requests, "May I have your business cards? I would like to call you when we come back to San Diego after graduation." Bill takes their cards, keeping two for Kathy and two for him. His heart scans for her house below as he flies toward his last college game.

Bowl Game

The bowl game against Alabama on New Year's Eve is their toughest game of the year. As anticipated, the two best teams battle each other the entire game, exchanging leads six times. Eli has the Irish defense operating in peak fashion as they display their game intentions early. During the first quarter, they hold Alabama to minus yards rushing. To start the second quarter, Notre Dame executes a 93-yard kickoff return for a touchdown. At the halftime pause, Bill and the team have a 14-10 lead as the coaches develop their remaining game strategy. Both teams reap touchdowns from their third quarter efforts. Early in the fourth quarter, Alabama runs a flea-flicker pass for a 25-yard scoring play to take a 23-21 lead. Unfortunately, they make a crucial mistake when their kicker misses the extra point. On his next drive, Bill pushes the offense down the field but the Alabama defense keeps the team out of the end zone as Notre Dame settles for a field goal and a 24-23 lead. Eli exhorts the defense to leave it all on the field over the game's final 4:26. From deep inside, he encourages, "Guys, Bill and the offense got us the lead and Alabama wants it back. If you give it everything you have for these next few minutes, you can walk away as a national champion with your heads held high. We have to grab at every ball, tackle every runner, and pressure every pass attempt. Make this game ours! Let's do this!" Responding to his clarion call, they make the field their own. The Irish finish 11-0 and receive the National Championship crown. Bill receives the bowl game MVP award but he gives the accolades to the defense and its efforts. The season gives Coach George Alan his first undefeated, untied season at Notre Dame and his third National Championship. The championship rings the Notre Dame team receives are the most magnificent rings ever given to a National Champion, thrilling Bill.

Sneaking off to dinner by themselves, Bill and Kathy celebrate the win immediately after the game. During the dinner, Bill decides to do something special for Kathy. Time and space meet as one in their hearts and minds. They know this is where they are supposed to be. Pulling his championship ring out of his pocket, Bill hands it to Kathy. Having already seen it, she opens the box to look at it again. As she closes the box to hand it back to him, he enlightens, "No Kathy, I want you to keep it because I love you. You have been by my side every moment."

As Kathy begins to cry softly, she utters with regret, "You're the greatest guy I know but I can't accept this. The thought alone is enough of a gift."

As she tries to give it back to him, Bill responds, "I love you more than anything or anyone. Let it remind you how much I love you. Please keep it." Kathy agrees reluctantly.

Arriving at the airport, Andy greets them both and brings an old friend, Deputy John Layton, with him. Deputy Layton brings three other deputies with him to help get them safely through the crowd to Andy's car. At Andy's car, Bill thanks the deputies for their friendship and care in the craziness. Wisely, Bill left his car at Andy's house away from prying eyes. Andy takes them to the privacy of Bill's car to allow them to drive back to South Bend themselves. It is a welcome solitude in the midst of the insanity. Their worst nightmares could not bring this treatment to mind as their world has turned upside down.

Driving back to South Bend, they discuss the serious articles about Bill and professional football. The articles anticipate he will be the first pick in the 1973 draft. Bill is everyone's All-American quarterback and Kathy is everyone's All-American sweetheart. Professional football teams call him for interviews to determine if his character is worthy of their first round draft pick. From all professional football teams, Bill receives letters, questionnaires, and forms. Contacting Irish team doctors and the head trainer, Russ James, the teams request Bill's medical and treatment records. His performance is not enough and they want to insure he is physically worth basing a team's future off his first selection in the draft. Suddenly, his world expands larger than it has ever been, pulling Kathy along for the ride and the media crush becomes extremely oppressive.

Kathy's Discussion

O nce back at Bill's apartment they sit on the couch and breathe a sigh of relief to be home and away from the overexcited throng. While snuggling to enjoy each other's touch again, Kathy begins crying uncontrollably. Extremely concerned, Bill's heart presses him to inquire, "Kathy, are you ok? Hon, what's wrong?"

Knowing she cannot conceal her hurt any longer, Kathy composes herself and begins, "I can't take all the pressure anymore. I have no *personal* privacy any longer and I can't take the invasion into *our* privacy anymore. My dream is to get married, to have children, and to live a normal life with my *husband*, not a public life. I don't want to live in some professional football city that could be anywhere in the country and maybe have to move at a minute's notice. I don't want to do all the things I'll have to do being a professional football player's wife. I just want us to be Bill and Kathy, the people that live in the nice house with the big yard on a small lake. I just want us to be regular people. I know now this isn't possible because you're *the* football player everyone wants to watch and be like. I know that you'll only destroy your dream if you stay with me and I can't ask you to do that." After uttering those words, she begins to sob again and chokes out, "I still love you so very much but I can't continue living the lives we live now with the prospect of that same life ahead of us. This is just not who I am. The Christmas break in San Diego convinced me even though I tried to deny it. I apologize that I hoped for too much because it took me four years to realize it. I would never trade these four years with you for anything except to have you with me forever. Would you provide me one last kindness by taking me to my apartment?"

Her words devastate Bill to his core like an Atomic bomb blast and radiate pain deeply into his heart, as she is the girl he wants to marry. They talked previously about getting married after graduation but set no definite plans or dates. Planning to wait until after the draft, they wanted to see for which team he would play. After that, they planned to set the wedding date in San Diego. Her words clearly stated that would never happen now. His heart screams in pain for the loss he feels. Wanting to hold her in his arms, he yearns to tell her everything will be all right. Longing for their relationship to be as it used to be, instead, he complies with Kathy's request and drives her to her apartment. Upon arrival, she requests, "Bill, would you mind waiting for a minute? I'll be right back."

Returning quickly with something in her hand, she intones, "Bill, please keep in touch with me. You have a special place in my heart always. I will love you forever." Walking up to his side of the car with deep sadness painting her face, she takes his hand and places his national championship ring in it.

Closing her hand around the ring with his hand, he replies softly, "Kathy, I want you to keep it. The ring is a symbol to remind you how much we meant to each other."

With sadness and emotional pain choking her words, she regrets, "Bill, I know how much you mean to me and always will. My heart has your image and all we have shared together irrevocably emblazoned on it. I won't need your ring as further proof we existed together. Please accept it back to remind you of our time together at Notre Dame and your efforts to garner the national championship and my love." As he gets out of his car, she hugs and kisses him for one last time with tears streaming down his cheeks.

Hurrying toward her apartment in tears, she leaves a choked, "Goodbye Bill," echoing in his ears and heart. Once inside, she collapses on her couch with their blanket for comfort and sobs uncontrollably. She loves him with all her heart. However, the media crush, the uncertainty of a permanent home, and the thought of lonely autumns without him were more than her love for him could overcome. Emotionally devastated and physically numb, Bill drives back to his apartment and drags his body through the door. Falling on the couch, he sobs from deep in his heart. His thoughts return to Sarah and to how perfectly they fit in all ways. Longing for the days when they were together, he aches for her friendship and the love they shared. With Kathy choosing to leave their love due to the pressure, his heart now pains for those days spent with Sarah.

Suddenly, Eli walks into the apartment after returning from Ft. Wayne. Hearing Bill's pained crying, he questions with great concern, "Hey Bill, you ok man. What's going on?"

Through tear-blurred eyes, Bill replies, "Kathy and I just broke up because she couldn't take the public lifestyle and the media crush anymore. She wanted us to be a normal couple, living a normal life in San Diego or even in Indiana. Unfortunately, football's potential nomadic future and the media pressure ended our relationship."

Feeling an emotional pile driver hit him, Eli attempts to cheer him up by saying, "There are plenty of girls who can handle your lifestyle. You'll find that one girl yet."

Reviewing memories of Sarah, Bill responds, "I found her once, Eli, but I let her go because we went to different schools several hours apart. She *is* the only girl who handled this lifestyle perfectly. She *is* the one girl I have truly loved since the first day of high school."

Confused, Eli exclaims, "Whoa Bill, hold up a minute. You're *still* in love with a girl from high school but you were going to *marry* Kathy. How the heck was that going to work?"

Calmly, Bill explains, "Yes, I love Kathy and wanted spend the rest of my life with her. However, the redhead and I *were* best friends, maybe still *are*. I was and I guess still am in love with her too. The problem was that the long distance relationship between schools didn't work for us. We both decided to move on with our lives at my first Purdue game. The breakup hurt me so much but her date challenged me at that moment in my deepest pain. I decided to meet his challenge and poured everything I had into that game. The result was a huge win for us. However, the Purdue game the next year at West Lafayette was a struggle. I was sure she was in the stands but I could never find her. We barely won that game and I was an emotional mess."

Excitedly, Eli remarks with determination, "Okay, we're going to find her. You're going to tell me who and where she is. I can't stand to see you in pain like this and I'm sure she can't either. I have to call her for you. I have to let her know how you really feel."

Dejected and emotionally drained, Bill replies as his mind again overrules his heart, "Trust me, she knows very well, and I know how deeply she loves me. The distance combined with the pressure was too much for her too. We needed each other for support. If she was here, I know we could have withstood the pressure. However, I don't want you to contact her. It's been four years man. I'm sure she's moved on."

Amazed at his emotional surrender, Eli comments, "Well, I'd like to know her name at least. Please, as your great friend and teammate for the last four years, let me try for you at least."

With a heavy heart, Bill responds, "I'm sorry my friend, I can't do that. I respect her privacy too much and I'll protect her still. Besides, she graduated from Purdue already. I'm sure of that. As far as you or anybody else knows, she is 'The Redhead.' That's all I'm telling anyone and no one else had better find out about her either." His tone speaks volumes and Eli agrees not to pursue the subject further. However, it hurts him to see his friend in such obvious pain apart from the one he loves.

Draft Day

As draft day for professional football arrives, Bill attends the national draft party as do many other players expected to be first round picks. Wearing a stunning Notre Dame blue colored suit, crisp white shirt, and a matching university tie, he is ready to meet an adoring nation. All the Indiana TV stations cover the draft party to report his selection position in the draft and the team that picks him. The head of professional football steps to the podium and says, "With the first pick in the 1973 draft, the Pittsburgh professional football team selects Bill Denton from the University of Notre Dame." Stepping to the podium, Bill accepts congratulations from the head of professional football, the coach, and the owner of the Pittsburgh team.

Sarah and her boyfriend watch the broadcast with several other couples. While listening as Bill speaks she thinks, "Wow, he hasn't changed a bit. He is the same humble person I loved so much, still praising his teammates and coaches. Amazing!"

While at the podium, Bill continues, "I thank Notre Dame for the opportunity to play there for four years and receive a world class education. However, I would be remiss if I did not thank God for the abilities he gave me to play this game. I have to thank my grandparents for the principles, work ethic, and traits they instilled in me. I want to thank Mr. Doug Tibbs who mentored me as a father after my parents and grandparents died. Finally, I want to thank the people in Pittsburgh for their faith in me as a person and a player. I will do everything in my power to justify that faith in selecting me number one."

Sarcastically, one person comments, "Can you believe this guy? Sarah, did you *really* know him in high school? Was he as big a jerk as he comes across on TV?"

Bristling immediately at the crass comment, Sarah leaps to Bill's defense, "Yes, I *do* know him and he *isn't* a jerk at all. Actually, he is the nicest, most respectful guy in the entire school. He has a great personality and everyone liked him for who he was not for what he was. He is as genuine in person as you saw him on TV. Now please excuse me, I have to visit the ladies room."

Quickly, rushing into the bathroom, Sarah fights back the tears as her heart swells with pride at seeing the man she knew has not changed. Reminiscing fondly about how much they meant to each other, she still loves him deeply. Gathering her thoughts and emotions, she composes herself and rejoins the party while her heart reaches out to touch Bill again.

Arriving in Pittsburgh

With the Draft Day party concluded, Bill stays in New York to meet the media blitz agenda for about a week then flies back to South Bend. After his Notre Dame graduation, he packs some clothes and flies to Houston to visit his aunt and uncle who pick him up at the airport. Bill called his uncle earlier to tell him to come in uniform and bring a couple more Houston Police Officers with him. If the past is any indication, he expects the crowd to be a little crazy. Finding a place to live in Magnolia, Texas just outside Houston, he wants to be close to his family, Uncle William and Aunt Susan. With both his parents and grandparents dead and Sarah graduated from Purdue, he believes he has nothing to hold him emotionally in Indianapolis. After a week, he meets with the Pittsburgh organization to negotiate his contract. With a 4.0 grade-point average and a degree in Business and Business Law from Notre Dame, Bill negotiates his own contract skillfully and successfully. No longer does he need to rely on his trust fund. His multi-million dollar contract provides him all the funds he needs now and in the foreseeable future. With his frugal nature and his investing ability, he can provide for himself and any future family. Yet his newly acquired wealth has its own drawbacks when seeking a potential woman with whom to share his life. The old question he faced in high school returns with an added twist. Does the woman want to date him for his money, for his quarterback fame, or because he is just Bill Denton, a sensitive, courteous, and loving guy?

Professional Life

As pre-season rookie camp begins, Bill's performance and work ethic convinces the Pittsburgh staff that they hit the sweet spot when they chose him. The veterans report to camp couple of weeks later. After two weeks of two a day practices, he impresses the veterans with his football knowledge and skills. Continuing to work after practice with his receiving corps, he hones their timing and routes to perfection, as he did in high school and college. His extra time spent studying the plays and knowledge of defensive schemes makes him an invaluable coach on the field. By the first game, Bill and the receivers operate as one and he is mentally ready for the most difficult defense. Commanding the team on the field, Bill will be a rookie starting quarterback in the first game.

Pushing the team to an amazing year for a rookie quarterback with a 10 and 4 record, he drives the team to a second-place divisional finish. Bill receives Rookie of the Year honors unanimously, heralding potential professional football greatness. During the next five seasons, Bill leads his team a first-place divisional finish each year and to 1975, 1976, and 1979 Championship victories. He is the Championship game MVP in 1979, the season MVP, and receives an invitation to the Pro All-Star Bowl eight years in a row. Pittsburgh continues to be a force in professional football under his leadership.

The 10-Year Reunion

During the summer of 1979, Bill has been out of South High for 10 years and receives an invitation to his high school reunion from the reunion committee. While reading the invitation, memories of Sarah flood his mind and warm his heart. Scanning for the date, he finds the reunion scheduled at the perfect time to allow him to attend. As a precaution, he does not pre-register to keep the media at bay. If the media finds out about this, he knows they would make it impossible for him and the others to enjoy the evening. Quietly and in relative privacy, he wants to speak with old friends, visit briefly with Sarah, and leave.

Walking down the hallway to the reunion hall entrance, his old friend from high school Jim Anderson walks toward him. Noticing Jim walking with purpose and oblivious to his presence, Bill chuckles, "Hey buddy, are you going to speak or walk right by me?"

Startled, Jim breaks his focus to find Bill standing before him. As they begin discussing their lives to this point, Jim says, "You know Bill, no one at work believes I know you."

With an idea popping into his mind, Bill replies, "I've got just the solution. If I send you some autographed Pittsburgh stuff for your office, I'm certain they'll believe you then."

Thrilled by the offer, Jim responds, "Bill, I want to thank you so much for offering to send me *any* memento. You've always been a good friend. You haven't changed at all and you've always been concerned about others' welfare. You're still the same guy I knew at South. Oh by the way, have you seen Sarah yet?"

Excited that she is there but nervous too, Bill replies, "No, I haven't' seen her yet. In fact, I just arrived."

Surprised, Jim says, "She's been asking everyone about you and if anyone has seen you here yet. One of the reunion committee told her none of them thought you were coming because you didn't register. You know she's right inside the door at the second table. You'd better say hello because she's been waiting to see you anxiously. I know you don't want to miss seeing her. She really hasn't changed at all since graduation."

Walking up to the table where Sarah sits, Bill waits politely for her to finish her conversation with another classmate. The person with whom she is speaking does not reveal with verbal or facial expressions that Bill waits behind Sarah. Oblivious to his presence, she continues talking with her back to him, enjoying the evening. As always, being ever courteous, he waits with great eagerness for her to finish. Finishing her conversation, the room waits with hushed anticipation of what will happen next.

Seeing an appropriate pause, Bill leans over close to her nervously and says, "Hey, I just wanted to say hello and then I'll leave you alone."

With those familiar tones racing through her mind, Sarah spins excitedly hoping her ears did not deceive her. When her eyes and brain confirm what her heart envisions, she screams, "Bill!" As her excitement breaches her inhibitions, she leaps into his startled arms and wraps her legs around him. Adding to this emotional Vesuvius, she gives him a long passionate kiss such as he has never experienced. With her heated emotions overflowing like a lava stream, the eruption surges through his overwhelmed heart. Finally, she says lovingly, "Bill Denton, from this moment on tonight, your slow dance card belongs to me. Don't bother to dance with anyone else because tonight is all about us." Speechless by this unexpected show of feelings, he agrees without hesitation. After all, it has been several years since he last saw her but his heart shouts it was only yesterday. While the vision of Sarah fading into the distance at Purdue still blazes in his memory, his heart fixates his gaze on Sarah longingly. Seeing the years of separation showing emotionally on his face, she inquires with concern, "Bill, is something wrong?"

Elated to be next to her again, he says with a warm smile, "No. Everything is fine. It's just that I have never seen you look more beautiful." Radiant in a "V" cut white dress that caresses her perfectly, the 2-karat diamond necklace Bill gave her highlights the vision she presents. A supernova could not look as white *hot*!

While Bill and Sarah reunite their hearts, another person sits in the seat beside Sarah's chair. As Sarah sits down, she decides to make room for Bill next to her. Strongly, she asks the person in the chair beside her, "Pardon me but I need you to move to another seat for me. Bill Denton is sitting in the seat you're in now." When Bill sits next to Sarah, their hands touch each other gently and their eyes get lost in each other's gaze lovingly. There is no need to exchange thoughts verbally as their hearts communicate perfectly through their eyes.

Suddenly, Bill breaks the silence of the heart with a smile and says, "I have a surprise for you." From several previous surprises, Sarah expects one of his beautiful handwritten notes. Instead, he pulls a ring box out of his coat pocket. A look of confusion and slight apprehension slides across her face. Before he gives the box to her, he says, "Well, I'm sure you're trying to guess what's in my hand. You can wear it, put it in a drawer, or put it with the Notre Dame Camp MVP trophy that I'm sure you still have."

Very confused by his words and the ring box, Sarah chuckles,

"Yes, it *is* on my desk at my office in Florida." Anticipating the look to arrive on her face, Bill hands her the box with no additional comment. As she opens it, a huge smile of surprise grows quickly on her face and she exclaims, "Bill, it is *so* beautiful."

Relieved at the warmth emanating from her smile, he explains, "It is the professional championship ring that the player's wives received." While in complete disbelief at the amazing gift, she tries it on excitedly. Of course, it fits her right ring finger perfectly.

Initially amazed at the fit, she questions, "How did you know…" Then, she pauses mid-sentence, as he always knows everything about her. The years melt away as their hearts entwine again in a special emotional tie. Not wanting to break their hearts' bond, they spend the evening visiting with everyone together. As the reunion winds down, Sarah says shyly, "The girls I came with have already left and I don't have a ride home. Are you available?"

With a thrilling opportunity presenting itself, Bill chuckles, "You know that everyone saw us together tonight. The years melted for them as easily as they did for us. They left because they knew I would take care of you."

"Like you always have," she laughs. Their hearts continue an unspoken desire as they drive back to her parent's house. Memories of wondrous times past overflow their hearts and minds as they walk to her door. Spectral visages of neighborhood walks hand-in-hand glide down the street of their memory as they peer into the darkness together from her porch.

Counting stars with her in his mind, Bill's heart screams to stay but he says with hesitation, "I hope I'll see you again sometime. I guess I should go." As he turns and begins to walk away, the memories shower her heart in a torrential downpour.

Suddenly, drowning in thought, she says emphatically, "Not that fast mister, you're not going anywhere. We still have a lot of catching up to do."

Waiting desperately for those words, he sighs, "I hoped you felt the same way I did. Is our couch still available?" Turning with a seductive smile, she takes his hand and leads him through the door.

Envisioning times past with him here, she offers, "Would you like a soda?" He nods affirmatively as she directs him to the couch. Returning with the sodas, she sits next to Bill on her parent's new couch while time and space fold to the moment as the conversation pours again from their hearts. Their times together at South weave through the conversation as if the events were yesterday. The Christmas dances, Homecoming, Brown County, Michigan, Grandview Lake, the many neighborhood walks, shared blankets, even snow angels, and hot chocolate each share a poignant moment in their discussion. All their past love wafts magically through the atmosphere in the room. Her emotions flow as she speaks about her life, her husband, and their jobs in Florida.

Realizing she has monopolized the time, she inquires, "Bill, you're married aren't you?"

With her question baring deeply hidden emotions, he replies sadly, "No Sarah, I'm not. I dated a very nice girl for nearly four years at Notre Dame but the public life demands finally got to her."

Remembering the girl she saw on TV many years ago, Sarah interrupts, "Was she the girl wearing the 'Protect My Man' t-shirt? I saw her on one of your televised games. I'm glad you let her wear the shirt *I* wanted to wear for you. I'm sorry it didn't work out for the two of you."

Showing the pain of Kathy's leaving and Sarah's good-bye in college on his face, he continues, "She told me she couldn't survive the media blitz while I played professional football. She just wanted a normal life out of the public eye. Sarah, you're probably the only woman on the planet who could lead this kind of life with me. The only problem is you're married now."

Seeing his pain and feeling it in her heart, she empathizes, "I'm sure you'll find somebody someday," wanting to add a note of hope.

Responding quickly, he declares, "I never will but I'm ok with that." The conversation continues after the awkward moment and revelations. Suddenly, Bill offers, "I could stay here and speak with you all night. I have no plans that I wouldn't change in a heartbeat for you."

With mixed sensations flooding her thoughts, Sarah responds, "I wouldn't mind that at all but I'm still married. I just can't trust my own emotions. I'm sorry to have to end the evening but I have a plane to catch in the morning. Besides, I need to get some sleep before the flight."

Disappointed, he observes, "I understand. I have a flight tomorrow as well. My plans are to fly back to Pittsburgh in the morning for some team-related community activities." They walk to the door together with their passions shackled. As he reaches for the door handle to leave, Sarah questions keenly, "Would you mind staying for one more question?"

Wanting to stay longer anyway, Bill concedes, "For you always, what it is it?"

Unloading a burning in her heart, Sarah probes, "Why did you stop dating me for a time in high school?"

Surprised by the question, he shuffles his feet and says, "Because, I thought you wanted to date other guys. I was deeply hurt and didn't think I was the type of guy you wanted to date. I didn't really think I had anything to offer you."

Looking at him lovingly with all the depth in her beautiful eyes, Sarah pulls him close and says softly, "I apologize for hurting you. I never wanted to date anyone but you. I just wanted to hear you say you loved me. I made a huge mistake. I thought if you saw me dating someone else, you'd tell me how much you loved me and ask me not to go out with the guy."

Stunned by the response from Sarah's heart, Bill intimates, "Well, this is an amazing revelation. My problem was I didn't have confidence enough to say those simple words to you. I wish I had realized that 10 years ago. Ok, I have one last question for you this evening if you don't mind?"

With one emotional burden lifted, Sarah replies with a huge smile, "Well, since we're opening our hearts, fire away."

Gathering his courage, he says, "I would have waited for you in college. I know the distance between schools was great and football was very demanding. However, I thought that I was holding you back from achieving *your* dreams. Would you have waited for me?"

Transforming her feelings into words carefully, she says, "I cheered for you in each game I watched on TV. When you played at our school for the last time, I had to cheer silently but I cried as I watched you walk into the tunnel for the last time and out of my life." Then, Sarah pauses and comments, "It would have been better for both of us if I *had* waited." As he again turns to go, she pulls him back, wraps her arms around him, and gives him a long, passionate kiss goodbye to fixate the moment in his mind.

On to The Hall

Buoyed by his memories of Sarah and the reunion, he leads his team to one last championship game and receives one last MVP in January 1980. After the championship, the team changes dramatically from the first ones that he led to victory. After three subpar years of winning less than ten games a season, he pulls the team to two more first place finishes in the division. Finally, after twelve years as a professional player, he announces, "Fans, teammates, Pittsburgh owners, staff, and coaches, today I am announcing my retirement from professional football. Twelve years is enough pounding and I want to retire at the top of my game. I do not want someone to provide me a gracious exit in a future rebuilding program. I do not want to become an aging player past his prime grasping for one last bit of glory. I want to leave the game I love with my head held high, unbowed, and my passion strong. All of you have been a remarkable part of my life that I will cherish forever. I cannot find words to express the depth of feeling I have for the support and love you have shown me all these years. I hope that God has allowed me to bring some joy into your lives through the game I love. I hope that my passion became your passion as we journeyed together. So, with my final 'Thank you so very much for the love and faith in me', I will turn and walk into the sunset of my playing days and into the dawn of a new phase of my life. God bless and keep you all. I leave you with an appropriate Irish blessing, 'May the road rise up to meet you. May the wind be ever at your back. May the sun shine warm upon your face and the rain fall softly on your fields and until we meet again, may God hold you in the hollow of his hand.'"

The years pass quickly and Bill's play and stats keep him in the minds of the voters for entry to the Hall of Fame, winning MVP and Pro All-Star Bowl honors. After retiring, Bill waits the required number of years to be eligible for the ballot and voting. Ballot eligibility finally arrives for Bill and he receives the necessary votes for enshrinement in his first year. For the induction ceremony, he invites Mr. Tibbs and his family, all the boys, Andy, Pete, D. J., Jordon, Joey, their wives, and their kids to attend the ceremony. Asking his old coach from Notre Dame for a special favor, Coach Alan agrees to introduce him to the attendees during the ceremony. The proceedings occur better than expected in the Hall's home city and on the last night, everyone has their kids in bed early. Sitting around a couple of tables in the hotel lounge, they share the joy of the moment with Bill. Having all the boys and Mr. Tibbs with him makes this a very special night. The wives make the family atmosphere extra special but Bill's elation is subdued and the guys all know why. As the wives excuse themselves to allow the men to discuss football history and old times, finally, Jordon, who is still the crazy one, utters what the rest of the group is thinking. In the most serious tone the guys have ever heard from him, he says, "Bill, you have it all finally, championships at every level of football, a member of the Hall of Fame, personal fame, fortune, and the trophy for the top college football player, in short, everything."

Preparing to toast him, Andy, Bill's constant confidant and protector among the guys, speaks up, "Guys you're dead wrong. Bill could have had everything but he is missing the mirror in his life, his equal, and without her he has nothing." Bill nods in agreement. Andy continues, "He could have had everything because all he had to do was ask her. We all know she would have been here in a heartbeat." Knowing Andy is right, Bill ponders why his heart could not convince his mind to make that call. His mind still rationalizes that he protected her privacy but the emotional cost is very high. With restraint, those in the room toast Bill's accomplishments.

Everyone knows Andy is speaking about Sarah but no one comments further as they can see the pain in Bill's face. Truly, he misses the one woman who could make this night complete. With the evening activities drawing to a close, the group discusses a few subjects that are more pertinent before breaking to go to their rooms and families. When Bill enters his room, his heart bears the weight of only one thought, "This should be the greatest night of my life but it isn't because I was too afraid to share it with Sarah." Sitting on the side of his bed, he weeps uncontrollably. His heart aches for Sarah's touch, her conversation, and her beauty near him more at this moment than at any time in his life. Sarah watches the day's activities on TV while crying silently in her heart. Her heartache is as great as Bill's as she longs to have shared this moment with him personally.

Life After Football

L eaving the heartache of his induction celebration behind, Bill places Sarah in a special corner of his heart. However, knowing life continues, he decides to move on emotionally. Working as a commentator for professional football games, he laughs at the juxtaposition of roles with him on the other end of the microphone in football now. Drawing on his God-given gift of understanding while the game unfolds, his talent is in constant demand and sports bureaus consider him the best in the business. Investing his earnings wisely from his playing years, he doesn't have to work but chooses to do so. He enjoys the emotional release and reward the games provide while keeping his mind focused. However, his heart remains a protected commodity from all others.

Reserving a special excitement for five-year fragments of life, he attends every reunion hoping to catch a glimpse of Sarah and to spend that precious time with her. When she does not arrive due to *her* life commitments, his emotions carry him through the evening with friends but his heart remains cloistered within its tower room. In the years when her presence lights the room, his self-imposed prison gates open, his heart releases, and the times apart melt again. Other people in the room fade as the two create their own world for a few hours and entwine their hearts again with fun and laughter. Unfortunately, the times together grow increasingly infrequent as life draws them in different directions.

As he has not received reinforcement of the bond they once shared for many years, his heart grows weary. Suddenly reaching for a relationship from her past, Sarah sends Bill a hand-written card in the mail. Including her email address and cell phone number in the note, she asks him to keep in touch. Buoyed with excitement, he responds quickly with an email in return, stoking the embers of their love. Continued emails between them fan their love's fire. They exchange holiday greetings and occasionally, emails asking what's happening. In the interim, Sarah moves back to Indianapolis and re-marries. Even with his connections, Bill has remained unaware she divorced from her first husband. His desire to protect her from the media's prying glare worked perfectly, keeping knowledge even from him.

Lunch

Suddenly finding his business schedule taking him to Indianapolis, Bill emails Sarah asking if she would be available to have lunch with him. Over 40 years have passed after high school, yet his heart still yearns to be near her for any reason. The email informs, "I'll be there on business, but I only have three days. So, if you can't make it, I'll understand." Providing the dates, he prays her heart still hungers enough to join him. Returning his email with great excitement, she says, "Lunch sounds great! I need to get some items downtown on one of those days. So, I can mix business with joys of the heart." Setting the time and place with her, Bill's excitement gnaws at him from his heart. Finally, the two of them can enjoy being together despite time's unkindness to them.

Time crawls until he arrives in town. He has a morning interview with a local TV station regarding football and his current career. The full interview content begins with his football career highlights then shifts to his views of moving into the broadcast booth from the field. Planning to air the interview quickly, the station schedules him on the six o'clock and eleven o'clock broadcasts. All the while, his heart focuses on lunch with Sarah in a short time. Finishing the interview, he rushes to the restaurant to meet her. In their late 50's and looking great, the eagerness of youth permeates their thoughts of each other. It is a beautiful summer day in Indianapolis as he waits outside the restaurant eagerly and signs some autographs. Suddenly the air wafts familiar tones to his ears, "Bill, Bill." Turning to orient his ears toward the sounds, his eyes fixate on the vision floating his way. The most beautiful woman he has ever seen walks toward him and 45 years melt in the moment. The sunlight highlights her face perfectly and the light breeze through her hair enhances her beauty to the point of weakening Bill's knees. With a preamble of caresses and kisses on each other's cheeks, Sarah walks through the door as Bill holds it chivalrously. The host directs them to their table and describes the day's lunch specials. After make their food decisions, Bill places their orders as usual and their hearts entwine in life discussions.

As the food arrives, Bill opens the vault of his stored emotions verbally, "I have something I need to tell you. I can't let any more time pass between us without letting you know."

As he pauses for a moment, Sarah replies, "Sure what is it?"

Gathering his courage to fight the deep desire to lose himself in her eyes, he continues, "Everyone knows about the Redhead. I've told the reunion story a million times and everyone knows why I never married. I had trouble convincing myself I was good enough for you to date. Because of that fact, I had trouble telling you I loved you when you wanted me to do so. The way I was raised I wouldn't have ever done anything disrespectful to you. I always tried to be there for you when you needed me."

Remembering a wonderful evening a few years ago, Sarah says, "I think I remember someone mentioning that a few years ago. If I recall correctly, it was at mom's house after the 10-year reunion, is there more?"

Anxious to continue, he answers, "Yes, there is. First, I love telling the reunion story. It was one of the best nights of my life. You wore that white V cut dress…"

Interrupting momentarily, she interjects with a big smile, "And I looked pretty hot in it as I recall."

Responding to her words, he adds, "Yes you did. You looked more beautiful than my heart ever remembered. You jumped into my arms, wrapped your legs around me, and gave me that passionate kiss. That moment is etched in my heart and mind permanently. You told me all the slow dances were just for us. Your girlfriends left you in my care early. Knowing I was there to take you home, they were not concerned for your welfare that night. I took you back to your mom and dad's and then you popped the big question. I'll never forget that night."

Remembering her college days without Bill, she says, "I should have dated you or guys like you but it's probably good you didn't wait for me in college."

Puzzled by her words, he says, "Why do you say that?"

Revealing some of her past, she confesses, "I made some very poor lifestyle choices in college. I wouldn't have wanted to involve you in my bad decisions."

Countering with his protective nature, he adds, "If I had been there you wouldn't have made those choices and acted on them."

Making a counterpoint, Sarah probes, "How can you be so sure?"

With the Lancelot in his character coming forth, Bill explains, "Because I wouldn't have let you and you know that's the truth. Even if you got mad at me, I wouldn't have let you act on those decisions because I cared so much about you."

Realizing the truth in his words, Sarah says, "You're right, you always were my Knight in Shining Armor. You were always there to protect me and encourage me."

Returning to the present, Bill offers, "So here we are having a nice lunch and getting to spend a little time together."

Enjoying the time together again, she agrees, "Yes this is nice just being together. Our problem is our path's never crossed at the right time after high school."

Confessing his biggest shortcoming in their relationship, he explains, "Yeah that's a great regret I have. We never were together at the right time after high school. Do you ever wonder why I never got married?"

Pondering his words, she questions, "Yes I do sometimes. So how is it a guy like you never got married or was never in the gossip magazines with rumors flying all over the place?"

Exasperated with his emotional stumbling, he says, "That's what I've been trying to tell you and I can't seem to find the words so I'll confess it again…I'm *still* hopelessly in love with you. I've *been* in love with you for over 40 years now. No one has ever come close to you. You've always been my best friend. It all started the day I spilled the soft drink on you and it continues to this day. When I bumped into you, your beauty swept me away like a tsunami."

Caught off-guard by his strong revelation, Sarah puts her hand over her mouth, fights back the tears, and exclaims, "Oh my!"

Continuing his emotional earthquake, he says, "Never in my private life, especially in high school, could I bring myself to verbalize these deep feelings to you in this way. *It's* true I said I loved you but these feelings are so much stronger. I just wasn't confident enough to take that next step. That's why I let you go in college. I didn't want to hold you back from your dreams yet my love was so strong for you, strong enough to let you go. So there you have it. I'm intensely in love with you, lost hopelessly in the depth of your eyes and heart. Sarah, I have been so for over 40 years."

Overcome with so many different emotions, Sarah confesses, "I can't express to you how that makes me feel. If *only* our paths had crossed at the right time."

Echoing her sentiments, Bill confesses, "If *only* I had more of the confidence off the field that I had on the field."

With their lunchtime ending quickly, Bill and Sarah leave the conversation with an elephant in the room of their relationship. They both hope in their hearts that maybe there is still a chance for their paths to cross. As time runs short for lunch, they grow misty eyed at the thought of leaving each other. Prefacing their leaving with hugs and kisses, they say goodbye and plan to keep in touch. As they start to walk away, Bill speaks in a tone and confidence she's never heard before, "If your path *ever* takes a new turn, let me know first." While walking away, Sarah turns back, smiles seductively, and again walks out of his life, etching another memory in his heart. This time she ponders his words deeply in her heart.

The Phone Call

T hree years pass after the stunning revelation and suddenly Bill's cell phone rings. The caller ID reveals Sarah as the caller. Thinking he would not see her until the next class reunion, he answers, "Hi Sarah. Wow, this *is* a surprise. How *are* you?"

With excitement crackling in her voice, Sarah says, "Well, I'm fine. Oh, what the heck, I'm not *married* anymore. Bill, did you ever get married?"

As his heart skips a beat at her words, he replies joyfully, "No, I never did and I'm not seeing anyone either." His emotions strain at the precipice, hanging on her next words.

Sarah gets right to the point, "Bill, now is *our* time. Now, finally, our paths are crossing at the right time. I couldn't tell you how I really felt at the reunion or at our lunch. I was too afraid to verbalize what my heart knew. Now that I'm not married, I wanted you to know that I have been in love with you since the day you spilled the soft drink on me. I wanted you in my life so much that I bungled our relationship badly. You have always been the one with whom I wanted to spend my entire life. I just didn't know how to express it and I let college life tear me away from you. I cried so many times when I saw you on TV but couldn't reach you. We had gone on to separate worlds and I thought you had moved on with your life. However, when I saw you play pro football, my heart would not let you go and I cried inside with each televised game. I couldn't let my husband know how I felt about you. I couldn't damage what I had for a possible false hope. Now, I want your heart to come home to me forever. If you're still in love with me, I want to spend the rest of my life with you. If you want that as much as I do still, would you please come and be with me."

Her words ignite the embers in his heart to roaring flame as he says, "Yes, with all my heart, I'm still in love with you. I have *always* been in love with you! I'll be on the first flight out of Houston. As soon as I know the flight and time, I'll let you know when I'll arrive in Indianapolis. My heart will fly to you on angels' wings. I knew God would answer my prayers about us. I can't wait to have the life we always longed to have."

Together Again

Filled with a joy and rapture in his heart, Bill steps off the plane. Finally happier than he has ever been in his life, his heart says they will be together as they always should have been. As he walks into the airport, he spots the most beautiful woman in his world, Sarah. While they are in their late 50's now, the passion in their kiss makes them look like high school kids. Sharing a tearful and happy reunion with him, she says, "I have a little secret desire to share. I want your heart to come home to me every night from wherever you are forever."

"I'll be there as long as you want me. My heart *is* yours forever," he responds and continues, "I have something special for you too." He reaches into his pocket, pulls out a rectangular box, and hands it to her. With a puzzled yet excited look, she opens the box and the tears begin to flow down her cheeks as she exclaims, "Bill, this couldn't be. Is it really..."

Interrupting her thoughts and words, he replies immediately, "Yes, Sarah. I gave you this same ruby heart necklace a lifetime ago. I kept it safe all these years after you gave it back to me at the Notre Dame game. It kept you near to me all these years."

Feeling so much love filling her heart, she requests softly, "Please

put it on me, Bill. I want you near my heart again as you used to be."
While he places the necklace gently around her neck, Sarah grasps it
in her hand, closes her eyes, and holds it near her heart as she used
to do. Memories of Bill and the necklace sweep her back in time and
she is with him again in their youth as she always has been in her
heart. As they are leaving, people stop them for questions. The public
still wants to shake Bill's hand and get his autograph after all these
years. Sarah waits at his side patiently, fully understanding who he
is and why people want to meet him.

Moving the reunion to the baggage claim area, they sign more
autographs along the way and eventually find Bill's luggage. While
walking to Sarah's car, their paths cross with more well-wishers
and autograph seekers. Each person receives a handshake, a brief
discussion, and an autograph. Getting the luggage in the car, the
couple drives to Sarah's house joyfully. However, on this occasion,
she refuses to let him stay in any hotel and be away from her heart.
Hearing his commitment to her in their phone conversation, she is
not letting him get away for any reason this time. The years fade in
their hearts and minds while the best times of high school repeat
themselves as Sarah and Bill are together every minute of every day.
Days blur into weeks and weeks rush onward while their shared joy
and emotional contentment grow. With their future lying before
them, they embrace it with the relish of youth coursing through
their thoughts and hearts.

Making up for lost time, they visit the places they used to
go that history has not removed and enjoy nature as they used to
do. They have dinner at a couple of restaurants owned by two old
friends of Bill. The Oaken Barrel Brewing Co. is located Greenwood,
Indiana south of Indianapolis. With each visit, Bill's friend, Kwang
Casey, greets them and reserves a special place for them. While they
sample other offerings from him during various visits, their favorite
dish is Kwang's Dynamite Shrimp. On their first visit to Kwang's

together, Bill starts to introduce Sarah to Kwang. However, Kwang interrupts exclaiming, "You're the Redhead, aren't you? I've heard so many wonderful stories about you and Bill wasn't kidding. You *are* beautiful."

Blushing, she says, "Yes, I'm the Redhead. My name is Sarah Ormond."

For this special couple, Kwang discusses with his staff, "These are special people to me. Please keep any other patrons away from them to allow them some privacy. Anything they want, please see that they receive it." Always enjoying a quiet dinner and their treatment at Kwang's restaurant, Sarah and Bill thank him when they leave and most often follow their visit with a movie visit. Everywhere they go, history has restored them again as the royal couple.

Frequenting Bill's other favorite restaurant just south of downtown, the Greek Islands Restaurant serves great Greek food whenever their palates desire. Bill's favorite entrée is Souvlaki, which contains marinated pork, potatoes, and peppers. On their first visit, the owner, another good friend of Bill, greets them as they walk in. Recognizing Sarah instantly from Bill's descriptive stories of her, he says, "Well, I'd know you anywhere, Sarah. You're the Redhead, aren't you? I've heard so much about you over the years. I'm George Stergiopoulos, the owner of this fine establishment."

Red-faced with his comment, Sarah confesses with a big smile, "Hello George. I'm Sarah Ormond and yes, I *am* the Redhead." Whispering to Bill, she says with a chuckle, "Do you always have to tell everyone about the *Redhead*?"

Sarah has her favorite places to frequent as well. Visiting Brown County and Nashville, Indiana frequently, they have lunches and dinners at the Artists Colony Inn and Restaurant. Strolling along the landscaped, brick walkway to the entrance of the tempting boutique inn, Bill and Sarah pass a waiting area of elegant wooden benches. Opening the door and entering, the inviting 19th century style colonial décor impresses them visually with its beamed ceilings, Oriental rugs, Windsor chairs, large stone fireplace, and especially friendly staff. The light color walls above the wooden chair rails keep the room bright and display the quality works of local artists. Requesting a table by the fireplace, their minds and hearts wander to warm memories of younger days spent snuggling on the couch at Sarah's house. During their frequent visits, it becomes their favorite seating spot in the restaurant. While Sarah prefers the homemade soup and salad, Bill prefers the grilled tenderloin and Sun fries, which are house specialties. Frequently, they enjoy the variety of delectable desserts offered but especially the apple crisp and homemade pecan pie. During the warm weather, they have dinner outside on the porch seating often. It affords the scenic view Sarah loves to share with Bill while watching the people shuffle by as they shop the town between stealthy, warm kisses. Spending several weekends in Nashville, they stay in the Inn's rooms where their favorite room is the Will Vawter room with a balcony overlooking the ice cream shop. The room delights with two mahogany, queen-sized, four-poster beds, armoire, and wooden plank floors while the furnishings with camel and persimmon colors of an earlier time bring the love in their hearts for each other to full blossom.

Sneaking off for coffee, tea, froothies, and warm conversation in Nashville, they stroll north on Van Buren past the Big Woods Village shops to Molly's Lane across from the courthouse. Walking down Molly's Lane and through the red door of the Common Grounds Coffee Bar, a visual festival of tropical colors around the bar area greets them. Their friend Iris, who owns the coffee bar, welcomes them warmly like family as she does everyone. Moving past the mosaic-top table seating, they browse the vintage china cabinet and bookcase filled with jars of exotic and traditional loose-leaf teas to decide if they want tea, coffee, or something else. The covered baked goods on the display case next to the teas draw their eyes and palettes toward the coffee bar. The baked goods are all tempting but the large cinnamon rolls and scones are among their favorites. Continuing to browse along the long coffee bar seating, their eyes find the wine rack behind the bar stocked with flavored syrups for coffee, froothies, and other unique non-alcoholic beverages.

Making their beverage and food decisions, they continue to browse through the hidden treasures of the shop's vintage and unique books, art, and glassware. They always find something special that catches their fancy. As Iris gives them their order, the collection of teapots and tea cozies begs for their attention. Moving from the eclectic tropical décor around the coffee bar, they walk past patrons surfing the Internet on the shop's Wi-Fi. The couple decides to sit on the traditional couch renewing memories of earlier days spent together at Sarah's house. While sitting cozily on the couch, they enjoy the music and spending time reading and relaxing with their hazelnut coffee and Nilgiri tea. The time passes joyfully as they listen to discussions of current news and watch other patrons pursue their passions.

Driving home from one such Nashville excursion, Sarah holds Bill's hand as in high school. Resting her head on his shoulder, she says lovingly, "Bill, I love that God manipulated circumstances and time to return us to each other. We should have been here all along. I'm sorry it took such a circuitous path to reach this point together." With her words, Bill smiles as he laughs in his heart and steals a kiss at a stop light. During the remaining drive home, Sarah says, "Bill, I think it's time to find a church and plan the ceremony." He agrees while looking deep in her eyes and they both start to tear up. Following his heart, Bill pulls into a parking lot at Trafalgar. While their journey home stops, they hold each other tightly. Resuming their drive, Bill caresses Sarah the rest of the way home. Clearly, their love is all-consuming as it spans the decades.

The Ceremony

A
rriving at St. Jude Catholic Church the next day, they meet with Father Doug Hunter. While planning the ceremony and the accompanying proceedings, Bill says, "Father Doug, as soon as we know when the date will be, we'll let you know."

Understanding completely, Father Doug replies, "I'll make sure the church is available for whatever date you need. I have no problem with that."

After setting their plans with Father Doug, Sarah and Bill drive back home caressing each other in relief. Joy returns to their hearts as they defeat the years with their love. Arriving at home again, they spend quiet time moments of love together, watching movies and toasting each other with hot chocolate. During the movies, they snuggle and caress on the couch with perfectly blended hearts as if they were still teenagers so many years ago.

Turning to Stony again, Bill says, "Well Stony, that's the entire story of how we ended up here. One last thought, Sarah confessed to me a few days earlier, 'You're the only man with whom I've been truly in love. I'll love you forever.' I've never been happier in all my life than I was then. Of course, I echoed the same to her."

Suddenly the door opens and Father Doug walks in the room saying, "Ok Bill, it's time." Both old and new friends fill the sanctuary waiting for Bill to take his place beside the only woman with whom he has been truly in love. Bill and Stony follow Father Doug to the altar where Sarah waits. Bill kisses Sarah lovingly on both cheeks and finally takes his place beside her. Father Doug nods at Bill to start.

Bill begins confessing to the audience, "As you know, I have been in love with this wonderful woman all my life. She has been the object of my heart's desire since I spilled a soft drink on her at my first varsity football game. Circumstances and indecision interrupted our time together but it could not quench our love for each other. There have been stories written about us and the love we share. Like many other special love stories in history, our story will live on long after we are gone. Love lives forever and is the stuff of legend. Sarah, I will love you forever." Suddenly in a somber tone, he continues, "However, when a friend dies, you accept that fact with sadness, yet life moves on. When your best friend dies, you accept that fact but with a deeper sadness while life moves forward more slowly. When a close family member dies, you accept that fact with a heaviness of heart as life grinds forward. But, when your best friend and the only woman with whom you've ever been in love dies, it leaves an deep, aching emptiness that one *cannot* quench. It is a feeling that escapes all description as life stops emotionally. One *can't* describe it especially, if you know in your heart you missed opportunities to fight to keep that person in your life. You missed opportunities to take that next step in your life, to make that one decision and forever change your life. Instead, you spend the rest of your life thinking ***if only*...**"

Recommended Playlist

For your reading enhancement, the authors recommend the following playlist while enjoying the book.

Somebody's Baby/Jackson Browne: **Sarah**, Paragraph 1, "he bumps into a dream"

Eye of the Tiger/Survivor: **Sarah**, Paragraph 6, "At the start of the second half"

Hushabye/Jay and the Americans: **Pizza**, Paragraph 7, "When Bill arrives home"

Pretty Blue Eyes/Steve Lawrence: **Maddie**, Paragraphs 3, "Helping the cheerleader to her feet"

Holding out for a Hero/Bonnie Tyler: **Building the Deck** Chapter

Hey There Lonely Girl/Eddie Holman: **Pizza Night With The Boys**, Paragraph 2

The Look Of Love/Diana Krall: **Movie Night** Paragraph 6, "As they walk in"

This Magic Moment/Ben E. King & the Drifters: **Senior Summer** Chapter

Moon River/ Ben E. King & the Drifters: **Homecoming**, "Relieved with his words"

Wouldn't It Be Nice/Beach Boys: **Homecoming**, Paragraph 10, "As Sarah walks to her room to change clothes"

God Only Knows/Beach Boys: **Uneasy Signs** Chapter

Put Your Head on My Shoulder/Lettermen: **Time Running Short** Chapter

A World of Our Own/The Seekers: **Redshirt**, Paragraph 2

Shape of a Heart/Jackson Browne: **A Tearful Meeting**, Paragraph 4, "Regaining his composure first"

Langstrom's Pony/Dirk Freymuth: Paragraph before **Game Time** after breakup with Sarah

Our Winter Love/Bill Purcell: **Party Time**, Paragraph 6: "While Eli rushes to get the clothes"

Valley of the Dolls/Dionne Warwick: **Christmas Break** Paragraph 2, "With the media intrusions"

The Hungry Years/Neil Sedaka: **Kathy's Discussion**, Paragraph 2

Same Old Lang Syne/Dan Fogelberg: **The 10-Year Reunion**, "Bill leans over to her"

My Way/Frank Sinatra: **On To The Hall** Paragraph 2, "Induction Ceremony"

Should Have Never Let You Go/Neil Sedaka: **Lunch,** Paragraph 2, "Lunch with Sarah"

Times of Your Life/Anka Back: **Together Again** Chapter

Once Upon a Time/Tony Bennett: **End of the Story after last sentence**

Credits

There are over one hundred true events rolled into the lives of the two main characters in the book. If you would like details of those events, please email your request to ifonly6969@comcast.net .

Author Biographies

James Anderson is a retired Business Analyst and IT pioneer concluding 35 years at Herff Jones Inc. December 31, 2012. Taking the company to electronic word processing, spreadsheets, and presentations from their manual counterparts, typewriters, ledgers, and overhead projectors, he built and managed the company's first nationwide, private computer network and email system between its manufacturing plants' mini-computers. He wrote over one hundred programs to support the manufacturing environments and data communication between them. Using the training manuals and programs he wrote, he trained the office staff and data entry personnel at all plants. For the last thirteen years before retirement, he tested, debugged, and improved the HJ automated sales program while supporting and training the HJ Scholastic Sales offices in its use. His writings include poetry, short stories, technical and training manuals. Married 35 years in 2012, he and his family reside in Indianapolis, IN.

Bill Rowley currently retired after 32 years of teaching. He obtained a Bachelors Degree from Ball State University and Master's Degree from Indiana University. Bill has written a column for a local newspaper and training lessons for various businesses. He currently resides in Indianapolis, IN.

Joey Mulinaro attends Ball State University and creates videos for local activities through his Baby Kangaroo Productions. He resides in Indianapolis, IN and during school at Ball State, in Muncie, IN.

Ruby Heart Necklace Giveaway

The purchase of this book entitles the buyer to one entry in the Ruby Heart Necklace Giveaway. On Valentine's Day, February 14, 2014, three fortunate individuals will have their names drawn from all valid entries received by January 31, 2014. Each of the three names drawn will receive one manufactured ruby heart necklace in the giveaway. To enter the giveaway, please mail this original page including the hearts graphic completed with your name, shipping address, email, and phone number to the address below. Only fully completed, original entry forms are accepted as valid entries. No duplicate forms will be accepted.

Send entry form to: Ruby Heart Necklace Giveaway
P.O Box 47009
Indianapolis, Indiana 46247

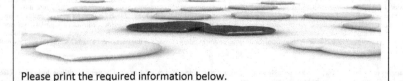

Please print the required information below.

Name:_____

Address:_____

| City | State | ZipCode |

Email Address:_____

Phone:_____

A limit of one entry per book, "If Only", purchase is allowed using the entry form page published in the book. Subsequent entries determined to be submitted in violation of this rule will be declared ineligible. No duplicate forms will be accepted.

All entries received by 11:59 P.M., ET, 1/31/2014 for this promotion will be eligible for our Ruby Heart Necklace Giveaway. *You will be entered into this Giveaway by completing and submitting the sweepstakes entry form to the address shown on the previous page of this book.* Entries submitted from this book and received after the deadline will be deemed invalid.

There will be a random drawing using all entries received by the specified deadline from which three names will be drawn and declared winning names. The Giveaway is only for retail purchasers of the book, "If Only" written by James Anderson, Bill Rowley, and Joey Mulinaro.

Prizes are as follows: The three names selected from all valid entries in a random drawing on 2/14/2014 shall each receive one manufactured ruby heart necklace with a retail value of $200.00.

Winners will be notified by email, phone, or by mail at the authors' option. The entrants named on the three winning entry forms selected in the random drawing will be considered the winners. The entry information listed on the submitted form is for notification of the three Ruby Heart Necklace Giveaway winners and sending the prize to those three winners. Acceptance of the prize constitutes permission to use the name and likeness of the winner for promotional purposes associated with the book, except where prohibited by law.

Authors' decisions are final. The winner selection method will not change. Any taxes are winner's responsibility. The Giveaway is open to U.S., U.K., and Canadian residents who are physically located and residing within their respective country of residence. Void where prohibited. **All giveaways are void in the province of Québec, and residents of that province are not eligible to enter or win.** Principals and employees of iUniverse, their affiliates and subsidiaries, their immediate families, the book's authors and their immediate families are not eligible. All federal, state and local laws apply.

By entering this promotion, each entrant accepts and agrees to be bound by these official rules and the decisions of the authors. iUniverse publishing and the book "If Only" authors are not responsible for any incorrect or inaccurate information, whether caused by website users or by any of the equipment or programming associated with or utilized in the Sweepstakes or by any technical or human error which may occur in the processing of submissions in the Sweepstakes. iUniverse publishing and the book "If Only" authors assume no responsibility for any error, omission, interruption, deletion, defect, US Postal delivery failure, delay in operation or transmission, communications line failure, theft or destruction or unauthorized access to, or alteration of entries. iUniverse publishing and the book "If Only" authors are not responsible for any problems or technical malfunction of any telephone network or lines, computer systems, servers or providers, computer equipment or software on account of technical problems or traffic congestion on the Internet or combination thereof, including injury or damage to participants or to any other person's computer related to or resulting from participating or downloading materials in this Giveaway. Entries become the property of the "If Only" authors and will not be returned.

The authors of the book "If Only" reserve the right to disqualify any entry determined to be the result of tampering including duplication of the original entry form published in the book "If Only" violation of the letter and spirit of the official rules. Any use of programmed, automatic or scripted entry methods will void all associated entries and individuals using such methods may be disqualified for future entry opportunity.

Sweepstakes eligibility will be based on date the mailed entry is received. Just mail each entry separately to the address below. We do not accept entries from a third party or entries sent in bulk.

Ruby Heart Necklace Giveaway
P. O. Box 47009
Indianapolis, Indiana 46247